THEY SHALL NOT PASS

THEY SHALL NOT PASS

CHRISTOPHER G. NUTTALL

Text copyright © 2018 Christopher G. Nuttall

ISBN-13: 9781983510021
ISBN-10: 1983510025

http://www.chrishanger.net
http://chrishanger.wordpress.com/
http://www.facebook.com/ChristopherGNuttall

All Comments Welcome!

A NOTE FROM THE AUTHOR

They Shall Not Pass is the direct sequel to *Never Surrender*, but features several characters from *Semper Fi*. Their backgrounds are detailed there. As always, I would be grateful for any spelling corrections, grammar suggestions, nitpicking and suchlike. Please send reports directly to my email address or through Amazon.

Thanks for reading! If you liked the book, please write a review. They help to boost sales.

CGN

PROLOGUE I

From: *The Day After: The Post-Empire Universe and its Wars.* Professor Leo Caesius. Avalon University Press. 46PE.

Brigadier Jasmine Yamane's escape from Meridian - and her attack on Wolfbane itself - was a significant tactical and strategic victory for the Commonwealth, in that it both boosted morale and crippled Wolfbane's ability to regenerate its naval forces and out-produce the Commonwealth. Certainly, the Commonwealth was quick to point to the daring prison escape and subsequent raid of enemy territory as a sign the tide was turning against Wolfbane. However, that was not entirely true.

It was true enough, to be fair, that Wolfbane would have difficulty keeping its fleet supplied with everything from replacement components to reinforcements. But it was also true that Wolfbane significantly outnumbered the Commonwealth in almost every category of starship. Indeed, if the Commonwealth had not enjoyed a significant technological advantage, Wolfbane would probably have crushed the Commonwealth in the first year of open warfare. The shortages would slow Wolfbane's ability to regenerate its forces, true, but would the crunch come in time to save the Commonwealth?

There was also a further problem that needed to be taken into account. No one, absolutely no one, had any real experience with a long-duration interstellar war. Interstellar conflict was almost unknown during the final years of the Empire, no matter how many planets fell to insurgents or declared independence as the Empire's grip started to weaken. Even Admiral Singh, one of the most capable officers in the Empire's final years, didn't appreciate what it meant to be fighting a long-term war. Why should she? She had no experience in handling anything more complex than brief and violent encounters between the Imperial Navy and a bewildering array of rebel and pirate forces.

It was inevitable, therefore, that both sides would make mistakes. The decision to send the Commonwealth Expeditionary Force to Thule, for example, was one such mistake, even though the logic made sense at the time. But the decision to attempt an over-clever envelopment of the Commonwealth Navy in the opening moves of the war was also a mistake, one less justified by then-current political concerns. In war, as has been noted for centuries, the simplest thing is difficult. Both sides failed to grasp the sheer complexity of what they were attempting to do.

But, despite its recent success, the Commonwealth knew itself to be in trouble. Wolfbane could bring attacks to bear along multiple axis of attack, while the Commonwealth - with far more limited resources - was forced to switch its forces from place to place rapidly, enduring the wear and tear on both equipment and personnel. (If Wolfbane had had access to any form of interstellar FTL communications, the Commonwealth would have lost fairly quickly; as it was, only the inability to coordinate offenses on an interstellar scale saved the Commonwealth from defeat.) The situation did not look good.

It was at that moment that Colonel Edward Stalker decided to gamble.

PROLOGUE II

Admiral Rani Singh, Governor-Admiral of Wolfbane, stood in her private observation blister, staring down at the blue and green planet below. It was *hers*, thanks to the death of Governor Brown, but she knew it seethed with resentment at how she'd claimed her role. She knew, from her network of spies, that far too many powerful people believed that *she* had killed the Governor, even though she'd merely managed to take advantage of his death. And some of them were only waiting for her to slip up before trying to take advantage of her weakness.

But they can't blame the destruction of the shipyards on me, she thought, darkly. No one in their right mind would allow an entire shipyard complex to be destroyed, even if it *did* propel her into the Governor's office. *But that won't stop them from trying, if I show weakness.*

Rani clenched her fists in irritation as she turned her gaze away from the world and up towards the endless darkness of interstellar space. She was a naval brat, pure and simple; she'd understood the military long before she'd formally signed up for a tour of duty. The navy was *organised*, people knew their place and did what they were told...*not* something that was common on Wolfbane. Governor Brown had ruled over a shifting morass of competing interests and power bases, allowing them to bicker amongst themselves while directing their energies towards the ultimate goal of galactic power. *She* knew how to win a battle or give orders, but managing so many different factions was far harder. And if she slipped, the knives would come out, aimed at her back...

The doorbell chimed. "Come."

She turned as the hatch opened, watching as Paula Bartholomew stepped into the chamber, the hatch hissing closed behind her. Paula was loyal, she had to be; her betrayal of her former superior would not be forgiven by anyone else. Using her was a risk - a person who betrayed once might betray again - but it had to be endured. Governor Brown had had years to put together his patronage network, the men and women who owed and served him; *she'd* barely had two weeks since the attack on Wolfbane. There were times when she wondered if it wouldn't be wiser to loot Wolfbane, then vanish as the world collapsed into chaos…

…But it wasn't in her to give up.

"Admiral," Paula said. "I have the final report for you."

Rani nodded as she turned back to the window. "And it says?"

"In the short run, we can continue to maintain the current operational tempo for the next six months to a year," Paula said, shortly. "But after that we will run into increasing difficulties in resupplying our forces. We'll have to slow the operational tempo quite significantly."

"So I feared," Rani said.

She shook her head slowly. No one had fought a war on such a scale in living memory; indeed, there had been no large-scale interstellar war for centuries. It was small wonder, she considered, that there had been more than a few hitches along the way. She and her personnel were learning as they went along. The only consolation was that the Commonwealth had the same problem.

"The industrialists did suggest suing for peace," Paula added, when Rani said nothing. "They argue that we could use a couple of years of peacetime to put the new weapons into production."

Rani shook her head, again. There were advantages to peace - particularly if she could keep everything she had captured over the last year of hard fighting - but peace would significantly undermine her position. The factions knew there was no other candidate to lead the military, no other candidate who could command the respect of the officers and crewmen. Removing her from power in the middle of a war would be disastrous. But in peacetime, anything could happen.

"The Commonwealth would grow stronger as they put *their* new weapons into production," she said, curtly. It was true enough. The Commonwealth had shown a truly distressing ability to innovate, something Wolfbane couldn't even *begin* to match. "Give them long enough and they'll find a silver bullet."

"There's no guarantee they will," Paula reminded her.

"There's no guarantee they won't," Rani snapped. Everyone had *known* that the Imperial Navy's technology was the peak of military potential, right up until the moment the Commonwealth had introduced shield generators. Who knew *what* certainty would be the next to fall? "What happens if they invent a weapon that can wipe out our entire fleet overnight?"

"That's absurd," Paula insisted. "Surely…"

Rani snorted, rudely. She would have thought the same, once upon a time. She'd clawed her way to office rank without selling herself to her superiors, even if said superiors had tried to punish her by exiling her to Trafalgar Naval Base. And she'd had the very last laugh when Admiral Bainbridge had been shot trying to escape. But now, the government and naval bureaucracy that had stifled innovation was no longer in existence. Who knew what would become possible in the future?

"We know very little for sure," Rani said. She turned to face the other woman. "Inform my senior officers that we will be proceeding with Operation Slam."

Paula bowed, then withdrew. Rani sighed as she turned back to the window. It was a gamble - life itself was a gamble - but there was no choice. Time was not on her side. The dice had to be rolled once again. If she won, she'd have the power and prestige to bring the industrialists and all the other factions to heel. And if she lost…she shook her head. She wasn't going to lose. Her life had been built on refusing to surrender when the odds seemed massively stacked against her…

And this time the odds are on my side, she thought. *Supreme power will finally be mine.*

She smirked. Empress Rani. She liked the sound of it.

CHAPTER
ONE

The real world is a messy place.
                    - Professor Leo Caesius. The Role of Randomness In War.

Jasmine Yamane gritted her teeth as the wind picked up strength, fighting to hold on to the sheer cliff face. The temperature plummeted rapidly, snowflakes drifting through the air, as she carefully let go with one hand and searched for the next handhold, an inch or two higher up the cliff. Grabbing hold, she tested it carefully before inching upwards, refusing to let the climb beat her. Maybe it had been a mistake, part of her mind noted, to attempt the climb without support, but she'd gone through worse on the Slaughterhouse. She firmly refused to allow something lesser to defeat her.

She inched her way up the cliff as the snow fell faster, cold flakes of ice brushing against her suit. The Mystic Mountains were known for sudden changes in the weather, just like the badlands to the south. She'd checked the forecast before setting out from the hut, but even the military-grade system assigned to monitor the planet's weather patterns hadn't been able to offer a reasonable prediction of what she might encounter. A civilian might have turned back, yet Jasmine had no intention of surrendering. Marines on deployment didn't have the luxury of abandoning a mission when they ran into a little snag.

But this weather might not be a little snag, she thought, as she finally reached the top of the cliff and pulled herself onto the ledge. The wind was growing stronger, so she secured herself to a rock before sitting down and staring at the view before her. *How many missions have run into trouble because of bad weather?*

She dug a ration bar out of her pocket and chewed it slowly as she took in the view. Giant mountains, rising up to vanish somewhere within the darkening clouds; great waves of snow hiding the rock beneath a layer of whiteness. The air was cold, but fresh and sharp. And nothing within view, save for Jasmine herself, to suggest that there was any human settlement nearby. Avalon really *was* a beautiful planet, at least in the regions untouched by human settlement. She hardly recognised Camelot these days, let alone some of the cities that had been towns when she'd first arrived on Avalon. The planet's population had almost quadrupled in the seven years since the marines had arrived, since the Empire had abandoned them, since Avalon had become the hub of a new interstellar civilisation…

And now we are at war again, she reminded herself. The sight before her could be destroyed, easily, if Wolfbane bombarded the planet. No one had deliberately targeted planetary populations from orbit for centuries, but that might change. All the old certainties had died with the Empire. *Who knows what will happen in the future?*

She looked down at her gloved hands, feeling a twinge of…uncertainty. The Colonel could say what he liked, but Jasmine blamed herself for the surrender on Thule. Even in the clear light of hindsight, it was hard to see what she'd done wrong, yet she was sure she *had* done something wrong. An entire military unit had surrendered in the opening hours of the war and *she* had been the one to issue the order. And even successfully escaping a POW camp and wreaking havoc in the enemy rear wasn't enough to wipe the slate clean. How could it be?

The Colonel said that everyone has a crisis of confidence eventually, she thought. *But how did he overcome his?*

It was a bitter thought. She'd gone through Boot Camp with flying colours, then survived the Slaughterhouse…only to discover, when she'd been assigned to her first company, just how much she still had to learn. And she'd survived that, only to discover that there was *still* much more to learn. By the time she'd been tortured on Corinthian, she'd been pushed right to the limits. And yet…

I never gave up, she told herself, firmly. *Too many lives were depending on me.*

She wished, as she carefully returned the remainder of the ration bar to her pocket, that she'd had a chance to go to OCS. Perhaps it would have made life easier for her, to learn the trade of an officer before taking marines into battle. But she was hardly the only person forced to learn on the job, after Avalon had lost contact with the remains of the Empire. Rumour had it that the Slaughterhouse had been destroyed, along with the infamous Death Zone. Even if she did manage to make it back to the Core Worlds, she would never be able to return to the Slaughterhouse.

You can't go home again, she thought. And that was literally true, for her. There was no way she could return to her homeworld, even if it had still been a matter of booking a ticket on the next ship. She knew there was no way she would have fitted in. *And you can't just stop either.*

She rose to her feet, testing the rope carefully, then took one last look at the white-covered mountains. Part of her was tempted to stay, to carry on exploring. She'd never really been tempted by the Survey Service, long before the Survey Service had been eviscerated by a dozen nasty budget cuts, but she could understand - now - the desire to see what lay on the other side of the hill. There were parts of the Mystic Mountains that had never been explored, even by the Mountain Men. It wasn't as if anyone wanted to settle in the mountains when there was good farmland to the south or west...

Unless they wanted to be alone, she thought, as she carefully tested the rope before starting to abseil down the cliff. Going down was always harder, she'd found; she preferred to abseil rather than attempt to climb down without precautions. If she injured herself so badly she couldn't trigger the emergency beacon, she would die up amidst the mountains, her body never to be found unless someone stumbled over her by sheer luck. *Being up here would be very far from everyone.*

Her lips quirked as she reached the bottom, then jerked the rope free. There had been a settlement on the Slaughterhouse, home to retired marines and their families. She'd often wondered if she'd wind up there, if she survived long enough to retire; now, she knew she would never see it again. But perhaps the handful of survivors might set up a new home in the mountains, miles from anywhere *civilian*. Merely *getting* there would provide the kind of challenge retired marines approved of.

Shaking her head, she turned and peered into the distance. A faint plume of smoke could be seen, rising up into the sky, as the snowfall trickled to a halt. She smiled - clearly, she was more resistant to the cold than her boyfriend - and started to walk, allowing the smoke to guide her back to the hut. It was the sort of thing, she noted as the hut came into view, that would never have been allowed on the Slaughterhouse. What sort of idiot expected a holiday hut in the middle of the Crucible?

The same sort of idiot who thinks he can pass the Crucible without a year of intensive training, she thought, wryly. *And the same sort of idiot who drinks himself into a stupor the night before entering Boot Camp.*

She pushed the thought to one side as she tramped up to the hut, opening the door and stumbling into the antechamber. The heat greeted her at once, sending sweat trickling down her back as she hurried to take off her shoes and remove her outer layer of clothing. She dumped the shoes by the door, then pushed open the inner door and stepped into the hut. A faint smell - she had never been able to identify it - greeted her as Emmanuel Alves rose to his feet, leaving a datapad on the table beside him. Jasmine gave her boyfriend a tight hug, then kissed him lightly on the lips.

"I heated up some soup," Emmanuel said, as she let him go. "Do you want some now?"

"Yes, please," Jasmine said. She'd spent the last week pushing her limits by climbing up and down the nearby mountains, but Emmanuel didn't have anything like the training he needed to accompany her. She didn't really begrudge it, even though it would have been nice to have the company. "It looks like it's going to snow again, later in the day."

"Joy," Emmanuel said. He walked over to the wood-burning stove and checked the heavy pan on top. "Should we be worried?"

Jasmine shrugged. Truthfully, the prospect of being trapped in the hut, buried under tons of snow, didn't bother her as much as it should have done. Years of training and experience had removed any tendency she might have had towards claustrophobia; months spent on various starships in cramped sleeping compartments had taught her how to endure even unendurable people. They could dig themselves out, if they wished, or signal for help. But she knew he might feel differently about it.

"Probably not," she said, finally. The hut's owners had sited it carefully, according to their brochure. Their guests could enjoy being in the midst of the mountains with minimal risk, although there was no way the risk could be eliminated entirely. "But it's worth keeping an eye on things if the snow starts to fall faster."

Emmanuel nodded as he ladled the soup into two bowls, then carried them over to the wooden table. Jasmine followed him, glancing around the hut and silently admiring the effort the original builder had put into his work. There wasn't anything that wasn't handmade, even the knives and forks. Even the water came from a stream and had to be heated on the stove, rather than warmed in a boiler. And it was more comfortable than anywhere she'd slept on the Slaughterhouse.

"Thank you," she said, as she sat down and started to sip the soup. "It's very good."

"All my own work," Emmanuel preened. "I opened those packets and mixed them myself."

Jasmine laughed. Trying to make military rations taste better had excited the imagination of countless soldiers, but there were limits to how much the addition of hot sauce or other flavours could improve the taste of recycled cardboard. She'd disliked marine ration packs until she'd tasted army ration packs, which were worse, and Civil Guard packs, which were unspeakably vile. It explained a great deal about the Civil Guard, she felt, that their officers couldn't be bothered attempting to source food from their postings, although they might well have a point. The Civil Guard was so loathed that it was quite possible that anyone selling them food would poison it first.

"You could probably get away with adding more sauce," she said, as she opened the breadbin. "It would add a little more kick."

Emmanuel rolled his eyes. "This isn't a Tabasco-swigging contest."

"A good thing too," Jasmine agreed. "I lost the last one."

She shook her head, feeling a strange mixture of pride and grief. Blake Coleman had challenged a trio of Imperial Navy crewmen to see who could eat the hottest sauce, just after the deployment to Han. She had no idea how he'd managed to swallow an entire bottle of Extra-Strong Chilli sauce, but he'd won the contest handily. She'd had to give up after trying to swallow something made of green chillies. And then Blake had died...she missed him, more than she cared to admit. It wasn't *right* that he'd died on a shitty little world, ruled by shitty little people who lorded over peasants who were just *waiting* for a chance to take power for themselves. No doubt the peasants had purged the aristocracy and then started fighting over the scraps of remaining power.

Emmanuel met her eyes. "Are you all right?"

Jasmine shrugged. Death was a fact of life. Blake Coleman had died well, unlike so many others she could mention. She knew he wouldn't want his friends to mourn him indefinitely, although he would have taken a perverse pride in the number of women who'd appeared, afterwards, to claim they'd been his soulmate. And yet, she missed him...

Maybe I shouldn't have let the Colonel promote me, she thought. *He wouldn't have counted it against me later on, would he?*

She snorted and pushed the thought aside as she finished her soup. Blake wouldn't have wanted her to be morbid either, she knew; he'd have teased her, endlessly, about taking a reporter to bed. But Emmanuel wasn't one of the paid shrills who'd blighted military operations from Earth to Han, getting soldiers killed by revealing classified information ahead of time. Indeed, Jasmine had to admit that Emmanuel was a *genuine* reporter, more interested in ferreting out the truth than spreading lies to push a political agenda. He *always* put his news in context.

"I think so," she answered, finally. She made a show of glancing at her watch. "Are you ready to go out this afternoon?"

"I suppose we might *just* find a decent restaurant *somewhere* up here," Emmanuel said, deadpan. "Snow for starter, rocks and ice for the main course, iced snow for pudding..."

"I meant going for a long walk," Jasmine said. Emmanuel was surprisingly fit, for a civilian, but he couldn't keep up with her. And yet he was light years ahead of the reporters on Han, who'd eyed her as if she was a dangerous animal permanently on the verge of breaking her leash. "A *very* long walk."

Emmanuel groaned, theatrically. "Must we?"

"There's a big reward on the far side," Jasmine said. "I'll make it worth your while."

"I'd be happy to chase you over the mountains," Emmanuel said. "But catching you might be tricky."

Jasmine smiled. Her mother had once told her that the secret to catching the right sort of man was to run away, yet not to run very fast. She'd never been quite convinced of the logic, personally, but she'd been a tough little scrapper even before she'd joined the marines. *And* her homeworld had a thoroughly practical attitude towards both firearms and personal defence. If she was caught by the wrong man, she could castrate him before she shot him…

Her wristcom bleeped, once. Jasmine frowned, then keyed the switch.

"Yamane," she said. "Go ahead."

"Brigadier," a calm female voice said. Jasmine straightened automatically. Technically, she outranked Command Sergeant Gwendolyn Patterson now, but she wouldn't dare to take liberties with the older woman. "I trust you had a pleasant vacation?"

"Yes, Sergeant," Jasmine said. She had the feeling her vacation had just come to a sudden halt. "The mountains are quite challenging, even in summer."

"Good, good," Gwendolyn said. "I've dispatched a Hummer to pick you and your boyfriend up for immediate transfer to Castle Rock. The colonel wants you back here ASAP."

"Understood," Jasmine said. She felt a flicker of the old excitement, despite her concerns about the past and her fears for the future. This was another deployment, she was sure. It couldn't be anything else. "ETA?"

"The Hummer should be with you in thirty minutes," Gwendolyn said. "Be ready to depart when it arrives."

The connection broke. Jasmine stared at the wristcom for a long moment, then looked up at Emmanuel. "We're being recalled," she said. "Both of us."

"It sounds that way," Emmanuel agreed. He didn't sound angry, but she knew he understood the realities of the job. *Both* of their jobs. "We'd better pack."

Jasmine nodded and hurried into the bedroom, picking her rucksack off the floor and dumping clothes and equipment into it willy-nilly. A lifetime in military service had taught her to travel light, thankfully. Emmanuel didn't have the same experience, but he'd learned rapidly. There were strong weight restrictions on what could be counted as personal baggage, at least on Commonwealth Navy starships. The Imperial Navy had been so keen to please the reporters that officers had often classed overweight reporter baggage as essential requirement, even though it was nothing of the sort. A reporter who tried *that* on the Commonwealth Navy would be lucky if his baggage was shipped home from the terminal, instead of merely being dumped.

"I don't suppose we have time for anything special," Emmanuel said, as he finished stuffing items into his bag. "Do we?"

"Not when we have to shut the hut down," Jasmine said. She'd had the same thought, but duty came first. "Sorry."

"It's all right," Emmanuel said. "You come far too close to breaking my bones."

Jasmine gave him a one-fingered gesture, then hurried back into the living room and turned off the water pipe, then glanced around to make sure they'd left nothing lying around. It was unlikely they'd have time to return to pick up anything, once the Hummer collected them.

"I thought we had another two days," Emmanuel added. "What do you think this is about?"

"The colonel said that his staff were working on a plan," Jasmine said. She'd been surprised when the colonel had agreed to her taking a week's leave, even if it *did* suggest he had a mission in mind for her. "It might be something *very* interesting."

Emmanuel leaned forward. "And decisive?"

Jasmine frowned. She'd hurt the Wolves badly, she knew, even if it had come at a terrible cost. She still had no idea what had happened to either Carl Watson or Paula Bartholomew - and killing Governor Brown had only elevated Admiral Singh to power. Jasmine had no illusions about the future. They might have won a battle, and embarrassed the Wolves, but the war was far from over.

"We will see," she said, as she heard the sound of the approaching aircraft. New-build Hummers weren't quite as fast as Raptors, but they'd be back at Castle Rock in less than thirty minutes. "We will see."

CHAPTER
TWO

This is perhaps best illustrated by an observation by the Imperial Marshals,
in their handbook. A story that hangs together perfectly is almost certainly a
premeditated alibi. The very flawlessness of the story is its flaw!
                    - Professor Leo Caesius. The Role of Randomness In War.

Colonel Edward Stalker sat in his chair in the War Room and studied the
starchart as he waited for his guests to pass through security and enter the
compartment. There was no way to avoid realising that the situation was
dire. The red and orange stars - stars owned or occupied by Wolfbane - were
closing in on the green stars, despite savage and desperate fighting around a
dozen stars at the edge of the Commonwealth. No matter how frantically Ed
switched forces from star to star, Wolfbane had a very definite advantage.

*They can pull their ships from the line for repairs, if necessary, while
we have to keep our ships in combat,* he thought, darkly. He'd never commanded a naval force, but the basic principles were identical to infantry warfare. A regiment, if pushed to the limits of its endurance, would
eventually break under constant enemy attack. *And some of our ships are
starting to break down.*

He scowled at the datapad containing the latest - highly classified -
reports. The newer starships were holding up well - they'd been built by
designers who no longer needed to stay within the limitations set by the
bureaucracy - but the older ships were starting to break down under the
pressures of warfare. A dozen ships needed urgent repairs, which they
weren't going to get. They were irreplaceable along the battle line…

And yet, if they break down in combat, we lose them anyway, he thought. *We need some way to tip the balance in our favour.*

He looked up as the door opened, allowing his guests to hurry into the room. Gaby Cracker, President of Avalon and First Speaker of the Commonwealth, gave him a tired smile as she took her seat, all professional despite the fact they'd been lovers for the past four years. She was followed by Brigadier Jasmine Yamane - looking better after a week's leave - and Colonel Kitty Stevenson, Commonwealth Intelligence. And, running a few minutes late, Commodore Mandy Caesius and Command Sergeant Gwendolyn Patterson. Ed had been surprised when the two women had developed a friendship - two more different women would be hard to imagine - but he was glad of it. Gwendolyn's position had always isolated her from the other marines.

"Close the doors," he ordered, as Commander Hiram Simpson entered the compartment. "I shouldn't have to tell any of you that this is a *secret* meeting. No one is to hear the details until we are ready to release them."

He glanced from face to face, knowing they would understand. Gaby had been an insurgent leader before she'd become part of the government. She understood the value of keeping information to a very limited circle, particularly when it was of tactical or strategic importance. The others were all career military, even Mandy. She might have started life as a bratty teenage daughter, but she'd grown up on Avalon. They'd all changed a great deal since they'd been cut off from the Core Worlds.

"First, a briefing," he added. He concealed a smile at their reactions. Gaby looked irked - she received too many briefings - while the others leaned forward, ready to hear just what Ed had in mind. "Commander?"

Simpson nodded, shortly. Ed could practically *taste* his nervousness. He was the lowest-ranking officer in the room and knew it. But he also knew his duty.

"As of the last report, Wolfbane has halted its offensive against Taurus to consolidate its position in the wake of Governor Brown's death," Simpson said. "Long-range scouts report that they have been bringing repair ships forward, trying to prepare as many ships as possible for the next offensive. Fighting continues on a number of worlds, but we consider it unlikely that any of the insurgencies can push Wolfbane off their world."

Ed frowned. They'd worked hard to arm and train stay-behind forces, but he was under no illusions about their chances of success. Wolfbane could call down fire from orbit on any insurgent position, if the insurgents showed themselves so blatantly. Holding an entire world didn't require vast numbers of troops, merely a starship or orbital bombardment platform ready to hammer targets at a moment's notice. The stay-behinds could sting, but it wouldn't be enough to do more than annoy their enemies.

"Our own forces are in critical condition," Simpson continued. "Our pre-war planning greatly underestimated the operational tempo we have to maintain and our supplies are starting to run out. Only our technological superiority gives us any advantage at all and...and that might come to an end, if Wolfbane obtains samples of our technology or has a breakthrough of its own. They now know that a great many things believed to be impossible are actually possible - and knowing is half the battle."

"True," Ed agreed. "We cannot assume we will maintain technological superiority indefinitely."

He waited patiently, silently gauging reactions as Simpson continued the briefing. Gaby looked concerned, despite herself; Jasmine was leaning forward, as if she was eager to get to grips with the enemy. Mandy looked worried - she'd skirmished with Wolfbane's fleet too many times - while Gwendolyn showed no visible reaction. But then, she wouldn't. A sergeant could not afford to show the slightest hint of doubt to subordinates, either in her own abilities or in the competence of superior officers. And then the briefing finally came to its inevitable conclusion.

"Assuming the operational tempo continues at its current pace," Simpson stated, "we will lose the war within the next two years."

Gaby choked. "That can't be right!"

"It is hard to predict the course of a war, Madam President," Simpson said. "There are too many random variables involved. One of our older ships might suffer a critical failure in combat, allowing Wolfbane to win a battle they would otherwise have lost. Or we may develop something that negates Wolfbane's numerical superiority. But, in many ways, two years is quite optimistic. If they push the tempo harder in the next six months, we may lose the war by the end of the year."

"We need a game-changer," Ed said, calmly.

"We could strike directly at Wolfbane," Mandy suggested.

"We'd never get a fleet through their defences," Ed said. "And we'd have to nuke the entire world. Quite apart from any moral considerations, Wolfbane would certainly do the same to Avalon and every other Commonwealth world."

He shuddered at the thought. For all of its flaws, the Empire had managed to prevent separatists, terrorists and insurgents from using weapons of mass destruction on a regular basis. The bastards had *known* that the Empire would stop at nothing to hunt them down, if they committed mass murder. But the Empire was gone and who knew if the successor states would uphold the old rules? Some of them might even see advantage in slaughtering entire planetary populations.

Not us, he told himself, firmly. He'd been far too close to one nuclear blast and he had no intention of being close to another. *Even if it costs us the war.*

He cleared his throat for attention. "I believe we have an option," he said. "It will be chancy, and perhaps quite costly, but it may be the only option we have."

The display altered at his command, focusing in on a single green star. He winced inwardly as he heard Jasmine's sharp intake of breath. She'd been captured and tortured on Corinthian, after all, and such treatment always left scars. He would have left her out of the mission entirely, if that were possible, but he was terrifyingly short of experienced and capable officers. If the devil had come to him and offered an entire regiment of marines, in exchange for his soul, he would have accepted without a second thought.

"Corinthian," he said. There would be time to chat with Jasmine privately later, if she had concerns of her own. "Once the home base of Admiral Singh, our old and new enemy; now, a loyal Commonwealth world."

"I should have killed her," Jasmine said, quietly.

"You couldn't have known what she'd manage to do," Ed said. Privately, he was more than a little impressed. Admiral Rani Singh's remaining formation should have rapidly run out of supplies and died, somewhere in the inky darkness of space. Instead, they'd made their way to Wolfbane and taken up high position in the government. "I wouldn't have expected her to be so quick to take Brown's place."

But it might just work in their favour, he told himself. Governor Brown was competent enough, but he'd worked hard to stack the deck in his favour before starting the war. He hadn't had the drive for power and military conquest that Rani Singh possessed in spades, or the sheer bloody-minded determination to win that characterised many of the marines. Ed had doubted Brown would take the bait, when it was waved under his nose, but Admiral Singh was another story. She'd be looking for weakness in his position and, if she saw a weakness, she'd try to take advantage of it.

"Over the next two months, we are going to have to consolidate our defence lines around the original Commonwealth stars," he said, simply. "We simply don't have the mobile firepower necessary to hold our current positions for much longer. This will place Corinthian outside our defence lines, a temptation to Admiral Singh. I believe, based upon reading her profile, that she will very much want to recover her former base, if only to prove that she cannot be permanently beaten. Right now, we don't have the firepower to keep her from recapturing the world."

Jasmine scowled. "That will be bad for anyone who worked with us, back then."

"Yes, it will," Ed agreed. That was, if anything, an understatement. Admiral Singh was known to be vindictive. "We've been evacuating much of the trained personnel to hidden shipyards and manufacturing complexes, but we haven't been able to strip the planet bare, simply because we need to keep those production lines running as long as possible. We cannot keep the world, but we can force her to expend her resources taking it by force."

He tapped the console, bringing up a map of the planetary surface. "The principal problem in holding a planet after losing control of the high orbitals is that the enemy can simply bombard the planet into rubble from orbit, well out of range of most planetary defence weapons," he stated. "The Empire was never keen on allowing planets to deploy weapons that might force the Imperial Navy to keep its distance. Now, however, we have our shield technology. We can project a force field over Freedom City and the surrounding environs, forcing the Wolves to land troops and take the planet from the ground."

"It sounds chancy," Jasmine observed, into the silence. "Can the shield hold?"

"As long as it has the power, it can hold," Mandy said, quietly. "But she'd still be able to bombard the remainder of the planet."

"She needs to capture Freedom City," Ed said. "Bombarding the remainder of the planet would be pointless and she'd know it. And if she did, her officers might well mutiny against her."

He tapped the map. "The point is that Singh will *want* to recover her former capital, want it very much," he added. "If everything goes according to plan, she will land troops herself and fight a conventional land campaign to seize the city. And we're going to be there to bleed her white. She will concentrate more and more of her resources on Corinthian, trying to dig us out without doing too much damage to the facilities. It should buy us time to get back on our feet and counterattack, trapping her forces against the planet."

"And even if she wins, it will cost her dearly," Gwendolyn observed.

Gaby frowned. "Will she survive?"

"I don't know," Ed said.

He studied the map for a long moment. In his experience, infantry campaigns tended to be long and drawn out, mainly because their enemies were smart enough not to come to grips with the marines directly. A more organised force would be smashed from orbit, but the force shield would ensure that was no longer a possibility. And if Singh committed herself to a ground campaign, the casualties would be horrific. But would they be enough to weaken her position on Wolfbane?

The Empire rarely cared about casualties, if the media wasn't involved, he thought. *But Wolfbane doesn't even begin to have the same level of resources.*

"It wouldn't be an easy campaign," Jasmine said, slowly. "It'll make Lakshmibai look easy - and we know she has data on *that* campaign."

"She's a naval officer," Ed said. "To her, eighty kilometres might as well be *eight*."

He smiled, remembering Admiral Valentine's insistence that the marines - and soldiers - could march over three hundred miles in a day. A

15

distance that was tiny on an interplanetary scale, a distance that a starship could cover in less than a second, was immense on a planetary surface. Even without hostile forces doing their level best to *stop* the march, it would have taken days to complete it. And, on Corinthian, his forces were going to be very hostile indeed.

And there's no such thing as terrain in space, he thought, dryly. Skimming through an asteroid field or punching it out with an enemy ship in a nebula only happened in bad entertainment flicks. *She isn't going to grasp how hard it can be to push through a mountain pass, even without the enemy making life interesting.*

"It is definitely not going to be easy," he warned. "Quite apart from the CEF, we'll be turning Corinthian into a battleground. The civilians will be evacuated, of course, but large parts of the region will be devastated."

"The planetary government will not take that well," Gaby warned.

"The planetary government isn't going to *survive* if Admiral Singh returns," Jasmine said, bluntly. "I think the leadership were all part of our little coup, weren't they?"

"Yes," Ed said. "They were all involved in the coup and purging her supporters from the planet, afterwards. They even renamed their capital Freedom City."

"She's not going to shower them with love," Jasmine said. "We may want to start thinking about evacuating them."

Ed shrugged. It was something to bear in mind, although he wasn't particularly keen on evacuating a government if the entire planet couldn't be abandoned. Far too many of the brushfires he'd had to deal with before their exile had been caused by planetary leaders who'd fled, the moment they realised they'd gone too far, leaving their people to deal with the consequences. He couldn't recall any governor who'd actually faced the consequences himself.

"We will consult with the government, of course," he said. "But the operation will need to begin as soon as possible."

Mandy leaned forward. "Colonel," she said, "how do you intend to lure Singh into the trap?"

Ed exchanged a glance with Kitty Stevenson. Only a handful of people knew about Hannalore Roeder and he wanted to keep it that way, even though he trusted everyone in the compartment implicitly. And yet, it *was* a good question. Admiral Singh might miss the preparations entirely, if there wasn't a direct link between Avalon and Wolfbane...

"Wolfbane has a number of intelligence-gathering rings operating on Avalon," he said, finally. "We believe they are all under our control. They'll be told that we will be pulling back from the defence lines, which is true, and that we will be stripping Corinthian of everything vital before we go. That's the message that will reach Admiral Singh."

"Unless there's a spy ring we don't know about," Jasmine said.

"True," Ed agreed. "But we will be spreading the story fairly widely. No one outside this room will know the truth until it's too late."

He smiled. "Officially, the CEF and a number of starships will be looting Corinthian," he added. "Admiral Singh will expect as much, of course. It will give her a strong incentive to move quickly. Unofficially, we will be digging in, preparing to resist her offensive when it comes."

Jasmine frowned. "We?"

"I'll be taking personal command of the operation," Ed said, firmly. "It was my idea."

He kept his face impassive. Jasmine might have expected it for herself, despite her doubts over her fitness for command, but the whole operation was *his* idea. He'd already sent far too many officers and men into combat without being there himself. And how many officers on Earth had agreed to ill-planned deployments and crazy tactical plans because they weren't the ones charged with making them real? The day he stopped being willing to take the field, to turn his plans into reality, was the day he should resign.

"I don't promise the plan will work," he concluded. "But I think it's the best chance we have to catch her with her pants down."

"It looks workable," Gaby said. "Is it?"

"If Admiral Singh takes the bait," Jasmine said. "A lot depends on her even *noticing* the bait being waved in front of her."

"We can take care of that," Kitty said. "And we can make sure that rumours spread, just to confuse any spies we *don't* know about."

"It may cause political problems," Gaby said. "If the other worlds get the impression that we're planning to loot Corinthian..."

Ed scowled. "Can you keep it under control?"

"Maybe," Gaby said. "But we will have to pay a price for it later."

"We will," Ed agreed. He tapped the table, thoughtfully. "We now move to the tactical planning for the operation…"

CHAPTER
THREE

Writers find this perplexing, of course. This is why most mystery stories tend to be very clear, with every last detail accounted for. The real world is a great deal more messy.

- Professor Leo Caesius. The Role of Randomness In War.

Jasmine kept her private thoughts to herself as the small planning team hashed out the tactical details of the operation, although she offered her thoughts and opinions based on her experience on Corinthian and Lakshmibai. She was, she suspected, the sole officer for a hundred light years who *had* commanded a fast-moving force trying to break through enemy defences, certainly the only one in the Commonwealth. But the warrior caste on Lakshmibai hadn't been anything like a competent enemy...

She pushed the thought aside as the meeting came to an end. The plan was a little vague, compared to the thousand-page outlines she'd seen before their exile to Avalon, but there was no way *every* possible variation could be planned for in advance. War was a democracy in the truest possible sense; the enemy got a vote. It was far better for the commander on the spot to have authority to react to the situation as it changed, rather than have to send for new orders from Avalon. The Empire had lost a dozen minor campaigns because the CO didn't have the authority to wipe his ass without orders from Earth, in triplicate.

"Jasmine," Colonel Stalker said. "Please remain behind."

Jasmine nodded and remained seated, feeling torn between anticipation and an odd kind of fear. Was she *ready* to go back into the field? Or was she about to be told that she was being permanently relegated to REMF status? *Someone* would have to remain on Avalon, after all, if Colonel Stalker was going to Corinthian. Normally, she wouldn't have a hope in hell of getting the post, but nothing had been normal for the past seven years. Her career path was a crooked mess.

"Jasmine," Stalker said. He sat, facing her. "How was your leave?"

"It was cold, sir," Jasmine said. She had always liked and respected the colonel, but they'd hardly been *friends*. He'd been her first commanding officer, after her graduation; there'd always been a distance between them. "But I managed to do plenty of climbing."

"I keep meaning to go climbing myself," Stalker mused. "Would you recommend it?"

"We could train mountain troops up there," Jasmine said. Marines were meant to be well-rounded, but some of the mountaineering troops she'd encountered on Han had been strikingly good, as long as they were in their element. "But I wouldn't climb some of the nastier mountains without another marine by my side."

"It would probably be wise," Stalker agreed. He leaned back in his chair, a movement that didn't put Jasmine at her ease. "What do you think of the operational plan?"

Jasmine took a moment to gather her thoughts. "It hinges on the assumption that Admiral Singh will fall for our trap," she said, finally. "The odds are in our favour, but she may have different ideas. Corinthian is simply less important than Wolfbane."

"Her profile makes it clear that she hates to lose," Stalker said. "Would you agree with that?"

"*I* hate to lose, sir," Jasmine said. "But I'm not sure I would walk deliberately into an elephant trap because of my wounded pride."

She rubbed her shaved head, thoughtfully. "It will look simple to her from orbit, I suspect," she added. "But it really is a gamble."

"Life is a gamble," Stalker said. "Right now, the alternative is to dig in and fight to the last or find a way to strike at Wolfbane directly. And that isn't going to be easy."

Jasmine nodded, shortly. The Wolves could muster the forces necessary to stop any deep-strike offensive, while launching an all-out attack on Avalon themselves. Trying to punch out Wolfbane might just cost the Commonwealth everything, yet hunkering down and hoping for the best wasn't a strategy either. Luring Admiral Singh into a minefield was the best of a set of bad options. She didn't like it, but she couldn't think of anything better.

"It should be workable, sir," she said. "If worst comes to worst, the CEF can go to ground and scatter until the navy recovers control of the system."

"That's one of the possible options," Stalker said.

"There's another concern," Jasmine added. "Is Admiral Singh going to be *ready* to launch a ground invasion? It isn't as though they're *expecting* to have to fight on the ground."

"Corinthian has been distributing weapons ever since the liberation," Stalker said. "They'll know that everyone and his wife is armed to the teeth, which will give them some incentive to bring a larger force. But you're right. They may have to delay matters long enough to summon additional forces from their nearby bases."

Jasmine nodded, slowly. The Imperial Navy had plenty of experience in landing occupation forces and then supporting them, but they had never considered a long conventional campaign without orbital supremacy. They'd simply never faced a peer power since the Unification Wars, so long ago that they'd passed well out of living memory. And now so much had to be relearned. It was frustrating, even though she suspected Admiral Singh had the same problem.

She looked up. "Is there anything we can do about that?"

"Probably not," Stalker admitted. "We're rolling the dice here, Jasmine, and the odds are pretty much stacked against us."

"I thought that was how we rolled, sir," Jasmine said. She couldn't help feeling a twinge of…concern. She'd never realised just how much commanding officers sweated bullets for the safety of their men until she'd become a commanding officer herself. "We can do anything, if we put our minds to it."

Stalker smiled. "I'm glad to hear you say that," he said. "What do you think of yourself, right now?"

"The job needs to be done, sir," Jasmine said, ducking the question. Two years at the Slaughterhouse and eight years on duty had taught her that whining and moaning helped no one, particularly not herself. "If you have a role for me in this operation, I will be happy to take it."

Stalker nodded. "I can't give you the CEF," he said, flatly. "The original formation has been almost completely rebuilt, with new officers in important positions. General Crichton Mathis currently holds command; he'll be my second on Corinthian."

Jasmine wasn't too surprised. She'd commanded the CEF in two campaigns, but the second had ended with surrender and a trip to a penal colony for her and her senior officers. And, of course, everyone she hadn't managed to get off Thule in time. She rather doubted that any of the surviving officers had much confidence in her after *that*. Mathis was a knight, rather than a marine, but he was a good man. A little unseasoned, perhaps, yet that was true of far too many officers these days.

"I understand, sir," she said. It hurt more than she'd expected, but it definitely wasn't a surprise. "He'll do a good job."

"I certainly hope so," Stalker said. "I have something different in mind for you."

He tapped a hidden switch, throwing up a holographic map of Landing City - no, *Freedom* City. Jasmine studied it, remembering how she and her men had sneaked into the city and brought down an entire government...and how she'd been captured, tortured and forced to escape under her own steam. She'd done well, she knew, but the whole experience had left scars on her soul.

But I escaped, she told herself, firmly. *It would be a great deal worse if I'd been rescued - or if I'd broken.*

The map wasn't too accurate outside the city, she noted. Corinthian had been settled long enough for accurate maps to be composed, but the drawers hadn't been too concerned with the unsettled regions to the north. The farmlands she recalled from her last visit existed only in outline, faint sketch marks that probably bore little resemblance to reality. Admiral Singh hadn't paid too much attention to the farmers either, only making sure they supplied enough food to keep the city alive. She'd been much more interested in establishing her power base and building an empire.

The colonel is right, Jasmine told herself. She'd studied Admiral Singh's file before the first mission. The older woman had been ambitious as hell, determined to make a name for herself…reading between the lines, it was clear she'd been exiled by her superiors, just for being too threatening to their careers. *Admiral Singh will want to recover her former base and wreak revenge on her enemies.*

"The map needs work," she said, pushing the thought aside. "We may need to get more up-to-date ones when we arrive."

"We will," the Colonel said. He altered the map so it showed the force shield, a spinning disc of energy hanging in the sky, ten kilometres above the ground. Jasmine had wondered if it would touch the ground, making it impossible for Singh to force her way into the city, but it didn't even curve into a bowl. "I believe she will try to land forces a safe distance from the force shield. She may assume that the force shield can actually be extended on command."

Jasmine frowned. "And can it?"

"Not without additional projectors, which we don't have," Stalker warned. "We did hope to produce a shield that covered an entire planet, but there are…problems…in how the different shield discs interact with one another. This piece of technology is a game-changer, but it needs to have the kinks worked out first."

"And if it fails midway through the operation," Jasmine said, "we all die."

"We would have to scatter very quickly," Stalker confirmed. He tapped the map again, pointing to a handful of possible Landing Zones. "I want you to take command of 1st Platoon, once again. Your job is to harass the enemy's rear, once they start landing in force."

Jasmine felt a flicker of excitement, mixed with an odd kind of regret. 1st Platoon - the 1st Platoon she'd joined and then commanded - no longer existed. The unit that bore its name consisted of newcomers, with hardly any continuity between them and their predecessors. A century or two of history was being lost…but what choice did they have? The Slaughterhouse was gone, if the rumours were to be believed. There would be no new marines to replace those who had died in the line of duty.

She pushed her feelings aside and leaned forward. "I have tactical command?"

"You have complete freedom to plan your operations," Stalker said. "Just make sure you hit them hard enough to keep them from bringing all their firepower to bear against us."

Jasmine smiled, relishing the challenge. "Yes, sir," she said. "I look forward to it."

"You'll meet up with the remainder of the platoon tomorrow," Stalker said. "Assuming the loading goes as planned, you'll have at least two weeks to brush up on your tactics and work your way through a number of possible options. Make sure you train hard too."

"Yes, sir," Jasmine said. It had been too long since she'd served as part of a fire team, although she *had* managed to improvise the escape from Meridian. "I'll make them regret ever hearing my name."

Stalker's lips twitched. "Admiral Singh may know you personally," he warned. "You probably don't want to be taken alive."

"Again," Jasmine said. Even if Admiral Singh didn't connect her with the person who'd sparked off a revolution on Corinthian, she'd know that Jasmine was an escaped POW. And an escaped POW could be shot out of hand, quite legally. "I won't let them capture me."

"Good," Stalker said.

He paused. "There is another issue," he added. "Your boyfriend will be accompanying the CEF to Corinthian, again. It's vitally important that we explain to the Commonwealth just what's going on - and why."

Jasmine looked down at the map. "May I ask why, sir?"

"Politics," Stalker said. He made the word a curse. "When we started, it was assumed that all worlds that joined the Commonwealth would be equal, once they signed the charter. In practice, worlds like Avalon - and Corinthian - are moving to dominate the Commonwealth, both because they have some degree of industrialisation and because they have room for immigrants with various skills. In doing so, they are accidentally crippling the other worlds in the Commonwealth by hampering their ability to industrialise."

"I thought they all had cloudscoops now," Jasmine said. "Surely..."

"They do," Stalker confirmed. "But there's a great deal more to industrialisation than merely having an effectively-endless source of fuel. They need experienced personnel who can help turn their dreams into reality, personnel who are in short supply because they can get better-paid jobs here."

He shrugged. "And then there's the problem of the war," he added. "There's a growing party within the government that believes we can come to terms with Wolfbane, if only to avoid losing what we've built over the past few years. And one that considers the entire war *Avalon's* fault. My screw-up on Lakshmibai gave the dissidents a chance to organise, which creates more problems for us. Without the war, things might have gone better, but right now we need our economy running at full power."

Jasmine put the rest of the picture together. "And that means a number of worlds are being screwed," he said. "And not in a good way, either."

"No," Stalker agreed. "If we're lucky, we can end the war and matters will normalise themselves before something explodes. But if we're unlucky, there will be a nasty explosion at the worst possible time, ripping the Commonwealth apart. We've learned too many bad habits as we struggled to prepare for the war."

He cleared his throat. "Back to the original subject, your boyfriend will be accompanying us to Corinthian," he said. "I trust this won't be a problem?"

"No, sir," Jasmine said. She doubted she could have talked the colonel out of it, even if she'd wanted to. Emmanuel would not have thanked her for denying him the chance to win the scoop of a lifetime. In his own way, he was as dedicated and daring as herself. "I assume we wouldn't be seeing too much of one another anyway."

"Probably not," Stalker confirmed. "He'll be briefed in on the operation tomorrow, then he'll go into the box. Make tonight count."

Jasmine nodded. It wouldn't be the first time she'd had to leave him behind when she went on deployment. Hell, she was hardly the only marine with a lover back home. She was too experienced to be embarrassed at the colonel's droll remark.

"If there are problems, I expect to hear about them," the colonel warned. "Once we depart, there will be no time to fix anything."

"Yes, sir," Jasmine said. "Do you anticipate any problems with the government of Corinthian?"

"They are going to be in deep shit if their world is...repossessed," Stalker observed. "They're not ruling over a planet that doesn't materially affect the balance of power..."

Jasmine nodded in grim understanding. Corinthian was *rich*, both in pre-established industries and human capital. Admiral Singh had good reason to want it, even if she hadn't already had a long history with Corinthian. And she would make sure to bring along enough firepower to cow the defenders, forcing them to surrender rather than fight or destroy their facilities. But she would run right into a trap. If, of course, everything worked as planned.

And if it doesn't, she told herself, *we'll just have to improvise.*

She looked back at the map and shuddered, inwardly. She'd spent weeks on the ground, getting to know the people; she'd met good men and bad, resistance fighters and criminals...and countless civilians who'd wanted nothing more than to keep their heads down and stay out of the fighting. And many of those people were going to die, when the storm of war raged over their heads. She had no illusions about just how badly Corinthian was going to be hammered. Lakshmibai had been devastated by the fighting, during the brief campaign...

But their society was permanently on the verge of collapse, she reminded herself. *This society had a chance to recover after Admiral Singh was forced to flee.*

"This will be a challenge, sir," she said, keeping her doubts to herself. "And if we can make her pay..."

"We need to bleed her white," Stalker told her. There was no give in his voice at all. "She has to suffer badly, Jasmine. She has to feel the losses."

Jasmine nodded. She'd heard enough about Wolfbane to be fairly confident that a failure - or even a partial success - would badly weaken Singh's position. But it would come at a terrible cost, for Corinthian, for Avalon...and for the young men and women who served Admiral Singh. She knew better than to think they were all evil, yet she knew many of them had to die...

"I understand, sir," she said.

Stalker held her eyes for a long moment. She wondered, absently, just what he thought of her. She'd offered to resign, twice. Would he have accepted if he hadn't been so terrifyingly short of experienced officers? She wasn't sure what *she* would have done if their positions had been reversed. But she didn't dare ask him. She wasn't sure she wanted to know the answer.

The colonel smiled, very briefly. "Good luck."

"Thank you, sir," Jasmine said. She rose, catching sight of their reflection in the wall-mounted computer monitors as she moved. They were very different and yet...there was something about them that was identical. Shared experiences, perhaps, or a shared outlook on the world around them. "I won't let you down."

CHAPTER
FOUR

The Battle of Camelot is a better example, at least for the military. On the face of it, the Crackers took a suicidal gamble and lost, badly. Their decision to attack Camelot - to attempt to cripple the remains of imperial governance on Avalon - was not only foolhardy, it was unnecessary.

- Professor Leo Caesius. The Role of Randomness In War.

"Is it wrong of me," Gaby asked as she climbed into bed, "to wish I was going with you?"

Ed considered it for a long moment. "Are politics finally starting to get you down?"

"Yeah," Gaby admitted. "Too many different factions, too many different opinions on just what we should do…it's not quite what I envisaged during the war."

"Nor I," Ed said. "I never expected all of this."

He waved a hand at the wall, indicating Castle Rock and Camelot, on the other side of the Sea of Dreams. Gaby had flown back to Camelot shortly after the briefing, while he'd stayed to talk to Jasmine and a dozen other officers. Piece by piece, the operational plans were becoming reality. It wouldn't be long before the CEF was assembled, ready to board its ships for the trip to Corinthian. And then he'd be leaving her behind while he went on yet another deployment.

"Everything was a great deal simpler during the first war," Gaby said. "This one…this one is complicated."

"You love it," Ed said. He'd never seen Gaby happier than when she was organising a political campaign, gathering support for her causes and bargaining cheerfully with her fellow politicians. It helped, he supposed, that so few of her fellows had any real long-term experience with politics. They hadn't yet ossified, unlike the Grand Senate. "Don't you?"

"I just wish this war was over," Gaby said, flatly. "Right now, the balance of power is skewing out of control."

She took a breath. "And there's something else I need to tell you," she added. "Something that might change everything."

Ed met her eyes, trying to read her expression. She sounded nervous, as if she wasn't quite sure how to talk to him. *That* was odd - and worrying. They'd been lovers for the last five years, after she'd become President. She knew him as well as anyone outside the marines, save perhaps for Professor Caesius. What was she so reluctant to talk about?

"I'm pregnant," Gaby said.

Ed felt his mouth drop open in shock. It took him several moments to form a coherent word or two. "Really? Pregnant?"

"I checked with the doctor this afternoon," Gaby said. She looked down at the bed for a long moment. "I wasn't feeling so good, you see. The doctor confirmed I was pregnant. I wasn't expecting it."

Ed stared at her, trying to wrap his thoughts about the concept of being a father. *His* father had been an unknown - and, now that Earth was gone, Ed knew he'd never know just who had fathered him. It wasn't as if he'd had many decent role models either, in his early life; he hadn't met anyone worthy of respect until he'd entered Boot Camp. What would his Drill Instructors have thought of him now? If they were still alive, where were they...?

I'm going to be a father, he thought. *But how?*

Glee and panic rushed through his mind. He had no experience with decent fathers, with men who set good examples for their children. The less said about his so-called stepfathers the better and as for the others... no, he couldn't think of them as anything other than monsters who'd deserved worse than to die when the city-blocks tumbled. No, he would have to learn from the Drill Instructors, but he couldn't treat a baby like they'd treated new recruits...

"That's wonderful," he said, finally. "How...?"

Gaby made a face. "The doctor said that my implant had expired ahead of time," she said, after a moment. "They didn't fill the reservoir completely back then, apparently. There was a shortage of contraceptive drugs."

"Or they were hoping you'd get pregnant and settle down with children," Ed said. The Old Council had probably thought a population boom was exactly what they needed. "I...it's wonderful, isn't it?"

"I think so," Gaby said. She smiled, rather tiredly. "There will be some tongues wagging, of course, but I don't think it's really much of a secret."

Ed nodded. Their relationship was one of the worst-kept secrets on Avalon. No one really cared enough to object, in any case. Gaby's father was long-dead, along with most of his family after the first rebellion had been brutally crushed. The handful of survivors thought the idea of Gaby having a relationship with Ed strengthened the settlement that had ended the war. There were a handful of traditionalists who would probably raise their eyebrows, but no one would really object.

"We should get married now," he said. He had never had much respect for marriage, after how the concept had been perverted on Earth, but it meant something on Avalon. "We can have it done right away..."

"It would be better to wait until my term in office ends," Gaby said. "I have another year to go."

Ed frowned. "Can you serve when you're pregnant?"

"I had better be able to serve," Gaby said. "If I resign now, Ed, there will be one hell of a power struggle over who replaces me."

"True," Ed agreed. Gaby had started her career as the post-war president of Avalon, enjoying the backing of almost all of the planet's factions. But now she held a position in the Commonwealth...and she didn't enjoy quite so much backing there. "We really do need to end this war."

He scowled as a thought struck him. "I can't stay."

"I wasn't going to ask you to stay," Gaby assured him. She sounded annoyed, rather than amused or angry. "I understood when I started dating you that you might have to leave for months or years."

Ed sighed. It was the old dilemma, rearing its ugly head all over again. A woman who married into the military might find herself alone, trying to bring up her children, while her husband was deployed elsewhere for months or years. Even the corps had problems keeping husbands and wives together, although it *had* offered living space on the Slaughterhouse to women who married active-duty marines. He'd been lucky, really; he'd gone to Lakshmibai, but otherwise he'd stayed on Avalon...

But he couldn't stay this time.

He cursed under his breath, torn between two imperatives. Part of him wanted to stay behind, to put command in the hands of Jasmine Yamane or General Crichton Mathis. He could do it, too; no one would question his orders. But the rest of him knew he *had* to go, he *had* to be with his men when they faced their gravest challenge. And yet, that meant leaving Gaby alone when she was pregnant...and taking the risk he might never return. He'd survived over fifteen years as a marine, but that conferred no immunity to death. A stray bullet could end his life as surely as it could end the life of the rawest of recruits.

Gaby rested her hand on his. "You can't stay," she said, softly. "You'd torment yourself, ever after, over what might have happened if you'd been there."

"I'd be worrying about you too," Ed said. It was silly, he knew; Gaby was a healthy young woman who would receive the very best of medical care. And yet he would worry...he looked down at himself and laughed. Gaby wasn't a marine, but she'd fought hard against overwhelming odds for years. She didn't need him patronising her. "Are you sure you'll be all right?"

"As sure as I can be," Gaby said. She touched her flat stomach lightly with her left hand. Ed watched, half-expecting to see a baby bump already there. "There's seven months to go before the baby's due, in any case."

Ed found himself lost for words. How *did* one be a good father? The young men he'd mentored had all been in their late teens or older, already formed by the time they were placed in his hands. He had no idea how to approach a child. It scared him on so many levels that he was tempted to run. And yet, the thought of just walking away was unthinkable. How many children on Earth had been lost to barbarity because they didn't have a strong and decent father-figure?

"I can't stay," he said, again. "Should we put the baby in an exowomb?"

Gaby shook her head. "My family has always gone for natural births," she said. Ed bit his tongue to keep from pointing out that there was nothing *natural* about modern medical treatment. "And besides, it's not an option open to many families here."

Ed nodded in reluctant agreement. Exowombs had been common among the upper classes on Earth - they still were, amongst the Traders - but they were rare on Avalon. Gaby hadn't come from a rich family, either. She probably *could* get an exowomb, if she tried, yet it would look very bad politically. And it just wasn't like her to claim an advantage when so many others were denied it.

"I have a son," he breathed.

"Or a daughter," Gaby pointed out. "I didn't want them to tell me what was coming."

Her eyes narrowed. "Would that bother you?"

"On Earth, it would have done," Ed said, honestly. It had been nearly seventeen years since he'd escaped the Undercity, but he still recalled the horrors he'd seen. When society collapsed, it was the girls who always got the worst of it. Rape and murder had been terrifyingly common, while suicide was the single biggest cause of death. "But on Avalon, it shouldn't be a problem."

It damn well wouldn't be, he resolved privately. *Avalon* took a much more practical view towards self-defence than Earth, where girls were denied anything they could use to fight back against the barbarians who infested the planet. *His* daughter would start learning to fight as soon as she could walk, training with daggers and pistols suited to a small pair of hands. If anyone tried to touch her, Ed was sure, it would be the last mistake he ever made.

"That's good," Gaby said, dryly. "I wasn't planning to check."

"I understand," Ed said. "Do you want to tell everyone now?"

Gaby touched her stomach, again. "I'll have to inform the Speaker," she said. "That's written into the laws, Ed; if there's anything that might impede my ability to handle my duties, I'm to report it before it becomes a problem. But otherwise..."

She frowned. "Do you want to tell anyone now?"

"I should inform Gwendolyn," Ed said. His friend would need to know, if only so she could tell him off for being distracted. He wanted to shout the news across the entire Commonwealth, but it was really Gaby's choice. Her opponents were the ones who would want to make hay out of the whole affair. "But otherwise…I can wait."

"Tell her," Gaby said. "But no one else, if you don't mind. The doctor says everything is fine, but I'd prefer to wait until the pregnancy is well-established."

Ed blinked in surprise - pregnant women on Earth wanted everyone to know as soon as possible - but he had no real objections. It wasn't as if he had many people to tell, in any case. The people he met were largely his subordinates, even Gwendolyn. Gaby was the closest thing he had to an equal and she was technically his superior. But then, there were so many legal headaches caused by the Fall of the Empire that it was probably better not to look at the matter too closely.

"I don't mind," he assured her. "It shouldn't be a problem."

"I don't have anything to gain from an early announcement," Gaby said. "I'll make a short one when the bulge becomes noticeable."

"I won't be here," Ed said. He scowled at the wall. "I honestly don't expect to be back for at least a year."

"I will endure," Gaby promised. "And after that, it will be the end of my term."

"I know," Ed said. He reached out and touched her belly, feeling nothing. Stupid, of course; the baby would be tiny right now, barely large enough to see. It would be months before the baby was large enough to kick, as his sisters had kicked before they'd been born. "You take very good care of yourself, all right?"

"Of course," Gaby said. Her mouth twisted in amused dismay. "But don't treat me like a china doll either. I'm not *that* fragile"

Ed nodded once, then kissed her, feeling a sudden burst of love and desire as her tongue entered his mouth. He wanted her, needed her. They wouldn't see much of one another over the next two weeks anyway, no matter what happened. There was just too much to do, even though the military was now a well-oiled machine. He'd check everything himself, just in case. He was the one who would be on the sharp end, if the shit hit the fan.

Gaby kissed him back as he climbed on top of her, reassuring himself that he couldn't hurt her or the baby. They'd made love countless times before she'd discovered she was pregnant. His hands traced her breasts as he slipped into her, her legs locking around him and pulling him close. He wondered, absently, just when their child had been conceived, then decided it didn't matter. Dating it all the way back to the first moments would be problematic. And then all rational thought was gone…

Afterwards, he watched her sleep, feeling an odd wave of protectiveness. Gaby didn't *need* his protection, not when she'd led an insurgency and then built a functioning government, but part of him just wanted to stay with her. And yet, he knew it was impossible. He couldn't claim something he'd deny to any other marine under his command.

And you might not be here when the baby is born, his thoughts mocked him. He rose, carefully tucking the blanket in around her body. Gaby was tough, but she was also pregnant…he told himself not to be silly. It was the baby he was worried about, not her. *What happens if there are… complications?*

He swallowed as he padded into the small office, where he'd set up a computer terminal attached to the military network. Modern medicine could work miracles, compared to what his long-distant predecessors had had to endure, but complications happened…particularly when people *wanted* them to happen. Gaby had enemies, powerful enemies; Admiral Singh, if no one else, had plenty of motive to try to arrange for an accident. He keyed the terminal, checking Gaby's health records. No one had flagged an alert since she'd first been captured, in the closing days of the war…

Idiot, he told himself. *She would have said if there was something very wrong.*

He closed the file and opened his personal file instead, digging up his will. It was an open question just how legal it was, these days; large tracts of Imperial Law had been wiped from existence, in the Commonwealth, at the stroke of a pen. But he had never bothered to update his will, not

THEY SHALL NOT PASS

when there was very little to give away. He had no family, no old friends who could be reached...

But that was no longer true.

He looked at the standard form for a long moment. His possessions, such as they were, had been assigned to his company, although quite how *that* would work out when he'd been in command was beyond him. It wasn't as if he had very much in any case. His remaining bank balance would be shared out for beer money. Like almost every other careerist, he'd been content to allow it to grow while the corps had fed and watered him - he'd known he didn't want to invest, even if there hadn't been concerns about insider trading - and there was quite a tidy sum. It would take the remainder of his company a few weeks to drink their way through it. But now...

His hands danced over the keyboard, rewriting his will. The money would go to the baby, held in trust until he reached his majority. Or she, he reminded himself. The child could easily be a girl, rather than a boy. Boys tended to have an easier time of it on Earth, but even they could lose their lives in the blink of an eye. If he'd been a little weaker, or a little more aggressive, he would have died or become a gangster, to die when he grew old or stupid or ran into someone stronger and luckier than himself. But on Avalon, a little boy could grow into a proper man.

He saved the file, then emailed a copy to Gwendolyn. She'd witness it, attach her e-signature and then send it back into the files. If something happened to him, the will would activate...he hoped nothing would go wrong, but it was better to be sure. Right now, he had something more personal to live for than the corps - or the Commonwealth.

Shaking his head, he rose to his feet and walked back into the bedroom. Gaby had shifted slightly in her sleep, her red hair spilling over the pillows. His heart almost stopped at the sight; he stared at her for a long moment, then climbed into bed next to her. She cuddled up to him in her sleep, rubbing against him. He wrapped an arm around her and closed his eyes.

Sleep tight, he told himself. *Tomorrow is another day.*

CHAPTER

FIVE

Unnecessary? The former council had already been arrested and removed from power, the governor had already agreed to concede the vast majority of the Cracker demands. Their desperate attempt to derail the slow shift against them - by striking directly at Camelot - risked everything. It could easily have pushed the governor into demanding harsh measures, instead of a political solution.

- Professor Leo Caesius. The Role of Randomness In War.

"I'm going to miss you," Emmanuel said, as they lay together afterwards. "You only just got back!"

Jasmine concealed her amusement, feeling an odd twinge of guilt. Emmanuel didn't know it, but he would be coming with her and the CEF. But she couldn't tell him, not when operational security came first. Far too many secrets had been blown because they'd been discussed openly, without regard for who might be listening in. She trusted Emmanuel, but she knew better than to take chances.

"I'll miss you too," she said, as she climbed out of bed and headed towards the shower. "But we will see each other again."

She smiled to herself as she turned on the tap, washing her body clean, then shook her head ruefully. It wasn't as if they would be together on Corinthian, even though they would technically be on the same *world*. No wonder the Colonel believed Admiral Singh would underestimate the task before her, Jasmine considered, if *she* could imagine that Emmanuel and her would be close together. She'd been in enough campaigns to know that a mere five kilometres could be brutal, if they were guarded by trained and experienced soldiers with plenty of heavy weapons.

The door opened. Emmanuel stepped into the shower. "It's 0700," he said. "When do you have to go?"

"I have to be at the base for 0900," Jasmine answered. She silently totted up the timing in her mind; half an hour for breakfast, half an hour to get to the base...there would be plenty of leeway if something went wrong. "Did you hear anything from your superiors?"

"I have to present myself at the main building at 0900," Emmanuel said. He climbed into the shower, his hands running over her body. "Before then, we have to empty the apartment."

Jasmine nodded, curtly. The apartment block was really for visitors from the Commonwealth, not a lone marine and her boyfriend. Whatever happened, they wouldn't be coming back after they left the complex. Her possessions would be stowed away until she returned, or handled in accordance with her will if she died. She didn't want to think about the possibility, but a lifetime of experience had taught her that *anyone* could die. Blake Coleman had seemed untouchable until an explosion had blown his body to bits. They'd never found the remains.

They made love with brutal urgency, washed again and then ate a simple breakfast before packing their bags. Neither of them had brought much, beyond a change of clothing and a pair of personal datapads. They'd have to go into storage too, Jasmine reminded herself. She was hardly the only marine to have a personal datapad, rather than a corps-issued terminal, but they posed another security risk. How many operations had been blown because a civilian-grade terminal had been turned into an unwitting spy?

"I'll see you soon," she promised, once the plates were washed and left to dry. She had no intention of leaving the apartment in a mess. "And I hope the interview goes well for you."

Emmanuel shrugged. "I'll have to go back into the office," he said. "Quite a few of the scoops I had before you returned couldn't be printed, apparently for planetary security."

Jasmine had to smile. "They do have a point."

"I know," Emmanuel said. He kissed her goodbye. "But who watches the watchmen who decide what threatens planetary security?"

Jasmine contemplated the problem as she walked downstairs, passed through the security checkpoint and jogged towards the marine barracks at the far edge of Castle Rock. Who *did* decide what threatened planetary security? She'd always tended to be careful, when it came to deciding what could and what couldn't be reported, but she knew from bitter experience that the rules could be interpreted differently. Admiral Valentine had been quite happy to reveal sensitive operational data to the media - and she was sure the rebels on Han had been delighted - yet he'd clamped down hard on anything that might cast doubt on his military competence. Who knew what would have happened, how many lives would have been saved, if the idiot had been removed from command before the shit *really* hit the fan?

She dismissed the thought as she stopped outside the barracks and pressed her hand against the scanner, allowing it to read the ID chip implanted in her palm. There was a long pause, then the door clicked, allowing her to push it open and step into the prefabricated building. It was the only place on Avalon that was solely for the marines, even though nearly a third of the company had died and another third had been distributed out to places where their skills could help build the Commonwealth. She scowled at the thought - there would be no new marines for years to come, even if they built a whole new Slaughterhouse - and then walked into the briefing room. Unlike so many others, it was reassuringly simple. A handful of chairs, a simple table and a projector. There was no need for fancy decorations in the corps.

"Jasmine," Lieutenant Joe Buckley called. "Welcome home!"

Jasmine allowed herself a smile. Joe Buckley had been one of her first comrades, back when she'd joined the company. He'd had a terrible reputation for getting into scrapes, but a reasonably decent reputation for getting out of them afterwards. She shook his hand warmly, then glanced at the other marines. Rifleman Thomas Stewart had been with her on Meridian, but the other four were largely unknown to her. They'd been in other platoons during the deployment to Avalon and then assigned out to various posts before she'd taken command of 1st Platoon for the first time.

"Thank you, Joe," she said, seriously. "I thought you'd left us for a wife!"

"The colonel called me back," Joe said, without heat. "Seriously, I was getting bored of training the youngsters."

"And a bit repetitive," Rifleman Henry Parkinson commented. "The training field was getting a little *too* organised."

"It isn't the bloody Slaughterhouse," Buckley snapped. "There are limits to what we can do to the poor little mites."

Jasmine glanced at him. "Is there any prospect of getting a new Slaughterhouse?"

"Not as yet," Buckley said. "I think Colonel Stalker doesn't want to take that step."

"Understandable," Rifleman William Randolph commented, darkly. "It would be a little like giving up."

Jasmine had to agree. The Slaughterhouse bound the marines together, reassuring them that a rifleman who'd been transferred from halfway across the galaxy would still speak the same language and look at the world in the same way. It had resisted all attempts to soften the training course or politicise the training cadre, concentrating on turning out the finest soldiers the galaxy had ever seen. Boot Camp was one thing - there had been a Boot Camp in each sector, preparing recruits for the Slaughterhouse, but a hundred different Slaughterhouses would rapidly lead to a hundred different kinds of marine. It could not be tolerated.

And yet we are terrifyingly short of manpower, she thought. 1st Platoon was meant to have ten marines, but she only had seven, counting herself. *There are no CROWs on their way to replace the fallen.*

"We need to be realistic," Rifleman Gavin Jalil observed. "None of us are going to see the Core Worlds again."

"That's not a bad thing," Buckley commented. "Have you ever tried to live there?"

"No," Jalil said. "But our universe is a great deal smaller than it was."

"Matter of opinion," Rifleman David Graf said. "It wouldn't be hard to send a starship to the Slaughterhouse, even if it *will* take a year before we hear anything back."

"Bit of a waste of resources," Jalil argued. "We have a war to fight."

"The war won't last forever," Graf countered. "For all we know, the Traders have already sent a mission to Earth."

"Or what's left of it," Jasmine said. Reports were vague, but most of them agreed that Earth had been destroyed and a tidal wave of anarchy was spreading across the Core Worlds. Even if they did manage to get back to the Core, it wouldn't be what they remembered. "I don't think we can count on any help."

She sucked in her breath. Some of the older marines had bitched and moaned about being sent into exile, but she'd known she wouldn't be leaving the corps for at least eighteen years in any case. She'd signed up for the long haul. Now, in hindsight, being exiled to Avalon might just have saved their lives. If the Core Worlds really had collapsed into anarchy, eighty-seven marines wouldn't have made much of a difference, while they'd been able to save Avalon from disaster. And then build a whole new society...

"This is an interesting debate," she said, "but it's not why we're here."

She took a seat and faced them, taking command. "Colonel Stalker is baiting a trap for Admiral Singh and the Wolves," she said, and ran through a brief outline. "Our job is to stay behind enemy lines and make their lives as miserable as possible."

"Sounds just like a rerun of what you did the *last* time you were on Corinthian," Buckley observed. "You just want to hurt the bastards as much as possible?"

"Last time, we had to overthrow the government," Jasmine reminded him. "This time, all we have to do is harry the invaders until they can be beaten."

"So we're still playing insurgent," Jalil observed. He leaned forward, excited by the challenge. "That's not going to be easy. Sneaking up on a military force is a little harder than sneaking up on a base..."

"We've done it before," Buckley said. He winked at Jasmine. "Remember when we broke into that Civil Guard base, wearing nothing but our birthday suits?"

"That was Blake's idea," Jasmine said. "And I don't think we're going to be trying it on Corinthian."

She smiled in happy memory. The marines had been tasked with testing the base's security to encourage the Civil Guard to close any holes before the Nihilists or another terrorist movement tried to steal weapons or launch an attack from inside the wire. Blake, always joking around, had suggested waltzing into the base wearing absolutely nothing. Somehow, the Civil Guardsmen had missed five naked men and one woman making their way through the fences and into the armoury. They'd been seated on the supply crates when the guards had finally caught up with them.

"Probably not," Buckley agreed. "Something might go wrong at the worst possible moment."

"More than that," Graf pointed out. "Any Guardsmen who stayed alive long enough to be folded into the Wolves would be reasonably experienced."

Jasmine nodded. The Civil Guard had always been a mixed bag, with some units considered reasonably competent and the remainder ranging between weekend warriors to thugs, rapists and looters. But the latter wouldn't have lasted long as the Empire fell apart, she was sure; the only way to survive was to gain experience and use it before time ran out. The guardsmen she'd met on Thule hadn't been *too* bad, compared to some of the units she'd seen on Han.

"We'll be borrowing some elements from the knights to serve as our op-force," she said, simply. "We cannot take the risk of assuming our enemies are idiots."

"Of course not," Buckley said. "The youngsters aren't much by our standards, Jasmine, but they're keen and they learn fast."

"It helps they don't have any bureaucrats messing with their training patterns," Graf added, deadpan. "They just have to cope with *you* teaching them what to do."

Buckley gave him a one-fingered gesture. He wasn't a trained Drill Instructor, Jasmine knew, but he was hardly the only person who had been given responsibilities that forced him to learn on the job. And yet, a surplus of ammunition alone would make his charges far more proficient shots. She'd wondered why the army soldiers had performed so badly on Han, only to learn that they were rarely allowed to fire their weapons for training purposes. There was just too much paperwork before they could go onto the range.

"We're not here to fight each other," Jasmine said, before Buckley could make a cutting remark. "Our job is to fight the enemy."

She went on, quickly. "Joe Buckley will be my second," she continued. "Below that, we'll go by strict seniority, but I don't envisage any problems. We've all seen the elephant. We can and we will argue out what we're going to do, if we have time."

"It strikes me that most of our operations will have to be worked out on the fly," Jalil said. "I don't see how we can plan if there are too many variables."

"Me neither," Jasmine confirmed. She tapped the projector to display the map. "There are simply too many possible landing sites within a hundred kilometres of the city. Or they may land some distance from the city, just to assemble their forces before commencing the advance. We'll do our best to guess where they might land, but it really won't be any better than a guess. If I was in charge of the landing operation, I'd make damn sure to lay as many false trails as possible before landing the main force."

"That's standard procedure," Jalil said.

"Insofar that there *is* a standard procedure for this," Jasmine agreed. "How many times have *we* made a forced landing on a planetary surface?"

"We have sneaked insertion teams down to the surface," Buckley reminded her. "But landing an entire army without orbital fire support? It's never happened."

"There *was* the landing on Thule," Stewart said, quietly. "But there *were* friends on the ground too."

Jasmine winced. Thule had been an elephant trap, all right, one they'd had no choice but to spring. Wolfbane had done an *excellent* job of laying the groundwork for a successful invasion, even though her escape from Meridian had more than evened the score. The bastards still had a major advantage over the Commonwealth...

"We'll go through the possible options now," she said, "and then start our training schedule."

"That's right," Buckley said. "How much fat have you picked up from being a Brigadier?"

Jasmine resisted - barely - the urge to stick her tongue out at him. The hell of it was that he had a point. She just hadn't had the time to keep up with her daily exercises, not even the intensive running that marked the start of every day in the marines. There was no doubt that she was still stronger and fitter than ninety-nine percent of the people she met, but she *had* let herself slip. Two weeks wasn't enough to repair the damage, yet it would have to do.

And I can rely on Buckley to chase me around with a cattle prod, if necessary, she thought, ruefully. Drill Instructors never forced their charges to do anything - they needed to find their motivation from within - but she was hardly a raw recruit. The marines under her command relied on her. *Joe won't let me slip any further.*

"Too much," she said, finally. "It's sitting on my ass all day, really."

"Sounds like a nightmare," Graf teased. "What were you thinking when you took the job?"

"*Someone* had to take command," Jasmine said. She hadn't done too badly on Lakshmibai, had she? "And it was quite an interesting challenge."

She shook her head slowly. The CEF had been better-trained than almost every other unit she'd seen of comparable size, but its collective reaction time was far slower than a marine platoon's. Striking a balance between giving the point men their heads and keeping a firm grip on her command hadn't been easy; indeed, she had a feeling she'd made more than a few mistakes on campaign. Being back in command of a small unit of highly-trained soldiers was a relief. She could rely on the marines to react instantly to any possible threats.

"Not that it matters right now," she added. She unfurled a sheet of paper, laying it out on the table. "How should we proceed?"

"Hit their landing shuttles," Buckley said, instantly. "It's what they did to us on Thule."

"If we can get a MANPAD unit into range," Stewart countered. "We might want to leave that task to the planetary militia."

"If the militia will fight," Graf said. "Can they fight?"

"The reports say they're good," Jasmine said. She didn't know for sure - she wouldn't, until she saw the militia personally - but Corinthia had good reason to keep a standing army in place. "And they should have enough HVMs to make life interesting for the landing forces."

"Then we stay low and slip out at night," Buckley said. "They'll need to set up supply dumps before they can muster the forces for a general offensive."

"Assuming they don't just give up," Stewart said. "Is Singh really going to over-commit herself?"

"I think so, if she takes the bait," Jasmine said. "Her pride was badly dented when we drove her off for the first time."

"That's something for the colonel to worry about," Graf said. He traced out a line on the map. "They'll practically *have* to secure this road, if they want to get supply trucks moving down to the city. We can do something with that, I think…"

Jasmine nodded, scribbling down a note. "An IED," she said. "Mine the road ahead of time."

"And a few more nasty surprises," Buckley added. "This should be an interesting mission."

"And too many innocents will be mashed in the gears," Graf warned. "Whatever happens, nothing is ever going to be the same again."

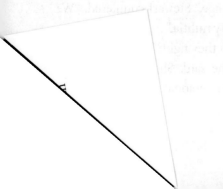

CHAPTER
SIX

Hindsight tells us that the Crackers took an insane gamble, but it didn't look that way at the time! They had no way to know just what decisions were being taken in Camelot (and Castle Rock.) How could they?
- Professor Leo Caesius. The Role of Randomness In War.

"Colonel," Emmanuel Alves said, as he was shown into Ed's office. "You wanted to see me?"

"I did," Ed said. He rose, nodding towards the drinks dispenser. "Do you want coffee?"

"Yes, please," Emmanuel said. "I've developed a taste for it."

Ed smiled as he poured two cups, then added milk and sugar. He'd grown used to drinking his coffee black, when he'd started at the Slaughterhouse, but in truth all that really mattered was that it had a good kick. There were times when he wondered if the entire Marine Corps ran on coffee. It was certainly drunk in vast quantities during deployments.

He passed Emmanuel his cup, then sat down behind his desk, studying the reporter. It was hard to trust *any* reporter, but he had to admit that Emmanuel was very different from the idiots and assholes who'd been assigned to shadow his unit on Han. The man actually had a working brain, for one thing, and an actual understanding of how the universe worked. But then, he *had* been on the fringes of the Crackers, back during the war. He might not have been a fighter, unlike so many others, but he'd been far from useless.

45

And he's dating a marine, Ed reminded himself. It was odd for such a relationship to last, but it had. *There's more to him than merely being a reporter.*

"You were on Lakshmibai, as I recall," he said, without preamble. "Your first embed went very well."

"Thank you, sir," Emmanuel said. "It was a very interesting experience."

Ed smiled, rather ruefully. It had been rather *more* interesting in the embassy complex, with howling barbarians struggling desperately to break down the doors and get their hands on the offworlders. He knew, all too well, just how close they'd come to total disaster, losing both the Commonwealth and Wolfbane representatives to the enemy. In hindsight, they'd badly underestimated the fanaticism of the planet's population.

"I'm offering you the chance to do another embed," he said. "The standard conditions apply, I'm afraid; you can back out now, if you wish, but afterwards you will be going into the lockbox until it no longer matters. Do you want to back out now?"

Emmanuel didn't hesitate. "No, sir."

Ed nodded. The reporters he'd known in the past would have demanded details, details he was unwilling to give without a clear commitment to either embed or remain in the lockbox until the operation was well underway. There might be some advantages to having hints of the overall plan escaping onto the datanet, but he wanted - needed - to keep the information as compartmentalised as possible. Admiral Singh couldn't be allowed enough time to think about her choices.

"There will be a major deployment to Corinthian," he said. He ran through the idea as tersely as possible. Emmanuel was more trustworthy than any other reporter, perhaps, but there were still limits. "Are you still interested in embedding with the CEF?"

"Yes, sir," Emmanuel said.

There was no hesitation, Ed noted. But he wasn't sure if that was a good or bad sign.

"Very well," Ed said. He smiled, rather coldly. "You'll be going through a brief refresher course, along with a handful of others who will be accompanying the CEF. If you change your mind at any point, you will be going straight into the lockbox. Any questions?"

"Just one," Emmanuel said. "I assume we will be following standard censorship protocols?"

"Correct," Ed said. "We do need to tell people what we're doing, but we can't allow information of tactical value to leak out."

"There will be a time delay," Emmanuel pointed out. "Surely…"

"It isn't something I want to test," Ed said, cutting him off. Emmanuel was right, to be fair, but there was no point in taking unnecessary chances. "The wrong piece of information, in the wrong hands, could be disastrous. Even if it's contained to the newsroom…"

He sighed. There was no way to be *sure* that all of the spy rings had been identified and quietly isolated. A single agent in the newsrooms - and that was where *he* would put an agent, if he could - could be disastrous. Simply knowing what the Commonwealth was trying to censor might be very helpful for the enemy. There was little more conspicuous than a man ducking for cover.

"This isn't negotiable," he concluded. "If you have a problem with it, say so now and you can go into the lockbox."

"I'll cope," Emmanuel said, dryly. "What happens now?"

Ed tapped his terminal. "You'll be escorted to the barracks; your refresher course starts tomorrow. Make sure you update your will, write a set of final letters and tie up loose ends before the course starts. You may not come back alive."

"Yes, sir," Emmanuel said. "And thank you."

"Thank me when you come back," Ed said. He disliked taking half-trained civilians into danger, even if there were certain advantages to the whole affair. But it was important to keep public support for the war. "And Emmanuel?"

Emmanuel blinked. "Yes, sir?"

"She didn't have the right to tell you," Ed said. He trusted Jasmine to keep her mouth shut, but it could cause problems when Emmanuel figured out that she'd known ahead of time. "I told her to keep it to herself."

"Yes, sir," Emmanuel said. "I understand."

Sergeant Lewis appeared and escorted Emmanuel out the door, taking him down to the guest barracks. Ed watched him go, shaking his head in quiet amusement. A reporter with a working brain, a reporter who understood...he'd always thought such people simply didn't exist. But then, on Avalon, a competent reporter could go far...and no one would complain if one was hanged for revealing classified information. Far too many people had fought in the war, on one side or the other, to take such matters lightly.

He finished his coffee, then returned to his paperwork. General George Grosskopf would take command on Avalon, in his absence, but he needed to tie up as many loose ends as possible before he departed. The various secret programs, so highly-classified that even Grosskopf didn't know they existed, had to be given orders covering every imaginable contingency, up to and including his death. He hoped - prayed - that there would be no trouble appointing Grosskopf as his successor, but he knew it wouldn't be easy. He'd started his career in the Civil Guard, after all.

His intercom bleeped. "Sir, Commodore Caesius is here to see you."

Ed glanced at the clock, then nodded. Commodore Mandy Caesius was twenty minutes early, but it didn't matter that much. Unlike Ed - or Jasmine - her problems were surprisingly simple. Either she had her opportunity to catch Admiral Singh with her pants down or she didn't. There was no middle ground.

"Send her in," he ordered. "And then hold my calls."

"Aye, sir."

The door opened. Ed rose in welcome, smiling at the young woman as she stepped into his office. It was hard, sometimes, to draw a line between the red-haired bratty teenage girl he'd met years ago and the competent naval officer facing him, but Mandy had had a harder path than far too many of her comrades. He would have hated her on Earth, he acknowledged, yet Avalon had been the making of her. And yet...there was a hardness in the young woman that worried him, sometimes.

She should have had months of therapy, after her return from pirate captivity, he thought, as they exchanged salutes. *But instead we put her back to work.*

"Commodore," he said. Mandy closed the door, then sat down in front of his desk. "I trust the planning session went well?"

"Well enough," Mandy said. "There are some issues that need to be explored further, but overall the squadron should be ready to do its duty."

Ed nodded. "No problems?"

"We will need to source additional supplies," Mandy warned. "A short engagement won't be a problem, but a long series of engagements is likely to cost us dearly. We certainly can't rely on drawing supplies from Corinthian."

"Of course not," Ed agreed. "Can you arrange freighter space?"

"Yes, but we'll need an interstellar supply dump," Mandy said. "Keeping the freighters will cause problems elsewhere."

Ed scowled. The Commonwealth had been producing its own freighters for the last four years, but there were nowhere near enough freighter bottoms to move everything the Commonwealth *needed* to move. Even with the help of the Trade Federation, there just wasn't enough to go around. The war was putting an ungodly strain on a structure that wasn't designed for such intensive overuse. Logistics were rapidly shaping up to be yet another Achilles Heel.

"We'll send them back once the supply dumps are established," he said. "Are there any other considerations?"

"It depends on just what Admiral Singh sends to take the planet," Mandy said. "Our cruisers are worth two of theirs, perhaps more, but she does have a numerical advantage. And if she wants Corinthian as much as you think, she'll send battleships too. They're old, but they have substantial firepower."

"True," Ed agreed. He'd read the reports from the shipbuilding commission. They had a design for battleships, but they'd warned that the design would eat up far too much of the Commonwealth's resources for limited returns. "Can you handle them?"

"It depends on how they've been modified, sir," Mandy said. "The last set of reports from a skirmish suggested that the Wolves have managed to produce and deploy improved missiles and seeker warheads. They're closing the gap between us. No sign of force shields yet, but my people think it's only a matter of time."

"I know," Ed grunted. "They know it's possible, don't they?"

"They do now," Mandy confirmed. She shivered. "Realistically, sir, if they close the gap a little more we're going to be in deep trouble."

Ed winced. Mandy, like Jasmine, had been captured…but while the Wolves had been fairly civilised the pirates had been nothing of the sort.

She'd managed to escape, crippling their starship as she left, yet the whole experience had scarred her badly. And yet, it had also given her a purpose. There was no one more ruthless in hunting down pirate bases and destroying them than Mandy Caesius.

"Then we will just have to try and stay ahead of them," he said. "Are there any other issues of concern?"

"My mother has invited my sister and myself to dinner, four days from now," Mandy said, slowly. "Is that going to be a problem?"

Ed hesitated. Technically, he should refuse to allow her to attend, but Mandy couldn't be kept on Castle Rock. She was splitting her time between the ships assembling in orbit and the training facilities near Camelot. Putting her in the lockbox would merely hamper his plans and add nothing to his security. And everyone attending the dinner would understand the value of keeping their mouths shut...

"Remember the rules," he said, firmly. "I don't want a single security breach."

"I understand, sir," Mandy said. "And thank you."

"Have your ships ready to depart on schedule," Ed ordered. "That will be thanks enough, I believe."

Mandy rose. "I'll do my best, sir," she said. "And thank you again."

Ed watched her go, making a mental note to check up on her when he had the time. Mandy had been through hell, a more hellish experience, in many ways, than himself. The Slaughterhouse had been bad, particularly the sections covering conduct after capture, but Mandy had never had any such training herself. He wouldn't have blamed her if she'd wanted to return to Avalon and never fly back into space, if she'd made that choice. And yet she was still fighting...

Better that than submission and surrender, he thought, tartly. *She's very definitely a fighter.*

He returned to his paperwork, working hard to tie up the final loose ends. Grosskopf would be formally taking command tomorrow, allowing them a chance to work out any problems before Ed departed for Corinthian. He'd have to be briefed into the secret too, Ed reminded himself; he trusted Grosskopf too, but the problem was still the same. The more people who knew, the greater the chance of an accidental leak. And while he wouldn't mind taunting Singh, there was always the prospect of her deciding it was better to concentrate on breaking through the inner defence line and mopping up Corinthian later.

It's what I would do, Ed reminded himself. But then, his career hadn't been marred by unpleasant superior officers. In some ways, Admiral Singh and Mandy had a great deal in common. *She'll want to rub their nose in their failure to keep her down...*

The terminal bleeped, again. "Sir, General Mathis is here."

"Send him in," Ed ordered.

He ground his teeth in frustration. Life had been so much easier when he'd been a mere captain of marines. Now, he spent half his time doing battle with bureaucracy and the greatest danger he faced was a paper cut. He'd have to make certain to spend time on the training ground himself, just to make sure he hadn't slacked. It had been far too long since he'd led men in combat. And to think he'd resisted the opportunity to take command for himself several times, just to ensure he had more experienced officers...

You do need experienced officers, his thoughts mocked him. *But you don't want to lose your edge either.*

He pushed the thought aside as General Crichton Mathis entered the room, one hand snapping up in salute. Ed rose, studying the older man carefully. Mathis had been a Civil Guard officer, which was a black mark on his record, but he *had* commanded a regiment during the Cracker War and the Battle of Camelot. And his men thought well of him, which was a good sign. The Civil Guard on Avalon had been good enough to hold the line, even if they hadn't been able to destroy their enemies. If they hadn't, they would have lost the war long ago.

"General," he said. It was odd, issuing orders to a man who held a higher rank than himself, but he'd never chosen to grant himself anything higher than colonel. "Please, be seated."

Mathis, a short man with a bulldog face, nodded curtly. "Yes, sir."

"You know the mission," Ed said. He'd spoken to Mathis personally, after the first planning session. "How quickly can the CEF be ready to depart?"

"We can have the advance units loaded onto ships within the day," Mathis said. He would have worked it out already, Ed was sure. Competent officers always planned for the worst, even as they hoped for the best. "The heavier units will require a couple of days to box up their gear, then another four or five days to load the ships. We can speed matters up, if necessary, by requisitioning supplies intended for the front lines."

"Very good," Ed said. Mentally, he added an extra day or two to the schedule. In his experience, nothing *ever* went like clockwork. Loading even a small military unit onto a starship could produce all kinds of head-aches. "I want you to give your men five days of leave, then start preparing for departure."

Mathis raised his bushy eyebrows. "Five days?"

"The remainder of the supplies won't be ready until then," Ed said. The CEF's transports didn't have stasis tubes, unlike the MEUs the Marine Corps had used to move its men and supplies around the Empire. There was no point in torturing his men by moving them to the ships before it was strictly necessary. "Once they're ready and loaded, we can proceed with the remainder of the loading."

"Yes, sir," Mathis said. "Do we have an official cover story?"

"I believe there's no need to make an explicit announcement," Ed said. Admiral Singh's spies would be more likely to believe something that *looked* like an attempted cover-up, even if it wasn't. "The men can be told they're going on deployment - again - but there's no need for anything else."

"Yes, sir," Mathis said.

Ed nodded. "Morale?"

Mathis showed the first hint of hesitation. "Most of the old sweats survived Thule, sir, and want a little payback," he said. "There were some... issues, because of the retreat, but overall they believe they've done well. The newcomers are less experienced, mostly; I've been keeping a pretty heavy training tempo going for the last two weeks. I think they'll perform well in combat."

"Good," Ed said. He kept his doubts to himself. No one ever knew how well a unit would perform until it saw the elephant, by which time it might be too late. "Are there any other issues I should know about?"

"There's some concern about leaving Avalon undefended," Mathis admitted, "but the sergeants have that well in hand. Most of the disciplinary actions have been fairly minor, too; a few incidents of drunkenness and a couple of idiots who fell asleep on watch. They were all handled in-unit."

"Very good," Ed said.

He nodded in approval. The knights had copied that from the marines, rather than the Imperial Army or the Civil Guard. They wouldn't regret it, either. The Empire had had far too many problems when minor disciplinary issues had to be kicked up the chain to senior officers, even when they could be handled by the sergeants and junior officers.

"See to your men, General," he added. "I fancy they're about to face one hell of a test."

"Yes, sir," Mathis said. He rose, saluting smartly. "I think they'll look forward to it."

CHAPTER
SEVEN

Indeed, their war against the planetary government was slowly losing steam. The combination of debt-relief and new soldiers - raised, trained and paid by the marines - was slowly draining their forces.
- Professor Leo Caesius. The Role of Randomness In War.

The sight before her, Mandy Caesius had to admit, was one she would never have seen on Earth. Hundreds of little houses, small gardens in front and larger gardens behind, lining a street as neatly as soldiers on parade. She'd hated the house, the first time she'd set foot in it, throwing a tantrum that had made her mother take to her bed in dismay and her younger sister flee into the garden. Now, as a serving officer, she understood just how lucky she'd been to have the house…and to leave Earth, before it was too late. She wished, desperately, that she could go back in time and slap her younger self silly. She'd deserved far worse.

She parked the groundcar outside, then climbed out, breathing in the evening air. Avalon had smelled odd to her, when they'd first landed, but now it was normal. Earth's ever-present stench of burning hydrocarbons and far too many humans in close proximity was gone, as was the poison in the air. She honestly didn't want to *think* about just how much crap she'd breathed into her system, once upon a time. Being exiled to Avalon was the smartest thing her father had ever done. And even though she'd hated being separated from her friends, she had come to realise that it had saved her life. None of her friends would have survived the Fall of Earth.

The door opened. "Mandy," Mindy called. "Come on! Dinner is waiting!"

Mandy shook her head in disbelief as she saw her younger sister for the first time in nearly a year. Mindy had always been more sporty than her - Mandy had never seen the point of ruining her body through excessive activity - but now she was muscular and lithe, remarkably like Jasmine in so many ways. Her head had been shaved completely, giving her an intimidating appearance that her green eyes did nothing to lighten. She would have been laughed at on Earth, Mandy was sure, but she would have been safe. And that was worth any amount of laughter.

"It's been too long," she said, feeling an odd lump in her throat. "What have you been doing with yourself?"

"I'm a stormtrooper now," Mindy said. She gave Mandy a tight hug, tight enough to make the older girl grunt in pain. "I was lucky to be able to come, really. We're shipping out in a week or so."

Mandy nodded slowly as her younger sister turned to lead the way into the house. Mindy had to be going to Corinthian, although it was unlikely she knew very much about their destination. It bothered her more than she cared to admit, really. Mindy was her little sister, someone she was supposed to look after...

We never really got over being on Earth, she thought, as she followed her sister, closing the door behind her. *None of us really recovered from spending our early lives on a hellish world.*

She pushed the thought aside and walked into the living room. The walls were covered in bookshelves and a fire burned in the grate, something that would have been flatly forbidden on Earth. Hell, they would *both* have been flatly forbidden on Earth. Digital records could be altered with ease, but print records were much harder to edit. The current trend for paper books on Avalon had always struck her as absurd, yet there might well be a point to it. No one wanted to give a government - any government - that much power for a second time.

"Mandy," her father said. "Welcome home."

He looked old, Mandy realised, as he rose from his chair. She'd known he was a good thirty years older than her - her parents had waited to have children until they were both settled - but she'd never really understood it

55

at an emotional level. They - Mindy too - had spent too much of their lives rebelling against their parents, against what little discipline their father and mother had tried to impose on them. The idea of seeing their parents as *people*…it wasn't something that would have occurred to them. But now…

"Father," she said, feeling her voice catch. "Are you well?"

"We've bought an entertainment box," her father said, wryly. "And I've spent too much time watching it."

Mandy snorted. Her father had never allowed her to have an entertainment box, even though all her friends had had them. She'd thrown hundreds of tantrums over it, she recalled; her younger self had been a right little brat. But now, with a real career, she no longer felt the impulse to sit down in front of the box and just wallow. Almost everything that passed for entertainment in the last decade of the Empire was alternatively vile, perverse, or a distraction to keep the plebs from thinking for themselves. And it was *very* good at keeping people distracted.

"I'm old," her father added. He gave her a gentle hug, then pulled her towards the table. "I don't know how long I'll live, even here."

"You're only fifty," Mindy said. "There are people here who have lived for nearly a century."

"Here," her father corrected. "Not on Earth."

Mandy swallowed. They'd never been upper class, but they *had* had a good life…until her father published a book that drew the ire of the Grand Senate. And yet, very few people on Earth lived past sixty. The support they needed just didn't exist. But on Avalon, where people were generally friendly and helpful…

"I'm sure you'll live a long time," she said. She cursed her younger self, once again. All the time she could have gotten to know her father, wasted! "Dad…"

"Don't worry about it," her father said. "I can't say I've done as much as you over the past seven years."

"You've done enough, one would think," Fiona Caesius said. Their mother stepped into the room, carrying a large bowl of stew. "They have yet to find respectable careers - or husbands."

Mandy and Mindy exchanged glances. Of the four of them, Fiona had taken exile the hardest. She had no useful skills on Avalon, nor did she have the time to learn anything that would allow her to find a proper job. The older woman wanted to return to Earth, to the life she'd led as the wife of a successful professor, not stay on Avalon and make the best of her new circumstances. And yet, that was simply not an option.

"They do have respectable careers," their father said. He motioned for the girls to sit down. "And they don't have to be bound by earthly laws."

"The military," their mother said. "It's a pit for losers, not for *my* children!"

Mandy felt her temper flare. Her mother had always talked down to her, something that had provoked more than a few nasty fights. But now…now she thought she understood what drove the elder woman. Fiona would never be able to accomplish anything on her own, not now. She'd been dependent on her husband - and the state - for far too long.

"It's a respectable career," she said, quickly. "And I earn more than father does."

"And I defend people who need defending," Mindy added. "Without the military, *Mom*, you'd be dead."

"I would have stayed on Earth," Fiona said.

"And died when the planet fell," Mandy said. Even if the stories and rumours were exaggerated, she couldn't imagine her mother surviving for long. She was no survivor to endure when the world fell apart around her. "It would have been the end."

Their father held up a hand. "Enough," he said. "It's rare for the four of us to sit around a table, certainly now that you two are adults. Let us not spoil it by bickering."

"She started it," Mindy muttered.

Mandy cleared her throat as her father ladled out the stew. "How is the university coming along, dad?"

"Slowly," her father said. "Everyone wants to learn how to build and maintain FTL drives, not study history and law. It's quite frustrating at times."

"At least they're not wasting their time," Mandy said. She knew from bitter experience that most of what she'd learned in school was useless. Children on Avalon learned so much more before entering their second decade. "What can we do with history?"

Her father jabbed a finger at her. "Don't you study the tactics of the past so you can prepare for the future?"

Mandy nodded, conceding the point. "But that's practical," she insisted. "History is rather less practical."

"Now you've set him off," Mindy muttered.

"History teaches lessons," her father said. "Far too many of the mistakes the Empire made could have been avoided, if it had studied its own history. Instead, it repeated the same mistakes over and over again."

He looked, just for a moment, old enough to recall the Unification Wars and the First Emperor. Mandy shuddered, inwardly. It couldn't be easy to learn the mistakes of the past, then watch helplessly as current generations repeated them. Perhaps it was why her father had written his book, even though it had cost him everything. He'd wanted - needed - to warn the universe about the decline and coming collapse of civilisation. But it had been too late to avert the final plunge into catastrophe.

"Those lessons have to be learned," her father added. "There is nothing new under the sun, not really. Human nature doesn't change."

"Enough of such gloomy talk," Fiona insisted. "Mandy, why haven't you brought a nice boy home yet?"

Mandy felt her cheeks heat. "I'm really too busy, mother," she said. "There hasn't been *time* to find someone, really."

Fiona pointed a finger at her. "You've already ruined your looks," she said, darkly. "What will you do when you're too old to attract a nice boy?"

"I'll survive," Mandy said. After everything she'd been through on the pirate ship, she was damned if she was interested in *anyone*. A life lived alone was quite an attractive prospect in so many ways. "I am not defined by the person I marry."

"But you'll need someone who can protect you," her mother wittered. "Not someone who'll dump you the moment you turn ugly."

Mandy bit down on her temper, hard. The hell of it was that her mother would have had a point, on Earth. They might not have lived in the Undercity, but even middle-class girls ran terrifying risks if they walked around without protection. She'd been lucky, really; she'd never really appreciated how she'd suffered until she'd been exiled to Avalon. Training girls to resist rape, with lethal force if necessary, was far more effective than telling idiots not to rape. But Earth had never wanted to put weapons in the hands of people who might turn them against the government.

"I carry a gun, mother," she said, tartly. Jasmine had taught her, once Mandy had taken her head out of her ass. "And I can use it, too."

Her mother's mouth opened wide.

"She's only joking," Mindy said. She gave Mandy a sharp look. "I've had dozens of boyfriends, but none of them wanted to stay around."

"You gave it up too quickly," Fiona said. She seemed to have forgotten Mandy's last comment entirely. "You have to get a man invested in you before you give it up, or he'll go away."

Mandy sighed. "We're not looking for husbands, mother," she said. She took a bite of her stew, wondering just who had cooked it. Her mother couldn't even begin to cook anything more complex than pre-pack-aged food. "We have careers and lives and the chance to do something important."

"Quite right," their father said. "There are other things in life than being married."

"Says the man," Fiona said. "It's not so easy if you're a woman."

"Jasmine manages it," Mandy said. "And so does Gaby Cracker."

Their mother snorted rudely, but said nothing else. Mandy sighed inwardly as she finished her meal, then walked upstairs to what had once been her bedroom. She'd half-expected to find that her mother was rent-ing it out, but instead it was practically a shrine to her. Two of the walls were covered with her awards from school - none of them worth the paper they were printed on - while the other two were still decorated with post-ers she'd brought with her from Earth. She cursed her younger self, yet again, as she sat down on the bed. How childish had she been to think there was nothing more important than decorating her room when she arrived on Avalon?

Stupid as well, she thought, recalling when she'd been tricked into tak-ing Sparkle Dust. If Jasmine hadn't come across her, she might well have been raped - or worse. And she would never have known for *sure* what had happened to her. *Stupid and childish and idiotic and...*

"Is it just me," Mindy said, "or is Mom starting to lose it?"

59

"She's been quietly losing her shit for a very long time," Mandy said. Their mother had been the perfect academic wife, right up until the moment they'd lost everything. She still shuddered in horror, remembering the screaming fits. Their friends had deserted them so quickly that none of them had quite recovered. "And she doesn't have anything to do."

Mindy shrugged, closing the door and leaning against the wall. Mandy was rather impressed at how she'd managed to sneak up the stairs without being heard, although she supposed Mindy had been taught to walk quietly in training. Her younger sister wasn't the girl she'd been any longer...but then, that was true of Mandy too. Mindy had never been *quite* so bratty either.

"There are options," she said, dryly. "Surely there's something she could do."

Mandy looked up at her. "Like what?"

"I don't know," Mindy said. "Military training?"

"Ha fucking ha," Mandy said. Her mother, like most people from Earth, had a bad case of hoplophobia. She would sooner pick up a neo-scorpion from the badlands than a loaded pistol, even in defence of her life. The idea that her daughter might be carrying a weapon had stunned her into speechlessness. "Do you think she'd last a day?"

She contemplated the problem for a long moment. What *was* there for an aging woman with no real skills? An aging woman who was unwilling to learn? She couldn't think of anything, really. The neighbours probably didn't care enough to help, if they realised Fiona *needed* help. And really, who could blame them?

"I'm damned if I'm letting her talk to me like that again," Mindy said. "Doesn't she realise we're our own people?"

Mandy shrugged. "Too many changes in her life," she said. "I think she just gave up trying to stay on top of things."

"You've had changes," Mindy pointed out.

"I'm younger," Mandy said. "If I fuck up now, I still have time to find a new career. I could go back to repair work, or take up farming, or even write books! Mom...doesn't have the time. Or anything, really."

She leaned back on the bed, surveying the room. It hadn't changed a bit from the last day she'd slept in it, even though *someone* had clearly been tidying up and dusting on a regular basis. Indeed, there was something a little *creepy* about the room, now she came to think of it. It might be playing games with her mother's mind, convincing her - on some level - that Mandy was still the sixteen-year-old who'd lost everything and been exiled to Avalon. No doubt her experiences on Lakshmibai hadn't helped either.

"I think they should move house," she said, suddenly.

Mindy gave her an odd look. "Why?"

"Because this house is probably messing with their minds," Mandy said. She stood, pacing over to her chest of drawers. "At the very least, we should move out permanently. Get our rooms emptied..."

"I have no idea what you're going to do with that crap," Mindy said. She jabbed a finger at the poster of a famous singer. In all honesty, Mandy couldn't remember his name or why she'd liked him. "Is there anyone here who might want it?"

"Maybe it should just go in the fire," Mandy said. She opened her drawers and frowned as she realised that half of her old clothing was still there. She'd never been able to bring herself to wear it, after she'd grown up, but her mother had kept it anyway. "And this crap can go in the clothing bank."

"If they'll take it," Mindy said. She pulled a miniskirt out of the drawer and eyed it. "What the fuck were you thinking when you wore this?"

Mandy coloured. "I don't think I was thinking at all," she said. The dress was so short that anyone watching her could see the bottom of her ass. She cringed at the memory of all the boys who'd whistled at her, the single time she'd worn it in public. "And I never wore it again."

"Oh, goody," Mindy said sarcastically. She tossed the miniskirt to Mandy, then headed for the door. "I'll empty my room, I think. You finish with yours."

Mandy nodded. By the time they left, she could have the room empty, stripped bare of everything that had once belonged to her. And when they returned, perhaps they could find something else for her mother, something that would allow the older woman to make something of her life...

It's true, she thought, grimly. She wasn't the person she'd been - and she was glad of it. *You just cannot go home again.*

CHAPTER
EIGHT

Indeed, while the underlying causes of the war were not addressed, there was a good chance the planetary government would come out ahead. To the Crackers, there could be no worse fate. They gambled everything on a victory.

- Professor Leo Caesius. The Role of Randomness In War.

"So," Gaby said. They stood together, a short distance from the line of shuttles that were departing the spaceport and heading to orbit. "This is goodbye?"

Ed nodded. He'd resisted the option to board earlier, even though most of his officers and men were already loaded onto the giant starships. On the face of it, he'd wanted to be on Avalon to cope with any unexpected surprises, but they both knew he'd chosen to remain behind with Gaby for a few days more. And yet, time had finally run out.

"It is," he said. "I should be back soon."

"Soon," Gaby repeated. Her lips twisted. "I thought the prediction was seven months, at best?"

"At best," Ed confirmed. "I wish I could stay with you."

He felt a flicker of guilt at his words. Leaving her behind was one thing, but leaving her behind when she was pregnant was quite another. He hadn't understood just how it would change his feelings until he'd actually faced it. Part of him was insistent that he shouldn't leave her at all. And yet, the rest of him was itching for the fight. There would be no political debates, no compromises over everything from funding to weapons design, merely a chance to get his hands around the enemy's throat. The CEF would either win victory or suffer a disastrous defeat. There were no middle grounds.

"No, you don't," Gaby said. She smiled, rather sadly. "You're just like my father, always keen to get stuck into the enemy. You've been pacing around here like a caged lion, always hoping the bars will vanish and you'll be able to make your escape."

Ed smiled back. "Was I really that bad?"

"I'm afraid so," Gaby said. She leaned forward, standing on tiptoes to kiss him. "If the child is born before you return, he or she will be named as we chose."

"It would be easier if you checked the child's sex," Ed pointed out. In truth, he wasn't sure he wanted to recall his parents or siblings, even though Avalon prized the idea of keeping names in the family. "At least we'd know what we're having."

"I don't want to find out," Gaby said. She glanced upwards as another shuttle screamed over the field, heading up to orbit. "Come back as fast as you can, all right?"

"I will," Ed promised. "And make sure you don't exert yourself too much…"

Gaby elbowed him. "I'm giving birth, not going for a life-threatening operation," she said, tartly. "Women have survived giving birth for thousands of years."

Ed kept his thoughts to himself. Modern medicine - and Gaby would have the very best - would ensure that nothing went wrong, but he'd been on too many planets suffering from social collapse to feel sanguine about the future. Women who should have had no difficulty bringing a child to term had lost the baby, simply because they didn't eat the right things or suffered from a lack of medical care. The marines had been quite popular in places, simply because they offered medical assistance to the locals, but it had been nothing more than a drop in the bucket and everyone knew it. He had a nasty feeling that there were countless planets, right across settled space, that had suffered a terrifying drop in population…

"You're brooding again," Gaby said. "Is that normal for you?"

"No," Ed said. "But I do have a great deal to brood about."

He shook his head. Seven years ago, he'd known his place; he was a company commander, reporting to the regimental commander. But now… he had *no* superiors, as far as he knew; he certainly had no idea what had happened to the marines he'd known on Earth and the Slaughterhouse. Cold logic told him that Stalker's Stalkers couldn't be the only surviving marine company, but cold logic wasn't very reassuring when he peered towards the former Core Worlds. None of the rumours made him feel any better about the future.

"Well, stop it," Gaby said. "You're meant to be gung ho about going to war, not brooding over matters you can't help."

Ed shrugged. "I'll do my best," he said. "Goodbye, Gaby. I love you."

He gave her one final kiss, then turned and walked towards the shuttle, refusing to look back until he reached the hatch. Gaby was standing there, looking alone; she waved once and then turned to walk back to the waiting aircar. She'd be back in her office, Ed was sure, before he was in orbit. And then…he fought down a mad impulse to run after her as he walked into the shuttle, the crew chief slamming the hatch shut behind him. He found a seat and pulled his datapad from his belt as the pilot ran through the pre-flight checks and then launched the shuttle into the sky. As always, there were too many pieces of paperwork that demanded his urgent attention.

And it would be worse if we were on Earth, he thought, darkly. *There were more paper-pushers in the military than there were fighting men.*

He opened the readiness reports and read through them, one by one. Jasmine Yamane confirmed that 1st Platoon - or what was left of the once-proud unit - was ready to deploy, once they reached Corinthian. She'd even attached a proposal for making an orbital drop down to the surface, rather than using a shuttle. Ed was honestly tempted for a long moment - it had been years since he'd done anything more challenging than a parachute jump above Castle Rock - but dismissed the idea. Orbital drops could be deadly, even to experienced marines. And there was no need to repeat their first landing on Corinthian.

It would be fun, he thought, a little wistfully, *but too much danger for no return.*

He sighed, then moved to the second report. General Mathis confirmed that the CEF was loaded onboard its ships, with no desertions and only a handful of minor disciplinary problems. Ed hadn't expected anything else, if he had to be honest; the CEF was far better trained and motivated than any comparable unit from the Imperial Army. And then, there were very real consequences for anyone who dared return to their post late, unlike in the army. A soldier who overstayed his leave could expect nothing more than a slap on the wrist.

Which explains why so many units did so badly when they were tried in combat, he thought, peering out the porthole as the shuttle passed through the upper wisps of atmosphere and entered orbit. *They'd allowed themselves to get sloppy long before they faced their first combat test.*

He clicked through the remaining reports on the datapad - ammunition stockpiles, medical supplies, emergency procedures - and returned it to his belt, taking a moment to close his eyes and centre himself. Even with modern starships, it would take three weeks to reach Corinthian - older ships needed over a month - and he would have plenty of time to catch up with his exercises. And yet, he'd probably find himself going stir-crazy inside a week. The stasis tubes had made so much more sense.

And yet we can't devote the resources to producing them here, he thought, tiredly. *It will be years before we have the productive capability of Earth, let alone the Core Worlds.*

The thought was a bitter one. All the old certainties about orbital industries had fallen with the Empire itself, once workers were allowed to think for themselves again. Ed - and the Commonwealth - had developed a system for *rewarding* innovation, rather than squashing it out of hand. And the results were all around him: faster, better-armed starships that could outrun or outfight anything of comparable size from the Imperial Navy. *And* a hundred other innovations that would change the universe forever.

A few more years, he thought, in quiet frustration. *A few more years and we would have overrun Wolfbane and the rest of the former Empire with ease.*

He opened his eyes as a low thump ran through the shuttle, the artificial gravity field quivering for a long moment before settling down.

The hatch opened seconds later as the atmosphere matched, automated systems checking everything before allowing the passengers to leave the shuttle and board the ship. Ed found the delay inconvenient, as he rose to his feet, but he had to admit it was necessary. The extensive safety regulations written into law by bean-counting paper-pushers hadn't prevented accidents when hatches were inadvertently opened to vacuum. It was far better to give the people on the spot the responsibility for handling the matter.

"Colonel," a young man said. "I'm Commander Tygart, XO. Welcome onboard CSS *Defiant*. I'm to escort you to your quarters."

"Thank you," Ed said. He saluted the Commonwealth flag, then turned to the XO. "Shall we go?"

He smiled at the young man's back as Commander Tygart led him through a maze of corridors, feeling the starship humming around him as if she was eagerly anticipating the chance to set sail on the interstellar sea. There was little pomp and ceremony in the Commonwealth - certainly not the hour-long ceremonies the Imperial Navy had been fond of, once upon a time - but there were certain matters that still needed to be honoured. The vessel's commander was her *commander*, no matter how badly she was outranked by her ship's guests. An Imperial Navy admiral would probably insist on being taken to the bridge, or the CIC, but Ed knew better. He would wait until the captain called on him.

I'd hate it if someone was looking over my shoulder too, he thought. *It would certainly undermine me in front of the crew.*

"You and your Sergeant have been assigned the same cabin," Tygart informed him, as they stopped in front of a hatch. "I was given to understand that that would be acceptable...?"

Ed concealed his amusement with an effort. "More than suitable, Commander," he said. The shipboard officer would probably be horrified at the thought of trying to catch forty winks in a foxhole, with enemy shells landing all around the position. "Indeed, it is quite luxurious."

Tygart gave him a surprised look and keyed the hatch. It opened, revealing a small cabin with barely enough room to swing a cat. Two beds, a small food dispenser and a single terminal...it was hardly the peak of luxury. Ed hated to think what Admiral Valentine would have said, if he'd been told he was expected to share such a tiny space with someone else; *he* was used to cabins that could have passed for football fields. Probably have ordered the starship's commander removed from command and put in front of a court martial board, he suspected. It wasn't as if it was a harmless little prank like stealing supplies, abusing one's crew and plotting barratry.

"Thank you," Ed said. He dropped his carryall on the bunk, remembering the younger man's shock when he'd insisted on carrying it for himself. "I'll be in here until departure."

"Yes, sir," Tygart said.

He saluted, then turned and left the tiny compartment. Ed watched him go, fighting down a flicker of amusement mixed with concern. The Commonwealth Navy was *young* - it was barely six years old - yet far too many of its experienced officers had picked up bad habits from the Imperial Navy. Pomp and circumstance was all very well, in its place, but it was far more important that the navy knew how to fight. The only consolation was that the war had been doing an excellent job of burning out the deadwood.

Except they lose ships when they die, Ed thought. *And crewmen we cannot afford to lose.*

He sat down at the desk and keyed the terminal. As he'd expected, there were a hundred new messages, all of which demanded his attention. He sighed, forwarded half of them to Grosskopf and started to read through the rest. Anyone who believed he would overrule Grosskopf without very good reason needed to be sent away with a flea in their ear. If Ed hadn't had total confidence in the older man, he wouldn't have left him in command on Avalon.

The final message was from Kitty Stevenson. Ed read it twice, then fed the message into the starship's internal shredder. It was impossible to delete *all* traces of a message from the datanet - which was how the spy ring had been detected - but he could make life difficult for anyone who tried. If Kitty was right, the messages that *should* inform Admiral Singh that Corinthian was going to be stripped of everything vital were well on their way. The trap had been laid...

And now we have to see if she falls into it, he thought. He stood, wishing he could pace in the tiny cabin, then forced himself to lie down on the bunk. The starship was quivering slightly, indicating that she was finally leaving orbit. *The die is cast now...*

There was nothing else he could do, he knew; not now. All he could do was wait.

Jasmine allowed herself a tight little smile as she stopped outside an unmarked hatch, then pressed her finger against the buzzer. *Defiant* had left orbit an hour ago, entering communications blackout almost at once. She rather suspected that General Mathis was dealing with a swarm of complaints from his subordinates, who'd expected to be able to send messages until the ship crossed the phase limit and jumped into phase space, but her marines were more experienced. *They* would have rewritten their wills and sent their last messages long before boarding the shuttles and heading to orbit.

And they'd know to be careful what they said, too, Jasmine thought. *They learned about communications security at the Slaughterhouse.*

She smiled to herself as the hatch slide open. Her entire body was aching, in a manner she hadn't felt since Boot Camp and the Slaughterhouse, but the pain was weakness - her weakness - leaving her body. She hadn't really grasped just how far she'd fallen, despite everything she'd done on Meridian, until she'd run through the training course again and again. A marine platoon could not afford a weak link, she knew through experience, and she was damned if she was *becoming* a weak link. The pain was deserved, but it was also proof that she was getting better...

"Jasmine," Emmanuel said. He turned in his chair and smiled at her. "Why am I not surprised to see you?"

"You have a working brain," Jasmine said. She stepped into the compartment, allowing the hatch to close behind her. She'd been twitted, more than once, about sleeping with a reporter - wasn't that sleeping with the enemy? - but Emmanuel *did* have both a brain and common sense. "And you knew I wouldn't be around for a while."

"I went straight into the lockbox," Emmanuel said. He didn't sound angry, somewhat to her surprise. Most of the reporters she'd met on Han would have been furious, if someone had dared suggest they couldn't be trusted. But there was no choice. Even an accidental mistake - as opposed to deliberate wilful stupidity - could be disastrous. "But if what the colonel said was true, it will be worth it."

"I certainly hope so," Jasmine agreed. She looked around the cabin. "You're in the lap of luxury here, you know?"

Emmanuel looked doubtful. "Really?"

"Oh, yes," Jasmine said. "I'm crammed into a smaller cabin with six other marines."

"I don't believe you could all fit in," Emmanuel said. He waved a hand at the bulkheads, barely two metres apart. "Can you?"

"With great difficulty," Jasmine said. She shook her head. "But we have to get used to living in one another's pockets now."

"You would be welcome to stay here," Emmanuel said. "The bunk isn't much…"

Jasmine shook her head. "I have to stay with them," she said. "And I can't come visit you very often, either."

"It's three weeks," Emmanuel protested.

"And no one else is going to get their rocks hauled either," Jasmine said. "I can't take too much advantage of you."

She sighed, recalling the courses on group dynamics she'd been forced to endure at the Slaughterhouse. People - even marines - tended to get pissed if someone had an unearned advantage. As far as she knew, she was the only marine who had a lover on *Defiant*, although she was sure the other marines would be trying to get crewmen or crewwomen into bed. She wouldn't care, either, as long as they showed up for their training sessions.

"I don't mind you taking advantage of me," Emmanuel said, with a wink. "What do you make of the ship's crew?"

"Frightfully keen," Jasmine said. Promotion was fast in the Commonwealth Navy, thanks to the demands of rapid expansion. *Mandy* was certainly proof of that. "But largely inexperienced in warfare."

"The war's been going on for over a year," Emmanuel reminded her.

"Yes," Jasmine agreed. "But how many engagements has this ship seen?"

She shrugged. "Are you planning to write a story about it?"

"Maybe," Emmanuel said. "People do want to know what their tax credits are being spent on, you know."

"I know," Jasmine agreed. "Just remember to tell them that all this" - she waved a hand at the bulkhead - "is a paragon of efficiency, compared to the Imperial Navy."

"I will," Emmanuel said. "But I don't know how many people will believe it."

Jasmine shrugged. "There's a difference between looking good and actually *being* good," she said. "And often those military units that manage the former fail at the latter."

CHAPTER
NINE

And they were lucky, indeed, that the planetary government had already settled on a political solution. The loss of so many trained fighters - and irreplaceable equipment - would have crippled their cause for generations to come. Sheer bad luck and worse timing would have broken them.
- Professor Leo Caesius. The Role of Randomness In War.

General Mark Haverford had come to detest Thule.

The planet had been having a civil war when the Wolves had arrived, a civil war over an interpretation of their constitution that had led to disaster, when the interstellar economy collapsed into ashes. He'd expected, given that there were two sides to the war, that at least one of them would have welcomed the Wolves. But, instead, both sides seemed intent on attacking the Wolves, making it difficult for the planet's surviving industry to be put to use supporting the fleet as it advanced further into Commonwealth space. There were shootings and bombings on a daily basis, despite the presence of three divisions of heavily-armed soldiers. Indeed, were it not for the orbiting starships and bombardment platforms, he had a nasty feeling that his force would have been defeated long ago.

He scowled at the thought as the shuttlecraft approached the giant battleship, surrounded by five other battleships and forty smaller ships. Admiral Singh - no, Governor-Admiral Singh - had arrived in person, escorted by ships that could have made a difference if they'd been moved to the front instead. The reinforcements she'd brought with her were welcome, he supposed, but he had a feeling he was about to be relieved of command. He'd argued with her, when Thule had fallen to the Wolves, and she wasn't one to forgive and forget a grudge.

Maybe I should have fled, he thought darkly. *But where would I have gone?*

He rose to his feet as the shuttle docked, the hatch slamming open a moment later. A pair of officers waited for him, rather than the armed guards he'd half-expected. Oddly, it was surprisingly reassuring. Admiral Singh had a determination he had to admire, but she wasn't a particularly subtle woman. If she'd wanted to arrest him, she would have dispatched soldiers or boosted mercenaries, if she didn't trust the soldiers. He followed the officers through a maze of corridors and into the suite Admiral Singh had claimed as her own, reluctantly allowing a handful of bodyguards to confiscate his sidearm and anything else that could be used as a weapon before allowing him to step through the final hatch.

"Mark," Admiral Rani Singh said. "Welcome onboard."

"Admiral," Mark said. He wasn't fooled by her casual tone. She had to be evaluating his loyalties even as she spoke. "Thank you for your invitation."

He studied her thoughtfully as she studied him back. She was a tall woman, with long dark hair, dark brown skin and eyes so dark they were almost black. Her face was hard, her cheekbones almost patrician, as if she was deliberately projecting a message that she was untouchable. It was easy to see why several of her former superiors had wanted to take her to bed - he'd read between the lines, when he'd accessed her file - and why they might have lashed out at her, when she'd refused them. There was a hardness to her that was both a challenge and a threat.

And her superiors weren't known for their competence, he reminded himself. He'd been a lowly colonel before Governor Brown had taken control of Wolfbane, purging the sector of hundreds of worthless officers. *Someone like her should have been given a position suited to her talents or quietly eliminated.*

"Be seated," Admiral Singh said, finally. "There is much we have to discuss."

Mark sat, watching as she took the chair facing him. Her dark eyes never left his face, something that bothered him more than he cared to admit. She knew he wasn't one of her **biggest** fans, let alone a supporter. And yet, if she started lashing out at **officers** who hadn't proven themselves incompetent, *someone* would **panic** and stick a knife in her back before it was too late. She needed to *seem* willing to tolerate people like him until her position was beyond **challenge**.

The Admiral tapped a console, **sending** a command to the projector. A starchart popped into existence in **front of** them, showing worlds occupied by Wolfbane and worlds that **still belonged** to the Commonwealth. Mark knew little about interstellar **warfare**, but it looked as though the Commonwealth was slowly being **ground down** to nothingness. And yet, he'd been an officer too long to take **anything** for granted. A world that appeared pacified might no longer be **so** peaceful, when the occupation forces were drawn down. Thule had **never** known a day of peace since the war had begun.

"Our agents within the Common**wealth** have reported that their government is working to shorten their **defence** lines," Admiral Singh said, without preamble. "They are pulling **much** of their mobile firepower back to the inner worlds, abandoning **seventeen** stars to us whenever we choose to take them. Most of those **worlds** are largely worthless, I admit. They probably made the right choice **in** choosing to concede them to us."

Mark nodded, keeping his **expression** under tight control. A stage-one or stage-two colony world was **useless**, as far as supporting the logistics of interstellar war was concerned. He **might** be able to raid them for food and drink, but little else. Their **populations** lacked the training to become anything more than conscript **soldiers**. They certainly couldn't be drafted as spacers!

"If they win the war, they can recover them at leisure," he agreed. "And if they lose, it doesn't matter what happens to those colony worlds. We certainly won't be fighting over them."

"Correct," Admiral Singh said. Her lips curved into a cold smile. "And yet, one of those worlds is *far* from useless."

She pointed to a single star, blinking red. Corinthian.

Mark frowned, thinking hard. He'd heard that Admiral Singh had been kicked off Corinthian by a general revolt, a revolt sponsored by the Commonwealth. If she hadn't been lucky enough to stumble across the

Wolves, she would have died in the vastness of interstellar space when her remaining ships ran out of supplies. It was impossible to believe she was impartial about the whole affair - she was known to be vindictive - and yet, a chance to snatch control of Corinthian was one that couldn't be missed. The planet had had a respectable industrial base even before it had lost touch with the Empire.

But it looked too good to be true. "They're abandoning such a useful world?"

"So it would seem," Admiral Singh agreed. "Corinthian is really too far from their core to allow for mutual support."

Mark nodded, slowly. He was no naval expert, but Corinthian was nearly a month from Avalon at best possible speed. Trying to hold on to the system would pin a substantial enemy force down indefinitely, allowing the Wolves to wreak havoc elsewhere. Corinthian might be able to support the enemy's war effort, but the sheer distance between the threatened world and the rest of the Commonwealth worked against it. The defences wouldn't die on the vine, yet they wouldn't help others either.

"It doesn't make sense," he said. "They must know that they need every last scrap of industry they can get."

"They do," Admiral Singh agreed. "They're sending a substantial force to...*liberate*...the industrial base I built up before I was forced to leave. They'll strip Corinthian bare of everything from trained personnel to industrial modules, leaving a restive population that won't be too pleased to see me again. By the time they leave, Corinthian will be useless to both us and the Commonwealth."

Mark frowned. That made a great deal more sense. The trained manpower alone would make one hell of a difference, in the right - or the wrong - hands. He'd seen enough of the Empire's educational system to know that trained manpower was worth its weight in any rare substance one cared to name. And Corinthian had been a member of the Commonwealth for nearly three years. The possibilities...

He looked up into her disturbingly dark eyes. "They might have moved some of their own industrial base out there," he breathed. "There'll be a chance to capture some of their technology."

"It's a possibility," Admiral Singh said. Her voice darkened. "The research labs have been quite slow in understanding the principles of their technology, even though we now know such things are possible. Indeed, half of the...*scientists*...are convinced that we are misreading the sensor records. They simply don't believe that force shields are a viable technology."

Mark wasn't surprised. He hated to admit it, but most of the technology his force used would be understandable to a military officer from the days before the Empire. Scientific research had slowed to a crawl, in the final days of the Empire, and technological innovation had been strongly discouraged. The Grand Senate had been happy with its control of everything important, he recalled. They hadn't wanted to accidentally develop something that might upend the entire balance of power, let alone threaten their superiority. Their *scientists* hadn't been worthy of the name.

"The Commonwealth doesn't have that disadvantage," he commented. "Nor does the Trade Federation."

"No," Admiral Singh agreed. "They have the advantage of having an industrial base, without the corporate mindset that developed over a thousand years of squashing all the competition by fair means or foul. Right now, there's no room in their little heads for a genuinely original thought. And I can't even purge half the bastards without sparking off a civil war."

She leant forward, her eyes blazing. "You understand the potential benefits of securing Corinthian before they strip the planet bare?"

"Yes, Admiral," Mark agreed. "But they will have already begun the operation, surely?"

"They will not find it easy to pick up a whole industrial base and transport it home," Admiral Singh pronounced. Mark was inclined to agree. "And I imagine that my...*successors*...will resent losing so much of their hard work. They will not be inclined to cooperate, even at gunpoint. The Commonwealth will find it hard to carry out their mission within six months, let alone a year."

Mark rather suspected she had a point. Wolfbane had raided every nearby world for trained manpower and industrial modules and it had *always* faced resistance. Never enough to *stop* the looting, to be fair, but enough to cause problems. Experienced personnel had even killed themselves, rather than be taken from their families. Governor Brown had eventually issued orders that families were to be taken too, but too much damage had already been done.

"They may not even have the shipping space for non-essential personnel," he commented, thoughtfully. He'd handled evacuations, in the past, and they were always messy as hell. A person would be taken on the wrong ship or left behind…hell, the Commonwealth's attempt to evacuate Thule had failed miserably. "And the trained personnel will definitely resent being separated from their families."

"Quite," Admiral Singh agreed.

She tapped the console again, replacing the starchart with an order of battle. "My task force will advance to Corinthian as quickly as possible, destroying or driving away the Commonwealth ships within the system, before proceeding to secure the high orbitals," she said. "Once we take control, you'll be landing with a sizable force to take control of all the major cities and secure the personnel and facilities we need. You'll also be watching for the rebels who unseated me beforehand, so they can be punished as they deserve."

Mark winced at the hatred running through her voice. Admiral Singh had been an empress, to all intents and purposes, before she'd been kicked off the planet. Now, she held power, but not *supreme* power. She could have come to terms with Governor Brown if she'd met him as an equal, instead of a supplicant. He couldn't blame her for wanting a little revenge…

And she can't strike at her true enemies, he thought. *So she strikes at others instead.*

"That will require considerable manpower," he said, carefully. If anything, that was an understatement. Corinthian was heavily populated as well as heavily armed. "We may not have the resources on hand to cope with the mission."

"You will be withdrawing two-thirds of the infantry and supporting arms from Thule," Admiral Singh said, bluntly. "We hold the high orbitals and much of the orbital and interplanetary infrastructure. We'll keep control of the capital and a handful of other locations, but the remainder of this shithole can go to hell."

Mark forced his face to reveal no trace of his feelings. Thule wasn't as important as Corinthian, but he'd lost thousands of men trying to keep the planet under control. Never mind that half of them had been conscripts, men who hadn't really wanted to join the military; they'd died for Wolfbane, countless light years from home. It wasn't *right* to have their deaths be for nothing, although he doubted that Governor Brown had cared much before he died. Surely Admiral Singh would understand...

"Thule is immaterial to us, right now," she said, firmly. "I don't intend to waste any more resources securing the planet. We can clobber the insurgents from orbit if they raise their heads too high."

She shrugged. "But that will be your successor's job," she added. "I want you in command of the ground forces on Corinthian."

"Yes, Admiral," Mark said. A trap? Or was he merely the most experienced officer at her disposal? He didn't know anyone with more experience of sustained urban combat. "When do you intend to depart?"

Admiral Singh eyed him darkly. "How quickly can you load your men onto the transports?"

Mark thought fast, silently grateful for the vast number of contingency plans he'd drawn up - or, rather, had his staff draw up - for every conceivable situation. He'd assumed from the start that the deployment wouldn't last indefinitely, not with Governor Brown a penny-pinching bureaucrat. Moving his men back to entrenched positions and preparing for evacuation had always been a very real possibility...

"Two to three weeks, assuming we have enough shuttles on hand," he said. "But we don't have that many we brought in from out-system."

He scowled in bitter memory. It was a sore spot. The orbital industrial nodes surrounding Thule had produced a number of shuttles for his forces, but two of them had exploded in flight - apparently, the insurgents had sabotaged the flight computers. It had caused several near-mutinies when his men had refused to board the damned craft. A number of locals had died for their involvement, but it hadn't been enough to repair the damage they'd done.

"Use shuttles from my ships," Admiral Singh ordered. "I want to be on the way to Corinthian within the month."

Mark frowned. "That might be tricky," he said. "Moving men is one thing, but evacuating our supplies is quite another."

"It has to be done," Admiral Singh said. "If necessary, we'll send back for more supplies once we are established on Corinthian."

"If we can," Mark said.

He wasn't happy. In his experience, pre-war simulations of just how much ammunition would be expended in combat were almost laughably optimistic. His men had fired off millions of rounds on Thule, while losing over four hundred combat vehicles from light armoured patrol units to Landshark tanks. And hadn't *that* been a blow to morale? He'd always assumed the Landsharks were next to invulnerable, until they hadn't been any longer.

And yet, he had a feeling Admiral Singh wouldn't accept any excuses. She *wanted* Corinthian badly, so badly she was prepared to take the risk of commanding the operation in person, something that would rebound badly on her if the operation failed. There was no room for him to manoeuvre.

"I'll communicate with my officers at once," he said. "We'll dust off the contingency plan for troop withdrawal, then put it into operation. It will have to be a staggered withdrawal…"

He paused as a thought struck him. "We could always tell the insurgents that we're leaving for good," he added. It was risky - once his forces had a reputation for being liars, it was unlikely to vanish in a hurry - but it was a possibility. "It might stop them harassing our forces as they withdraw."

Admiral Singh's lips thinned. "I doubt they would believe us," she said. "They have to know we would not abandon the industrial nodes."

"True," Mark agreed.

"Hammer the insurgents from orbit," Admiral Singh ordered, curtly. There was no give in her voice at all. "Hit them whenever they hit us."

Mark winced. Admiral Singh was a naval officer, not a ground-pounder. She had no *conception* of what happened when a KEW struck its target. The resulting blast would not only obliterate the insurgent position, but everything around it. Hundreds of civilians - and Wolves - would be caught in the blast and killed. And any civilian survivors would be

THEY SHALL NOT PASS

thoroughly radicalised. His men had caught hundreds of insurgents who claimed they'd only begun to fight after losing loved ones to KEW strikes.

She doesn't give a damn about collateral damage, he thought. In space, there was rarely any such thing. Even a nuke could detonate without risking innocent lives. *And there's no way to talk her out of it.*

"I'll issue the best orders for each situation," he said. "Getting our troops out in reasonable order is the first priority."

"Understood," Admiral Singh said. She rose. "I'll expect you for dinner tonight, General. I have some operational matters to discuss with you."

"Of course, Admiral," Mark said. Thankfully, his second could start preparations for the evacuation, once he had his orders. "I look forward to it."

And that, he knew all too well, was a lie.

CHAPTER
TEN

Indeed, most observers fail to understand the role luck and timing play in military (and government) operations.

- Professor Leo Caesius. The Role of Randomness In War.

"You know, Captain," Commander Tygart said, "we could probably claim a record."

Mandy smiled, rather ruefully. "I doubt we could beat a courier boat," she said, as she studied the eerie lights of phase space. "And even if we did, it wouldn't last."

She smiled at the thought. Starships were getting faster, thanks to the wave of innovation unleashed by the Commonwealth. So far, the technology had remained mainly restricted to military ships, but that would change sooner rather than later. And when it did, the galactic economy would change once again. *Defiant* was the fastest capital ship in space, as far as she knew, but she'd soon be joined by others. And all the stars would grow closer together.

And that will make life more interesting, she thought, as she settled back in her command chair. Being a starship commander *and* squadron commander was awkward, but her crews were well-trained and used to making a number of decisions without having her looking over their shoulders. *We won't have as much freedom as we have now.*

She pushed the thought aside as she glanced at the timer, showing the last minutes ticking away before the squadron reached the phase limit surrounding Corinthian's star. Pirates had been known to lurk along the phase limits, watching for lone freighters they could ambush, but it was unlikely that any pirates would dare to tangle with a warship. If, of course, there were any pirates left. She smiled a smile of cold satisfaction when she contemplated just how many pirate ships had been captured or destroyed, along with their bases, in the years since she'd escaped from captivity. It wasn't enough - it would *never* be enough - but it was a *start*.

"Two minutes to emergence point, Captain," the helmsman said. "The drive is ready to recycle upon command."

"See to it," Mandy ordered, curtly. It was unlikely they would run into a problem that would force them to turn and flee, but she knew better than to take chances. The timing should work in their favour, yet luck might turn against them at any moment. "Tactical?"

"All weapons and sensors charged and ready, Captain," the tactical officer reported. "Shield generator is online, ready to go active."

Mandy forced herself not to show any sign of tension as the last few seconds ticked down to nothingness. It had been a boring voyage, even if she'd had time to chat to Jasmine and Mindy and run hundreds of simulations, based on what she expected to find when they reached their destination. But she knew from bitter experience that boredom was far better than running into an enemy squadron or being a helpless prisoner of a pirate crew. She felt for the poison tooth in her mouth with her tongue, feeling a wave of grim determination. One solid *crunch* and she'd die within seconds. It was an unpleasant thought, but she was damned if she was allowing herself to fall into pirate hands for a second time.

The ship rocked, slightly, as she dropped back into realspace. Mandy's eyes flew to the holographic display, watching grimly as red icons flashed into existence, only to turn blue as IFF codes were checked and rechecked. The remainder of the squadron had made it, thankfully. She'd heard too many tales of navigators who put the wrong coordinates into the phase drive and ended up thousands of light years from their destination...

"Preliminary scan complete, Captain," the tactical officer said. "Local space is clear."

Mandy nodded, although she still felt jumpy. The squadron had taken a least-time course to Corinthian, which made their arrival time and destination predictable to anyone with half a brain. If the enemy had managed to get an ambush in place, the first she'd know of it was when the missiles came screeching towards them out of seemingly empty space. But, as the seconds ticked by, she relaxed. The enemy, if indeed there *was* an enemy, had missed its best chance at scoring a devastating series of blows.

"Remain on tactical alert," she ordered, quietly. "Send a standard IFF pulse to System Command."

"Aye, Captain," the communications officer said.

"Helm, take us into the system," Mandy added. "Match course and speed with the transports."

"Aye, Captain," the helmsman added.

Mandy sat back in her chair and watched, grimly, as the squadron proceeded into the system, the display lighting up with hundreds of icons. Corinthian had been settled long before Avalon and it showed, although two successive governments hadn't been *quite* as enthusiastic about unrestrained capitalism and innovation as the Commonwealth. The system was dotted with radio signals, ranging from a dozen cloudscoops to asteroid settlements and small establishments on almost every planet. Indeed, it was clear that the level of interplanetary activity had tripled since her first visit to the planet.

And they're working on growing their manpower base too, she thought. Corinthian had had the same problems as most of the other worlds, but Admiral Singh *had* managed to overcome many of them before she'd been forced to flee. *Given time, they could rise to dominate the sector.*

She scowled, remembering some of the complaints she'd heard from junior crewmen. They wondered just what would happen if Avalon - and Corinthian - continued to dominate the worlds around them. The Empire, on a smaller scale? Or something worse? She didn't mourn for what she'd lost, when she'd been exiled from Earth, but she had to admit that the Empire had offered stability. But that had been a lie, held in place by force and threats...both of which had been in short supply when the end finally came. Now...

Once the war is over, we can work on growing other economies, she thought. She knew what the plans had been, before Wolfbane had cast a long shadow over the Commonwealth. Those plans could be dusted off and put back to work. *And it will make us stronger in the long run.*

"There's quite a few ships leaving the system," the tactical officer commented. "They may have seen us already."

Mandy doubted it. The message to Corinthian wouldn't even have reached the planet; they certainly wouldn't have had time to send a reply. And the freighters shouldn't have detected the squadron's arrival, not with civilian-grade sensors. But if Wolfbane had a few spy ships among the freighters…they might well have set off to report back to their masters. Or, perhaps, they were smugglers who feared being caught and trapped inside the phase limit.

Or it might be nothing at all, she thought, sourly. *There's no way to be certain.*

The communications console pinged, seven hours later. "Captain, Corinthian acknowledges our arrival," the communications officer said. "System Command would like to know what we're doing here."

Because they didn't expect us to arrive, Mandy thought. The arrival of an unscheduled fleet, in wartime, would cause some alarm, even if the fleet *did* have the right IFF codes. Who knew if an enemy spy could have obtained the codes? *They'll be getting ready to fight now, even though they think we're friendly.*

"Inform them that Colonel Stalker will explain, once we reach communications range," she ordered. There was no point in trying to hold a conversation when it took three and a half hours for a message to reach Corinthian, then a further three and a half hours for a reply to reach *Defiant*. "And request a suitable orbital slot."

She sighed, inwardly, as she rose to her feet and passed command to her XO. *Everyone* was paranoid these days, with reason. The *Pax Imperia* was long gone, replaced by a universe where the wolf was at the door… literally, for the worlds facing the prospect of being added to the Wolfbane Consortium. No one would allow a newcomer to enter firing range, let alone orbit, without being *very* sure of the newcomer's *bona fides*. Part of her found it depressing, as if some piece of her innocence had been stolen without her ever knowing why. And yet, she knew that only an idiot failed to lock her doors on Earth. Even in Imperial City, thieves were everywhere.

And the colonel is going to turn this system upside down, she thought. *They won't be pleased at hearing from him.*

She stepped through the hatch into her office and keyed a switch, activating the display. The system was slowly revealing its secrets, allowing her to see more and more detail…the locals wouldn't *want* to move, no matter the threat. But they had no choice. The Wolves would want Corinthian, even if Admiral Singh hadn't had a personal connection to the system. And Corinthian couldn't hold indefinitely against a powerful fleet.

The colonel will just have to convince them to go, she thought, as she sat down. *That's his job.*

"They've done a lot of work," Jasmine said, as she stood next to Colonel Stalker in the compact CIC. The compartment was largely empty, save for a pair of operators Mandy had loaned them. "It wasn't anything like this industrialised when I was here last."

"They needed time to build without Admiral Singh," Stalker said. "And since they already had an industrial base, it was natural for it to keep growing."

Jasmine shrugged, watching grimly as more and more asteroid settlements came into view. It was easy to hide an asteroid settlement from anything less than a close inspection, but she knew better than to take it for granted. If one of the ships that had left the system was a spy, she knew, Wolfbane would already have a pretty good idea where most of the settlements actually *were*. And even if they didn't, they had good reason to keep catching asteroids and melting them down for raw materials.

Not that there's any shortage, she thought. Thousands of years of mining hadn't significantly reduced Earth's asteroid belt, after all, although there had been plans to blow up one of the minor planets to produce more raw material. The plans had come to nothing, as far as she recalled; she was fairly sure she would have noticed a missing planet when she was last in the Sol System. *They can support a full-scale industrial node for centuries if necessary.*

The Colonel glanced at her. "Is 1st Platoon ready for deployment?"

"Yes, sir," Jasmine said. She was still disappointed that he'd rejected her idea for an orbital drop, but she did understand his logic. They'd be taking quite enough crazy risks when the enemy arrived, finally. "Do you want an escort?"

"I think it would be best," Colonel Stalker said. "And I'll want your impressions of Corinthian too."

Jasmine frowned. "Not all of them will be pleased to see me, sir," she said. She'd tried to resign, the first time, after completing the mission on Corinthian. "And some of them may bear a grudge."

"It can't be helped," the Colonel said. "All hell is going to break loose soon."

"Unless Wolfbane fails to take the bait," Jasmine said.

She looked up at the display. The logic of shortening the defence lines was sound, she knew, although part of her insisted it was the pre-lude to accepting inevitable defeat. There were good reasons to strip Corinthian of everything useful before ceding the world to Wolfbane and good reasons for Wolfbane to want to move fast, to intervene before it was too late. And yet, on an interstellar scale, the universe laughed at plots and plans. It was quite possible that Admiral Singh would continue her drive towards Avalon and leave Corinthian for later.

But she wants revenge, Jasmine thought. *And we're offering her the chance to take it.*

"Twelve hours until we enter orbit," the Colonel added. "I'll be taking a shuttle down to Freedom City as soon as possible. You and 1st Platoon will accompany me, as planned."

"Yes, sir," Jasmine said.

"And leave your boyfriend behind," he warned. "This meeting will have to be private."

Jasmine nodded, curtly. She was used to the ribbing - and besides, the colonel had a very valid point. No one, particularly a planetary govern-ment official, would want a public record of what was certain to be a very uncomfortable meeting.

"I imagine he'll be off-loaded with the troops," she said. She hesitated, then asked the question that had been bothering her for weeks. "What happens if they refuse to cooperate?"

The Colonel hesitated. "We cannot try to compel cooperation," he said, finally. "Even if we wanted to try, it would be devastating. The Commonwealth would not survive."

He cleared his throat. "If they refuse to allow us to land and deploy our forces, along with the shield generator and everything else, we will have no choice but to withdraw," he admitted. "And we will have to hope that the Wolves suffer when they try to take the system."

Jasmine watched him go, then turned her gaze back to the display. Corinthian had powerful defences; Admiral Singh had been determined to keep her capital safe and her successors, always aware she might return, had built on them. But there were problems, hundreds of problems, in defending a planet from a mobile fleet. A planet could neither run nor hide...

...And if they choose to fight without our help, they'll be slaughtered, she thought. *And then Admiral Singh will take whatever is left and turn it against us.*

She keyed her wristcom after taking one last glance at the timer. "Report to the shuttlebay at 0920, local time," she ordered. "Bring standard escort gear; make sure you get some sleep before we leave."

Her lips twitched as she turned and walked out of the CIC. Joe Buckley had remained faithful to his wife, much to Jasmine's relief, but the other marines had been working hard to lure as many crewwomen into bed as possible. They'd been quite successful too, she thought, if the bragging was any indication. At least they hadn't taken to collecting pairs of panties again, thankfully. She still winced when she recalled Sergeant Hallowell's reaction to Blake Coleman's collection, the night before all hell broke loose on Han...

Get some sleep, she told herself, firmly. *The long wait is over.*

"They're not taking any chances, Captain," the tactical officer reported, as Mandy stepped back onto the bridge. "They've got us locked with a hundred automated missile platforms."

"The first line of defence," Mandy commented. The platforms weren't much, but their mere presence would force an attacker to declare himself before he got into firing range of the orbital battlestations. "Hold position. Wait for them to call us."

She wondered, absently, just what was going on in the mighty battlestations. They'd had plenty of opportunity to get hard visuals of her hulls, confirming that *Defiant* and her sisters were Commonwealth starships. It wasn't as if she'd arrived in a fleet of ex-Empire ships that could have been flown by anyone from rebels to pirates. But they'd still be wondering what the hell was going on...

"Picking up a signal, Captain," the communications officer said. "It's from an Admiral Melaka."

"Put him through," Mandy ordered.

She glanced at the line of text under the screen. Admiral Melaka was a local-born naval officer, technically an officer in the Commonwealth Navy even though he hadn't been trained on Avalon. Like her, he'd been promoted rapidly; she was mildly surprised he hadn't been working for Admiral Singh. But then, that had probably been a factor in his promotion. Too many local officers had had ties to the former dictator.

"Commodore Caesius," Admiral Melaka said. He was older than she'd expected, although it could be that he was merely one of the rare people who reacted badly to anti-aging and rejuvenation treatments. Or it could be a fashion statement. "It's...*interesting* to see you here, at this moment. You came without notification."

"I'm afraid so, Admiral," Mandy said. "The entire mission was organised on very short notice."

Admiral Melaka cocked his head. "Indeed?"

"Colonel Stalker needs to speak directly to your government," Mandy said. She played enough word games with her father, when he was in a good mood and her mother was elsewhere. "Please would you clear his shuttle to pass through your defence grid?"

"It will be done," Admiral Melaka said. "I'll have a flight path forwarded to you shortly."

Just long enough to make sure the planetary leaders are briefed, Mandy thought. She didn't really blame Admiral Melaka for making sure his superiors were alerted, but she doubted they had time for playing games. *He doesn't know what's coming.*

"That would be good," she said, out loud.

Admiral Melaka nodded. "And your crews? Will they be requiring shore leave facilities?"

"Not at present," Mandy said. Commonwealth crews were quite well behaved, compared to some of the horror stories she'd heard from the Imperial Navy, but bad memories faded slowly. Admiral Singh's crews had probably not been too disciplined either. "I expect we will be talking again, shortly."

His eyes narrowed. "Aye, I can see it," he said. He'd picked up on *something*, after all. "I look forward to it, Commodore."

Mandy frowned as his face vanished, then glanced at the communications officer. "They've sent a flight path, Captain," he said. "It's a straight-line descent to Freedom City."

They definitely know something is up, Mandy thought. Admiral Melaka's file warned that he had very limited experience, but he was not a fool. The sheer surprise of their arrival had probably worried him badly. *That's good, right now.*

"Forward it to the shuttlebay, then clear Colonel Stalker for departure," she ordered. A straight-line descent meant no security games, which both pleased and worried her. "And then hold position here until further notice."

"Aye, Commodore," the communications officer said.

Good luck, Jasmine, Mandy thought. *You'll need it.*

CHAPTER
ELEVEN

There was, for example, a war back on Old Earth where one side made the mistake of switching its reserve forces from west to east, when the war in the west appeared to be going well.

- Professor Leo Caesius. The Role of Randomness In War.

Ed had only set foot on Corinthian once, shortly after Jasmine's coup had sent Admiral Singh fleeing into deep space. Landing City - it had been renamed Freedom City shortly after his visit - had impressed him, although it wasn't the kind of place he'd want to spend the rest of his life. The towering skyscrapers were far too close to the CityBlocks of Earth for his comfort, even though they were smaller and far less inclusive. He'd grown too used to open spaces to find them comfortable.

But it was clear that the city's planners disagreed. There were hundreds of new skyscrapers, running out in all directions from the government complex in the centre of the city. Much of the ring of farms surrounding the city had been obliterated, replaced by skyscrapers and other buildings as the city expanded to absorb the influx of newcomers. He hoped, despite himself, that the planet's population understood the wisdom of keeping their powder dry - and zero tolerance for crime. Without it, they'd rapidly lose control of their streets as the barbarity at the core of human nature reasserted itself.

He settled back in his chair as the shuttle dropped towards Government House and landed neatly on the landing pad. A handful of armed soldiers were within view, but none of them seemed inclined to storm the shuttle or do anything other than serve as a welcoming committee. Ed studied them through the porthole as he rose to his feet, silently deciding that they were probably better trained than the average City Guard unit. Admiral Singh, whatever else could be said about her, had understood the value of intensive training.

And even that didn't stop her forces from committing atrocities from time to time, he thought, grimly. *What's going to happen when she returns to Corinthian?*

Jasmine and 1st Platoon fanned out around him as he disembarked, taking a long breath as soon as he was outside the hatch. The air brought back unwelcome memories, reminding him far too much of Earth. It didn't stink *quite* as badly as humanity's homeworld, he conceded after a long moment, but he could taste the scent of industrialisation in the air. But perhaps that was not too surprising. Compared to most of the worlds within the Commonwealth, Corinthian had had a big head start. Even lawsuits filed by worlds Admiral Singh had looted to build up her industrial base hadn't slowed the planet's industrial growth.

A young man wearing a captain's uniform stepped forward, showing no sign of nervousness at meeting either Ed himself or the armed marines. Ed was moderately impressed, recognising the signs of special training. The guards would know how to handle guests from off-world, protecting their charges without causing offense. It spoke well of him, Ed decided, but how would he handle himself in a combat zone? It was quite likely he was about to find out.

"Colonel Stalker," the young man said. "Welcome to Corinthian."

"Thank you," Ed said. He couldn't help noticing that the officer didn't wear a nametag, a common precaution when diplomats with ruffled feathers could file reports and complaints that would put an end to an officer's career. The guards he recalled on Earth had taken a perverse delight in watching for opportunities to manhandle their seniors. "It's been quite some time since I was last here."

"Yes, sir," the officer said. "I am to conduct a brief security scan, then escort you and your marines to the briefing compartment. Is that suitable?"

"Of course," Ed said. "I quite understand the requirements."

He waited, patiently, as the guards ran sensors over their bodies, silently noting what they did and didn't do. Diplomats tended to get offended when told they needed to be strip-searched, which made it harder to keep them from smuggling weapons or other surprises into conference rooms. *Ed* was sure he could have gotten a weapon through security without too much trouble, even without implants that would send false readings back to the scanner. But then, anything short of a full search - including the removal of his uniform - would have been insufficient.

The thought made him smile as they were escorted down the stairs and through a network of corridors, each one lined with black-edged photographs of the men and women who had died in the fight against Admiral Singh. He wondered if Jasmine recognised any of them, but there was no way he could ask her in public. A large portrait hung at the end of the corridor, with a sign underneath that read *The Liberators*. He fought down the urge to laugh as he saw someone who was probably meant to be Jasmine. He'd wondered why none of the guards had seemed to recognise her, but if they expected her to look like her portrait…

"The President and the General are waiting for you," the escort said, as they stopped outside a large pair of doors. "Do you want your escort to remain here?"

"Jasmine, with me," Ed ordered. "The rest of you, wait here."

He walked through the doors and into a small conference room. It was smaller than he'd expected, strikingly plain. In *his* experience, planetary governments tended to build themselves the most ornate complexes they could, regardless of the cost. He'd even been in a complex where the walls were literally lined with gold. But Corinthian seemed to have avoided that particular trap. It was, he suspected, a legacy from Admiral Singh. She was smart enough to know that *power*, rather than the *appearance* of power, was all that mattered in the universe.

And if they realised they'd drawn that lesson from Admiral Singh, he thought as the two people in the room rose to face him, *what would they do with it?*

"Colonel Stalker," a rich contralto said. "And Jasmine. It has been a while."

Ed nodded. President Danielle Chambers looked young for her role, although he knew for a fact that she was the mother of two children. Her dark skin and darker hair suggested both youth and maturity, although the fact she was one of the handful of resistance leaders who had survived Admiral Singh had given her a very definite edge in the first planetary elections after Singh's flight. Beside her, General Conrad Hampton was a short and wiry sparkplug, an appearance befitting a retired marine. Ed gave him a smile that said, very clearly, that they needed to catch up afterwards. He'd invited Hampton to stay on Avalon, after his flight from Greenway, but the older man had declined. Corinthian needed him.

"Thank you for seeing us on such short notice," Ed said, as they sat down. "Time is short, so if you don't mind we will skip the formalities and get straight down to business."

Hampton smiled. "Glad to see that being a senior officer hasn't weakened you, Ed."

Ed frowned as a maid entered, carrying a tray of coffee, then reminded himself that it was still early in the morning. He'd had the ships switched to local time as soon as they'd entered phase space, but he still felt the after-effects of interstellar lag. It just didn't *feel* like morning to him. But then, he *had* slept for seven solid hours after the squadron had dropped out of phase space.

"I try to remain blunt, where possible," he said. He'd never had any patience for political games, even though he spent half of his time on Avalon doing nothing else. "I trust that won't be a problem?"

Danielle smiled. "If you can be blunter than some of the people I have to deal with," she said, "I will be very impressed."

Ed nodded slowly and waited until the maid had finished pouring coffee before leaving the room. She was probably trustworthy - anyone working in the building would have been checked thoroughly before being granted a security clearance - but there was no point in taking chances. Suborning someone so close to the planetary leader - someone so lowly as to pass unnoticed - was every intelligence officer's wet dream. A single spy in such a position could do a great deal of damage.

"The war has taken a turn against us," he said, bluntly. There was no way to make the news *good*, no matter how he tried to phrase it. "This planet is likely to come under heavy attack within the next two months, probably sooner."

Danielle studied him for a long moment. "Can you be sure?"

"No," Ed said. "But Admiral Singh is currently in command of the enemy forces, unless some kindly soul assassinates her. She has the means, motive and opportunity to attack Corinthian as soon as possible. Our best guess is that you will be attacked in force within a month."

He ran through a brief reprise of the strategic situation, watching them carefully. Danielle had learned to hide her feelings, he noted, but it was clear that she was appalled by the prospect of Admiral Singh returning to Corinthian. Hampton, by contrast, was obviously contemplating his contingency plans and wondering which one should be hastily updated and then put into practice. He, at least, would understand that Ed was trying to bait a trap, but what would he do with the knowledge? It would be hard to blame Danielle for not wanting to turn her homeworld into a combat zone...

Again, he reminded himself. *The people here know what will happen if Admiral Singh resumes control of the system.*

"We believe we can make a stand here," he concluded. "But it will require your cooperation."

"Your plan would seem to hinge on fighting a brutal battle on the surface," Danielle said. It was hard to read her emotions, but she didn't *sound* pleased. "Are you sure Admiral Singh will fall into the trap?"

"There's no guarantee of anything," Ed said. In truth, there were no guarantees that Admiral Singh had even realised she was being offered a chance to snatch Corinthian, no matter what the intelligence staff claimed. "But we believe she would be unwilling to let the chance slip past."

"And you're betting everything on an untested piece of technology," Danielle added. "If the shield generator fails..."

"The level of firepower they would need to break the shield would turn the planet's surface into ash," Ed said. There were so many redundancies built into the shield generator that even *he* was impressed. "Singh would have a very good reason to fight it out on the ground."

Danielle met his eyes. "And if we refuse to cooperate?"

"Admiral Singh is going to try to retake this system," Ed said, bluntly. "Corinthian is of vital importance - and she knows it. She'll be sure to bring along enough firepower to take the system too, if we fight a conventional battle. The only way to hurt her, the only way to draw her into a trap, is to fight an unconventional engagement."

"Which would devastate the planet," Danielle pointed out.

"How badly would it be devastated," Jasmine asked quietly, "if Admiral Singh retook control?"

Hampton scowled. "Very badly," he said. "We'd lose everything."

Danielle glanced at him, then looked at Ed. "What's your plan?"

"Land troops and build defences, while evacuating trained manpower and their families," Ed said. Cold logic insisted that trained manpower should come first, but common sense - and simple humanity - stated that their families had to be evacuated at the same time. "We set up the shield generator in place to cover Freedom City, then wait. When Admiral Singh arrives, she will have to land troops to secure the facilities she wants."

"Unless she decides to merely secure the high orbitals and call it a draw," Hampton pointed out.

"She cannot afford to lose," Ed insisted. "Everything we know about Wolfbane indicates that the system is dangerously unstable. Admiral Singh will only remain on top as long as she seems victorious and unstoppable. A draw would ruin her image."

Danielle frowned. "Conrad and I will need to discuss the matter," she said, rising. "Please will you wait here? Call the maid" - she jabbed a finger towards the buzzer - "if you need more coffee."

"Of course," Ed said. "But time is not on our side."

———

President Danielle Chambers had never really *expected* to be President. It had been enough of a surprise that Admiral Singh had left her alone, after the first resistance movement had been broken; she'd been reluctant to be dragged into the second, let alone remain involved in politics after Admiral Singh had fled. But Corinthian had been on a knife-edge since Admiral Singh's defeat and she was one of the few remaining citizens who had served in *both* resistance movements. She'd run for office because none of the other candidates seemed more interested in the planet than their own personal power...

And yet, part of her was still the scared woman who had withdrawn from the fight for the good of her children.

She swallowed hard, remembering the days when Admiral Singh's soldiers had patrolled the streets, keeping a wary eye on the population. The scars the bitch had left behind ran deep, she knew all too well; the prospect of returning to those days was not one anyone would welcome. Indeed, she'd thrown so much money into the planetary defences purely to ensure that Singh could not return. But if Colonel Stalker was right, all their hard work was for nothing. Admiral Singh was about to return.

"General," she said. She trusted Hampton rather more than she trusted some of her cabinet members. The man was reassuringly solid in the midst of chaos. "What do you make of it?"

"The logic is sound," Hampton said, gravely. "We may need to check with Amir" - Admiral Melaka - "but as far as I can tell we will be gravely exposed as the Commonwealth's defence lines contract."

"They pledged to protect us," Danielle said, without heat. She knew, all too well, that the Commonwealth was pushed to the limits. "Can we keep Singh from taking the high orbitals?"

"Probably not," Hampton admitted. "Amir may think otherwise, but I suspect that a determined offensive will allow Admiral Singh to wipe the defences out before taking the high orbitals and forcing us to surrender. If, of course, we fight a conventional war."

Danielle shuddered, inwardly. She knew what would happen if they surrendered. Admiral Singh would purge the planet of everyone involved in the government, from politicians such as herself to lowly civil servants, then start handing out the loot to her cronies. And this time, there would be no mercy for the families of the purged. Admiral Singh would kill her husband and children as surely as she'd kill Danielle herself. Everyone related to someone on the Admiral's hit list would die.

And yet, the prospect of a long and brutal war on the surface was almost as horrifying.

She had no illusions. A long war on the same scale as Han would be utterly devastating to the planet. By the time it ended, if it *did* end, Freedom City would be in ruins, while the planet's population would be sharply reduced. And it wasn't as if Corinthian had *that* many friends to help reconstruction. Admiral Singh, damn the bitch, had ensured that the nearby planets had good reason to refuse *any* help...

And I didn't make it any easier, she thought. In hindsight, alienating several of her neighbours had probably been a mistake. *They really don't like us.*

She looked at Hampton. "Can we win?"

"It gives us our best chance of hurting the bitch," Hampton said, flatly. "The blunt truth, Madam President, is that if we surrender, we will face devastating losses anyway. She isn't going to be content to secure the high orbitals and move on, not with us. She'll want us to support her forces as they press on towards Avalon."

"And surrender means a purge anyway," Danielle said. She rather doubted Admiral Singh would keep her word, if she pledged to spare lives in exchange for a hasty surrender. And even if she did, it would still be devastating for Corinthian. "So we have to fight."

"It looks that way," Hampton agreed. "But the cabinet won't be pleased."

Danielle shuddered. If she'd been able to choose her own cabinet... but she hadn't. She'd had to take politicians from all over the political spectrum, from industrialists who would want to seek an accommodation to former resistance soldiers who would want to fight to the death. Hell, she'd worried about what would happen if Governor Brown had been in command of the force invading her space. *He* would be happy to bargain with the industrialists...

And he would probably have kept his word too, she thought.

She turned and strode back into the conference room, Hampton following. "I will have to speak to the cabinet," she said, "but I believe they will agree that we have to fight. However, I do have a condition. I want the evacuation broadened to take relatives of people who are likely to be purged, if Singh wins the war."

"We need to put trained manpower first," Stalker said. "But we can hide others around the planet, if necessary."

"The cabinet will want guarantees," Danielle said. How long did they have? A month? Two months? Or much less? "Their families will be at risk too."

"We'll add them to the list," Stalker said. "But like I said, time is really not on our side."

"It isn't on hers either," Danielle said. Some of the industrialists had wanted to impose strict gun control, but it had found absolutely no political backing at all. The planet's population would never be unarmed again. "Give us a few weeks and we will be ready to fight."

And she hoped desperately that she was right.

CHAPTER
TWELVE

Unknown to that side, its western enemy was rallying - and the forces it had dispatched were caught in limbo, unable to do anything to assist its fellows to either west or east. By the time they reached their final destination, the matter was already decided.

- Professor Leo Caesius. The Role of Randomness In War.

Emmanuel Alves was no stranger to spaceports - he'd seen a dozen space-ports across the Commonwealth during his career - but he had to admit that the Freedom City Spaceport was easily the largest he'd seen, dwarfing anything on Avalon. Even the colossal military spaceport he'd visited on Lakshmibai was tiny in comparison. Hundreds of hangers for shuttlec-raft, dozens of terminals to organise passengers and shuttlecraft taking off every five minutes…he was relieved, despite himself, that he wasn't in charge of traffic control. It had to be an absolute nightmare.

He adjusted the camera on his shoulder as another Commonwealth shuttle landed, far too close to one of the terminals for comfort. The hatches sprang open a moment later, allowing a long line of soldiers to march out onto the tarmac, where they were greeted by military police-men who guided them towards one of the hangers. There, they'd be given a brief orientation and an introduction to the planet, then told to wait until the buses were ready to take them to the defence lines. He allowed the camera to pass over the soldiers - mostly young men, although there were a handful of young women too - and then turned and walked towards the nearest terminal. The guards eyed him sharply, then allowed him to pass through the doors and into the building.

It was chaotic. Emmanuel was no stranger to crowds, but the building was crammed with men, women and children. The latter were running around, arguing and shouting, while their parents were trying to maintain control or fight their own battles. None of them had expected to have to leave their homes, their friends, the lives they'd built for themselves, but there was no choice. Admiral Singh wouldn't hesitate to round up trained manpower and put it to use on her behalf. He panned the camera over the giant room, then zoomed in on a pretty teenage girl who was having a sulk. It was hard to be sure, but she seemed to be complaining about having to leave her pet behind.

Not that there would be room on the ships, Emmanuel thought, as he stepped to one side. A pair of officers were barking orders, rounding up the next set of evacuees. *A pet would consume life support that would be better saved for more humans.*

He smiled at the thought, then watched grimly as the officers fought to impose some order on the chaos. The older couples seemed to understand, save for a handful who bitched and moaned and wasted time. One woman in particular seemed insistent on suing everyone involved in the evacuation, even though it would be pointless. And, all the while, the children were running around, or crying, or fighting. The racket was deafening.

"STAY IN YOUR SEATS UNTIL CALLED," someone bellowed. "YOU WILL BE CALLED WHEN THE TIME COMES."

Emmanuel sighed and hurried through the exit, walking down to the terminal entrance. A line of guards stood there, checking IDs and baggage weights before allowing the new evacuees to enter the terminal. As he watched, a couple of bags were dumped in a waste trolley, despite protests from their owners. They'd been *warned* not to bring more than a single bag each, no matter what it was they couldn't bear to leave behind. There just wasn't the room on the shuttles to accommodate everything.

He took a handful of pictures, then nodded to the security guards as he walked outside. A long line of buses were waiting to be unloaded, their drivers looking frazzled. They'd be working under military command, Emmanuel recalled from the briefing; everyone who could drive a bus had been summoned to the colours and put to work assisting the evacuation. He rather doubted the drivers would get hazard pay, although they probably deserved it. He'd heard that a handful of fights had already been broken up by the guards.

"Better stay out the way," a harried-looking woman said. "You'll get shipped off to Earth if you're not careful."

Emmanuel nodded and stepped backwards as another bus opened its doors, allowing a swarm of men, women and children to disembark. The guards stepped forwards, keeping their weapons clearly visible, and started to chivvy the civilians into inspection lanes. A tough-looking man waved his fists at the guards, but quietened down in a hurry as he found himself the target of several rifles. Emmanuel had never been keen on watching civilians pushed around by the military, but what else could the guards do? They had to keep order somehow.

"Hey," a voice called. "You the reporter from Avalon?"

Emmanuel looked up. A young man, no older than himself, was standing there, wearing a press pass around his neck. "That's me," he said. "And you are?"

"Tad," the reporter said. He held out a hand, which Emmanuel shook. "*Corinthian News.*"

"Pleased to meet you," Emmanuel said. "I was hoping for a few interviews, but people seem to be rather busy."

"Tell me about it," Tad said. His accent was surprisingly strong. "A mate of mine tried asking for an interview with a spaceport worker, but she called the guards and he's currently under arrest."

"How unfortunate," Emmanuel said. He knew from Jasmine that reporters couldn't be allowed to get in the way, even if it *did* lead to be the best stories. It could also lead to the reporters becoming the news themselves. "Is he going to be all right?"

"I have no idea," Tad said. He shrugged "Normally, you can talk to anyone here, but as you can see..."

He waved a hand at the line of buses. "It's a right nightmare," he added. He lowered his voice, significantly. "Say...is this true?"

Emmanuel blinked. "Is *what* true?"

"That there's going to be an attack," Tad said. "That…" - he waved a hand around the scene - "that this isn't all just an attempt to loot our world."

"I believe it to be true," Emmanuel said, stiffly. He couldn't see Colonel Stalker deciding to loot a world for fun and profit - or Jasmine, for that matter. "Admiral Singh is likely to be attacking soon, you see."

"I see," Tad said. "But not everyone believes it."

Emmanuel sighed. It was something he'd never really understood until he'd started travelling between the stars. Word spread slowly, even within the Commonwealth, and news from hundreds of light years away often seemed less important than local affairs. It was hard to blame someone for not believing that Admiral Singh had not only survived, but prospered on Wolfbane. But she had and now she was out for revenge.

"It's true," he said, quietly. "We wouldn't be wasting time preparing defences if it wasn't true, would we?"

"I don't know," Tad said. "After Singh…there's so much people will believe - or won't believe, depending."

———

Mindy Caesius let out a breath she hadn't realised she was holding as the shuttle slammed into the ground, then sprang to her feet as the hatch banged open. The Stormtroopers lined up in rows and hurried out of the shuttlecraft, following directions from the military policemen that led towards a giant hanger. It was a bare and a barren space, she noted, as she slowed to a walk, but it provided some shelter from the racket as the officers fought to keep everyone in line. She'd seen enough quick-deployment exercises on Avalon to know they could disintegrate into chaos very quickly.

"All right, stand at ease," Sergeant Rackham bellowed. "We have a lot of shit to get through and there isn't much time."

Mindy winced. Sergeant Rackham was a tall man who had intimidated her more than she cared to admit, back when she'd applied to join the Stormtroopers. He'd ridden her constantly, alternatively insisting that no woman could pass the course and suggesting that she quit before she was seriously injured. It hadn't been until she'd completed the course that she'd realised he'd been driving her onwards, pushing her right to the very limit just to make sure she could handle it. She still loathed him - and she hadn't been pleased when he'd been assigned to the troop - but she trusted him.

"This is Corinthian," Sergeant Rackham continued, without lowering his voice. "You've read the briefing packets, so remember what they said! Follow the rules; anyone caught breaking them will be in deep shit! Stay with your unit unless you are given clear permission to leave and *behave yourselves!*"

She forced herself to listen as Sergeant Rackham ran through a brief overview of the cultural rules - Corinthian was considerably looser than Avalon, although rather less loose than Earth - and then joined the line of troopers heading towards the buses. The local drivers eyed them curiously, without the fear she'd felt - herself - when she'd seen her first soldier. But then, she reminded herself, Corinthian had been under occupation for three years. They might dislike off-world soldiers, but they wouldn't see them as wild animals.

The bus roared to life as soon as the last trooper was onboard. Sergeant Rackham slammed the door, then kept a sharp eye on his men as the bus lurched once, then started forward down a long ramp. Mindy stared towards the towering skyscrapers in the distance, feeling an odd flicker of *Déjà Vu*. Corinthian was nothing like Earth, but there was something in the skyscrapers that felt familiar, a sense that both attracted and repelled her. She'd expected the spaceport to be some distance from the city, yet as they drove onwards it was obvious that the spaceport was surrounded. The city had just expanded outwards at terrifying speed.

There'll be an accident one day, she thought, morbidly. *A shuttle will crash into a populated zone and all hell will break loose.*

She sucked in her breath as she saw a line of protestors, holding up banners that demanded everything from all offworlders being kicked off the planet to the immediate resignation of the planetary president. Most of them appeared to be young, no older than Mindy herself; they looked more like students than soldiers. She'd never seen anything like it on

Avalon, but student protests had been strikingly common on Earth. And none of them, according to her father, had done anything more than let the students blow off a little steam.

Trooper Hicks had another question. "Why aren't those bastards in the militia?"

"Silence," Sergeant Rackham snapped.

Surprisingly, the driver answered. "Because certain kinds of students have exemptions, assuming they keep their grades high," he said. "I'd imagine that lot have received draft notices by now."

Mindy shook her head in grim amusement as one of the protesters - a topless girl - danced into view, swinging her breasts as she held a sign aloft in the air. It attracted attention, she had to admit, but she could barely read the sign. Something to do with freedom of expression for all, something that puzzled Mindy. Corinthian was a signatory to the Commonwealth Charter, wasn't it? Freedom of expression was part of the charter.

The bus drove past the protesters, who didn't seem inclined to do anything more than shout insults and slogans, and headed further down the road. Mindy couldn't help noticing that the streets were almost empty, save for military and commandeered civilian vehicles. A long line of earth-moving equipment was slowly making its way to the lines, followed by a handful of other vehicles carrying supplies. She rather suspected the building industry was enjoying a boom time, even as the remainder of the planetary economy staggered under the need to evacuate as much of its trained personnel and industrial nodes as possible. But then, it was equally possible that the building industries had been rapidly nationalised, just to make sure they did their damned job without quibbles. She rather doubted she'd ever know.

She braced herself as the bus slowed to a halt, outside a gate guarded by armed soldiers and a pair of AFVs. The camp looked like a makeshift barracks, a neatly-organised set of tents surrounded by barbed wire. She'd slept in them before during countless exercises; they were uncomfortable, but heaven itself compared to sleeping in a muddy trench. She had a feeling she'd have enough of both before the coming war was over.

"All right, dismount," Sergeant Rackham barked, as the doors banged open. He jabbed a finger towards two of the larger tents. Mindy could see lines of computers and operators inside one, but the other was empty. "Get into the second tent and wait for orders!"

Mindy jumped to her feet and followed the others out of the bus.

———

"It looks like a giant radar dome," Danielle observed, as she studied the shield generator. She was no expert, but she'd expected something a little more...*dramatic*. "Is it really capable of protecting the city?"

"And a great deal more," Trader Engineer Susan Coomb assured her. She was a tall girl, young enough to make Danielle worry about her competence. And yet, the Traders were renowned for being among the most advanced faction in known space. "As long as the power holds out, the shield will remain firmly in place."

"Unless the enemy unleashes planet-cracking levels of force," Danielle muttered. She recalled Colonel Stalker's warning far too clearly. "Or if the power *does* run out."

"We've tied Gladys into the power grid," Susan said, "but we've also brought along nineteen fusion generators, three times as many as we need to keep the shield up. They will practically have to take out the shield generator itself to take the shield down, which will not be easy."

"They should be able to locate the generator," Danielle pointed out. She rather liked Susan's attitude, but she wasn't going to allow her feelings to sway her judgement. "If only by deducing the centre of the shield."

Susan grinned. "Oh no they won't," she said. "The shield is actually fuzzed, a little, just to keep someone from doing just that. They'll be able to tell that the generator is somewhere within five square miles, but nothing more precise. A random hit would be pretty bad, I admit, yet we've done everything we can to keep that from happening. They'd really have to have a stroke of very good luck to score a direct hit."

"They'll certainly try," Danielle observed. "Can't you curve the shield to prevent them from flying underneath it?"

"There actually *is* a very slight shield curvature, in line with the planet itself," Susan said, ruefully. "Doing what you suggest would be very useful,

Madam President, but the shield generators can't hold a curved shield in place for long. It would put too much stress on the field manifolds."

She launched into a long and complicated explanation filled with technobabble Danielle couldn't begin to understand, although she managed to force herself to keep listening until the younger woman was finally finished. Danielle had thought she'd had a fairly complete education, but it hadn't taken long for her - as President - to realise just how little she actually knew. The whole concept of force fields was new, in any case. Admiral Singh had grown up in a universe where there was nothing protecting a planet from marauding starships.

And let us hope the bitch gets gnashed to death when she tries to land on our world, she thought, coldly. *We are getting ready for her.*

She sighed as another flight of shuttles roared over the city, heading to the starships waiting in orbit. Ordering the evacuation had been one hell of a fight with her cabinet, once she'd convinced them that Corinthian was likely to come under attack. Even with the offer to evacuate their relatives too, along with the trained manpower, she'd had to call in every favour she was owed to convince the cabinet to declare martial law. And even with martial law, she knew there were people who were dragging their feet…

And if Admiral Singh doesn't show up in a couple of months, she thought wryly, *I'll be thrown out of office and hanged.*

"Thank you," she said to Susan. "How quickly can you power up the generator?"

"I intend to run power-curve tests once the final control circuits are in place," Susan said, glancing at her datapad. "Once Gladys is confirmed fully-functional, we'll keep her active - on low power - so we can bring her up at any moment. We shouldn't have any problems maintaining her power curves for several months, at least. There's a lot of redundancy built into the system."

"That's good to know," Danielle said. "And can you repair it while the system is active?"

"It would depend on what needed to be repaired," Susan said, after a moment. "But yeah, we should be able to repair the system."

Danielle nodded. Far too many of the devices the Empire had produced, in its last century of life, had been impossible to modify or repair.

It had been intended to save people from damaging their possessions, according to the corporations, but she knew the *real* purpose was to keep people from repairing a device instead of buying a new one. How many of the devices she'd owned had started to show problems after a few years of life? The Trade Federation, thankfully, preferred devices that could be repaired by the user.

"Of course, if the generator was under heavy stress, it might not be possible," Susan added, darkly. "But if that were the case, we would have more important things to worry about."

Danielle nodded, crossly. Susan was, if anything, understating the matter.

And if the generator fails, she thought, *we lose the war.*

CHAPTER
THIRTEEN

Another interesting problem facing the Commonwealth - which caused a great deal of debate prior to the Battle of Thule - was the Battle of Lakshmibai. It is beyond doubt that a single starship, from either the Commonwealth or Wolfbane, would have rendered the entire battle over in half an hour.
- Professor Leo Caesius. The Role of Randomness In War.

It was quiet at night, very quiet.

Jasmine lay on the ground, listening carefully as she crawled through the darkness towards the militia camp. An owl-like creature was hooting softly in the distance, but otherwise there was nothing to mask their approach. She peered through the darkness, her enhanced eyes picking out the pair of sentries on guard and scowled in disapproval as she realised that they were chatting quietly while smoking cigarettes. The light from one's match, as he lit a second cigarette, would blind his night vision for a few precious seconds.

At least they're not sleeping, she thought. Falling asleep on duty in Boot Camp would have resulted in weeks of Incentive Training, falling asleep on the Slaughterhouse would have been an automatic fail…but falling asleep on watch in a combat zone could get someone killed. *And yet it isn't much of an improvement.*

The three marines scouted the camp carefully, noting the enemy positions from the outside and planning their approach. It was clear that the militia hadn't done any real drills for years, she thought; they'd made a number of mistakes that would get them killed, if they were on the battlefield. They *knew* that someone was going to be probing their defences, yet they weren't watching for signs of an incoming attacker. And their camp was practically *designed* to allow someone to count the militiamen without needing to sneak through the wire.

Her lips thinned in disapproval as she monitored the guards on patrol. Even the merest imbecile knew to vary the timing, just to make sure no one could try to sneak through the wire while the guards were somewhere else, but this bunch hadn't bothered to read a tactical manual. Unless, of course, it was a trap...she puzzled over it for a long moment, then decided she'd need to spring it anyway. Who knew? Maybe the enemy CO had some fiendish plan that would catch all three marines before they could do any real damage.

She glanced at Thomas Stewart and Joe Buckley. It was hard to read expressions on their blackened faces, but neither of them looked very impressed by the camp. Jasmine briefly contemplated capturing the guards first - it would be thoroughly embarrassing to the locals if she succeeded - before dismissing the thought. There was just too great a risk of setting off an alarm before they got into position to do some real damage. Sneaking under the wire would be far more effective.

Holding up her hand, she communicated her intentions and waited for their nods, then turned and crawled towards the wire. Up close, it was nowhere near as impressive as it looked from a distance; they'd established a fairly solid line separating the camp from the rest of the great outdoors, but it wasn't pinned to the ground or wired to sound the alert if anyone tampered with it. The Imperial Army had had a regular problem with men sneaking off to the nearest bar, she recalled, and their senior officers had eventually stopped responding to alerts. It was amusing, although not in a good way, that Corinthian's militia had the same problem.

She lifted the wire quickly, maintaining a silent countdown in her head, and crawled underneath, bracing herself for an alarm or gunfire. Neither happened; she held the wire up long enough for Stewart and Buckley to join her, then remained low as the guards made their next sweep around the fence. Marines were taught to watch for something - anything - out of place, on the grounds it was better to sound the alarm over nothing than get throats slit while they were sleeping, but whoever had trained the militia hadn't done a very good job. The report she intended to make to her superiors was growing longer by the minute.

They've had five fucking weeks to prepare, she thought, as she watched the guards vanish into the darkness. The damned idiot was *still* smoking his cigarette! *Five fucking weeks and they can't even maintain a decent night watch!*

She found herself hoping that it actually *was* a trap as they rose and hurried soundlessly towards the five tents. If someone had tracked them, lured them into the camp...no, only a complete idiot would take such a risk. Maybe it would work, in bad fiction or worse flicks, but she would hand in her Rifleman's Tab if someone tried it in the real world and it actually worked. The grenades she and her fellows were carrying were enough to ensure a high casualty rate, whatever else happened. She briefly considered deliberately breaking a twig, just to see if it provoked any reaction, then shook her head. Right now, she wasn't particularly inclined to do the militia any favours.

Buckley held up a hand, signalling *idiots*. Jasmine nodded in agreement, feeling a flicker of unearned sympathy for the militia. Joe Buckley had been a tough instructor, according to Mindy; he'd be drawing up his own list of issues to report to their superiors. And he might even be assigned to *fix* them. She held up a response, ordering the pair of marines to unhook their grenades from their belts and get ready to hurl them into the tents. As soon as they were ready, she counted down from three and hurled the first grenade.

It screamed as it struck the tent, emitting a sound fit to wake the dead and enough strobe lighting to disorientate a marine. Jasmine hit the ground automatically, silently glad of the blockers in her ears, as the other grenades detonated. The noise was deafening, but she could hear militiamen screaming in panic and see the guards running back towards the gates. Her lips thinned again - they could have rolled under the fence, just as the marines had done - and she motioned for the other two to stick with her as the CO stuck his head out of the lead tent.

And they put their commander in the newest tent, she thought. No doubt they saluted him on the battlefield too. A sniper would have a field day. *Aren't these bastards lucky they got us instead of the Wolves?*

Buckley pointed his pistol at the commander's head. "Bang," he said, as the guards finally charged into the enclosure. "You're dead."

"Fuck," the commander said.

"You're fucked," Jasmine agreed. She cleared her throat, then tapped a switch on her terminal. The grenades deactivated; silence descended, broken only by groans of pain and muffled curses. Their ears would be ringing for hours. "How many men do you have here?"

The commander - he was a captain, she recalled - blinked in shock. "Forty," he said, rubbing his ears frantically. "Forty men…"

"They're all dead," Jasmine said. The militia might be nothing more than weekend warriors - if indeed they bothered to assemble *that* often - but they needed to be better. "The exercise is over. Assemble your men, once their ears recover, and we will go over your series of mistakes."

"We could have killed you," one of the guards protested.

"We could have gunned you down long before you ran back into the camp," Buckley sneered, nastily. "Why didn't it occur to you to hit the deck the moment the grenades went off?"

Because they thought they weren't real grenades, Jasmine thought. She wouldn't have been so casual about tossing them around, either, if they *had* been real. *And because they wanted to salvage something from the fuck-up.*

She cleared her throat. "The exercise is over," she repeated. "We will discuss your mistakes shortly."

The commander looked furious, muttering something about his uncle, but Jasmine ignored him. Martial law had been declared. If his uncle was foolish enough to make a fuss, he wouldn't have a career for much longer. She turned and walked away, taking advantage of the chaos to sweep the camp and make a note of their other mistakes. Honestly! What idiot built the latrines so close to the camp? She hated to think what her drill instructors would have said if *she'd* designed the camp. Probably something nasty about wanting to get her men killed.

She tapped her terminal, sending in a brief report, then strode back to the centre of the militia camp. The militiamen were looking sullen, their beauty sleep in tatters; she would have felt sorry for them, if she hadn't had to fight for over three days without respite on Han. There were limits, even for marines. She wondered, vaguely, if they were going to give her any trouble, then decided it was unlikely. Once they stopped screaming in outrage, they were certain to realise that Jasmine could have killed them, if she'd been a genuine enemy.

"You were told that your camp would be raided," Jasmine said, once the militiamen were lined up facing her. "And yet the precautions you took were laughably ineffective."

She paused, giving them a moment for her words to sink in. The sun was starting to rise, allowing her to see them clearly. They didn't *look* very promising, she had to admit; several of them were alarmingly old, two were suspiciously young and a number looked more like overweight businessmen than soldiers or spacers. She made a mental note to check up on them, then dismissed it for later. Corinthian, like all of the Commonwealth worlds, could recruit whoever it liked for its militia. War - and death - was no respecter of age.

"There was far too much cover around your camp to hide us as we approached," she said, waving a hand towards the trees and tall grass. "You should have camped somewhere with a clear field of fire, making it harder for anyone to sneak up on you. And then you didn't take any precautions with the fence. All we had to do was lift up a few wires and crawl underneath."

Which they are probably not used to doing, she thought. Crawling through mud - or worse - disgusted city-folk, she recalled. She'd always thought of it as an odd taboo, given what she knew city-folk tolerated. *But they'll learn as soon as the bullets start flying.*

The commander coughed. "The alarms kept going off."

I was right, Jasmine thought.

She glowered at him instead. "A single false alarm is far better than having your men slaughtered in their sleep," she said. "Being inconvenienced is less unpleasant than being dead!

"In addition, your guards followed a predictable routine as they walked around the wire," she added. "It was easy for us to time our crawl to the fence and get under it before the guards made their next sweep. They didn't even notice anything out of place! And then it was too late to keep us from killing forty men. All we had to do was stand and throw grenades!"

There was a long chilling pause. "You did some things right," she conceded. "But it was not enough to save you from three raiders."

She looked at the commander, who seemed furious. God alone knew what sort of chewing out he'd get from his superiors, when her report reached them. *They* wouldn't lose sight of what would have happened, if the attack had been real. Losing forty men for nothing would be bad, very bad. And it would cause a great deal of damage to morale. She hoped - prayed - that the militiamen would take the lessons to heart. The next attack might well be real.

"We'll be back later this afternoon to discuss tactics," she concluded. "And then we will be running another set of exercises. You need to do better."

Gritting her teeth, she turned and led the way towards the gates, striding out into the countryside. They weren't actually *that* far from where she'd landed, the first time she'd set foot on Corinthian. The countryside might have been designed for a defending force, she'd thought at the time, although it was unlikely Admiral Singh would have played war with the farmers when she could have obliterated them from orbit. This time, though, with the shield in place…a handful of thoughts ran through her mind. Heavy weapons sited *there*, long-range weapons hidden to the rear *there*…there were all sorts of options.

"What a bunch of clowns," Buckley commented, as they took their bearings and headed down towards the local HQ. "Did they really do *anything* right?"

"They're not drilled daily," Stewart pointed out. "We were hammered into shape at Boot Camp before we ever saw the Slaughterhouse. They barely got a day's training each month between Singh's departure and now. The real wonder is that they did as well as they did."

Jasmine snorted. The militia's shooting stats were excellent, thanks to the shooting clubs that dotted the cities, but they were sadly lacking in every other field. They didn't know how to march, they didn't know how to advance towards the enemy…she hated to think what they'd do when they stumbled into an ambush, as they would from time to time. The natural reaction was to flinch back and it was almost always the wrong one.

"They've had more time in the field recently," she said. "You'd expect them to improve, wouldn't you?"

"They need intensive training," Buckley said, firmly. "And they're not going to get it."

Jasmine had to agree. Corinthian had an army, a civil guard and the militia, the latter consisting of every able-bodied man and woman who wasn't in either of the first two. In theory, everyone could be conscripted; in practice, trying would blow a hole in an already badly-weakened economy. The planet had quite enough troubles without adding economic collapse to the list.

Although the economy won't last long, once Admiral Singh arrives, Jasmine thought. She knew what Colonel Stalker intended to do, if the planet fell to the enemy. The facilities that couldn't be evacuated would be destroyed. It would ensure that Admiral Singh won nothing, whatever else happened. And yet she knew it would weaken the Commonwealth significantly…

She looked up into the lightening sky. There were flickers of light high overhead, vast arrays of battlestations and industrial nodes - and starships - orbiting the planet. The latter were being moved now, pushed into deep space where they would be hidden until the fighting finally came to an end. It was tempting to believe that the orbital fortifications would be enough to keep the planet safe, but she knew better. Admiral Singh wouldn't have any trouble battering them aside, once the mobile forces were withdrawn.

A pity we didn't spent more money on improving the fortifications, she thought, although she knew it had never been a possibility. *We needed more mobile units instead.*

They kept walking down towards the HQ, passing lines of soldiers drilling in fields or carrying out shooting practice under the eye of senior NCOs. Jasmine had seen the defences surrounding Freedom City - five weeks of concentrated effort had turned the city into a fortress - but she knew the city had to be guarded by outer layers of defences - and raiding parties, ready to harass the enemy when they arrived. Admiral Singh might take the city anyway, yet she'd take hideous losses. Jasmine just hoped they were enough to weaken her position.

A civil war on Wolfbane would help us, she told herself. *And even a year's delay would be long enough for us to put new weapons into production.*

"I feel like whining," Buckley announced. "Do we *have* to go back this afternoon?"

"Pass your bad feelings down to them," Jasmine told him, dryly. "It's character-building."

"Sergeant Roth kept saying that, didn't he?" Stewart recalled. "*Everything* was character-building, as far as he was concerned. It concentrated the mind wonderfully."

"Yes," Buckley agreed. He snickered. "It concentrated our minds on new and interesting ways to murder a drill instructor and get away with it."

"I'm not sure that was *quite* what he had in mind," Jasmine said. Sergeant Roth had retired shortly after she'd graduated, if she recalled correctly. Somehow, she found it hard to imagine *anything* killing the tough old man. "Who could kill him?"

"He used to say that anyone who *did* kill him would get his job," Buckley reminded her, mischievously. "No one had the nerve to try."

Jasmine had to smile, recalling her first day in the unarmed combat pit. Sergeant Roth, knowing his new recruits had completed Boot Camp, had offered - in all seriousness - to stand aside for anyone who thought they could beat him. They'd get his job *and* a Rifleman's Tab, without having to complete the course. But they'd spent six months learning the ropes at Boot Camp, long enough to know they couldn't beat him.

"Better watch your backs," Stewart said, changing the subject. He lowered his voice. "That captain - whatever his name was - is probably the sort of person to think that arranging an accident for you is the best way to avoid explaining himself to his superiors."

"He'd have to be mad," Buckley said. "What's he going to do? Tell the colonel we walked over a landmine and got blown to smithereens?"

"Some people can be very stupid indeed," Jasmine reminded him. "And he may not be thinking too clearly."

She broke off as her terminal buzzed, flashing up an urgent signal. All thought of the militia fled as she took it in. All hell was about to break loose.

"That's the orbital alert," she breathed. She could hear alarms in the distance as soldiers were summoned back to their camps. "They're here!"

CHAPTER

FOURTEEN

Lakshmibai had no planetary defences, no network of ground-based or orbital weapons. A hail of KEWs would be enough to smash the planet's forces from orbit, allowing the Commonwealth Expeditionary Force to march to the planet's capital and recover the diplomats without serious risk.

- Professor Leo Caesius. The Role of Randomness In War.

"Captain," the sensor officer said. "I just picked up a FLASH-signal from the long-range sensor platforms. A number of ships just crossed the phase limit."

"Send the alert," Mandy ordered automatically, cursing the time delay under her breath. The warning was at least three hours out of date. "And put what you have on the display."

"Aye, Captain," the sensor officer said. "They're on a least-time course from Thule."

Mandy frowned, contemplating the possibilities. Thule wasn't *that* far, relatively speaking, from Corinthian, but intelligence had suggested that the occupied world was being used as a base for thrusts deeper into the Commonwealth. But then, if Admiral Singh had had to put the operation together on the fly, she would have needed to draw forces from every forward base under her control. Stripping Thule bare, with the Commonwealth in no state to mount a counteroffensive, might make a great deal of sense.

She put the thought out of her mind as the long-range sensor reports popped up on the display. Seven battleships, at least thirty smaller warships…and seventeen heavy freighters and troop transports. It was more than she'd expected, she had to admit; they might have underestimated Admiral Singh's desire to regain control of Corinthian. Or she might have decided not to take chances. Losing the battle, Colonel Stalker had said, would undermine her position on Wolfbane. Better to bring vast amounts of overkill than risk an embarrassing defeat.

"Nothing *new*," she mused. "Do they show any signs of being modified?"

"Not as far as I can tell, Captain," the sensor officer said. "But they may be mounting additional weapons and point defences and we wouldn't know until they opened fire."

Mandy nodded, stroking her chin with a finger as she contemplated the display. The Wolves had been launching new starships, but they were all based on the Empire's designs. They'd been strikingly conservative, which had puzzled her until she'd realised that Wolfbane was effectively run by giant corporations. Innovation was neither desired nor encouraged. They must *hate* the simple fact that the Commonwealth and the Trade Federation were forcing them to innovate after so long.

But those battleships have a lot of missile tubes, she thought. In days gone by, a single battleship had been more than enough to cow all opposition. *Seven* battleships could dominate an entire sector with ease, the mere threat of their weapons keeping the population in line. *They may be looking to overwhelm our defences by swamping them.*

She closed her eyes as she contemplated the latest reports. Wolfbane had added extra missile tubes to its ships, after the Commonwealth had taught them that their imagination was far from adequate, but they had to know that wasn't enough. What other surprises might be hidden in the enemy hulls? How could they adapt what they had to overcome her new technology? A year of hard fighting had been more than enough to convince her that her advanced weapons didn't make her invincible. Wolfbane had taken heavy losses, but they could afford to replace them. The Commonwealth could not.

"Deploy a full sensor shell," she ordered, quietly. Corinthian already had a pretty good deep-space tracking system, but she wanted additional stealthed platforms of her own. Admiral Singh would destroy the local network as she decelerated. "And then keep the fleet at yellow alert."

"Yellow alert, aye," the tactical officer said.

Mandy leaned back in her chair, trying to project an air of calmness she didn't really feel. If Admiral Singh redlined her drives, her ships would be in firing range within six hours; if she took a more leisurely approach, she'd be in orbit within eight or nine. Mandy rather doubted she'd take the risk of coming in slower, even though it would give her the chance to capture a number of deep-space stations and industrial nodes. The longer Corinthian had to prepare, the tougher the fight Admiral Singh would face. She was too old a hand to allow the enemy more warning than strictly necessary.

She might even hope she wasn't detected, when she came over the phase limit, Mandy thought. It was what *she* would have wanted, if the positions had been reversed. Did Singh know that the Commonwealth had improved its sensors, along with everything else? Or was she smart enough to assume the worst, even as she hoped for the best? *We can't keep her from realising that she's been detected for long.*

"Captain," the communications officer said. "We are receiving a private signal for you from System Command."

"Put it through," Mandy ordered.

She nodded politely as Admiral Amir Melaka's face appeared in the display. They'd worked together closely over the last six months, even though she was a starship commander and he was a system defence officer. Indeed, she'd added a suggestion to her report insisting that the concept of separating the two responsibilities be discontinued. Melaka knew the problems facing her and her squadron, but not every officer was so understanding. Besides, switching from starships to fortresses and then back again would broaden their minds.

"Commodore," Melaka said. His voice sounded strained. He'd be lucky to survive long enough to be purged, if Admiral Singh took the planet. "I believe we have guests."

"It looks that way," Mandy agreed. "Admiral Singh has arrived in force."

Melaka looked pained. "There's no mistake?"

"Not unless there's someone else with seven battleships," Mandy said. "We're too far from the enemy ships to get a positive ID, but it's hard to imagine who *else* they could be."

"Understood," Melaka said. He didn't sound pleased. "I assume you intend to follow Plan Theta?"

"It gives us the greatest chance of carrying out our mission *and* scoring a few hits," Mandy confirmed. "There's no choice."

She didn't blame him for sounding annoyed. Plan Theta might have suited the Commonwealth, but it left the local defenders badly exposed. She would have raised more doubts about the whole plan if she hadn't known that standing in defence of Corinthian would be a good way to get her entire command wiped out. Hell, it was what *she* intended to do to Admiral Singh.

"Very well," Melaka said. "I'm ordering the evacuation ships to depart in three hours, mark. I don't want to take chances."

Mandy nodded, even though she knew it was ballsy of him to order the evacuation without permission from his political superiors. *They* would probably complain, pointing out that Admiral Singh couldn't possibly reach Corinthian for a *further* three hours. But leaving then would give the ships the best chance of hiding within the inky darkness of interplanetary space, as they made their slow way towards the phase limit. Admiral Singh wouldn't have a chance to hunt them down before it was too late.

"Very good, sir," she said. "And good luck."

"You too," Melaka said.

His face vanished from the display. Mandy nodded to herself, then looked at her XO.

"The alpha crews are to rest for five hours," she ordered. Even if Singh *did* redline her drives, her crew should have enough time to rest before going into battle. "Order the beta crews to take control and watch the sensor nodes. The enemy might well have sneaked ships into the system ahead of time."

"Yes, Captain," the XO said.

The howling alarm brought Ed out of bed, one hand groping for the sidearm he kept on the bedside cabinet. He'd have preferred to bed down with the CEF, but the planetary government had insisted on him sleeping in their underground command bunker, deep underneath Freedom City. He forced himself to relax, lowering the sidearm, as he glanced at the terminal. The blinking alert confirmed that the enemy had reached the system, but it would be at least six hours before they attacked the planet.

He put the sidearm back on the table, then hastily dressed before returning the sidearm to its holster and hurrying out the door. The bunker was cold, dark and claustrophobic; surprisingly, the government hadn't bothered to spend money on making it slightly more liveable, even though government ministers would be the ones staying there. For once, he wasn't sure that he approved. Men had been known to go crazy when trapped in similar environments, even elite soldiers. He wouldn't have gambled on retaining his own sanity indefinitely if he'd been trapped in the bunker.

At least they can still go to the surface, he thought, as he walked into the war room. *But that may be about to change.*

There were no guards so far underground, merely a handful of operators sitting in front of consoles, chatting rapidly into their headsets. He frowned in surprise; he could see the logic, but it still struck him as insecure. Putting the thought aside, he looked up. A giant holographic display hung in the air, showing an ever-expanding red sphere that marked the point where the enemy ships had first been detected. Admiral Singh could be *anywhere* within that sphere, he knew, but he would have been surprised if she wasn't driving on Corinthian as fast as possible. She would almost certainly assume she'd lost the element of surprise as soon as she'd crossed the phase limit.

Unless her plan depends on us not detecting her, he thought. *She might choose to believe she hasn't been detected…*

"Colonel," a female voice said. He turned to see President Danielle Chambers, her dark eyes shadowed. "It has begun?"

"Yes, Madam President," Ed said. He'd worked with her long enough to develop a keen respect for her mind, although he would have preferred someone with extensive military experience. "The enemy fleet has been detected."

Danielle sagged, very slightly. "I would have preferred for you to have been wrong," she said, as she led the way into a smaller conference room. Another holographic display, the twin of the one behind them, dominated the compartment. "Nothing is ever going to be the same again."

Ed nodded, shortly. He understood how she felt, even though he had come to believe that change was the sole universal constant. The Grand Senate had tried to freeze the Empire in stasis, only to watch helplessly as their mighty civilisation started to crumble into rubble, unleashing chaos and war in its wake. Danielle had rebuilt her entire planet, after Admiral Singh had fled. The thought of losing everything she'd built had to be nightmarish.

And I wouldn't be too pleased at the thought of enemy boots on Avalon, he thought. It was a bitter thought. He'd once had no home, save for the Marine Corps; now, Avalon was his home. *Even if we drove them off, we'd have to rebuild the entire planet.*

"Tell me," Danielle said. "Is there any way to know just how long it will be before the planet comes under attack?"

"No," Ed said. "It depends on just how quickly she makes her approach."

He studied the display for a long moment, mentally untangling the angles and vectors drawn out by the plotting computers. "She could be here in less than six hours, Madam President, or she could be here in nine or ten. I doubt it will be any longer."

"Unless she wants to devastate the cloudscoops," Danielle said. "That would cripple our economy."

"Not for long," Ed said. He glanced up as the door opened, allowing General Hampton to enter the compartment, "We can rebuild cloudscoops quickly these days."

"She'd need to take the planet first," Hampton said. "It's the only way she'd be able to convince the crews to surrender."

Ed shrugged. In truth, there was little particularly innovative about Commonwealth-designed cloudscoops. The Empire's colossal - and hugely expensive - designs were a matter of law and custom, not practicality. Someone had probably paid the Grand Senate a colossal bribe to ensure that cheaper designs were banned, on grounds of public safety. It had helped give the designers a stranglehold over the economy. Indeed, he would be surprised if Wolfbane wasn't already duplicating them.

Danielle looked at Hampton. "What's happening up there?"

"The population is ready, what's left of it," Hampton said. "I've started moving the remaining vital personnel to the shuttles for the last flight out, then sending non-combatants to the shelters well away from the war zone. They should be safe there. There's nothing to attract Admiral Singh's attention."

And let's hope he's right, Ed thought. It was generally agreed that planetary governments couldn't be allowed to use their populations as human shields - putting a defence station in the middle of a city would draw fire, no matter how many innocents were nearby - but Admiral Singh would have to be insane to start bombarding civilians at random. *If she does, we can do the same to her.*

He scowled at the thought as Hampton continued to outline the precautions the planetary government was now putting into effect. People died in war, he knew; it was a reality that no one, no matter how well-meaning, could escape. And yet, he had never liked the idea of indiscriminate mass slaughter. The thought of unleashing nuclear weapons on Wolfbane was horrifying, but if Admiral Singh killed civilians at random he'd have no choice. They couldn't allow Admiral Singh to set a precedent...

We'd have to demand that they surrender her for punishment, he thought. *Or our own population would demand retaliation.*

"We are as close to ready as we ever will be," Hampton concluded. "Colonel?"

Ed looked up. "Yes, we should be ready," he said. "Has the shield generator begun its power-up sequence?"

"It has," Hampton confirmed. "And we've given the entire quadrant as much protection as possible."

Unless they use nukes, Ed reminded himself. *I wonder if the thought will cross Singh's mind?*

He pushed the thought out of his mind. "Then we should be ready," he said. "It won't be long now."

"No one has done anything like this for hundreds of years," Hampton said. "Are you confident?"

Ed shrugged. He would bet on the marines over an army unit twice their size, but Hampton was right. No one had fought a full-scale war on a planetary surface for hundreds of years, even though the Slaughterhouse and the various infantry training centres had included intensive ground-based combat in their scenarios. There were too many things that could go wrong, from Admiral Singh refusing to play by the rules to the shield generator failing or the lines breaking at a crucial moment.

But they'd covered all the bases they could.

"I am as confident as I can be," he said, truthfully. "And whatever else happens, we'll give Admiral Singh something to remember."

———

Emmanuel was no stranger to human misery. He'd watched farms burned to ashes for daring to support the Crackers, then stared helplessly as bodies were carried out of blown-up buildings in Camelot and the other larger cities on Avalon. And then he'd gone to Lakshmibai, where the population had wallowed in squalor. He still had nightmares about starving children, denied food and water because of their caste, staring at him with big black eyes. And yet, there was something truly terrible about watching the final stages of the evacuation.

Freedom City had practically become a ghost town over the last three weeks, as the trained manpower was shipped to orbit and non-essential personnel were transported to safe zones on the other side of the continent, but now things were changing rapidly. He walked down a shopping boulevard, where he'd picked up a handful of trinkets for his family back home, and shivered as he realised just how deserted it was. In the distance, he could see industrial workers being loaded onto buses, ready to start the trip out of the city. Who knew if they would ever be able to return?

He swallowed as he peered into abandoned restaurants, the chairs piled on the tables, the food counters wiped clean and dry. There was no point in going in - people had been shot on suspicion of looting - but he made sure to get a number of pictures before restarting his walk towards the defence lines. A burst of chatter made him jump, one hand reaching for the pistol at his belt, before he realised that a radio had turned on, broadcasting an emergency bulletin into the empty shopping mall. He was the only person in earshot.

And this place is going to be devastated, he thought, as he reached the end of the road. *It will never be the same again.*

The last bus was already on its way, leaving him feeling isolated and alone, abandoned at the heart of a towering city. He shivered as he looked up, spotting the faint shimmer in the air as the force shield came online. He'd half-expected it to cut the skyscrapers in half, but it looked as though there was plenty of clearance between their roofs and the shield. He sucked in his breath, remembering what one of his contacts had said. Hundreds of thousands of people had worked hard for apartments in those skyscrapers, often going into debt just to make sure they had somewhere to live near their workspace. And now the skyscrapers were going to be torn apart by the fighting.

There will be snipers and observation posts up there, he thought. *And the enemy will respond by hitting them with shellfire, knocking them down to rubble.*

He keyed his recorder. "This is a city on the edge," he said, quietly. He wasn't planning any live broadcasts, but he wanted to record his impressions before it was too late. "The civilians are gone, the government is in hiding. And now the defenders wait for the enemy to arrive."

CHAPTER

FIFTEEN

Indeed, even Pradesh - a city located in a bottleneck, between two mountains that were impassable to a mechanized force - would not have survived an orbital bombardment. The locals might have gambled that the prospect - the certainty - of heavy civilian causalities would prevent a bombardment, but they would almost certainly have been wrong.

- Professor Leo Caesius. The Role of Randomness In War.

Admiral Rani Singh knew it was unprofessional, but she couldn't help feeling a kind of unholy glee as the Corinthian System slowly revealed its secrets to her. This was *her* system, the system she had captured early in her reign and turned into an industrial powerhouse; it pleased her, on so many levels, that the population had taken the ball she'd tossed them and run with it. Wolfbane, for all its virtues, was a balancing act, not a world guided by a single mind. Once the rebels were purged, Corinthian would be hers again.

"Admiral," the tactical officer said. "I'm picking up thirty-three warships orbiting Corinthian, backing up five heavy battlestations."

"Commonwealth ships, I assume," Rani said. "Do we have any IDs?"

She frowned as she contemplated the display. Whatever happened, she wouldn't make the mistake of assuming their tonnage indicated their firepower. The Commonwealth's damned innovations had given their cruisers the same effective firepower as her battlecruisers. It was fortunate indeed that she'd been able to talk Governor Brown into starting the war. A few years delay and Wolfbane would have been effortlessly crushed. As it was, she knew she had to win quickly before it was too late.

"No, Admiral," the tactical officer said, finally. "Their drive signatures are indistinct at this distance."

Rani shrugged, unsurprised. "Bring the fleet to red alert," she ordered, curtly. She'd chosen not to risk redlining her drives - two of her battleships were in poor states, despite her repair crews best efforts - and the enemy had had plenty of time to see her coming. "Launch tactical probes, then transmit the surrender demand."

She leaned forward as more and more detail appeared on the display. Corinthian's rebel government had thrown a great many resources into building up their defence network, she noted, but their inexperience was showing. It *looked* good - and it would intimidate anyone without substantial firepower - yet it lacked the ability to keep her from hammering the defences into scrap metal. They should have concentrated on mobile firepower, she considered, as question marks appeared over the battlestations. It was unlikely their damned innovations would be enough to keep her from taking control of the high orbitals.

And then they can surrender or get crushed, she thought, coldly. *And I don't care which.*

"Admiral," the communications officer said. "There has been no response."

Rani glanced at the timer, then nodded. They were barely a light-minute from the planet; the defenders had had plenty of time to read her message and transmit a reply. She hadn't really expected one, even though the defenders had to know they were badly outgunned. Indeed, she'd only really sent it to convince the weak sisters on Wolfbane that she'd *tried* to be reasonable before opening fire. The morons had no idea what it took to actually fight and win a battle.

"As expected," she said, calmly. "Continue on our present course."

There was a long pause. "Admiral," the tactical officer said, finally. "The enemy fleet is breaking orbit."

Rani felt a stab of disappointment, mixed with relief. The chance of catching a substantial enemy force and smashing it to rubble was not one to be discounted, but the Commonwealth Navy was a dangerous foe. Matched with the orbital battlestations, it might be capable of doing some real damage, even trapped against the planet. She was prepared to endure some losses to recover Corinthian, but there were limits. Her enemies wouldn't see the victories, only what they'd cost.

"They're angling for a long-range engagement," the tactical officer added. "Admiral?"

"They'll be right on the edge of our missile envelope," Rani mused. She couldn't fault the enemy commander, even though the odds of either side inflicting much damage were very low. Indeed, the smart choice would be to grit her teeth and take the enemy fire without a response, conserving her missile loads for later targets. "Swing a handful of drones in their direction, then put the point defence on standby."

"Aye, Admiral," the tactical officer said.

———

"They're not moving in pursuit," the sensor officer reported.

Mandy scowled. An inexperienced officer might have allowed her to lure him into a stern chase, giving her plenty of time to wear him down, but Admiral Singh was too smart for such a simple trick. Indeed, she'd been careful not to take her eye off the prize. Her fleet was progressing towards Corinthian, ignoring the Commonwealth ships.

"Five minutes to engagement range," the tactical officer said.

"Hold your course," Mandy ordered, calmly. "And hold the range open, once we enter firing range."

She sucked in her breath as the seconds ticked down to zero. There were no clever tricks, no cunning ploys…merely the clash of squadron against squadron. Her modified missiles might have made a difference, if she'd chosen to use them, but she knew that they were a secret that had to be kept. Admiral Singh *might* be training her point defence crews on missiles that flew faster and harder than anything known to exist, yet it was possible she wouldn't believe in them. There was nothing to gain by tipping her off before the missiles offered Mandy a chance to win a decisive victory.

Admiral Singh's ships didn't change course, either to open the range or close it. Mandy felt sweat trickling down her back, wondering just what the older woman was thinking. Rani Singh was ruthless enough, she knew from Jasmine, to soak up losses if it gained her something in exchange, but it would cost her badly. The Commonwealth Navy would court martial Mandy for expending her crews callously; Wolfbane would probably have to assassinate their ruler.

And that raises another question, Mandy thought. *Is it really Singh in command over there?*

"Captain," the tactical officer said. "We will be entering missile range in thirty seconds."

"Fire at will, as soon as we enter range," Mandy ordered. "And follow up with a spread of drones. We need to see how they react to us."

———

"Admiral," the tactical officer said. "The enemy ships have opened fire."

Rani nodded, resisting the urge to snap at the officer. She could see it on the display, thousands of red icons detaching from the enemy ships and roaring towards her fleet. It was impossible to be sure, but it didn't *look* as though there were any unpleasant surprises waiting for her. The missiles might be numerous - no one had fired such a large salvo for hundreds of years - yet they looked conventional. Maybe the Commonwealth had been reluctant to risk developing new missile systems that might well be duds.

"Reposition the fleet, then deploy decoys," she ordered. It wasn't pleasant, but she needed to preserve her battleships, even at the expense of her smaller ships. "The point defence is to open fire as soon as the missiles enter firing range."

"Aye, Admiral," the tactical officer said.

Rani forced herself to watch, silently evaluating both the enemy missiles and her own crew's performance. The situation was far from perfect - there were a *lot* of missiles bearing down on her - but it did have its advantages. Her ships had plenty of time to chart out firing solutions *and* adjust their positions, throwing off whatever missile locks the enemy had managed to secure at extended range. Warheads were rarely very smart. If they lost their locks, it was quite possible they would go for a decoy, rather than an active warship.

The point defence opened fire on command, picking off hundreds of missiles as they closed in on their targets. She smiled, rather coldly, as her first impressions were confirmed. There wasn't anything special about the missiles, certainly nothing that could be used to get them through the defence grid. A handful *would* get through, she knew, through sheer weight of numbers, but they wouldn't be decisive. Her fleet would barely be scratched.

"*Hamilton* is gone," the tactical officer said. "*Sutherland* has taken heavy damage and her CO is requesting permission to abandon ship."

"Granted," Rani said. In the bad old days, a commander who ordered his crew to abandon ship could expect a court martial, something that had ensured a great many unnecessary deaths. She knew better than to persecute an officer for something outside his control. It was something of a miracle that *Sutherland* had survived the four hits she'd taken. "Order SAR teams to pick up the lifepods."

"The enemy fleet is opening the range," the sensor officer reported. "They'll be out of missile range in two minutes."

"Let them go," Rani ordered. There was no point in giving chase, not now. A stern chase was invariably a long one, even if one side *didn't* have faster ships. "Do we have an accurate scan of the high orbitals?"

"Yes, Admiral," the tactical officer said. "I have missile locks on the defence network."

"Then prepare to fire," Rani said. "Angle the firing patterns to sweep as many of the defenders out of the orbitals as possible."

And be careful you don't accidentally hit the planet, she added, silently. A missile striking Corinthian, at a reasonable percentage of the speed of light, would be utterly devastating. It would certainly ensure that she couldn't recover anything of value, along with slaughtering billions of people and prompting the Commonwealth to retaliate in kind. *That would be the end of everything.*

She scowled. Shortly before the war, Governor Brown had dispatched a couple of starships towards the Core Worlds. One had returned, bringing news of planets scorched clean of life; the other hadn't returned at all. Rani knew herself to be ruthless in pursuit of power, but there was nothing to be gained by mass slaughter. Planets couldn't become part of her empire if their populations were exterminated. The very thought was horrific, even to her.

"Two minutes to firing range," the tactical officer reported. "All weapons are online."

"Fire on my command," Rani said.

"They're out of range," the tactical officer said. "Captain?"

Mandy scowled. She'd expected - hoped - that Admiral Singh would fire a barrage back at her, but the damned woman had held her fire. And she couldn't fault the bitch either, no matter how much she wanted to. Throwing thousands of missiles at Mandy's squadron would simply be throwing good money after bad. It had to be frustrating to *know* she could inflict more damage on the enemy, *if* she was willing to take losses herself, but Admiral Singh had done the right thing.

"Hold our course," she ordered. It felt like running away - and, in truth, that was *exactly* what she was doing, leaving Mindy and Jasmine and Colonel Stalker behind as she fled into the depths of interplanetary space. It might have been part of the plan, but she didn't feel comfortable with it. "Launch a final set of drones, then update both the Colonel and the picket ships."

She leaned back in her command chair, cursing herself under her breath. Once, she wouldn't have cared for her annoying little sister; now, she wished she had more time to know the young woman her sister had become. But she couldn't reverse course, she couldn't go back to help the planet. She had to stick with the plan, even though she knew it would kill her to watch helplessly as her sister died.

"Continue as planned," she ordered, feeling a little of her heart grow cold. "And keep updating the colonel until we're out of range."

It was very cold in the fortress's CIC.

Admiral Amir Melaka watched, grimly, as the enemy fleet grew closer, readying its weapons for the final push. It wouldn't be long before they opened fire, tearing through the planet's defences as if they were made of paper. Commodore Caesius had insisted that they would have been better off building more warships and, in the privacy of his own mind, he accepted that she had a point. But the planetary government had chosen to put self-defence ahead of mobile firepower and he hadn't had the nerve to contradict them.

In hindsight, he knew, that had been a deadly mistake. He was well-aware of his own limitations as a senior officer. He'd been promoted, at least in part, because he'd had no role in Admiral Singh's government; indeed, he'd been too junior to do anything more than keep his head down and pray not to be noticed by his seniors. And yet, he was damned if he was just surrendering control of the high orbitals to the wretched tyrant. His family had worked too hard to fit into Corinthian to allow Admiral Singh to ruin it.

And besides, they're on their way to safety, he thought. He knew he wasn't likely to survive, but it didn't matter. His family would go on. *They'll remember me with pride.*

"The enemy fleet is locking weapons on the defence platforms," his sensor officer reported, grimly. Like the remainder of his crew, she was a volunteer. All non-essential personnel had been shipped out-system, just to keep them out of enemy hands. "They're getting ready to fire."

"Order the platforms to start shooting as soon as the enemy open fire," Amir ordered, trying to keep his voice calm. The platforms wouldn't last long, once the enemy started picking them off. He had few illusions, too, about the giant battlestations. They were meant to be backed up by battleships. "And then launch missiles at will."

The display flickered. "Enemy ships are coming into range," the sensor officer said. "They have locked on."

———

"You may open fire when ready," Rani said.

She smiled, coldly, as the fleet unleashed a hail of buckshot. It wasn't something she would have taken into combat against warships, but it was hellishly effective against automated platforms. The targets couldn't dodge; hell, they'd have problems realising they were under attack until it was far too late. It was a shame the buckshot was useless against heavily-armoured battlestations, but she had nuclear-tipped warheads for *them*.

"The platforms are opening fire," the tactical officer reported. "And they're launching pre-placed missiles."

Rani frowned, darkly. *That* could be trouble...her probes hadn't detected the free-floating missiles. She made a mental note to have a few words with the sensor crews - the missiles were a nasty surprise - and then watched, grimly, as the missiles slipped into her point defence envelope. Three of her ships were hit, one badly, but the surprise couldn't be repeated. She knew what to expect now.

They must have transhipped their stockpiles to orbit and just left them there, she thought, coldly. *Did they have some warning we were coming?*

"Admiral, the battlestations are coming into range," the tactical officer said. "They're locking missiles on us."

"Fire," Rani ordered.

Moments later, the battleship shuddered as she unleashed the first huge salvo.

Amir cursed savagely as the seven battleships opened fire, hull-mounted missile pods adding their weight to the wall of missiles slashing towards him. It was worse than it seemed, too; his point defence platforms were programmed to prioritise missiles that might strike the planet itself. He couldn't fault the defence planners - even if a strike was purely accidental, it would be devastating - but it weakened his defences significantly. Every missile that was marked a potential genocide threat forced his automated platforms to target it exclusively.

Bitch is probably doing it deliberately, he thought, as the torrent of missiles roared down on his position. The battlestation couldn't alter position, certainly not fast enough to save itself; he winced, again, as his automated platforms continued to die. He wasn't quite sure how Admiral Singh was targeting them, but it was working. *We're in deep shit…*

He glanced around the compartment, feeling bitter regret. His crews were fighting desperately, but there was no way they could take out *all* the incoming missiles before it was too late. Admiral Singh had simply swamped his defences. He'd scored a handful of hits on her ships, yet nowhere near enough to slow her down. And the exchange rate was very much in her favour.

The missiles struck home…

———

"All, but one of the fortresses have been destroyed," the tactical officer reported. "The final fortress is heavily damaged. It won't last long."

Rani nodded. She was surprised the surviving fortress hadn't tried to surrender, now it had been battered into uselessness. Its point defence had even stopped firing. But in the end, it didn't matter. All that mattered was that her ships were slowly settling into the high orbitals, plotting their firing solutions for attacking the planet itself. Unless, of course, the population saw sense and surrendered…

"Admiral," the sensor officer said. "I'm detecting…"

He broke off. Rani glared at him. "What?"

"I'm detecting a force shield in the upper atmosphere," the sensor officer said. "It's holding solid, right above the capital city."

Rani stared in disbelief. She'd expected improved point defences and missile warheads, not *this*. "A force shield on a planetary scale?"

"Yes, Admiral," the sensor officer said. "The capital city is shielded from us."

He swallowed. "If my calculations are correct," he added, "taking it down would require enough firepower to devastate the planet."

Rani felt her temper flare. *How dare they?*

Cold logic reasserted itself. Devastating the planet would not only deprive her of any loot, but start a civil war. "Is there any way to take the shield down without hurting the planet?"

"We'd have to destroy the generator," the sensor officer said. He pointed at an image of the city. "It's somewhere within that rough location."

She tapped her console. "General Haverford, report to my office," she ordered. "You have an operation to plan."

CHAPTER
SIXTEEN

The problem facing the diplomats, however, was that Lakshmibai and its history simply didn't register, compared to the spacefaring power of Wolfbane. It was decided to send the starships away to prevent the Wolfbane ships ambushing Commonwealth ships (or vice versa). The prospect of being attacked by the planetary natives never crossed their minds.
- Professor Leo Caesius. The Role of Randomness In War.

Danielle watched, fighting down the urge to cry, as the final battlestation exploded, showering pieces of debris into the gravity well. They *looked* too small to make it through the atmosphere and strike the surface, but she knew from endless briefings that it was a very real concern. Hullmetal was tough, very tough. A handful of chunks that survived passage through the atmosphere would do a great deal of damage.

She looked at Colonel Stalker, wondering how he could be so impassive. Didn't he realise that hundreds of good men and women had just died? More people had died in a matter of minutes than had died during the years Admiral Singh had controlled the planet! She knew the crews had been stripped down to the bare minimum, she knew the remaining personnel had all been volunteers, but it was no consolation. Decades of work and years of investment had just been casually brushed aside. A single damaged battleship and a handful of smaller ships was no fair exchange for the battlestations.

"They didn't repeat their demand for surrender," she said, quietly.

"They've detected the force shield," Stalker said. "They would have started bombarding their targets now, in preparation for a landing, if they hadn't."

Danielle scowled. "So what do we do now?"

"We wait," Stalker said. She hated him at that moment, hated how he could be so dispassionate when her world's very survival was at stake. "The ball's in her court now."

———

"The force shield is genuine," Mark said, in disbelief. "It isn't a trick?"

"A piece of debris struck the shield and was disintegrated," Admiral Singh said, tartly. "It's real."

Mark studied the display, wondering why the thought of building a force shield on a continental scale had never occurred to him. But then, he'd never realised force shields were *possible* until he'd seen them deployed in combat. Why *not* scale one up to the point where it could shield a city and the surrounding landscape? If one had the technology and the power, one could make it happen.

"We need to take that city," Admiral Singh said. "It has to be captured before the facilities can be destroyed."

"That might be tricky," Mark said. He'd brought two divisions from Thule - and a third division from Wolfbane - but he hadn't expected a long campaign. Corinthian was supposed to surrender, like most worlds, when the high orbitals were captured. But that damned force field changed everything. "We'd need to adjust the plans at breakneck speed."

He scowled at the map, thinking hard. Luckily, they *had* done some planning to establish a forward base that would be independent of the local spaceports, but it wasn't enough to handle every requirement. He'd need to scale up the plans considerably, which would cause no end of problems. And he'd have to do it under fire, if the intelligence reports were to be believed. Every man, woman and child on the planet below owned a firearm and knew how to use it.

"I can put a forward deployment team here, Admiral," he said, tapping a patch of farmland seventy kilometres from the city. "And then start funnelling in more supplies, under cover from the orbiting starships. It would still take upwards of a week before we were ready to start extending our control, let alone advancing on the city. I'd really be happier landing further away from the shield."

"It can't be extended," Admiral Singh said.

Mark glanced at her. "How can you be sure?"

"The field has a radius of fifty kilometres," Admiral Singh pointed out. "That forces us to land at *least* fifty kilometres from the city, depriving us of our chance at a quick victory. If they could extend the shield still further, they would have done it. It would make life difficult for us."

"You're right," Mark conceded. There was no point in bickering about it. "Do I have your permission to plan and conduct an opposed landing?"

"I want boots on the ground within a day," Admiral Singh said. "And I want that city in our hands within two weeks."

"It will depend on what opposition we encounter," Mark said. He'd never had to fight without orbital firepower backing him up. The enemy would have the same problem, of course, but they'd had several weeks to draw up contingency plans. There were hundreds of steps they could take to make his life miserable, if they'd thought of them. "I can't promise a victory within two weeks."

"Time is not on our side," Admiral Singh hissed.

"And expending thousands of lives to take one relatively meaningless city will not work in our favour," Mark pointed out. "This is not Thule, Admiral. My forces have only the faintest idea of what they're going to encounter. As long as that shield is in place, there's no real hope of a quick victory."

Admiral Singh made a visible attempt to control herself. "Very well," she said. Her voice sharpened. "You may plan your operations as you wish."

And take the blame, if something goes wrong, Mark concluded, silently. It was almost *familiar. You'll put the blame on me to safeguard your own position.*

He watched Admiral Singh stalk out of the office, then turned his attention to the orbital imagery. The force shield had an unexpected side-effect, he noted; it fuzzed orbital surveillance to some degree, making it harder to see what was under the shield. He didn't know if the enemy had done it deliberately, but he rather suspected they had. Orbital observation would have been a powerful advantage, if he'd been able to use it. The only consolation was that the enemy wouldn't have it either.

His feelings were mixed, he had to admit, as he called for his planning staff. Part of him relished the challenge, the prospect of a ground campaign that was more than taking surrenders or fighting a bitter insurgency. But the rest of him knew that it would be a nightmare. The enemy would fight for every last inch of ground, while his troops were on the end of a very long supply line. Hell, he'd have to send back to Thule and the other forward bases for additional ammunition. His most optimistic calculations suggested that they'd be running short within a week.

Good thing we can produce bullets and suchlike on site, he thought. He'd had to argue heavily to convince the shipyards that duplicating a pair of Marine Corps MEUs was worthwhile, but it had definitely worked out in his favour. *Without that, we'd soon be short on everything.*

"I want to put advance forces here, here and here," he said, tapping the map when his planning team had assembled. "And then start landing the first elements here."

He had to smile at their reactions. Landing armoured units in the middle of farmland would be difficult, if only because the muddy ground would rapidly become impassable. But there were few other options. Even if he dared land shuttles on the highways, they'd be broken into debris soon enough by the tanks. It would take time and effort to set up a prefabricated base and he doubted he had the time. No matter what she'd said, he suspected Admiral Singh would be peering over his shoulder as often as possible.

"This is a challenge," he said. "And let's face it. It beats chasing insurgents around on Thule."

"One might say it's almost beautiful," Jalil said.

Jasmine snorted rudely as she stared into the sky. Pieces of debris were slowly plummeting through the upper atmosphere, burning up as they fell towards the ground. It *was* almost beautiful, she had to admit, but so was a KEW on its way to its final destination. A person might admire the sight from a distance, the person underneath would be unable to escape before it was far too late.

She glanced at the terminal, wishing she had a clear picture of just what was happening above the atmosphere. They'd hurried to their preplanned rendezvous point as soon as the alert was sounded, even though she'd wanted to return to the militia camp and make sure they'd learned something from the night battle. But now it was too late. The radio spoke briefly, panicky mutterings echoing through the airwaves, yet she'd heard nothing of value. It was unlikely that anyone would take the risk of sending a message through the airwaves when there was a very real chance it would be intercepted.

And the shield plays merry hell with radio waves too, she thought. It hadn't been anticipated, according to the brief message they'd received; no one had operated a planetary shield for more than a few seconds, during tests. She hadn't bothered to follow the technobabble she'd been given, merely noted to herself that radio signals were unreliable. *We may be completely cut off from Colonel Stalker.*

She looked up into the sky, silently trying to pick out Admiral Singh's warships as they entered orbit. But there was nothing, save for the falling debris and a slowly darkening sky.

"The warships are too small to be seen easily," Stewart commented. Jasmine glanced at him, wondering how he'd practically read her mind. "But we'll see them landing soon enough."

Jasmine shrugged. She'd gone through all the simulations, putting herself in the enemy's shoes, during her stint in the planning cell, but none of them had been able to put any definite timing to the enemy's moves. It was quite possible that Admiral Singh would order an immediate landing, they'd reasoned, or that she would settle for mining the high orbitals and withdrawing, devastating the system on the way out. She shook her head slowly as the sky grew darker, tiny lights moving high overhead. The enemy fleet was still in orbit.

"And that raises a different question," Jasmine said. "Where are they going to land?"

An hour passed slowly before the terminal buzzed, once. She picked it up and read the microburst message quickly, then passed the terminal to Stewart. Colonel Stalker had warned them that the enemy ships were dropping lower, perhaps preparing to launch drones and armoured units directly into the planet's atmosphere. She hoped - prayed - that the microburst was as undetectable as the boffins claimed, certainly at long-range. They needed them to report back to the colonel, once they knew where the enemy were landing...

"Look," Rifleman William Randolph breathed.

Jasmine followed his pointing finger. A handful of streaks of light were falling from the sky, a number falling slowly while others were descending with terrifying speed. She mentally matched their trajectories to the maps she memorised and swore, inwardly, when she realised they were targeted on farmhouses. Most of the buildings had been abandoned, their crops taken to Freedom City and their farm animals marched well away from the prospective warzone, but some of the more stubborn farmers had chosen to stay put. She hoped they'd had the sense to abandon their homes, as the KEWs crashed down, yet it was unlikely that they had any idea of what was going on.

"Nineteen hits," Stewart muttered, as flashes of light flickered in the distance. The sound reached them seconds later, crackling thunderclaps that sent shivers down her spine. She knew the sound all too well. "And after them, the invasion."

"They're taking a leaf out of our playbook," Jasmine breathed. The smaller flecks of light were too slow to be KEWs...impatiently, she reached for her binoculars and peered towards the enemy troops. "Armoured men dropping directly from orbit."

"And heading towards one of the predicted LZs," Jalil agreed. She passed him the binoculars, allowing him to take a look. "Is it just me, boss, or are they falling slower than us?"

"Probably never tried a jump into opposed territory before," Buckley said.

Jasmine shrugged. "Pack up your gear," she ordered, as she tapped a command into the transmitter. In theory, a microburst report would reach Colonel Stalker without drawing enemy fire, but just in case she ordered the terminal to send the signal once they were a safe distance from the hide. "We move out in five minutes."

There were no more KEWs falling from orbit, she noted as they left the hide and headed towards the enemy landing zone, but there were dozens of other troopers. The first batch had landed in one of the predicted locations, as Jalil had said, although unfortunately it wasn't a bad choice. There were no armoured units nearby, ready to charge forward and smash the LZ into rubble. If there had been, they would have been spotted from orbit and wiped out the moment they left their camouflaged bunkers. She slowed the march as they approached one of the farms, taking a moment to look for survivors. But there was nothing left of the farmhouses, save for giant craters in the ground.

"Let's hope they got out in time," Buckley breathed.

"Definitely," Jalil agreed. "They were good people, weren't they?"

Jasmine nodded, keeping her thoughts to herself. The farmers hadn't really needed much training, although *their* role in the militia had been geared towards individual hunting and sniping rather than serving as an organised unit. She'd been impressed by their stealth, even though the marines still had a slight edge. And their shooting skills were first rate. She recalled a young girl, barely old enough to marry, casually shooting birds out of the sky just to show what she could do. If that girl was dead…

She shook her head. If that girl was dead, along with her friends and family, they were merely the first of many.

They reached the bottom of a hill and climbed slowly, weapons at the ready. They'd scouted the hill two weeks ago, but it was just possible the enemy had noted its existence from orbit and decided it would make a good vantage point. Jasmine's eyes swept the darkness, watching for signs of movement or trouble, yet there was nothing, not even tiny animal and insect nightlife. Even the owls seemed to have decided to stay quiet. The KEWs had probably shocked them badly.

She slowed as she reached the summit, peering into the distance towards the LZ. Thirty or forty men, wearing suits of armour, stood on the ground, quartering it with practiced efficiency. There was no sign of armoured vehicles, although she hadn't really expected *them* to be dropped from orbit. She glanced up as she heard the unmistakable sound of a shuttle making a combat drop, weaving madly from side to side in a desperate attempt to avoid any incoming MANPAD fire. But there was none…it grounded sharply, its hatch opening seconds later. An AFV - a design she recognised from basic training - glided out into the night, its weapons searching for targets. It was followed rapidly by two more, which followed the first into a patrol pattern.

"Oh, for a HVM," Stewart muttered.

Jasmine shook her head. Colonel Stalker's orders were clear. The enemy were to be allowed to establish their FOB in peace, just to ensure they didn't get discouraged. Every fibre of her body augured against the decision - she'd been taught it was better *not* to give the enemy time to get organised - but she understood his logic. If someone as ruthless as Admiral Singh decided she couldn't have the planet, and there was no risk to *her* forces, she might just decide that no one else could have the planet either.

She placed a visual sensor in position to record the landing zone, then pulled back enough so they could be sure of breaking contact without being detected as more and more shuttles landed. There was no way to be *sure*, but it looked very much as though the Wolves were adopting a standard pattern for landing and securing a planetary target, even though they probably hadn't anticipated the shield. Indeed, some of the weaponry they were deploying would have made more sense for a force landing to take control of a spaceport, rather than a number of fields in the middle of nowhere. But it would probably still work out in their favour.

"That's a smaller force heading towards the nearest road," Stewart muttered. The enemy vehicles had lit up their headlights, much to her surprise. They must be sure of not running into trouble…or, perhaps, they hadn't expected to have to land in the dark. "Once it gets there, it will be in a position to intercept anything heading south."

"From the city," Jasmine agreed. She rather doubted that anything would get close enough to threaten the LZ, but she understood the pre-caution. The hills might be swarming with sniper-farmers, after all; there was definitely a marine platoon watching the landing. It wouldn't be long, too, before the enemy decided to sweep the hill for potential trouble. "We may need to fall back ourselves."

She placed another pair of sensors in position to monitor the landing, keying their transmitters to keep the microbursts as low-power as possible, then led the way back down the hill, away from the enemy position. They didn't dare get caught now, not when it would throw the entire plan off kilter. Behind her, she could hear dozens of shuttles dropping out of the skies, landing, unloading and then blasting off again into the darkness.

Whatever else can be said about them, she thought, *they have nerve.*

"We'll be back," Jalil muttered, as they started to move cross-country. "And we'll have a surprise for them when we do."

"Semper Fi," Jasmine agreed.

CHAPTER
SEVENTEEN

Indeed, luck favoured the Commonwealth when the CEF was also dispatched to Lakshmibai, in a test of its ability to rapidly deploy from Avalon to a prospective trouble spot. Without it, everyone on the mission would have been killed by the locals.

- Professor Leo Caesius. The Role of Randomness In War.

Mark tensed as the shuttle lurched from side to side, its pilot trying desperately to ensure that any watching gunmen had no chance of scoring a hit before he got his cargo and passengers to the surface. He had to fight down the urge to vomit, knowing it was almost certainly futile. If a soldier with a MANPAD was hiding near the LZ, waiting for an opportunity to take a shot, the HVM would strike the shuttle and turn it into a fireball long before either the pilot or crew could react. The shuttle lurched one final time, the internal compensators struggling to dampen the stress running through the hull, and grounded with a terrifying crash. Mark jumped to his feet as the hatch slammed open, following his escorts into the fresh air. He took a long breath as he sprinted away from the shuttle, towards the handful of prefabricated buildings his engineers had already erected. The air smelt foul.

Too many shuttles landing and taking off, he thought. *The Empire's beancounters would throw a fit if they knew.*

He smirked at the thought, then glanced around, hastily taking in the soldiers, armoured vehicles and SHORAD defence stations scattered around the LZ. His officers had done a good job, he noted; any attack on the LZ would have to be made in force to have a chance of success, but orbital bombardment would break up any substantial enemy force long before it reached its target. Behind him, he heard the sound of the shuttle taking off as four more came in to land, unloading more soldiers onto the ground. Officers and sergeants hurried forward to greet the new arrivals, then point them to stations along the perimeter. The outer edge of the LZ was constantly expanding, allowing his engineers to lay the groundwork for a colossal FOB.

If nothing else, he thought as he stepped into the building, *it will be good practice for later operations.*

"General," Colonel Steve Ferguson said. "Welcome to Corinthian."

"Thank you, Steve," Mark said. He glanced around, taking in the handful of communications consoles and the big holographic display, then looked back at his subordinate. "I assume command."

"I stand relieved, sir," Ferguson said, tonelessly. Mark rather doubted he was *pleased*, but at least it would allow him to return to his infantry regiment and take command. "So far, there has been no enemy contact, but we did stumble across a pair of observation sensors. They self-destructed as soon as we removed them from their positions."

Mark's eyes narrowed. "Newly-placed?"

"We assume so, sir," Ferguson said. "There were no tracks in the surrounding area, but we have to assume that we're being watched."

"There are too many hills nearby," Mark agreed. A single man with a handheld sensor could monitor everything from a safe distance, as long as he was careful. Given the terrain, he might even be able to stay in place once the hills were occupied and patrolled. "And they clearly had a good idea of where we'd land."

He didn't like the sound of it. It wasn't common for anyone to consider potential landing zones on their planets, not when anyone in control of the high orbitals could dictate terms at will. But Corinthian had a force shield…he wondered, grimly, if someone had deduced that Admiral Singh would make a grab for her former capital. Or had the force shield been part of a bargain with the Commonwealth? Corinthian would be stripped of its trained manpower and industrial base in exchange for something that would give them a fighting chance, when the Wolves arrived? He wasn't sure *he* would have made that decision, but he could see why Corinthian might have taken the risk. It wasn't as if its government had any hope of coming to an agreement with Admiral Singh.

"We have advance forces in place, as planned," Ferguson said, pointing to the display. "I believe we can press forward to seize the highways at selected points, sir, although that will almost certainly bring us into contact with enemy partisans. If the farms we destroyed had any survivors, they will want a little revenge."

"And there are untouched towns and hamlets to the north," Mark agreed. He suspected the enemy would have ordered them evacuated, as soon as the LZ became clear, but there was no way to be sure. They would have to be secured as soon as possible, if only to avoid becoming bogged down in urban combat before reaching Freedom City. "Push the advance forces forward, but make sure they have armoured and air support in place."

"Yes, sir," Ferguson said. He paused. "As yet, we don't have any of the helicopters in the air, but we've been launching drones over the past two hours. I request permission to start steering them to support the advance units."

Mark scowled. They could produce nearly unlimited quantities of bullets and other basic supplies, but replacing the drones would take a great deal longer. Hell, hardly anyone had anticipated *needing* drones before the war began. And while the drones flew so high they were impossible to see with the naked eye, an enemy with a MANPAD could easily pick one out and launch a missile that would blow it out of the sky.

And they won't leave them in place, either, he thought. *There's no way they can take the risk of allowing us to watch them.*

"Granted," he said, reluctantly. Losing the drones was expensive - the beancounters would bitch and moan all the way to the bank - but better to expend a drone than a living man. "But try to keep them away from enemy fire if possible."

Ferguson nodded, his expression unreadable. "Yes, sir," he said. "Right now, everything is proceeding as planned."

"Good," Mark said.

He turned his attention to the orbital map. The enemy forces would be lurking under the main body of the force shield, but if he was any judge, the land between the LZ and the outer edge of the force shield would be swarming with insurgents. Admiral Singh had made sure of it, just by convincing the local government that it was better to go down fighting rather than coming to an arrangement. And while he doubted the insurgents could stop him, he was sure they'd slow him down. It would be quite awkward to explain.

Because the Admiral has no understanding of what it's like to fight on the ground, he thought, darkly. *She will expect speedy results when there are none to be found.*

He looked back at Ferguson. "How are we coping with the landing schedule?"

"Proceeding as planned, so far," Ferguson reported. "The lack of enemy interference has helped, sir."

Mark scowled. He would almost have preferred to *see* the enemy, even if incoming missiles or mortar rounds would have screwed up his timetable beyond repair. An enemy force that wasn't visible was planning something, he knew from long experience. The locals knew their world far better than any of the invaders *and* had a cause, a good reason to put their lives on the line to defend their land. If they weren't attacking him, it meant they were planning something else. And it might explode in his face at the worst possible time.

"Keep expanding the defence lines as we set up the FOB," he ordered. The more he had on the ground, the more exposed he'd feel. If someone was watching the deployment from a safe distance, they'd be able to call in long-range fire or missile strikes as soon as there were enough targets to justify the expense. "And have those nearby hills swept as soon as possible."

"Yes, sir," Ferguson said.

And the Admiral will expect us to move at once, Mark thought. *But if I sweep the area first, it will look like I'm doing something…*

The plan wasn't much, he knew. It was a desperate dodge, one he'd used before the Empire had collapsed into ruins. Bureaucrats in military uniforms had been fooled; Admiral Singh, an experienced naval officer, might not be so easily tricked. But it was all he had.

———

Lieutenant Ryan Osborne kept his rifle at the ready as the small platoon advanced across the farmland, watching carefully for any sign of enemy activity. The landscape was surprisingly familiar - he'd grown up on a farm before deciding he didn't want to spend the rest of his life staring at the back end of a mule - but that didn't mean it wasn't dangerous. He'd spent six months on Thule after he'd been commissioned, promoted to lieutenant after the previous officer had been killed in an IED blast; he knew just how dangerous countryside folk could be.

And they have a better reason to fight than the city-folk, he thought, as they reached the remains of a farmhouse. *The land is theirs.*

He sucked in his breath as he saw the burned-out ruins, his eyes flickering automatically to the crater where the KEW had struck before traversing to a pair of wooden barns that had - somehow - survived the blast. It bothered him, more than he cared to admit. The barns looked solid, but they should have been flattered by the shockwave. If they'd survived...why? He motioned for half the platoon to remain behind, weapons at the ready, while he led the way towards the nearest barn, feeling sweat trickling down his back. The briefing had made it clear that the entire population was armed to the teeth, often with military-grade weapons. They might not have his force's training and experience, but they certainly knew the terrain and where best to site their weapons for maximum effect.

Up close, the barn was simple, little different from the structures he recalled from his homeworld. No prefabricated buildings for a farm so far from the capital! He felt a flicker of homesickness as he tested the door, watching carefully for unpleasant surprises; he used the tip of his rifle barrel to open the door, allowing him to step inside. One of his soldiers retched - the barn clearly hadn't been vented in a long time - as Ryan peered into the darkness. The barn was empty, save for piles of manure on the ground. No doubt the farmer had kept his pigs in the barn when they hadn't been roaming the fields.

He stepped forward, inspecting the ground carefully. He'd been a farmer, after all; he knew all the tricks. Hiding money and supplies from the taxman was practically second nature; farmers all over the galaxy believed, often with reason, that the intruders wouldn't go poking through animal shit just to check there was no hidden basement underneath the barn. He would have been surprised if the basement had survived the KEW strike, but the barn itself had survived...

Nothing, he thought. He made a mental note to report the barn as a possible barracks, once it was cleaned and vented, then led the way back outside. *Nothing worth mentioning at all.*

They inspected the second barn, but found nothing more than a handful of pieces of equipment and a tractor. He checked the tractor, wondering if it could be pressed into service, only to discover that someone had removed a number of components from the engine, along with the fuel. There was no fuel dump within the farm, as far as he could tell; no doubt the farmers had had a communal supply, somewhere nearby. It wasn't as if the tractors required vast amounts of fuel. But it would probably have been blown up or removed by now.

"Lieutenant," Sergeant Hove said, as the platoon reformed. "We found a body."

Ryan nodded and allowed Hove to lead him to the corpse. It was a middle-aged man, arms muscular and hands calloused from working the farm. A piece of flying debris had struck him in the back, killing him instantly. Or at least Ryan *hoped* it had been instant. He was quite happy to watch insurgent shitheads die slowly and painfully, but the farmer before him could easily have been his father. A strong and stern man, with limited book-learning but a great deal of common sense and experience...

He wanted to take the time to bury the man, but there was no time. "Did you see any traces of anyone else?"

"No, sir," Hove said.

"They must have left his body here," Ryan said. *Someone* had clearly had a plan, although he was surprised the other farmers hadn't buried the body before departing. The thought of eventually giving oneself back to the soil was a tempting one, for farmers. "They're probably in the hills."

He looked up, gritting his teeth. The hills would make excellent territory for insurgents, particularly ones composed of farmers who knew how to shoot and move quietly. If it was up to him, he would have ordered the hills burned to the ground, but that decision was well above his pay grade. Instead, he tapped his radio, reporting on the surviving farm and the dead body. Someone would bury the corpse eventually, he was sure, or burn it to ash with a plasma grenade. Corpses littering the landscape were sure vectors for disease.

A low humming sound echoed over the landscape as they resumed their probing, a pair of Landshark tanks advancing forward in support. Ryan scowled in disapproval at how they churned up the land beneath their treads, knocking over fences and smashing through cornfields with gay abandon, but he had to admit he was glad to see them. His body armour was very limited, he knew through experience, while the tanks were practically invulnerable to anything an insurgent force might reasonably have at its disposal. If they ran into an enemy position, he might just let the tanks charge forward while his men brought up the rear.

"No enemy in sight," he heard one of his men muttering. "Where *are* they?"

Ryan scowled, inwardly. They had *all* fought on Thule. They knew, all too well, that a rifle could be lurking behind every blade of grass. There were places where patrolling soldiers *knew* they would be ambushed, where the enemy could move unseen before opening fire from concealed positions and then retreating in the face of the inevitable bombardment. To be allowed to move openly, without being fired upon…it felt unnatural. Part of him almost wished the enemy would get on with it.

I'll have to watch them, he reminded himself.

It was a bitter thought. He cared nothing for the insurgents, but his superiors would be unimpressed if his men committed an atrocity against seemingly-innocent civilians. It wasn't easy to convince men hundreds of miles from the front that there was no such thing as an innocent civilian, that civilians were guilty - at the very least - of allowing the insurgents to move freely amongst them, unopposed. He knew it wasn't fair - he'd seen the punishments the insurgents had meted out to anyone who showed even a *hint* of collaborationist tendencies - but he found it hard to care. He'd seen too many good men killed, directly or indirectly, by civilians.

"They're hiding under their shield," he snapped. That too was a bitter thought. He wasn't used to operating **without** air cover, let alone the ability to call down orbital fire on any **target that** proved too stubborn for his men. "We'll be coming to grips with **them** soon enough."

———

"It looks like the enemy has been **evacuating** the region," Mark said, grimly. "There have been no engagements, Admiral, and the only bodies we've found are men and women who **were** killed by the KEW strikes."

Admiral Singh's mouth thinned. "They knew where we would be landing?"

"They probably tracked the orbital **drop**," Mark said. Given the KEW strikes, it would take a very stupid enemy *not* to guess they were about to be on the front lines. Bombarding **farmhouses** would have been pointless petty spite otherwise. "Even if they didn't, Admiral, there's no way to hide the endless stream of shuttles."

Admiral Singh looked displeased, **but** she didn't bother to argue. "I assume your forces are ready to deploy **further?**"

"We're just sweeping the **surrounding** countryside now," Mark said. Hadn't Admiral Singh promised him **complete** control? "Once we have our forces built up, we will be ready to take **the** offensive into the nearest towns and hamlets. That will allow us to seize **roads** leading directly to the capital."

"Move fast," Admiral Singh ordered. "Are there any other problems?"

"We will need more supplies," Mark said. "Can we send to Wolfbane for additional forces and pieces of equipment?"

Admiral Singh's expression darkened. "It will take time," she said. "Can you not take the city with what you have on hand?"

"I don't know," Mark admitted. He didn't really blame her for being annoyed. By any reasonable standard, they'd come loaded for bear. But they hadn't taken the force shield into account. "I would prefer to have too much firepower than too little."

"Send your request," Admiral Singh ordered, finally. "And push the offensive forward as fast as possible. The enemy must be crushed and broken."

"Yes, Admiral," Mark said. "It shall be done."

He assumed she thought he could just point his tanks at the enemy and crush all resistance under their treads. It sounded good, but it would be suicide in practice. There was no point in trying to argue with her, but he'd keep advancing forward carefully anyway. Thrusting forward too fast might result in disaster.

"Good," Admiral Singh said. "I want to be in Landing City by the end of the week."

CHAPTER

EIGHTEEN

There would, of course, have been brutal revenge afterwards. But the prospect of future punishment did not deter the locals from attacking the diplomats. They too were unable to comprehend the sheer power of the outsiders.
- Professor Leo Caesius. The Role of Randomness In War.

"They're quite efficient," Command Sergeant Gwendolyn Patterson observed. "I'm not sure *we* would do so well, under the same circumstances."

It was galling, but Ed had to agree with her. The Wolves were landing their shuttles and unloading them at an astonishing rate, suggesting either a high degree of pre-planning or considerable experience. A Marine Corps regiment might be able to match their speed, but he rather doubted an Imperial Army unit could have done anything along the same lines in twice the time. Admittedly, no one was trying to impede their activities, yet it was still alarming. The Wolves might be ready to advance forward long before he'd expected to meet them.

"No one has done anything like this for centuries," he said. "But they probably had plans in place to land at the spaceports and take control of Freedom City."

He shrugged, watching the microburst feed from the handful of sensors that had survived the enemy's sweep of the hillsides. The sensors themselves were extremely difficult to find - he recalled ducking them during a training exercise at OCS - but unmistakable once they were found. There was no doubt that the Wolves knew they were under observation. A wise commander would assume that he hadn't managed to find all of the sensors, even though he'd had the hills searched thoroughly. It was what *he* would have done.

"Lieutenant Pearson ran the calculations," Gwendolyn added. "Assuming the Wolves continue to deploy at their current rate, they will be ready to take the offensive in less than a week."

Ed nodded in agreement. The Wolves had picked the best of several possible LZs; they were far enough from civilisation to make it harder to slow them down, yet close enough to civilisation not to need to spend weeks hacking their way through difficult terrain. Unless he missed his guess, the enemy commander would start expanding his line of control over the next couple of days, fanning down towards the nearest inhabited settlements. The risk of running into insurgents was balanced by the need to keep insurgents as far from his LZ as possible.

"So we have to stop them," Danielle said. The President gave him a sharp look. "Can't you hit them now?"

"They need to commit themselves first," Ed said. "And then we can hurt them."

Privately, he agreed with her. Training and experience both argued that their best chance to score a decisive blow was now, while the Wolves were unloading their troops. But hitting the enemy too hard before they were overcommitted might just cause them to cut their losses…he'd gone over it, time and time again, but Danielle was clearly having problems coping with the thought of leaving an enemy force untouched, even though it was looming over her capital city. Realistically, it was hard to blame her. Corinthian had too many problems right now, even without a full-scale invasion.

"We do have raiders in place," Gwendolyn pointed out. "Give us a couple of days, then we can start pricking at them."

"Or someone else will start taking pot-shots at the bastards," Hampton snapped. "You know half the farmers in the area refused to leave?"

Ed nodded. Practically, the Wolves would expect a certain amount of armed resistance in any case. There was no way to keep the farmers from sniping at the Wolves whenever they had a chance, just as they'd sniped at Admiral Singh's troopers and imperial taxmen. He just didn't know the threshold between Admiral Singh's decision to carry on, whatever the cost, and a decision to cut her losses and withdraw. How badly did she have to be hurt to stop her?

"I think Admiral Singh will ignore minor losses," he said. "The real question is just how she plans to keep her forces supplied."

He scowled as he studied the shuttle timetable. The Wolves had to be pushing their gear to the limit, but it was working out for them. Their speed at unloading a set of orbital freighters, without a transhipment facility, was quite remarkable. And, behind them, a pair of starships that *had* to be copycat MEUs. Given just how many warships Admiral Singh had clustered around the MEUs, it was clear that she was aware of their importance. He ran through the calculations in his head, not liking the results. Admiral Singh should have no difficulty keeping her forces supplied with bullets and ration packs until the fighting came to an end.

But she has to be short of heavier equipment, he thought, grimly. *Taking out even one or two of those Landsharks won't do her any good.*

"There isn't much left for her to take in the region," Hampton assured him. "All heavy equipment was withdrawn under the shield."

Ed nodded, curtly. The farmers had plenty of small weapons, but nothing that would make a decisive difference. Maybe the Wolves would take food, if there was any left, to supplement their rations…

He pushed the thought aside. "Mandy may have a chance to hit the bastards in orbit," he said, instead. "Taking out one or both of the MEUs may tip the balance if done at the right time."

"I doubt she'll be able to sneak up to the ships," Gwendolyn said. "Admiral Singh isn't taking chances with them."

"No," Ed agreed. "But we can probably use their over-protectiveness against them."

He looked at Gwendolyn. "We'll give them a couple more days, then start interfering with their logistics," he added. "Pass the word to 1st Platoon."

"Aye, sir," Gwendolyn said. "They're still quite close to the enemy FOB."

And that means that there's a very real prospect of being stumbled over, Ed thought. He knew his men were experienced, but the Wolves couldn't be treated lightly. *And if that happens, the original plan will go right off the rails.*

Jasmine pressed herself into the earth, cursing silently as the enemy patrol grew closer and closer. Seven men, making their way up the wooded hillside with calm professionalism, taking care to beat the bushes as they passed. It wasn't particularly stealthy, but they weren't *trying* to be stealthy. They were the beaters, trying to flush out the game.

And that means there's probably a larger force in front of us, she thought. The trees and bushes provided a great deal of cover, but that wouldn't last. If she tried to keep ahead of the loud and noisy threat, she'd probably run into another enemy force waiting for her. But if she stayed where she was, there was the very real risk of being discovered and caught. *We need to sneak past the beaters and hope there isn't a follow-up force…*

She held up her hands, silently flashing orders to Stewart and Buckley. Thankfully, the remainder of the platoon was well out of the way, monitoring the enemy from two other vantage points. If something happened to the three of them, there would still be four other marines in the area, ready to unleash some serious grief when the order to engage the enemy finally came. But if the beaters pushed any closer, it was possible they'd be unable to avoid opening fire and revealing their presence far too soon.

Gritting her teeth, she slipped down the hill, keeping one hand on her pistol. Their passage was almost completely silent, but accidentally disturbing the wildlife would reveal their presence as surely as snapping a branch or stumbling into a pit. Thankfully, the beaters were making enough noise to drown out whatever noise they did make…Jasmine wondered, idly, if they'd stumbled across one or more of the sensors or if they were merely patrolling for the hell of it. *She* would have made sure to patrol the surrounding hills constantly, just to keep her people alert and focused. *And* make life hard for anyone who tried to sneak up on the FOB.

The noise of the beaters grew louder, suddenly, as they appeared in the distance. Jasmine braced herself, remaining still…very few people could spot a marine in a gillie suit hidden amidst the foliage, but it was quite possible the beaters knew what to look for. The three men in her view were laughing and joking amongst themselves, even as they kept moving forward with deliberate speed. They rustled the leaves constantly as they approached her position, one so close she could have reached out and touched him, then kept moving. If they spotted the lurking marines, they showed no sign.

She didn't relax. The beaters were loud, too loud. If she'd had the manpower, she would have added a second layer of beaters, with strict orders to remain silent as they crawled up the hill. She waited long enough for the beaters to fade into the distance - yet still close enough so they provided covering noise - and then slid down the hillside, as silently as she could. If the enemy had a second line of beaters…

…But it didn't look as though they had, she decided, as they reached the bottom of the hill and headed north. She hated to be optimistic, but it was possible that the enemy had limits on its manpower - or, perhaps, hadn't really expected to find anything. Shaking her head, she kept moving, keeping under the trees as much as possible. The forest would provide both cover and food for as long as they needed it, although she wanted to check out the nearest homestead before heading back to the hide. She glanced up as she heard something high overhead, then cursed inwardly when she saw the helicopter. KEWs provided considerably more punch, at far lower cost - they were really nothing more than rocks dropped from orbit - but helicopters offered far more accuracy. If - when - the Wolves started hunting insurgents, the helicopters would be deadly weapons. Their sensors, if nothing else, would have a very good chance of picking up someone sneaking nearby.

"I could down it with a missile," Stewart muttered. "One good shot…"

Jasmine scowled. The pilot clearly wasn't *expecting* trouble, judging by his flight path. If she'd been in command, the pilot would have been busted down a grade or two, if she didn't beat the living daylights out of him for gross stupidity. A helicopter was a simple beast - Avalon had been producing its own variants on the standard designs for years - but shipping one across interstellar distances was hardly cost-effective. Shooting the helicopter and a trained crew out of the sky would have a *very* interesting effect on enemy logistics.

"Not yet," she said, reluctantly. She *wanted* to take the shot, damn it. "The colonel was quite clear that we were to evade detection as long as possible."

It was nearly an hour of walking before they heard the sound of someone talking ahead of them and dropped to the ground, instinctively. Jasmine assumed that they'd run into an enemy patrol, but as she braced for combat it became clear that the voices weren't getting any closer. She listened carefully, picking out individual words with her enhanced ears. The language was Imperial Standard, but the accent was very definitely Wolfbane. She'd heard it before, far too often, on Meridian. Their guards had talked with a similar accent.

They're not alert, she thought, as she heard laughter echoing through the trees. *And they're not supervised either.*

She crawled forward slowly, keeping her ears pricked for trouble. A long wooden cabin sat in the middle of a clearing, by a small pond. She didn't recall seeing it on the maps - indeed, judging by its appearance, it was quite possible that it had *never* been recorded by the cartographers. Four soldiers stood in clear view, drinking alcohol straight from the bottle, as they watched a crying girl slowly start to undress at gunpoint. Behind her, kneeling against the wooden wall, an older couple and two young men strained against their bonds, their faces twisted with horror. Jasmine had no doubt that all five of the locals would be killed, their bodies burned to a crisp, after the soldiers had had their fun with the girl. Whatever else could be said about the Wolves, they didn't encourage atrocities. The soldiers would be executed - or sent to a penal unit - if they were caught.

Her duty told her that they should avoid contact, that they should withdraw and allow the whole tragedy to play itself out, but she couldn't just *leave*. Marines were meant to *protect* the population and she was *damned* if she was just turning her back and walking away, regardless of the risk. She crawled back long enough to signal the situation to her comrades, then returned to the clearing. The girl was slowly taking off her shirt, one button at a time, as the soldiers catcalled and shouted at her to move faster.

"No guns," Jasmine signalled. She drew her ka-bar from its sheaf and braced herself, testing the weight. It had been a long time since she'd taken a knife to a gunfight, but she didn't want to risk attracting attention. "On my mark."

The soldiers whooped and leaned forward as the girl undid the last button, allowing her breasts to bobble free. Jasmine sprang, throwing herself forward at lightning speed; she buried the knife in the neck of the nearest soldier, trusting her comrades to deal with the others. He jerked violently, then collapsed as she yanked out the knife. The other three died just as quickly.

"We're here to help," Jasmine said, addressing the girl. Her eyes were wide and staring, as if she didn't quite believe what had happened. She'd probably never been in any real danger from her fellow humans before, not in a farming community where everyone knew everyone else. "Cover yourself."

She checked the bodies, just to make sure they were dead, then nodded to Stewart to free the prisoners as she removed anything that might be of value. A handful of grenades, including two plasma grenades…no doubt they'd intended to put the bodies in the cabin and swear blind that the locals had attempted to resist, forcing the soldiers to burn the house and destroy the evidence. The weapons were standard-issue, no surprise; she checked their radios before placing them under the bodies. There was no point in trying to take them with her, not when they could be tracked easily.

"Thank you," the older man said. "Who *were* they?"

Jasmine glanced at him. "Wolves," she said. "Didn't you hear the radio?"

"We're Forsakers," the older man said. He sounded torn between taking offense and being grateful for having his family saved from certain death. "We don't *have* radios."

"The Wolves have invaded this planet," Jasmine said, deciding it would be better not to delay matters. "You're all in terrible danger."

She was genuinely surprised by the meeting. A Forsaker? She'd never encountered any, although she'd heard of them. An agricultural cult, determined to return to a pre-technological paradise that had never really existed. They'd stuck around longer than most such cults - actually *living* without technology wasn't as easy as far too many people thought - but she was surprised to meet one on Corinthian. It was hardly a low-tech world.

Maybe that's why they remained Forsakers, she thought. The young woman was being comforted by her mother, while her brothers were collecting weapons. *They weren't forced to do everything for themselves.*

"You need to move," she said. "This place is not safe."

"God will protect us," the older man said.

Jasmine frowned. "We won't be here a second time," she said. There was no way the Wolves could fail to notice that four of their soldiers hadn't returned. "If they send more troopers out here, you *will* be discovered."

She left the men to argue - the women seemed unwilling or unable to join the discussion - and helped Buckley and Stewart dig a grave by the edge of the clearing. It would probably not pass unnoticed, if the Wolves made a proper search, but it was the best they could do. They dumped the bodies in the graves, then covered them with soil. She was tempted to rig up a nasty surprise for anyone who tried to dig up the bodies, yet it would only provoke retaliation.

"We should just burn the bodies," Stewart said. "Those idiots aren't going to last long here, if they don't move."

Jasmine shrugged. "That would be quite visible," she said. A plasma fire would be seen from orbit. The soldiers might have had a cover story in place, but she couldn't risk detection. "And we'd better get moving. Those bastards will have friends."

She spoke briefly to the Forsakers, warning them of the dangers of staying in their home, and then led the way northwards. A handful of shuttles passed overhead, some slowing enough to make her wonder if the enemy had started work on a second LZ, but there were no other signs of enemy contact. By the time they reached the hide and compared notes with the other marines, she was tired and cranky. But she had to make her report before she went to sleep.

"Poor girl," Jalil commented, once they'd finished outlining what had happened. "To be stuck with a family like that."

Buckley frowned. "You think they'll insist she has to marry her brother?"

"No," Jalil said. "They're not *that* sort of people. But I once dated a girl who escaped a Forsaker commune. They're not *bad* people, but they have very firm ideas of a woman's role in society. And now she was almost molested...well, I wouldn't care to be in her shoes."

Jasmine shuddered. "Maybe we should have taken her with us."

"She would have complained," Jalil said. "Most of them think that's the way the world is supposed to be."

"At least she's still alive to complain," Buckley said. "And who knows? After what happened, they may realise the error of their ways."

Jasmine had her doubts, but she kept them to herself.

CHAPTER
NINETEEN

Indeed, as Ed is fond of remarking, one should not have blind faith in the efficiency of the military machine. Bad officers, bad NCOs and simple bad luck can reduce a crack regiment to a mob within months. A handful of battles have been decided simply by the enemy commanders not being up to their jobs.

- Professor Leo Caesius. The Role of Randomness In War.

"Soldiers do not go missing," Lieutenant Ryan Osborne said, as the platoon advanced along the half-beaten track. The trees had been cut back enough to allow his men to move two abreast, but beyond that they pressed together so closely that a large enemy force could be shadowing them in the undergrowth and they'd never know it. "Even if they *are* inexperienced idiots."

Sergeant Hove gave him a sharp glance, but said nothing. Ryan understood anyway, without the need for words. *He'd* been an inexperienced idiot too, when he'd arrived on Thule as a newly-commissioned officer. It was astonishing just how fast someone learned when he was put under heavy fire, if he survived the experience. But the platoon that was now reporting that four of its men were overdue had been shipped directly from Wolfbane. Their experience was limited to training exercises and simulations, neither of which could capture the vagaries of the battlefield. A beaten foe might keep running...or he might turn and face you, one final time.

Ryan scowled as they hurried down the track, wondering just what had happened. Had the soldiers managed to get lost? Or had they run into an insurgent camp and been killed - or captured? Wolfbane didn't pay ransoms for soldiers - a decision that made more sense to beancounters who were in no danger of being kidnapped - and if they had been captured, it wouldn't be long before they were killed. Unless, of course, they were interrogated first…

But that isn't likely, he thought, as the track widened suddenly. *What would a common soldier know that would help the enemy?*

He tensed as he saw the wooden cabin in the middle of the clearing, a single young man standing outside it. Had the soldiers come along the track? It was impossible to be *certain*, although they *should* have stumbled across the cabin. He barked a command to the young man, ordering him to summon everyone else out of the cabin. Moments later, five people stood in front of him; an older man who eyed him with wary defiance, two young men who eyed him with open hostility and two women, both of whom seemed determined not to make eye contact. The younger woman was pretty, despite her shapeless dress; he reminded himself, sharply, that there were strict rules against fraternising with the locals. There would be a brothel soon enough, if he was any judge. His superiors had decided it was better to ship whores in from Wolfbane rather than risk having their men sneaking over the wire and being brutally killed by the insurgents.

"We're looking for four of our men," he said, shortly. They'd speak Imperial Standard, whatever else they spoke. "Have you seen anyone else?"

"No," the elder man said, shortly. "We do not get visitors here."

Ryan wasn't too surprised. He might have been born a farmer, but there was something a little creepy about the cabin. There was plenty of wildlife in the surrounding forest to keep a family alive - and he could hear the sound of hens clucking and pigs grunting around the far side of the cabin - yet the isolation would have worn him down, eventually. Surely the locals needed *some* contact with the nearby hamlets?

"We have to search your property," he said, curtly. "Remain here and you will not be harmed."

He nodded a command to Sergeant Hove, then stepped through the wooden door and into the cabin. It was like stepping back in time. A faint pungent smell hung in the air. The only illumination, save for the windows, came from candles perched neatly in alcoves carved into the walls. There was nothing within eyeshot, save for a pair of rifles, that couldn't be made by hand. He glanced into the bedrooms and shook his head in disbelief. A blanket made from sheepskin couldn't possibly be as comfortable as something made from modern materials. There was no toilet; he puzzled over it for a moment before deciding they probably crapped in the woods. He couldn't help feeling a little sick as he emerged from the cabin, breathing in the fresh air with relief. How could anyone live like that?

They swept the rest of the property quickly and efficiently, but found nothing save for a number of hens. He was tempted to buy - or requisition - a number of fresh eggs, yet he was too concerned about the missing men. If they were somewhere within the forest, where? It was quite possible they were lost, but they *had* been carrying emergency beacons. Hell, if worst came to worst, all they had to do to call help was light a fire.

"Nothing, sir," Sergeant Hove concluded.

"Call it in," Ryan ordered. "And tell HQ that they're going to need more men to sweep for the lost boys."

He took one last look at the odd little family, then turned and headed back to the track, his men falling in behind him. If they were lucky, they'd stumble across something before getting roped into a long search that would take them away from their mission. Or, perhaps, the four men would be abandoned by their superiors. Losing them would hurt, but the mission was more important.

"Those boys are going to be trouble," Sergeant Hove predicted. "Their pride was hurt when we trampled through their home."

Ryan shrugged. There was no shortage of idiots on Thule willing to get themselves killed, in the hope they would take a Wolf with them. He doubted the young men behind them had the training or equipment to be really dangerous, although it was possible he was wrong. A single sniper with a hunting rifle could do a great deal of damage, if he hit the right person.

"If we see them fighting, we kill them," he said. There was already a detention camp on the far side of the FOB, but rounding up civilians at random would probably be counter-productive. "Until then, we ignore them."

———————

"They found nothing," Mark said.

"Yes, sir," Colonel Ferguson said. "The sweep of the forest turned up nothing, beyond a handful of hermits and a couple of tiny homesteads."

Mark cursed under his breath. He understood losing soldiers in combat, but *missing* soldiers was far worse. There would always be uncertainty over their fate. It had been nine hours since their absence had been noted, more than long enough for their kidnappers - if they had been kidnapped - to bundle them out of the danger zone and go to ground. Or, if they had merely been killed, there was plenty of space to hide the bodies. He no longer found it possible to believe that they'd merely gotten lost.

He scowled. "Captain Voss, the man who should have kept them in line?"

Ferguson looked up. "Yes, sir?"

"Demote him," Mark said, firmly. It was a harsh punishment, but he saw no choice. Voss was, at best, a third-rate officer. He might improve, given time and experience, yet there was *no* time. "And have the remainder of the platoon reassigned to CROW-duty."

He allowed his scowl to deepen as he studied the map. Four soldiers, missing somewhere within a largely-impassable forest. Killed, kidnapped…or had they deserted? It wasn't impossible, although they'd have to be complete idiots to realise they wouldn't be able to hide indefinitely. He made a mental note to have their platoon mates interrogated, then dismissed the matter. There was no more time to waste.

"Have one company remain on search duty, but redirect the others to the advance guard," he ordered. More and more soldiers were being landed, every day; the FOB was rapidly expanding as the engineers reconstructed buildings and sited defences. "We don't want to give the enemy a chance to react."

"Yes, sir," Ferguson said.

Mark dismissed him with a nod, then turned back to the map. The small town of Cheshire was largely intact, but that would change quickly if the enemy put up a fight. Orbital observation suggested that the enemy had evacuated much of the town, yet there were enough people left to convince him that they *were* planning something. He would have preferred to flatten the town from orbit, but he needed the road and rail network largely intact.

As if the enemy were planning to leave it intact, he thought, coldly. *They'll do what they can to mess it up before it's too late.*

He pushed the thought aside as he started to issue additional orders. Maybe he couldn't flatten the town, but he could make damned sure the enemy had no time to slip reinforcements into the settlement or turn it into a base of operations long before he stormed through the gates. Once his forces were blocking all the roads, the locals would be trapped and isolated.

And if they refuse to surrender, he told himself firmly, *we will take the city by storm.*

———

Jasmine read the message with a strange mix of emotions. On one hand, Colonel Stalker hadn't reprimanded her for killing the enemy soldiers, even though she risked revealing their presence and destabilising the entire plan. But, on the other hand, there was an unspoken yet unmistakable warning in his words. Her decision could have had far-reaching consequences, even though it didn't *seem* to have changed anything...

"We're to advance to the nearest vantage point to Cheshire," she said, once she reached the end of the message. "And then we're to deploy the MANPADs."

"At last," Buckley said. "I was getting bored here."

Jasmine nodded. It had been a day since they'd killed the would-be rapists, a day in which they'd lurked in the hide, catching up with their sleep while waiting to see if the Wolves would direct their forces in their direction. She'd had the entire platoon packed up, ready to move on a moment's notice, but it seemed to have been unnecessary. SIGINT suggested that the Wolves had been delayed, searching for their missing comrades. She hoped, silently, that they hadn't stumbled across the bodies.

They'd kill the Forsakers, if they found the bodies, she thought, grimly. *I hope they had the sense to run.*

She pushed the thought out of her mind as she closed the terminal and buckled it to her belt, then joined the others outside the hide. The sound of shuttlecraft was, if anything, growing louder. Buckley had spent two hours tracking them with his handheld sensor, finally concluding that the Wolves were stacking up the shuttles to keep the landings under some kind of schedule rather than setting up new LZs. It made a certain kind of sense, Jasmine had to admit, but it also suggested a certain degree of overconfidence. They had to be fairly sure they weren't going to run into someone with a MANPAD.

"Cheshire is ten kilometres to the west," she said, once she'd run through the content of the message. There was no point in trying to keep it to herself. Someone might well get killed on the mission - and that someone might be her. Leaving her subordinates in ignorance would ensure the mission failed with her. "We'll head for Hill #352 and set up an OP there."

"That's quite close to the town," Stewart pointed out. "They'll sweep for trouble there, surely."

"It *is* on the other side of the river," Jalil countered. "They may not put it at the top of their list."

"That's not a treacherous river," Stewart reminded him. "You don't need an armoured combat suit to cross it."

"We'll check carefully before we reach the summit," Jasmine said. They'd had one close call and she didn't really want another, even though it wouldn't be long before they'd be ordered to hit the enemy as hard as they could. A running battle midway up a hillside could go either way. "And if the Wolves are present in force, we'll pull back and find somewhere else."

She glanced at them, then led the way through the forest. It wasn't a long march, compared to some of the routine marches she'd done on the Slaughterhouse, but it was *real*. Showing themselves, even for a brief second, could be disastrous. She felt an itching between her shoulder blades as she contemplated unfeeling automated eyes, staring down from the high orbitals. It was unlikely that anyone, even Admiral Singh, would waste a KEW on a handful of insurgents, but the chance to pick off seven marines was not one to be dismissed. And if Admiral Singh knew who was leading them…

The thought made her smile. She didn't know - couldn't know - if Admiral Singh had drawn a connection between Jasmine Yamane and the person who'd fomented a revolution on Corinthian, forcing her to flee in disarray. It was quite possible, she had to admit; her name was well-known on Corinthian, despite strong suggestions that it would be better to keep the details as concealed as possible. And yet, she'd given her *real* name when she'd been captured on Thule and she'd just been shipped to Meridian, rather than isolated and executed at Admiral Singh's whim. It was possible that there was another *Jasmine Yamane* in the files - there had been millions of men and women in military uniform before the Empire collapsed into ruins - but equally possible that Admiral Singh hadn't realised who she'd captured.

Because she's a vindictive bitch, Jasmine thought. She'd read the files, after Corinthian had been liberated. Admiral Singh had slaughtered her former enemies with an unholy glee, even though she hadn't embarked on random purges. *If she knew who I was, she would want me dead.*

She pushed the thought aside as she heard something moving in the undergrowth, lifting her rifle before she saw the fox springing from cover and bounding into the distance. There were people who *hunted* the creatures, she recalled from her briefing; farmers viewed them as pests and rich idiots enjoyed the idea of chasing the animals over hill and dale. Jasmine saw why farmers didn't like foxes, but she took no pleasure in hunting dumb animals, even ones that could be dangerous. Hunting humans was far more challenging - and they had a tendency to fight back.

The sun was high in the sky when they reached the lower base of Hill #352. They circled it slowly, watching for signs of an enemy presence, then climbed up the rear of the hill until they found a point that overlooked Cheshire. The Wolves had already arrived, in force; Jasmine didn't need anything more than the naked eye to pick out a dozen AFVs and five Landsharks lurking on the approach roads, their guns dominating the scene. A handful of prisoners were sitting on the ground by one of the tanks, their hands bound behind their backs. She briefly considered another rescue, but it would be suicide. There was a small army within view.

And more on the way, she thought, as yet another shuttle entered the planet's atmosphere and headed towards the enemy FOB. The town's defenders were badly outnumbered. *They would be wise to surrender, if they thought they might survive the experience.*

Her expression darkened as she silently surveyed the scene. Two helicopters were clattering through the sky, keeping a wary distance from the town; this time, at least, the pilots seemed much more aware of potential danger. They were ducking and weaving at random, trying hard to throw off any targeting sensors that might be aimed in their direction. It looked very much as though the Wolves were moving deliberately, rather than making a quick thrust into the town. She had a feeling that their commander had been trained by the Imperial Army; his tactics were slow and ponderous, rather than the quicksilver blows she'd been taught at the Slaughterhouse. But she had to admit they were effective.

"We appear to be alone up here," she said. "Do you concur?"

"Yep," Buckley said. "They're not interested in the hill."

Jasmine shrugged, then took a passive sensor from her carryall and turned it on, checking for active sensor emissions. Not entirely to her surprise, there were three drones orbiting over the town as well as the helicopters, while the shuttles were using active sensors of their own to make sure they didn't accidentally crash into another shuttle. Mid-air collisions were rare - at least off Earth, where there had often been at least one a week - but there were so many shuttles flying through the atmosphere that it was a very real possibility...

She returned the sensor to its place, then removed the HVM launcher from the bag and snapped it together. Beside her, the other marines readied their own weapons, checking and rechecking to make sure they were ready to take out their targets. The drones were probably basic surveillance models, but they might well be armed. There had been a fuss over arming drones in the army, she recalled, yet the Marine Corps hadn't hesitated. Admiral Singh would probably not hesitate either.

And whoever is on command on the ground would definitely see the advantages, she thought, as she lifted the launcher to the sky and hunted for a target. A shuttle *had* to be targeted, whatever else they hit. The enemy logistics needed to be hampered. *And taking down the drones won't hurt either.*

"Ready," Buckley said.

"Ready," Stewart echoed.

Jasmine braced herself as the next shuttle came into view. She wondered, idly, what it carried; troops, supplies…but it didn't matter. All that mattered was giving the wolves a bloody nose.

"Fire," she ordered.

CHAPTER
TWENTY

Lakshmibai provides yet another example. The planetary caste system ensured that the Kshatriyas (warriors) were the only ones considered for military service. (In fact, being born into the Kshatriyas ensured that one would either be expected to serve or bear the next generation of warriors.)
- Professor Leo Caesius. The Role of Randomness In War.

Ryan started as he saw the first HVM shoot up from the hillside, a streak of light that moved so quickly that it had struck its target before he realised quite what had happened. The shuttle seemed to stagger as the missile slammed into its hull, then rolled over and plummeted out of the sky, trailing fire and smoke. Four more missiles followed, two targeting the helicopters while the remaining two headed up into the sky. The shuttle crashed hard, the explosion echoing across the valley.

"They're on the hillside," Sergeant Rove snapped. "Sir?"

Ryan didn't hesitate. "Deploy the platoon," he ordered. The hill was on the wrong side of a river, but they could ford it easily. And if not, the tanks could certainly drive through the water with men perched on their hulls. "Call for reinforcements…"

He thought fast. "Seal off the hill," he added, sharply. "Don't let them get away!"

———

Jasmine dropped the launcher on the ground as soon as the missile was in the air, then turned and led the marines down the rear of the hill. There was no point in trying to keep and recycle the launcher, something that had always annoyed the beancounters; they were no longer any use once the missiles had been fired. Indeed, carrying the damned things would slow the marines down at the worst possible moment. Behind her, a thundering explosion told her that at least one of the missiles had scored a direct hit. She glanced up just in time to see the remains of a helicopter dropping from the sky.

She smirked to herself - *that* would teach the Wolves not to be over-confident - and then kept moving, sacrificing stealth for speed. The Wolves had probably studied at one of the army's training facilities - hell, they might even have a graduate of a Marine Corps Boot Camp in command. They'd try to keep the marines from slipping away by surrounding the hill, then searching it inch by inch. Unless, of course, they just called in a KEW strike. There was nothing stopping the Wolves from flattening the hill from orbit.

"We know we got the drones," Stewart muttered. "They'd have thrown something back at us by now if they hadn't."

Jasmine shrugged, glancing back to see a plume of smoke rising up on the other side of the hill. She hoped the shuttle hadn't crashed into the town, but there had been no way to be *certain* where the craft would come down. The shuttle was large enough to crash, rather than be blown to smithereens; the helicopters would have been blown apart in mid-air. Their crews would have died before they knew they were under attack.

She felt a stab of guilt, which she pushed aside savagely. The troops on the shuttle, assuming there *had* been troops on the shuttle, would have been dangerous, if they'd ever been allowed to land. Part of her thought that shooting at defenceless men was dishonourable, but those men hadn't been POWs or innocent civilians. Killing them while they were on the shuttle was safer and simpler than killing them on the ground. She couldn't allow herself to feel any regard for their lives as long as they were opposing her.

A clattering sound echoed in the distance; she glanced north to see a pair of helicopters heading towards the hill, bobbing backwards and forwards as they tried to evade any potential missile locks. There were none, she knew; there was no one left on the hillside, unless the enemy troops had already reached the bottom. She kept a wary eye out as they made it into the forest, but there was no sign of trouble. The enemy hadn't had time - yet - to prevent them from escaping.

"We need to keep moving," she said. Leaving traps for their enemies was second nature by now, but speed was of the essence. "And hope we make it out of the envelope before it's too late."

"They'll call in KEWs," Stewart predicted. "They'll never catch us now and they have to know it."

Jasmine was inclined to agree. The enemy didn't have anything close enough to the hill to intercept them before they made their escape. All that was required was a decision to call in a KEW strike...who had that authority? The Imperial Army had never been keen on issuing Forward Fire Controllers to individual units, but the Marine Corps had thought differently; hell, *she* had the training to call in air or orbital strikes. Who knew what the Wolves thought about the matter?

She pushed the thought aside and kept moving, picking up speed as they plunged further into the forest. She'd find out soon enough.

———

Mark sucked in his breath sharply as the first alerts popped up on the display; a shuttle, two helicopters and two drones, blown out of the air by man-portable HVMs. He wasn't surprised that the enemy had finally shown their teeth, now his forces were enveloping Cheshire and readying themselves to push down to the capital, but it was a headache.

"I'm clearing all air traffic out of the area," an operator called. "All orbiting shuttles are to remain in orbit; I say again, all orbital shuttles are to remain in orbit!"

"Pick up the landing schedule," another operator barked. "Get them all down on the ground."

And hope to hell some bastard with a mortar isn't taking aim at the FOB, Mark thought, grimly. The FOB was protected by SHORAD units, but a single shell that made it through the network of laser defences would be devastating, if it struck a shuttle. *They won't be content with just taking out a single shuttle...*

"Colonel Mustard reports that his men are heading towards the launch site," Ferguson said, sharply. "He's confident that they'll be able to catch the missile crews..."

Mark shook his head. He'd fought insurgents long enough to know that the cowardly bastards wouldn't stick around for a fair fight. HVMs were single-shot weapons; they'd fire their missiles, then run for their lives without sticking around to watch the fireworks. And he didn't dare send his remaining helicopters after them. He'd lost too many craft on Thule when they ran into a HVM the enemy had kept in reserve. No, there was only one option.

"Call in a KEW," he ordered. They had to move fast, before the enemy had a chance to escape the blast radius. As soon as they were off the hillside, they'd head off in a random direction and vanish. "I want that hill flattened into the ground."

"Our troops are heading towards it," Ferguson pointed out.

"Then tell them to take cover," Mark snapped. He admired initiative - he certainly wasn't going to reprimand whoever was on the ground - but there just wasn't time to set up a cordon and catch the bastards. "Call down the KEW."

"Yes, sir," Ferguson said.

———

Ryan's headset buzzed. "Code Red, Danger Close," it barked. "I say again, Code Red, Danger Close."

"Get down," he bellowed. Code Red meant an incoming KEW strike; Danger Close meant that it would be impacting alarmingly close to their position. He glanced for cover, but saw nothing. "Danger Close, Danger Close!"

Ryan hit the ground, covering his head with his hands, as Sergeant Rove took up the cry. KEW strikes were accurate, but not always *that* accurate. It was just possible that the strike would come down right on top of them, slamming into the ground before they knew they were in trouble. He was suddenly very aware of his own fragility. A single KEW, a rock little bigger than his head, would smash him and his platoon so thoroughly that no one would recover anything bigger than DNA traces, if they were lucky. He covered his ears as time seemed to slow down...

...And then the earth shook violently. The sound was deafening, even though his covered ears; he was silently grateful for the implants he'd been given in basic training. Without them, he would have been deafened. He heard pieces of debris crashing to the ground, followed by splashing sounds from the direction of the river. Gritting his teeth, he looked up at the hillside and stared in astonishment. The hill had been cleaved in two, smashed and scattered trees lying everywhere. If the insurgents had been there, when the KEW hit, they were gone. There was nothing left of them.

He pulled himself to his feet slowly, glancing at the river. Hundreds of trees had fallen down the hillside and landed in the water, damming it quite effectively. The water was already building up behind the make-shift dam, although he doubted it would be long before it found a new way through the debris and down to the sea. He wondered, absently, if flooding would pose a problem, but decided it wouldn't. There just wasn't enough water in the river to do more than muddy the ground.

"Call it in," he ordered, once he'd checked his men for injuries. No one had been hurt, thankfully. "Ask if we should sweep the remains of the hillside."

"Yes, sir," Sergeant Rove said.

———

The blast came without warning. Jasmine was picked up and thrown forward, tossed almost casually into a tree as the shockwave roared through the forest. She heard the sound of trees toppling in the distance as she caught herself, gritting her teeth as she fell to the ground and landed badly. She'd regret that, she knew, even though nothing was broken. An injury, even a small one, could be disastrous on campaign. There were no proper medical facilities for miles.

And spraining your ankle now could end our lives, she thought, numbly. *They cannot be allowed to catch us.*

"Ouch," Stewart said.

Jasmine gave him a sharp look as she picked herself up. "Everyone all right?"

"Got a nosebleed here, boss," Buckley said. "I'm going to die!"

"You'll outlive us all," Jasmine said, sharply. His nose looked fine to her. Joe Buckley's reputation for horrific bad luck hadn't got him killed yet, although he'd argued that it proved he merely had *very* bad luck to remain alive and escape the afterlife. She hadn't found that argument very convincing. "Anyone else?"

She allowed herself a moment of relief as she realised no one was seriously hurt. The KEW - it couldn't have been anything else - had come down too late to kill them, even though they'd been caught by the shockwave. She glanced up towards the clear blue sky, wondering if the enemy was considering another shot, then reminded herself that there was no point in worrying about it. They'd be smashed before they knew it, if the enemy caught a glimpse of them and called in additional fire.

"Move out," she snapped. "We want to put some distance between us and them before it gets dark."

She contemplated the problem as they started to walk, keeping under the forest canopy as much as they could. It was quite possible the enemy would send infantry into the forest after them. *She* would have classed it as a fool's errand, but the enemy CO might think differently. Losing a shuttle would *sting*. Indeed, depending on how many they'd brought with them, it might cause all sorts of long-term logistics problems. If nothing else, it would make a mess of their landing schedule. She'd seen it herself on Thule.

And they'll know it too, she thought. *They'll hate it.*

———

"There were no survivors," Ferguson said. "Advance elements secured the remains of the shuttle, but all they found were bodies."

Mark clenched his fist in rage. Three hundred men - two companies of infantry and one company of logistics support officers - were dead, blown out of the sky and killed by a single missile. Capturing and killing the insurgents who'd fired the shot would be immensely satisfying, but it wouldn't bring the dead back to life. And losing the shuttle was almost worse. The landing operation had placed so much pressure on the shuttles that it was quite likely a number of craft would break down over the next week, simply through normal wear and tear.

And we can't guarantee keeping the region around the LZ swept clean of insurgents, he thought, darkly. It had been a persistent problem on Thule, although the insurgents had been short on advanced weapons. They'd grown too dependent on Wolfbane as a source of supply, never realising that the weapons could be deactivated at will. *A single shot will be enough to slow down the landing schedule again.*

He shook his head. The Admiral was not going to be pleased.

"Have the bodies brought back here for storage," he ordered. He studied the orbital imagery of the KEW strike for a long moment, then shrugged. "And then order the forward elements to advance into Cheshire. The town is to be taken intact."

"Aye, sir," Ferguson said. "The locals have been erecting defences."

"Then crush them," Mark snapped.

He turned to study the map. "I want a series of heavy patrols run around the LZ before we start shipping more men and equipment down to the surface," he said. "The enemy is to *know* they're there. In addition, I want the shuttles and helicopters to take full precautions. I don't want to lose another craft to enemy fire."

"Yes, sir," Ferguson said. He paused. "What about the hermits?"

Mark scowled. The patrols had stumbled across a number of tiny settlements, only a couple larger than a single family farm. He honestly had no idea how they'd managed to avoid going mad from the isolation, although there were times when he had to admit the attraction of being spared the attentions of idiots. But such tough self-reliant folk would be natural insurgents, being both stealthy and excellent shots. They'd even know how to keep themselves alive in the forest, rather than hunting food at the local store. Such skills had been practically unknown on Earth for years.

The Wolves had left the hermits alone. But that might have been a mistake.

"Round them up," he ordered. They already had a detention camp; it would just have to be expanded, long enough to hold the hermits and any other civilians they swept up. The population of Cheshire couldn't be allowed to get in the way, unless they had useful skills…but then, they probably couldn't be trusted. "Put them in the camp. And warn the men that I expect to see them treated decently."

"Yes, sir," Ferguson said.

Mark dismissed him, cursing silently as he studied the map. His troops were far better trained and disciplined than any regiment from the pre-fall Imperial Army, but counter-insurgency duties could wear down the strongest of men. The mixture of fear and frustration could lead to madness…or a sheer lack of concern for the civilians that could lead directly to atrocities. He'd had four men hung for rape on Thule, even though there had been military-run brothels at all of the major bases. The bastards had just wanted to make the locals *suffer*.

"Sir," one of the operators said. He sounded hesitant, as if he were reluctant to be the bearer of bad news. In the old days, Mark had to admit, it would have been a valid fear. His old superiors had never liked hearing bad news. "I've reformatted the landing schedule, but there are quite a few kinks in it."

Mark bit down the response that came to mind. There had been little margin for error - or unanticipated attacks - in the original schedule. Of *course* there were a few kinks in the new one! Shuttles that had been tasked to do one thing had been redeployed, which meant that a number of other tasks would be delayed, causing a knock-on effect that would eventually shatter the schedule completely. Compensating for that would not be an easy task.

"It's understandable," he said, firmly.

"But I did have an idea," the operator said. "We could ground one of the freighters…"

"Oh," Mark said.

He managed - somehow - to avoid laughing. As solutions went, it was innovative…and completely useless. Grounding a bulk freighter was theoretically possible, but getting it back off the ground would be impossible. Nothing larger than a light freighter could land and take off from a planet without a great deal of help. He'd given some thought to dropping the supplies on the surface, but they didn't have the equipment on hand. It wasn't something anyone had ever anticipated.

They did it during the Unification Wars, he thought. *And they still do it...*

He looked up. "We'll stick with the shuttles, for the moment," he said. A colonial dumpster would be perfect, if they could get their hands on one or more. Could one of the MEUs put a dumpster together? Or a captured industrial node? Corinthian had certainly supported colony missions in the past. "But well done for at least considering it."

"Thank you, sir," the operator said.

Mark shook his head in amusement - grounding a freighter *indeed* - and then turned his attention back to the display. His forces were finally moving into place to take Cheshire by storm, rather than trying to starve the defenders out. He just didn't have time to be clever...

And I need to win a victory, he thought. Losing a shuttle was annoying, but the delays promised to be worse. *The Admiral will definitely not be pleased if we run into more problems.*

CHAPTER
TWENTY-ONE

The belief that they were the ultimate warriors did give the Kshatriyas some advantages, but the simple inability to grasp that military perfection required realistic training, experience and competent officers weakened them. Their only opponents, prior to the CEF, were poorly-armed peasants, driven into desperate revolt by unbearable living conditions. The Kshatriyas had very little trouble in squashing those revolts.

- Professor Leo Caesius. The Role of Randomness In War.

"You really shouldn't be here," John said.

Lily eyed him mulishly. He might be her boyfriend - and they'd already started talking about getting married - but he didn't *own* her. She was a crack shot and she was damned if she was simply abandoning her home, even if the children and half the women had been evacuated as soon as the Wolves began to land. If her father had reluctantly agreed she could stay behind, her boyfriend could like it or lump it.

She shrugged and glanced towards the barricade. It had taken four days with earth-moving machines to put it together, blocking all access to the town. Cheshire might well fall - no one seemed to think they had a chance - but they'd make the enemy pay. Watching one of their shuttles being blown out of the sky had only heightened their determination to resist. Her grandfather, among others, had settled Cheshire. None of their descendants wanted to surrender to the invader or walk away. They recalled Admiral Singh all too well.

"They're coming," someone shouted.

180

"I'd better get into position," she said. She gave John a quick kiss, then kissed him again for luck. "Goodbye."

"See you on the other side," John called after her. "But run if you have to."

Lily scowled to herself as she hurried into the house and climbed up the ladder onto the rooftop, where she'd already set up a perch. She'd never hunted humans - she'd never needed to defend herself - but the principle wasn't that different from shooting birds or small animals. Hell, she'd even killed one of the wild boars with a single shot from her rifle, much to her father's surprise. The wretched beasts were very tasty, but they were crop-destroying pests that needed to be killed.

What is it, she asked herself, *that makes men so irritatingly protective?*

She mulled the thought over and over again as she peered through her scope towards the enemy positions. There wasn't much in sight, save for a pair of armoured vehicles and a handful of men. She wasn't even sure why the watchers thought the enemy were on the move, unless they'd seen something that had faded away by the time she reached her perch and readied herself. And then she saw the tank rumbling into view.

Her heart sank as she took in the massive vehicle. It was huge, easily as large as a house, studded with weapons that moved constantly, searching for targets. The immense main gun didn't move, but it didn't have to. It was pointed directly at the barricade. She fought down the urge to run for her life as the tank moved closer, willing herself to stay in place despite the trickle of fear making its way into her gut. She'd told John too many times that she would be staying to run now.

She heard shots cracking out from the men manning the barricade, but the tank didn't slow or return fire. It just kept coming. She searched for a target, sweeping the tank with her scope, yet there was nothing. Sparks were flickering on its armoured hull as bullets bounced off, as if the defenders were searching for a weak spot. She rather doubted that such a spot existed, not on a tank. They needed something far more powerful to tear through its armour.

The tank smashed into the barricade and crushed it, effortlessly. Lily stared in horror, watching as men toppled from their perches only to be crushed under its treads. *John* had been there, supporting the gunners;

was he alive or dead? She saw a stream of men running from the nearest building, heading to the fallback position…was John amongst them? The tank kept moving forward, an explosion blasting out on its hull as someone hurled a grenade at the vehicle. Others followed…she saw a young man running forward, carrying a whole bag of grenades. He scrambled onto the hull and pulled the pin. The explosion blew him to bits, but it didn't even scratch the tank…

And then the tank opened fire, a deafening rattle splitting the air as machine gun bullets tore through the air, seeking out the defenders. Lily saw a building disintegrate under the impact, bullets tearing through its walls as if they were made of paper. A pair of men ran forward, carrying yet more grenades…the gunners blew them away, casually. The tank kept moving, even as the defenders broke and ran rather than face it any longer. Lily wanted to damn them for cowards, but she knew the only reason she hadn't run herself was that she was frozen in horror…

The entire building shook, violently, as the tank brushed against it. Lily snapped out of her shock as the walls tottered and fell, turning to run as the rooftop smashed down into the rubble. She dropped her rifle as she fled, but she didn't have time to recover it. The tank was moving onwards and there was no safety anywhere, not any longer.

And it dawned on her, as she ran, that she hadn't fired a single shot.

———

Ryan advanced carefully into the town, silently noting the remains of the barricade and the dead bodies. The former wasn't a bad piece of work, he had to admit, but they'd criminally underestimated the sheer mass and power of Landshark tanks. All the tankers had had to do was give the barricade a *push* and it had fallen over, burying too many of the defenders beneath it.

Cheshire had been a nice town, once upon a time, but now half its buildings were nothing more than piles of rubble. There was no resistance as the soldiers advanced, the handful of survivors too stunned to do more than stare as they were rounded up and marched to the centre of the town. He doubted any of them would dare to cause trouble while they were sitting under the Landshark's guns, but if they did a single burst of machine gun fire would ensure they wouldn't cause it for very long.

"Sir," Sergeant Rove said. "The lower half of the town hasn't been cleared…"

He broke off as a shot snapped out from a nearby building. A soldier tumbled to the ground, badly injured. Ryan swore as he unhooked a grenade from his belt and hurled it into the building, hoping desperately that it would be enough to stop the sniper. There was always *someone* who thought they could put up a fight. The explosion shattered the wooden walls, sending the building tumbling to the ground. He led the way forward, carefully, and probed through the rubble. The sniper had been killed by the grenade, then crushed under his own roof.

Asshole, he thought, as they began to sweep the next set of buildings. The wounded man was checked by a medic, then carried off to the aid station. *You could have got a lot of people killed.*

The platoon fanned out, carefully. There was no joking, no quiet comments when they thought he couldn't hear. The men were on edge after the sniper. Ryan glanced into a couple of buildings, but wasn't too impressed. The people had been relatively wealthy, yet they'd built their homes from wood? And yet, if he were forced to be honest, he had to admit it did have some advantages. Expanding their homes - and carrying out repairs - would be easy.

"Looks like a glory hole," one of the soldiers muttered, as they glanced at the wall. A handful of bullets had gone through the wood, leaving a gaping hole in their wake. "Not big enough for me, of course."

"You nearly shot your cock off by stuffing it up a gun barrel," another said. Ryan cringed at the thought. "And…"

"Shut up, the pair of you," Sergeant Rove snapped. "Keep your eye on your surroundings or something will put a bullet in your ass!"

Ryan kept his face impassive as they reached three more buildings. They looked empty, but he used hand signals to split the platoon into two groups and then led the first group into the building. It was a small family home, judging by the furniture, but it was completely deserted. And yet, it looked as though it had been cleaned and tided before the family departed. It made him wonder just what they'd been feeling…

They thought they could just come home, he told himself. *But their town is never going to be the same again.*

———

Lily sat in a corner of the house, shaking with fear and horror. Everything had caught up with her the moment she'd found cover, even though she knew the wooden walls wouldn't last any longer than the barricade if the tank decided to crush the house. She'd seen too many men die - for nothing - to do anything more than collapse. Cheshire had never had a chance, she knew now. They should just have fled or surrendered the moment the enemy troops showed themselves...

She looked up as the door crashed open, knowing it was already too late to flee. Two men stood in the doorway, weapons sweeping the room. She didn't need to see their uniforms to know they weren't friendly. The mere act of kicking their way into the house was quite enough. They stared at her, their weapons pointed at her chest, then motioned for her to stand. Lily stared back, too frightened to move.

"On your feet," one growled. "Now!"

Lily couldn't move. The soldier nodded to his comrade, then stamped over to her, caught hold of her shirt and hauled her to her feet, spinning her round and pushing her against the wall. She heard someone else entering the house as her captor's hands roamed her body, checking her belt and pockets before slowly creeping up to her breasts. His touch was repulsive; she tried to twist away from him, only to find herself pinned helplessly in place as he groped her.

And then her captor was yanked away from her. She turned, just in time to see an older man punch her former captor in the face.

"Behave yourself," he growled. "Or you'll be spending the next month in a penal battalion, if it doesn't kill you first!"

He turned to face Lily before she could do more than stare. She gasped in pain as he caught her arms, pulled them behind her back and snapped a plastic tie around her wrists with practiced ease, then took firm hold of her shoulders and pushed her towards the door. Lily tested her bonds as covertly as she could, but discovered that the plastic tie was effectively unbreakable. If they wanted to kill her - or worse - there was nothing she could do to resist.

Outside, Cheshire lay in ruins. The upper half of the town was almost completely gone, save for a couple of buildings that had somehow survived. Dead bodies lay everywhere; bile rose in her throat as she recognised a couple of the dead. Andrew, who'd been the first young man to kiss her; Tammy, who'd been married only five months ago. She blinked away tears as she remembered the wedding; Tammy, dressed in virgin white, walking down the aisle, her father by her side. And to think she'd been talking about having kids!

Soldiers were everywhere, weapons at the ready as they watched for potential threats. She shuddered at the way some of them looked at her, although none of them did any more than look. The man holding her had protected her, at least, but why? He'd punched one of his own men? Did he want her for himself?

A handful of prisoners, their hands bound, sat in front of a tank. Most of them were boys, she noted, although a couple were girls. She looked for John, but didn't see him. Her boyfriend would never forgive himself if he'd run from the fight, yet she would have been forever grateful if he had. But there was no sign of him. He'd either escaped captivity or died in the brief one-sided fight.

Lily sat down where she was bid, fighting down the urge to cry. She was a prisoner. She no longer had any control over her own life. If they wanted to kill her, they could kill her; if they wanted to rape her, or beat her, or put her to work…they could. They could do anything to her. She tested the bonds again, but they remained resolutely unbreakable. And even if she did manage to stand, they were right in front of the tank. There was no escape.

I'm sorry, she thought. She wished she'd listened to John. Or to her father. *I should have run.*

————

"Trooper Eula got a little grabby," Sergeant Rove reported. "I gave him a clout instead of sending him to a penal unit."

Ryan nodded, curtly. He'd seen the bruise. Trooper Eula might spend the next few hours bitching and moaning about his sergeant, but if he had any sense at all he'd be grateful to be spared a penal battalion. A penal unit would be assigned the most hazardous or unpleasant jobs, everything from clearing minefields to digging latrines and carting supplies around the battlefield. The odds of an individual soldier completing his month on penal duty were not high, although there had been a number of legendary survivors.

"Make an unofficial note of it," he said.

He scowled, inwardly. An *official* report would have sent Trooper Eula to the nearest penal unit, but there had to be *some* record. They had strict orders not to mistreat the locals. A would-be rapist - or even a groper - could cause no end of problems, when the fighting came to an end. Trooper Eula might have to be handed over. And their superiors would do it without a second thought.

Idiot, he thought, crossly. *You could just wait long enough for them to set up the brothel at the FOB.*

"Yes, sir," Sergeant Rove said. No doubt he would already have composed the report for his fellow NCOs. "I moved the victim to the prisoner cache. I think she'll be fine."

Ryan hoped he was right. He was tempted to quietly release the prisoner, by way of apology, but he knew it would be pointless. Orders had come down from General Haverford himself, making it clear that all enemy civilians were to be rounded up and transported to the POW camp near the FOB. Ryan had no idea what they were going to do, once they had so many prisoners the camp couldn't handle them all, but that was well above his pay grade. He couldn't deliberately defy an order without a far better reason.

"I hope so," he said, shortly. "And the remainder of the platoon?"

"Held up well," Rove said. "But this wasn't much of a test."

Ryan nodded in agreement. The defenders hadn't realised what they were facing and they hadn't had time to recover from their mistake. A little forethought would have made Cheshire a more dangerous environment, although he doubted General Haverford and his officers would bother to play war with civilian insurgents. Flattening the entire town without damaging the road network would have been straightforward, if the town couldn't be preserved intact. A few dozen booby traps would have made taking and holding the town much harder.

"We'll just have to keep reminding them of it," he said. He glanced at his terminal, then nodded to himself. Follow-up units were already advancing into Cheshire. It wouldn't be long before they started the advance to the next target. "And make sure they don't get overconfident by the time we slip under the shield."

————

"On your feet," a voice barked.

Lily sighed, then struggled to stand upright. Her hands were numb; she had a nasty feeling that her hands would never recover, even if her bonds were removed at once. The guards kept a sharp eye on the captives, their weapons following their every move. She glanced around, taking one last look at her former home, as the captives were ordered to start walking up the northern road. It was clear they were on their way to a camp.

She swallowed hard as she saw the next pile of bodies. A pair of earth-moving machines were digging a giant pit in the ground, while soldiers piled up bodies nearby. It was a mass grave, she realised in horror; they were planning to dump the bodies into the pit and cover them up, without bothering with any funeral rites. She wanted to protest, but what was the point? One of the prisoners had gotten lippy with a guard and received a rifle butt in the face for his trouble. She would just have to hope that God would accept the souls of the dead, even if they weren't given a proper funeral.

Of course He will, she told herself. *And we can remember them too.*

A handful of soldiers whistled at the young women as they were marched past. Lily forced herself to stand upright and glare at them, despite feeling vulnerable. The soldiers seemed amused by her defiance and waved, cheerfully, as she kept walking. Beside them, the guards kept easy pace. She couldn't help wondering if the guards thought their bound captives were really dangerous…

Gritting her teeth, she marched onwards to an uncertain future.

CHAPTER

TWENTY-TWO

This ease led to a whole host of bad practices. Looting was uncommon (the rebels very rarely had anything to loot) but the Kshatriyas frequently engaged in rape and other atrocities. Military discipline, in fact, was so poor that lower-caste workers who supported the military were often killed or raped, purely for fun.

- Professor Leo Caesius. The Role of Randomness In War.

"They're not slowing down," Danielle commented.

Ed nodded, shortly. A week of skirmishing had bled the Wolves, but it hadn't cost them dearly enough to slow them down. Indeed, their tactic of turning colonial dumpsters into drop ships had solved most of their logistics problems in one fell swoop. He'd missed the implications of the dumpsters, when he'd first realised that they could be captured; in hindsight, it had been a blunder of dangerous proportions.

"They're brushing along the edge of the shield, without actually entering territory covered from orbital strikes," he said. "It won't last."

Danielle glanced at him. "Are you sure?"

"They can't hold the siege indefinitely," Ed said. "The only way to actually *beat* us is to advance on the ground."

He shook his head, slowly. The figures were unreliable, but he was fairly sure the main thrust of the advance would begin within a week, perhaps sooner. Using the dumpsters had probably caused some problems at the other end, yet they wouldn't be anything the logistics officers couldn't handle. He would be astonished if they took longer than two weeks before beginning their advance. They had to know that he'd already had far too long to prepare for them on the ground.

But not in towns and villages unprotected by the shield, he thought. Stealth drones had made it clear that the Wolves were taking prisoners, evacuating the survivors to camps near the FOB. He had no idea what was happening to them there - no drone had survived long enough to send back pictures - but he doubted it was anything pleasant. *They barely slowed the enemy for more than a few hours.*

"And in the meantime they're tearing the land apart," Danielle said. "Countless lives are being destroyed."

Ed bit down the urge to remind her, sharply, that he'd strongly advised her to order a general evacuation. Thousands *had* left the land, of course, but thousands more had stayed where they were, either to fight or in the simple belief that the war wouldn't touch them. But they'd been wrong. Even clear non-combatants were being rounded up and sent to the camps. The planet would have one hell of a mess to clear up, afterwards, but the Wolves didn't give a damn. They didn't care about the farms.

"It won't last," he reassured her, instead. "They'll be advancing against us soon enough."

He glanced at the last set of reports from the drones. The Wolves were bringing forward short-range artillery pieces, setting them up for a general bombardment. Thankfully, they didn't seem to have anything large enough to throw a shell all the way into Freedom City, but that might change if the war lasted a few years more. Using dumpsters as drop ships…what else would the bastards reinvent?

"I think we'll start seeing raiders soon enough," he said. "And then all hell will break loose."

"It's already broken loose," Danielle said. "And it won't be long before the pieces start to fall in unpredictable directions."

———

Mindy tensed, lifting her rifle into firing position, as the farm truck advanced down the road towards the checkpoint. It shouldn't have been moving at all - the government had issued strong orders that all vehicles were to be moved out of the war zone or immobilised - but it wasn't hard to put such a simple vehicle back into service. She took a breath and regretted it, instantly. The stench from the vehicle reminded her far too much of the farm she'd stayed on, the year before she'd entered basic training.

"Pooh," Stormtrooper Robins said. "What a stench!"

"Smells like one of yours," Mindy shot back. "Are you ready?"

Robins nodded, curtly. Mindy stepped forward, tapping her mike, then bellowed an order for the truck to stop. It was already too close for comfort, really. She hadn't been a soldier during the Cracker War, but she'd heard the stories of truck bombs from the old hands. A truck crammed with explosive could do *real* damage, if it went off in the right place...

She winced, remembering the other stories. There had been soldiers who'd opened fire on vehicles that simply didn't stop, only to find they'd shot innocent civilians, and soldiers who'd held their fire too long and been blown up when the bomb exploded. It was never easy, she'd been told, to make the right decision at the right time, while someone millions of miles away would be happy to tell her what she really *should* have done. The fact that those armchair soldiers had the benefit of hindsight was something they were quite willing to ignore.

The truck lurched to a halt. She breathed a sigh of relief, then walked forward, keeping her weapon in plain view. This was always the part she hated, feeling naked even though she was wearing body armour as well as her urban combat outfit. If there was anyone in the vehicle who felt like causing trouble, he'd have a free shot at her. Her platoon would riddle the truck with bullets, of course, but she'd probably be dead.

Or nursing my wounds, she thought. She'd had a bullet fired into her armour during training and it had felt like a punch in the gut. *That would be very bad.*

The door opened, jerkily. "Step out of the vehicle slowly," she barked. It was important not to allow any appearance of weakness, she'd been taught. "Keep your hands where I can see them!"

She watched as a middle-aged man stumbled out of the vehicle. "Who are you?"

"I'm Godey," the man said. The accent, at least, matched the others she'd heard. "I have a number of women and children in the truck."

"They'll have to get out," Mindy ordered. She didn't dare relax. The Crackers had fought a relatively clean war, but there was no shortage of factions that would happily use women and children as human shields. Or as cover for a bomb. "Now, if you please."

Godey nodded and turned to shout a command. The rear doors opened, allowing nine women and seventeen children to spill out onto the road. They had to have been packed in like sardines, Mindy thought, or soldiers in a helicopter. She swept her eyes over them and relaxed, very slightly, as it became clear that they were genuine refugees. There had been quite a few walking into the defence lines over the last few days.

She keyed her mike. "Sergeant, this is Caesius," she said. "I've got one man, nine women and seventeen children here. Can I send them for processing?"

"Search them first," Sergeant Rackham ordered. "I'll get the escorts moving now."

Mindy closed the channel, then leaned forward. "You'll have to be searched, then you will be escorted through our lines," she said. "Please don't try to resist."

Godey hesitated. "What will happen to us?"

"I don't know," Mindy said. She had no idea what would happen to them afterwards; they'd probably be taken to the other side of the city and shipped to a refugee camp on the other side of the continent. Unless, of course, they had useful skills. "Please stand still and hold out your arms."

She searched each of the refugees quickly, then pointed them towards the checkpoint. A handful of newcomers were already standing there, ready to escort the refugees through the lines. She couldn't help feeling a twinge of guilt at the relieved expressions on their faces, as if they had finally reached safety. They didn't seem to know that the Wolves were already at the door, probing under the force shield. It wouldn't be long until they launched a full-scale thrust towards Freedom City.

"Poor bastards," she muttered, as the refugees were marched off. "Out of the frying pan and into the fire."

"Looks like it," Robins said. "I..."

He broke off as a dull roar split the air. Another truck was roaring down the road towards them, its driver holding his foot to the gas. Mindy cursed, realising that they were caught out of the blockhouse, then lifted her weapon. Robins copied her as the truck came closer, refusing to slow down. It was already too close...

She lifted her rifle and shouted a warning. The truck didn't stop. She hesitated for a long moment, then squeezed the trigger, aiming at the driver. The truck seemed to flinch, then exploded into a colossal fireball. Mindy hit the ground as pieces of debris flew over her head, careful to keep her rifle at the ready. There was no way that was anything but a bomb.

"Good shot," Robins said. He pulled himself to his feet, peering towards the remains of the truck. It was nothing more than smouldering wreckage. The first truck, far too close to the blast, had caught fire. "That driver must have had his hand on the trigger."

"Or someone set it off remotely," Mindy said. Technically, a WARCAT team should try to recover DNA samples, but she suspected it would be pointless. The blast would have scattered the driver's body to the four winds. "Either one works."

Her earpiece crackled. "Good work, Caesius," Sergeant Rackham said. "Return to the blockhouse."

Mindy nodded. "On the way," she said. She looked up at Robins. "What was the point?"

Robins shrugged.

"If they'd gotten a bit closer, they could have done us some serious harm," Sergeant Rackham said, when they reached the blockhouse. "And even by detonating where they did, they make us jumpy. Bastards."

"Yeah," Robins agreed. "The next truck we blow up might be crammed with innocent children."

Mindy shuddered.

———

"They're genuine, as far as we can tell," Sergeant Rackham said. "But we're keeping a sharp eye on them until we get their sorry asses onto a boat."

Emmanuel Alves nodded. He hadn't really expected much from the latest tour of the defence lines - solid walls of defences, solid soldiers who were solidly confident they could hold the Wolves back indefinitely - yet he had to admit that it had produced *something* worth recording. Avalon had never developed Earth's perverted taste for blood sports - he recalled some of the exported programs with a shudder - but live footage showing their men at war would be warmly welcomed. The population needed to feel that their soldiers were fighting for the right side.

And that Admiral Singh's next target might be Avalon itself, Emmanuel thought. *There aren't that many more targets worth occupying.*

He recorded the refugees as they were loaded into a truck, their faces torn between relief and fear. The destroyed truck might be all they had left, if they had fled in the wake of the landings. It was unlikely they had much cash with them, if any. Corinthian had never been a cashless society, unlike some of the odder worlds nearer Earth, but most people kept their money in the bank. And the banks had been closed when the enemy fleet entered the system.

Poor bastards, he thought. *They have nothing but the clothes on their backs.*

"It will be on the next courier to Avalon," he said, slowly. "Shall we go look at the trenches?"

Lieutenant Angel Patterson - his escort and minder - looked worried. Emmanuel barely managed to keep himself from rolling his eyes at her. After Jasmine - and Mindy and a number of other young women who wore military uniform - Angel was a joke. She was tall, blonde and busty enough that he had a nasty feeling he knew *precisely* how she'd gotten her promotion. Her uniform should have been tailored to hide her oversized breasts as much as possible, but instead it was tight around her chest and hips. She carried no weapon, which was something of a relief. He'd fired enough guns himself to suspect that the safest person in the room would be the person she was trying to hit.

"The trenches are unsafe," she said, finally. She threw a concerned look at Sergeant Rackham's retreating back. "We should return to the city…"

"I have clearance to go everywhere," Emmanuel said. It was true enough. "But you can stay with the car, if you like."

Angel hesitated, then led the way towards the nearest trench. Emmanuel couldn't help noticing the very unmilitary way she swung her hips. Whoever had promoted her hadn't done her any favours at all. On Avalon, she would be summarily dismissed from the service; here, without such a strong military tradition, it was quite likely she'd simply be ignored, if she tried to give orders. About the only thing he could say in her favour was that she wasn't *trying* to issue orders.

Jasmine would fall over laughing, he thought as he followed her. *And then tell her to get that uniform off before she disgraced it any further.*

He smiled at the thought, then stepped into the trench. The early earthworks had been little more than holes in the ground, but six weeks of effort had created a network of bunkers, heavy weapons and underground tunnels that would make it immensely costly for anyone who tried to break into the city. Hundreds of armed soldiers were manning the defences, checking their weapons and preparing for the onslaught. Emmanuel couldn't help wondering, as he inspected one particular fortification, if Angel realised she was actually standing far too close to him. It wasn't seductive, he thought; she wanted *protection*. He rolled his eyes at the thought and waved to a lieutenant who was supervising proceedings. The lieutenant looked as though he'd sooner have his teeth pulled out than talk to a reporter, but he didn't say anything out loud.

Too busy staring at Angel, he thought, wryly.

"A great deal of effort has gone into the network," he said, instead. "Do you think it can hold?"

"There's no such thing as an impregnable defence," the lieutenant said. He didn't give his name, something Emmanuel had found depressingly common in his career. The only soldiers who willingly gave their names to reporters were their minders. "However, we are confident that we can seal off a breach and then crush the attackers before they can withdraw."

Emmanuel frowned. "Even a charge led by Landsharks?"

"They are not indestructible," the lieutenant said. "The tanks are tough, but even their armour can be broken with the right weapons. And if they charge too fast, they will be cut off from their infantry and smashed. We have heavy weapons to the rear to hammer their forces if they try anything so foolish."

Emmanuel frowned. "Can you still fire shells under the shield?"

"Of course," the lieutenant said. "But if they hit the shield itself they detonate."

"Of course," Emmanuel echoed.

He walked up and down the fortification, silently noting all the innovations that the defenders had worked into the system to make the attackers miserable. They'd think they'd cleared one fortification, he thought, and then discover enemy forces popping up in their rear. It would force them to break off their advance and clear the rear, again. And, judging from the sheer amount of concrete - and hullmetal - worked into the fortifications, no amount of enemy shelling would be enough to shatter them. The Wolves would have to clear them, inch by bloody inch. It would cost them dearly.

"It's time to go," Angel said. "You have a dinner tonight with General Scott."

Emmanuel groaned, inwardly. General Scott was *old*, a man who had somehow survived Admiral Singh's reign without being purged or forced into her service. He'd had a glance at the man's record, only to discover that General Scott had spent most of his career in logistics, rather than on the front lines. Admiral Singh had probably considered him neither a potential enemy nor someone who could be useful. Given that he was so boring that Emmanuel suspected his voice could be adapted for use as a weapon, he wasn't too surprised.

"I suppose," he said. General Scott was honestly concerned about his troops, but there was little else positive about him. And he fussed over them too much to understand that their lives were always in danger. "Shall we go?"

Angel relaxed a little as soon as they were outside, walking towards the car. Emmanuel glanced at her, then turned to look northwards towards the advancing enemy. He'd heard bangs and cracks to the north earlier, when he'd first arrived, but now he couldn't hear a sound. And yet, he knew the Wolves were lurking somewhere out of sight, readying their offensive...

"After General Scott's dinner," Angel said, "where do you want to go?"

Emmanuel shrugged. "My room," he said, flatly. "I need to get some sleep before the big offensive begins."

Angel gave him a sidelong look. "Alone?"

"My girlfriend is on the front lines," Emmanuel said. He had to fight to keep the smile off his face at her shocked reaction. Clearly, she hadn't expected *that.* "So yes, alone."

She didn't say anything else as they climbed into the car and started to drive, heading to the centre of the city. Emmanuel looked from side to side, shaking his head at all the buildings that had been turned into fortresses. The Wolves might think that cracking the defensive line would allow them access, but they were in for a very nasty surprise...

Angel cleared her throat. "You have a girlfriend in uniform?"

"Yes," Emmanuel said, flatly. He didn't understand Angel - the more he thought about it, the more he thought there was something wrong with her - but he had no intention of allowing himself to be seduced. "I do."

CHAPTER
TWENTY-THREE

To be fair to the Kshatriyas, they were good at putting on parades. They looked very good when they were marching around the city, wearing their fancy uniforms and showing off their precision steps. But they received almost no training in actual fighting, which meant that their first encounter with a professional force was almost always their last.

- Professor Leo Caesius. The Role of Randomness In War.

It was very quiet on the bridge.

Mandy watched the display, feeling a flicker of amusement as *Defiant* drew closer to her target. There was no way sound could pass through a vacuum, yet the crew spoke in whispers, as if they feared the enemy could hear every word they said. The grim awareness that they were far too close to a pair of enemy starships pervaded the compartment, reminding her that one mistake might prove fatal. In theory, the Wolves shouldn't have a hope of peeking through an enhanced cloaking device, but no one knew for sure.

She studied the target thoughtfully, silently cursing Admiral Singh - or one of her officers - under her breath. The industrial node was basic, so basic that it barely deserved the title. It had certainly passed largely unnoticed when the planners had contemplated what needed to be removed from the system and what needed to be rigged to blow, in the event of the Commonwealth losing the battle. And yet, its mere presence had given Admiral Singh an advantage. Time would tell if it was a *decisive* advantage.

We should have thought of colony dumpsters, she told herself, tartly. Avalon's dumpsters had only been broken down completely two years ago, even though the planet had been settled for over a century. She'd seen them herself, when she'd landed on the planet for the first time, but she hadn't given any thought to the implications. No one had. *But someone on the other side beat us to it.*

"Get me a solid lock on the enemy ships," she ordered, glancing at the sensor officer. "Do we have a tactical breakdown yet?"

"No, Captain," the tactical officer stated. "There's no hint of how the ships have been modified, *if* they've been modified."

Mandy scowled. The Imperial Navy had designed its starships on a modular pattern, primarily to make repairs nothing more than removing a damaged component and slotting in a new one. But it also made it impossible to be *certain* what she was facing. The destroyer and light cruiser Admiral Singh had assigned to protect the industrial node might carry a standard weapons load, in which case she could kick their asses without serious problems, or they might be crammed with new and better weapons. There was no way to be sure without actually engaging the enemy, at which point she would be committed.

And if we fail to take out the industrial node, they'll move more ships to defend it, she thought, grimly. Indeed, she was surprised the Wolves hadn't moved the node to Corinthian to make it easier to defend, although she supposed there was a very real risk of taking fire from the ground. *They'll know what we know.*

She contemplated the tactical position for a long moment. If she fired on the node, both enemy ships would have a free shot at her hull; if she engaged both ships, they might overwhelm *Defiant* before she could take them out and destroy the node. In hindsight, she should have brought additional ships, but she knew she dare didn't reveal just how many starships were lurking near Corinthian. A raider or two wouldn't trigger any significant alarms - the Commonwealth Navy had been raiding behind enemy lines ever since the war began - but an entire squadron would raise hackles. Admiral Singh would start to wonder if she was being played.

"Lock weapons on the cruiser," she ordered. Unless the Wolves had come up with something she'd never heard of, which she had to admit was a valid possibility, the cruiser would be the most dangerous opponent. "Prepare to fire."

"Weapons locked, Captain," the tactical officer said.

"Fire," Mandy snapped.

The enemy ship was caught by surprise, she noted as the barrage of missiles roared towards its target, but there was nothing wrong with her reaction time. Her CO swung the ship around, launching decoys and engaging with point defence even as he plunged *towards* the missile swarm. A civilian would have been horrified, but it actually gave him the best chance of surviving the barrage and getting his own hits in before it was too late. His companion reacted too, adding her point defence to the cruiser's even as her sensors sought out *Defiant* and locked on. No cloaking device could hide a ship that was firing missiles.

"Shield raised," the tactical officer said. Both enemy ships opened fire, launching their missiles as fast as they could. "Impact in thirty seconds…"

Mandy sucked in her breath as the enemy cruiser fought for survival, feeling an odd mix of emotions. The cruiser was the enemy; she had to be destroyed. And yet, she couldn't help feeling a kinship too with the enemy spacers. They were doomed, yet they fought hard to strike back and survive for a few seconds more. And they nearly made it, evading two-thirds of the missiles she'd fired. The remainder slammed into their hull, blowing the cruiser into an expanding wave of debris. She glanced at the display, hoping to see distress signals from lifepods, but it looked very much as though the enemy hadn't had time to abandon ship before it was too late.

"The destroyer is picking up speed," the tactical officer reported, as enemy missiles started to slam into *Defiant's* shield. They hadn't had time to reprogram them to evade the shield, even though it was a standard tactic by now. Any hopes that force shields would make the Commonwealth Navy invincible had faded quickly, after the first battles. "She's trying to ram!"

"Evasive action, continue firing," Mandy ordered. The destroyer didn't have any other option, not now her consort had been destroyed. Ramming *Defiant* would destroy both ships, an exchange that would be solidly in their favour. "Take the bastard out!"

She tensed as the enemy destroyer came closer, before staggering to one side as a direct hit shattered its left drive node. Mandy allowed herself a flicker of relief as the enemy ship spun out of control, leaking atmosphere from a dozen gashes in her hull. Her main power had either failed or been shut down, according to the sensors. She no longer posed any real threat.

And it will take years to repair her, she thought. Unless she was very wrong - and she had a great deal of experience with ships that had been mistreated or badly damaged - it would be cheaper to scrap the hulk and build a whole new ship. *There's no point in finishing the job.*

"Let her go," she ordered. If there were any crew left on the destroyer, they'd be trying to evacuate, not continue the fight. Admiral Singh wouldn't blame them for being so badly outmatched, would she? "Raise the node. Inform them that they have five minutes to board the lifeboat and evacuate."

"Aye, Captain," the communications officer said.

Mandy settled back in her chair, keeping a wary eye on the display. A holographic sphere was already expanding out at the speed of light, showing just how far any emergency message from the enemy ships had reached. It wouldn't be long before Admiral Singh knew the node had come under attack and dispatched reinforcements, although Mandy was sure she would have completed her grisly task and vanished back into cloak before more enemy ships arrived. But it was quite possible that enemy reinforcements were closer than she expected.

And if they do show up ahead of time, she thought, *I will have to blow the node and retreat at once, even if it means slaughtering the workers.*

She gritted her teeth at the thought. The RockRats who ran the node had refused to evacuate, when the warning had been issued, but that didn't mean they should be sentenced to death. She'd trained with RockRats, worked with them...there should have been no real danger, not when their technology was so primitive. And yet, Admiral Singh had found a way to put it to use. The more she thought about it, the more it worried her. What *else* had been overlooked?

"They're launching the lifeboat now, Captain," the tactical officer said. He sounded amused. "It's a primitive piece of crap."

Mandy shrugged. "At least they can repair it easily," she said. She understood their logic, but it made no sense in a war zone. "A reaction drive is very simple compared to anything *we* have."

She smiled at the thought. RockRats and planet-bound agrarian settlers had quite a lot in common, although both sides would have loudly objected to the comparison. They never used anything more complex than strictly necessary. The lifeboat slowly making its way out of the asteroid belonged to an era before drive fields and phase drives, before hullmetal and force shields. A laser beam could slide through her hull as easily as a hot knife through butter.

"They'd better hope Admiral Singh is in a forgiving mood, Captain," the XO said. "That ship isn't going to get very far before enemy ships arrive."

"No, it isn't," Mandy agreed. "Communications, offer to take them onboard."

"Aye, Captain," the communications officer said.

Mandy nodded, slowly. The RockRats might just abandon their principles long enough to board *Defiant*, if they realised the alternative. Or Admiral Singh's minders - she assumed they were on the lifeboat too - would force the issue. *They* might have very good reason to want to go into a brig, rather than be picked up by enemy ships. *Someone* would have to take the blame for the whole affair.

And if Admiral Singh starts blaming her crews for something well beyond their control, she thought, *it will make them discontented and fearful. And that might just lead to a mutiny.*

Shaking her head, she waited to see what would happen.

———

It was bad news, of course.

Rani had known it from the moment the young ensign had passed through her bodyguards and entered her office on *Orion*. The young man - he looked too young to shave, too young to be doing anything more serious than playing games and flirting with girls - had been nervous, so nervous he'd almost forgotten to salute. Rani had been amused, although she'd hidden it well. She didn't have a habit of shooting the messenger.

She took the datapad and read the report quickly, cursing under her breath. The report lacked detail - she made a mental note to have a few words with the writer - but the gist of it was clear. There would be no more dumpsters for her forces. It wasn't a major headache - she'd produced enough in the last week to get the remainder of her army down to the surface - yet it was a hassle. She'd need to revert back to shuttles to get the next wave of troops down.

Unless we produce more dumpsters and have them shipped to Corinthian, she thought. But that would be another problem. Dumpsters weren't *designed* to be dismantled and put back together, not once they'd been forged. Weakening the layers of hullmetal that allowed them to pass through the atmosphere without harm risked disaster. *We'll need a colony support vessel to make the landing.*

It was a bitter thought. She hadn't secured one - as far as she knew, there were none within Wolfbane's territory - and constructing such a ship would take years. The Empire had used them to settle entire worlds, transporting everything the colonists might need for the first five years in one massive vessel. Paired with a colonist-carrier, it could found a new colony in a single voyage. If there were any left along the Rim, there was a good chance that the Commonwealth had already secured them.

She mulled it over for a long moment, using the issue to distract herself from her other problems. Perhaps the huge vessels the Empire had used could be slimmed down. Or phase drives could be attached to the dumpsters themselves, then removed before the dumpsters began the final part of their journey. She wrote a handful of queries for her designers, cursing their corporate masters under her breath. In theory, it should take less than six months to produce something as simple as a freighter, but in practice the corporations spun it out to nearly two years. No *wonder* there was such a shortage of shipping when it took so long to replenish the merchant marine!

They'll give me a shot at their necks sooner or later, she told herself, firmly. *Or I can relax the anti-competition rules and see what happens.*

She shook her head curtly, then returned her attention to the real problem. Her forces were brushing against the force shield, making their way towards the capital city. She was damned if she was going to call it *Freedom* City. And yet, matters were proceeding far slower than she would have liked. What was so bloody difficult about crossing eighty kilometres?

It wasn't as though she was asking her officers to sail around the world or travel from one star system to another! The longer the fleet remained tied down at Corinthian, the greater the chance of the enemy inflicting some major damage elsewhere.

The display in front of her made it clear that her forces were practically *inching* forward, even though the resistance was very limited. A handful of missile attacks, a couple of destroyed bridges...it was hardly enough to slow an entire army! And half the region had been evacuated ahead of time. She didn't give a damn about civilian casualties, at least outside the city itself, but there was hardly any real resistance. The remaining civilians could stay in POW camps until the war was over.

She glanced back at the report. No more dumpsters. No more shortcuts to getting forces down to the surface. She'd sent messages back to Thule and Wolfbane, ordering the immediate dispatch of additional ground forces - and supplies that could not easily be replenished - but it would be at least six weeks before anything arrived. And withdrawing more heavy equipment from Thule would weaken her grip on *that* world...

Impatiently, she keyed her console. "Get me a direct link to General Haverford."

"Yes, Admiral," the communications officer said. She sounded scared, much to Rani's irritation. Communications officers knew what was going on ahead of everyone else, even if it was meant to be classified. She wasn't about to shoot people for bringing her bad news...or for merely being there when she was in a vile mood. "I'll raise him now."

It was nearly ten minutes before Haverford's face popped up in front of her, by which time Rani's temper had risen to boiling point. He looked tired - it was midnight on the planet below, she recalled with a flicker of guilt - but it wasn't as if he was on the front lines. No, he was in the FOB, safe and secure in the rear. The enemy hadn't even been able to fire a mortar round or two into the FOB, let alone hit it with something lethal.

"General," she said, curtly. "The industrial node is gone."

Haverford winced. "They took it out?"

"Correct," Rani said. The wretched report might not have given many details, but she could guess. A single nuclear warhead would be more than enough to blow the asteroid into dust or melt the equipment to slag. No one had any inhibitions about using nukes in space too, unlike planetary surfaces. "There will be no more dumpsters for at least two months - and that's assuming we can find a way to get them here."

"Understood," Haverford said. "We may be able to put together smaller dumpsters in the MEUs."

"It's a possibility," Rani said. "But they also need to keep pace with your demands for ammunition."

She eyed him for a long moment. "Are you sure you're not overstating your requirements?"

Haverford looked back at her evenly. "I would far sooner have too much ammunition than too little," he said. "Many of our early battles on Thule made it clear that pre-war estimates of just how much ammunition we would use were hopelessly inaccurate. If we hadn't been able to call down KEW strikes at will, Admiral, we would have lost hundreds of outposts when the ammunition ran out."

He paused. "And we're not talking about an ongoing insurgency here," he added, after a moment. "We're talking about a thrust directly into a line of defences, *without* KEWs."

Rani nodded in irritation. That damned shield! If it didn't exist, the battle would have been over within an hour. But it did exist, constantly reminding her that the Commonwealth was far more innovative than Wolfbane. It was just another reason to get on with the war before it was too late, before they were too far behind to catch up. Who knew what *else* might be being invented in the other successor states?

"Then you are to take the offensive as soon as possible," she ordered, flatly. "No more delays, General. I want that city taken!"

"We can try," Haverford said. "But Admiral, no one has done anything on this scale for hundreds of years."

"Then it's high time we remembered how to do it," Rani snapped. "You have your orders, General."

She tapped a switch, closing the channel before he could raise any more pettifogging objections. The city *would* be taken - and, if they were lucky, the shield generator would be **taken** intact. And then the battle would be over…

"And then I can strike at Avalon itself," she muttered. "And put an end to this whole damned war."

CHAPTER
TWENTY-FOUR

The officers, in fact, were often worse than the men. Having acquired their positions through birth, rather than merit, they were a mixed bag. Some were good officers, by their standards; others were cowardly autocrats who believed their birth made them superior to their soldiers.

- Professor Leo Caesius. The Role of Randomness In War.

General Mark Haverford prided himself on being a calm and composed man, under all circumstances. But he found it hard to resist the temptation to swear loudly as Admiral Singh's face vanished from the display. Didn't she realise just how hard it was advancing forward, now his forces were under the shield? Of course she didn't! She only cared about capturing the city and to hell with however many good men died in the fighting.

He glared at the display, then turned his attention to the map. The advance had slowed, at least in part, because the locals were constantly setting traps and sniping at his forces, as well as destroying bridges or rigging them to collapse when his men tried to cross them. It wasn't costing him much, in material terms, but it *was* costing him time. Merely pausing long enough to sweep the countryside or put a new bridge together delayed the advance, giving the enemy time to emplace the *next* set of traps. His men were holding together better than he'd expected, given the constant threat and frustration, but there had already been a handful of nasty incidents. There were just too many men used to having their way cleared by orbital strikes in his force,

And she wants us to move faster, he thought. *I don't know how!*

He ground his teeth in frustration. The outer edge of the defence line was growing closer, a point where he would have to commit himself to a major thrust right into the teeth of enemy fire. Training and doctrine called for the defences to be outflanked, but there was no *way* to outflank them. The damned city was *surrounded* by heavy defences. He'd looked at ways to try to get a force up the river, yet every last scenario he ran past the planning staff ended in disaster. There was just no shortcut to victory, no way to drop commandos into the enemy base or break their morale in a single blow. It was going to be a long hard slog through the network of bunkers and fortifications, a slog that would be immensely costly. He shuddered to think of just how many men would be killed or wounded in the coming battle.

But he had his orders. There was very little wriggle room.

He tapped his console, summoning Colonel Ferguson. If *he'd* been woken at midnight - clearly, the Admiral hadn't bothered to check a chronometer before placing the call - it was time to spread the misery. He pasted a calm expression on his face as the younger man entered the compartment, reminding himself sternly that he couldn't trust *anyone* completely, not when Governor Brown had seeded commissioners and spies throughout the military. It said something about the bastards, he felt, that most of them had promptly switched their allegiance to Admiral Singh when she'd taken control.

"General," Ferguson said. He managed to look dapper, despite having only a couple of hours sleep since his return from the front. "You called for me?"

"We are to thrust the offensive forward as fast as possible," Mark said. He knew Ferguson would see the problems, but they didn't dare discuss the matter openly. Who knew who might be listening? "Start putting Plan Beta into operation, Colonel. I want advance units ready to make the thrust within two days."

Ferguson frowned. "Plan Beta?"

"We don't have the forces in place to launch Plan Alpha," Mark said, curtly. Ferguson was just covering his ass, he was sure. "Besides, Beta also gives us a much better option for cutting our losses and falling back, if the first stages fail."

He scowled as he turned back to the console. Losing the dumpsters would *hurt* in the long run, although his logistics officers were working hard to sort out the colossal pile of supplies that had been dropped near the FOB. Plan Alpha was pretty much ideal - insofar as anything was ideal, given the limited room for manoeuvre - but it would take at least another two weeks to get everything in place for a broad offensive. They'd have to gamble on breaking through at the point of contact, then clearing the enemy defences before thrusting forward into the city.

"I believe that a number of regiments have been recalled for Intercourse and Intoxication," Ferguson said. "They'll have to be rushed back to the front."

Mark nodded without taking his eyes off the display. Men weren't machines, he knew from bitter experience; hell, even *machines* needed constant maintenance and replenishment to keep them going. He'd allowed five regiments who'd distinguished themselves in battle to fall back long enough to visit the FOB's new facilities, *after* squashing complaints from a whole number of REMFs who hated the thought of seeing muddy soldiers in muddy combat uniforms waiting in line outside the brothels. Sending a handful of the loudest whiners to the front had done wonders for *his* morale, even if it hadn't done anything for theirs.

"Move them back," he ordered, quietly. He turned his head to look at the younger man, meeting his eyes. "I want the offensive to kick off in two days from now."

"Yes, sir," Ferguson said.

He saluted, then left the compartment. Mark scowled at his retreating back before turning his attention back to the display. A handful of raids - and a pair of drones, before they were shot down - had told him things he didn't want to know about the enemy defences. They were robust, erected by experts who knew precisely how best to fuck up a major armoured and infantry assault. Landsharks were the most powerful tanks in human history, as far as he knew, and yet even they would bog down in the defence lines. Clearing the way into the city would require a full-scale assault, which would be immensely costly...

And if we don't take the city, he thought numbly, *I don't know what the Admiral will do.*

———

"They're picking up the pace," Jasmine noted. Stewart, Buckley and herself hid under camouflage netting, watching as an enemy convoy made its way down towards the front lines. The remainder of the platoon lurked nearby, awaiting their cue. "That's nineteen lorries and a quartet of escorts."

"Got it on tape," Buckley said. He returned the portable sensor to his belt and reached for his rifle. "I'm sure the Colonel will be glad to see it."

"I'm not," Stewart said. "How many men can you shove into a truck like that?"

"Thirty, if you cram them in really tight," Jasmine said. The enemy convoy slowly faded into the distance, a pair of helicopters flying overhead as they headed north, back towards the nearest enemy airbase. "Maybe more, if you forced them to lie down."

"Blake was always talking about the day he managed to cram ten marines into a shuttle," Buckley said, softly. "He said the answer was *ten*."

Jasmine knew the punchline, but played along anyway. "You can fit more than ten marines into a shuttle."

"Yes, but they didn't have any more marines," Buckley said. "So they had to make up the difference with some of the locals..."

"And then the MPs came along to bitch about you stinking up the shuttle," Stewart said, dryly. "I recall the rest of the story."

"There's another convoy coming," Jasmine said, sharply. "Grab your weapons."

"Finally," Buckley said. "I thought we were going to be lying here all day!"

Jasmine ignored him as she studied the oncoming convoy. It was larger, thirty trucks escorted by six AFVs. One of the trucks was uncovered, allowing her to see a number of soldiers sitting in neat rows. They were laughing and joking, from what she could see, although she suspected there was a worried edge to it. The easy part of the war was now over; they knew as well as she did. Their next step would be to attack the defence lines directly.

"They're sending heavy weapons too," Stewart muttered. "You want to hit them instead?"

"No," Jasmine muttered back. Four of the trucks were towing artillery pieces - they looked like standard-issue howitzers - but she was more interested in the soldiers. They were the ones who would be using the weapons, after all. "Put a missile into the lead AFV, then target the trucks."

"Understood," Stewart said.

"Pass the word," Jasmine ordered. "We hit them hard, then fall back."

She sucked in her breath as the enemy convoy came closer. The AFVs were a problem, even though they were following the road rather than travelling cross-country. Their heavy machine guns could make mincemeat of her position, even if their sensors couldn't track the marines; they could certainly call in helicopters, if necessary, to provide covering fire. She eyed the visible soldiers for a long moment, then silently calculated the best time to hit the convoy. Too close and they might be caught if - when - the enemy counterattacked; too far and the enemy wouldn't be badly hurt. It was just a matter of timing...

"Fire," she snapped.

Stewart launched the antitank missile, aimed directly at the first AFV. Its guns began to traverse with striking speed, but there was no hope of stopping the missile before it slammed into the vehicle's side, punched through the armour and exploded inside. The crew had no chance to escape before the fireball blew their vehicle aside. Jasmine barely noticed, too busy hosing down the trucks with machine gun fire. The other AFVs were turning, their weapons already blazing fire; one was struck by another missile and destroyed, a second managed to evade a third missile through skill and luck.

"Go," she ordered, as bullets started to crack through the air above them. She thought she could hear a helicopter in the distance. "I think we've outstayed our welcome."

Ryan had been half-asleep when the attack began, dreaming of a girl he'd met in the officer's brothel who had been more than just a quick lay. She'd been friendly and chatty and even though he knew it was all an act, he couldn't help being drawn to it. The remembrance that there was more to life than long hours of boredom, punctuated with moments of sheer terror, was worth any price. Indeed, he had already made plans to see her during his next period of leave…

And then the truck ground to a halt as explosions shook the vehicle and bullets started cracking through the canopy.

"Get out," he barked, jumping to his feet and shoving the door open. His men were sitting ducks as long as they were in the truck; he snatched up his rifle, dived out of the door and hastily glanced around for cover. "Get out now!"

He cursed as he hit the ground, crawling away from the truck before it was too late. There was damn-all in sight, save for a hillside that seemed to have been turned into a firing position. An AFV was burning brightly, flames billowing up towards the sky; he hoped, desperately, that the ammunition wouldn't start cooking off before he and his men were well away from the vehicle. Two more were driving towards the hillside, their guns blazing as they swept the area with fire. Ryan rather doubted they were hitting anything - it certainly didn't look as if they were doing more than firing at random - but at least it would give the troops time to get organised. He glanced towards the lead truck and swore when he realised that it had been badly riddled with bullets. It was increasingly unlikely that Captain Casey, the convoy commander, had survived.

Bastards must have targeted him deliberately, Ryan thought. The entire convoy had ground to a halt, the surviving drivers concentrating on evacuating their vehicles rather than moving onwards. But then, who knew *what* lay ahead of them? This whole area was supposed to be *safe*! *Now what*?

Training took over. "Form up on me," he bellowed. Lieutenant Tammy was nowhere in sight, either dead or wounded. That made *him* the senior surviving officer, as far as he could tell. No one had ever won a medal by waiting for the official confirmation that he was in charge before taking action. "Sergeant Rackham, take the second assault squad. I'll take the first!"

His eyes swept over the soldiers as they were hastily organised into two groups. A handful hadn't thought to grab their weapons before escaping the trucks; they'd have to stay behind, hoping desperately that the enemy hadn't planned anything more elaborate than a quick ambush. If they had, dozens of soldiers were probably about to die. He looked towards the AFVs as another explosion echoed out over the hillside and cursed, again, as one of them rolled over an emplaced mine and was flipped over by the blast. The crew would be safe, he was sure, but the vehicle itself would be out of action until it could be repaired.

"Sergeant, take the right fork," he ordered. He could see two helicopters on the way, but he didn't dare delay any longer. "I'll take the left - go!"

He led his squad forward, feeling sweat prickling down his back as they advanced past the ruined AFV. They'd learned to be careful when giving chase in the last few days. The enemy seemed to have an unlimited supply of mines and diabolical ingenuity when it came to placing them in awkward positions. He'd seen too many men carried off, their legs missing, after they put their foot down on top of a mine. The damnable bastards were trying to wound his soldiers, rather than kill them outright. Rumour had it that hospital beds were already overflowing back at the FOB.

Should just start conscripting the local civilians to help, he thought. The helicopters swooped overhead, heading towards where the enemies had to be. *They'll have good reasons to assist...*

He swore as a missile lanced up from the ground, striking one of the helicopters and blowing it into flaming debris which showered down on the ground. The other helicopter opened fire, strafing the enemy position with missiles and machine gun fire. Ryan held up a hand, calling a halt, then cursed as one of his soldiers toppled to the ground. There was a sniper, perhaps more than one, lurking nearby. He realised his own mistake a second later and jumped forward, hastily shifting position. Giving orders openly marked him as an officer - and officers were invariably targeted by snipers.

The force advanced forward, slowly, towards the flaming remains of an enemy position. Ryan hadn't expected much, but there was nothing to be seen but shattered trees and debris. If there had been any enemy troops caught within the bombardment, there was nothing left of them. It wasn't encouraging. He briefly considered probing further, then dismissed the thought. There was too much risk of running into another ambush - or a MANPAD.

"Sir," Sergeant Rask said. "I picked up a message from FOB Three. They're dispatching a force to escort us the rest of the way."

"Understood," Ryan said. "The sooner they get here, the better."

He took one last look at the mangled remains of dozens of trees, then turned and led the way back to the convoy. The enemy had struck them a blow and - probably - escaped. He tried to tell himself that they'd hit an enemy soldier or two, but he couldn't even begin to convince himself. There was just no way to be sure.

And this will delay us still further, he thought, darkly. *Damn it.*

————

"I'm sorry," Stewart said. "He's gone."

Jasmine winced. Rifleman Gavin Jalil had been a good man, but he'd taken four bullets to the back during the escape and no one, not even a marine, could survive such trauma. His implants had kept him alive for a short period - and done what they could to make his final moments more comfortable - but now he was dead. She couldn't help wondering if his armour had actually made matters worse, before realising it hardly mattered. There had been far too much trauma.

"Fuck it," she said. "Just...fuck it!"

She fought down a surge of bitter grief and anger. Losing someone - anyone - was never easy, but Jalil was a *marine*. How many of the original Stalkers were still alive? Eighty-four marines had been exiled to Avalon; fifty-six, by her count, were still on active duty. Jalil was completely irreplaceable until they re-established the Slaughterhouse or set up something along the same lines.

"Put him in the bag," she said. She wanted to take his body back to the city, then back to Avalon, but she knew it was impossible. "We'll bury him nearby and come back for him afterwards."

She bent down and removed the Rifleman's Tab - and one half of his dog tags - then nodded to Stewart. He wrapped a bag around the body while the other marines used entrenching tools to dig a foxhole-like grave. It would suffice, Jasmine told herself, as she made a careful note of its location. Jalil would be recovered after the war and given a proper burial, in line with his will.

I'm sorry, she thought, honouring her comrade with a moment of silence. Jalil had been a good man, just like everyone else who'd graduated from the Slaughterhouse. She'd liked him. And he'd had a girl on Avalon. She would never see her lover again. *You deserved better.*

In the distance, she could hear the sound of thunder.

CHAPTER
TWENTY-FIVE

Indeed, the question of just who was in command was often decisive in battle. An officer who ran, after encountering an enemy that actually fought, would often be followed by the remainder of his men. The NCOs would often be unable to rally the men, if indeed they tried. Some units barely brushed up against an enemy before disintegrating into a rabble.

- Professor Leo Caesius. The Role of Randomness In War.

"They're coming," Ed said, quietly.

Danielle gave him a sharp look. "Are you sure?"

"Unless they're posturing," Ed said. It was possible, but he rather doubted it. Time worked in their favour, not Admiral Singh's. Barring an accident with the shield, the Wolves simply *had* to take the city or keep the planet under guard indefinitely. "They're assembling too many forces in place to be doing anything, but planning an assault."

He scowled as he studied the reports. Hundreds of tanks and other vehicles, thousands of soldiers…massing in what were self-evidently jump-off positions. And, behind them, hundreds upon hundreds of guns, ranging from long-range artillery pieces to vehicle-mounted heavy mortars. He wondered, absently, just how much ammunition the Wolves had brought along, if their MEUs couldn't keep up with the demand. Firing off thousands of shells, in the certain knowledge that most of them would be intercepted before they hit their targets, would be immensely costly.

But we're ready, he told himself. *As ready as we're ever going to be.*

Danielle frowned. "How many people are going to die?"

"Too many," Ed said. "But most of them will be on their side."

"You could be wrong," Danielle pointed out.

"The conventional wisdom is that you need a three-to-one superiority at the point of contact to guarantee success," Ed said. In truth, it was impossible to be sure just how the odds were truly stacked. "In this case, the conventional wisdom is deeply insufficient. We have a very solid position; they have very little room to be clever. They'll be advancing on us over their own dead bodies."

He looked down at the map, wondering just what his counterpart was thinking. A handful of prisoners - the Wolves seemed to like using their penal battalions to probe defences - had named their ultimate superior as General Mark Haverford, but they hadn't known enough to allow Ed to locate the man's pre-Collapse file. There were dozens of men with that name listed among the millions of soldiers and spacers who'd served the Empire. Hell, he might not have been a serving soldier at all, merely someone who'd put on the uniform after the collapse and somehow worked his way up to power. It had been six years, more or less, since Wolfbane had slipped out of Earth's grasp. A great deal could have happened in that time.

"They have a lot of bodies," Danielle pointed out, dryly.

"They won't take enough ground to bury their dead," Ed said. "Not this time, anyway."

Danielle frowned. "What would *you* do? In their shoes, I mean. What would you do if you were presented with the same problem?"

Ed considered it. "Try to wear the defenders down," he said, after a moment. "But time is pressing, really. They don't have the time to grind us down without exposing themselves."

He considered it for a long moment. Just what was Singh thinking? And Haverford? It was hard to get a sense of his opponent's personality, but so far the man hadn't made many mistakes - if any. Losing a shuttle or two had to be annoying, yet he'd recovered neatly and even *benefited* from the experience. A calculating mind, perhaps; one smart enough to see opportunity and cunning enough to think outside the box. And yet, there were few options left. The Wolves had a blunt choice between attacking the city in force or pulling back and conceding a draw.

Or waiting for the shield to fail, he thought. *But can they afford to wait that long?*

———

"Everything is in place, sir," Ferguson said.

Mark glanced at the time. Local dawn was breaking over the city, but he doubted the defenders would be half-asleep. Dawn had been seen as an ideal time to attack for so long that just about every military force worthy of the name was careful not to allow someone to catch them on the hop. And, unlike a mobile force, the defenders of the city had plenty of manpower. Half of them could be asleep while the other half manned the ramparts.

We haven't done anything like this for centuries, he thought. No matter what happened, victory was going to come at a very high price. *And if we lose…*

He pushed the thought aside. Admiral Singh's patience was at an end. He hadn't been told *directly* that he was on the verge of being relieved, but he had enough experience to read it between the lines. His successor wouldn't hesitate to order the attack, piling on the infantry and tanks heedless of their losses. He couldn't allow that to happen, not after he'd worked so hard to minimise casualties. The only thing he could do was send the command.

"Contact all units," he ordered. "We will proceed as planned."

He took a long breath. "The offensive starts at 0900."

And may God have mercy on our souls, he added, silently.

———

Mindy felt a chill running through her as she peered towards the enemy positions, two kilometres from the outer edge of the defence line. The warning from higher-up had been clear, too clear; the sound of engines echoing in the dawn merely underlined the simple fact that they were about to be attacked. She checked her rifle, again and again, as the sun slowly rose higher in the sky. It was hard to escape the sense that she was about to be tested to the limit.

"The sounds are growing louder," Cornwallis said. Mindy gave him a sidelong glance. He sounded as nervous as she felt, even though he was a veteran of Thule and Piker's Peak. His experience was far greater than hers. "I think this is it!"

A flicker of flame billowed out in the distance, great tongues of fire licking up towards the sky. Mindy stared at it, confused. Had someone hit the enemy rear and destroyed their ammunition stockpiles? And then it struck her, as she heard the sounds of shells falling towards their targets. The enemy had opened fire! She glanced up, just in time to see flashes in the sky as shells were intercepted by laser stations and destroyed...

And then the ground shook as the surviving shells slammed into the fortifications. Mindy braced herself, hearing the sound of something crashing to the ground, but it looked as though the fortifications had survived intact. She glanced up at the overhang, then relaxed slightly as there was no sign of it coming down on their heads. More and more shells crashed down, the noise deafening despite the implants in her ears. She had the nasty feeling that an unprotected civilian would have been deafened within seconds, if she'd been far too close to the explosions. The noise was growing louder and louder. She gritted her teeth as she forced herself to watch for incoming threats. In the distance, she could see missiles lancing out towards the city, ducking and weaving to avoid point defence.

"They're dumb shells," someone said.

"Of course they are," Sergeant Rackham said. He didn't sound nervous at all. "The bastards just want to make us keep our heads down. They're not going to waste expensive guided shells on us."

They might, Mindy thought. If a smart warhead was lurking amongst the dumb shells launched on ballistic trajectories, it might evade detection long enough to hit one of the point defence stations. *And once they take out the point defence, they can wear the rest of us down.*

"Contact," Collins screamed. "Incoming! I say again, incoming!"

Mindy stared. A line of vehicles - a couple of Landsharks and a handful of AFVs that looked like giant bulldozers were advancing towards the fortifications, their guns already blazing madly. The tanks were firing rapidly, hurling shells into the teeth of the outer line, while the smaller vehicles were falling behind. Bullets were already pinging off their armour, slowing them down not at all…she cursed under her breath, then sighed in relief as a plasma warhead found one of the AFVs. It exploded, revealing a number of soldiers lurking behind its armour. The survivors hastily dropped to the ground as their cover was torn away, hurling grenades towards the defence line. She covered her eyes hastily as she saw the white-hot glare of a plasma grenade, followed by several more.

A missile struck one of the Landsharks, toppling the giant vehicle onto its side. The crew must have been shocked, she thought, but they kept firing until another missile came down and shattered the tank. She breathed a sigh of relief, then winced as a line of soldiers ran towards the fortifications, using the burning remains of the tank as cover. A dozen men fell, but the rest kept coming. Behind them, another wave of tanks hurtled forward, firing constantly. She heard the noise of explosions growing louder as a helicopter swooped low along the defence line, only to explode in midair. Mindy couldn't help wondering, as the remains crashed to the ground, if the crew had had the extreme ill-luck to be hit by a shell fired by their own side. There were so many shells in the air that it was possible…

"Here they come," Rackham shouted. "Fire at will!"

Cornwallis laughed. "Which of them is Will?"

"Fire, you fucking idiot," Rackham bellowed.

Mindy moved her rifle from target to target, squeezing the trigger whenever she thought she had a clean shot. The scene before her was nightmarish; hundreds of soldiers, some using the bodies of their dead comrades for cover, running towards her, shells slamming into the defences from the enemy tanks and guns. Explosions billowed up amidst the advancing hordes as the defenders returned fire, calling down shells on enemy positions. She felt a trickle running down her leg as *something* exploded far too close for comfort, but she ignored it and kept firing, switching out magazines one by one. And yet the enemy were still getting closer…

A low rumble ran through the complex. "Fall back," Rackham snapped, as dust and grit started to fall from the ceiling. "They've breached the outer layer!"

Mindy cursed, snatched up her rifle and hurried to the door as Cornwallis set the first layer of traps. Any enemy stupid enough to roll through the firing slit would get a very nasty fright - and, if he was unlucky, he'd survive the experience. Cornwallis followed her a moment later as more explosions shook the complex, although she wasn't sure what had caused them. The enemy might have hit an ammunition dump, she thought, or they might be clearing the corridors with brutal efficiency as they fought their way into the complex. There was no way to know.

The tunnel gaped open in front of her and she practically dived into it, following the rest of her platoon as they moved to the next defensive position. She shuddered as the ground shook, time and time again, but the tunnel was solidly-constructed. And yet, they hadn't really anticipated so many dumb shells being hurled into the teeth of their defences. The threat just hadn't registered.

But we're hurting them badly, she told herself. *They have no choice, but to keep coming into the teeth of our fire.*

———

Ryan crawled towards the enemy position, forcing himself to keep moving despite roiling waves of fear in his heart. The enemy fortification was nothing more than an oversized blockhouse, yet it was terrifyingly effective at sweeping all the approach routes with machine guns and missile fire. He'd watched in horror as five Landsharks were killed in quick succession, the final tank barely managing to make it to the line before being turned into a blackened hulk. The never-ending roar of incoming shellfire made it hard to hear anything, despite his enhancements. It was quite possible that his men would be accidentally killed by their own shells.

He reached the side of the blockhouse and unhooked a pair of HE grenades from his belt, setting the timer for two seconds before rolling them both through the firing slit and into the fortification. Someone shouted in shock, a second before the grenades exploded and set off a chain reaction of smaller explosions. Ryan glanced up at two troopers who had followed them, then indicated the gap to them with his hand. They crawled through the firing slit and into the fortifications at terrifying speed.

"Clear," one shouted.

Ryan nodded and followed them through the gap, fighting down claustrophobia as he made it into the compartment and fell to the ground. Inside, it was dark and shadowy, the tattered remains of two bodies lying on the floor. It didn't look as though there was any point in stripping the bodies for intelligence, but he checked them anyway as more soldiers made it through the gap. The point men opened a door in the rear of the room, then hurled another set of grenades down the corridor. Ryan glanced up, trying to gauge the strength of the roof, yet there was no way to know just how much it could take.

It's survived a massive bombardment, he thought, morbidly. The point men were advancing now, throwing grenades ahead of them into side rooms, just to make it impossible for the enemy to muster resistance. *It'll survive a few grenades.*

The complex was going dark, the remaining lights flickering and failing. There were no windows, no way to see out into the daylight. He slipped his night-vision goggles over his eyes, cursing under his breath. The goggles were far from perfect, but they would have to do until they got some proper light into the bunker. Turning on their flashlights would only reveal their positions to anyone lurking in the darkness. And yet, as they pushed further into the complex, it was starting to feel deserted.

He shuddered, torn between fear and a strange sort of admiration for the massive complex. It was fairly basic, as far as he could tell, and yet it had been erected at terrifying speed. And there were more and more of them surrounding the damned city. Just how much of his unit had been killed, trying to break into even *one* of them? How many more would die before the lines were broken and the city itself lay at their mercy.

They've woven the suburbs into their defence line, he thought, grimly. *This could get very nasty.*

He whirled around as he heard an explosion behind him, followed by shooting. A grenade exploded, the light throwing the scene into stark relief. Five men - or women; it was impossible to tell - had appeared from nowhere, attacking his men in the back. He lifted his rifle and fired, holding his finger down on the trigger to produce a spray of bullets. It was risky - bullets would bounce off the walls and ricochet around randomly - but he had no choice. He saw bodies fall to the ground and ducked himself, realising that the enemy must have built a tunnel underneath the bunker.

No, he thought, as the point men hurried back to join him. *They built several tunnels.*

They'd hidden it well, he realised, as they stumbled over the entrance. It had been concealed behind a concrete block, solid enough to resist anything less than an antitank weapon. The first point man started to advance down it, only to jump backwards as an explosion shook the tunnel, sending pieces of debris falling from the roof. Moments later, the entire structure collapsed into rubble. The tunnel was thoroughly blocked.

"Damn it," Ryan breathed.

"We could have had someone caught down there, sir," Sergeant Rove pointed out, as he stepped into view. "That would have been fatal."

Ryan looked past him, at the men who'd been rounded up and sent into the fortification. He didn't recognise *any* of them. He'd memorised the names and faces of every man in the company, making mental notes of their strengths and weaknesses, but the men in front of him were strangers. He didn't want to ask, but he forced himself to push forward anyway.

"Sergeant," he said slowly, "what happened to the others?"

"Gone, sir," Rove said.

Ryan shook his head, unable to quite comprehend the magnitude of the losses. There had been one hundred and fifty men in the reformed company, ranging from experienced sweats who'd served on Thule to newcomers who'd just finished Basic Training. Captain Lancaster, Lieutenant Ava, Lieutenant Omar…were they all dead? Omar had been a great help to him, when he'd first been assigned to the company; Ava had made sarcastic remarks that always seemed to have a worthwhile point. And Captain Lancaster…he'd thought there wasn't *anything* that could kill that motherfucker…

"Fuck," he breathed. "There were two whole *regiments* assigned to support the tanks!"

"Yes, sir," Rove said. His voice was flat, but it was easy to tell that some of the men behind him had been badly shaken. "And if we don't get reinforcements soon, we're going to be tossed back out as easily as we came."

"Fuck," Ryan said, again. He wanted to sit down and shake, but he knew his duty. "Put in a call for reinforcements and supplies, then we'll sweep the rest of this shithole for nasty surprises. And then we'll try to force our way onwards."

It was hard, very hard, to force any enthusiasm into his voice. If he and Rove were the only survivors of their company, and it certainly looked that way, a hundred and forty-eight men were dead or badly wounded. And if they pushed on…

No one is fooled, he told himself. *You're not very enthusiastic either.*

CHAPTER
TWENTY-SIX

Other officers, the ones who wallowed in atrocities - one officer had a harem of women taken from various villages, the sole survivors after his men had had their fun - were often unable to command in a competent manner. They might be able to hold their men, but didn't really comprehend that they might be facing someone dangerous and therefore took no real precautions.
                          - Professor Leo Caesius. The Role of Randomness In War.

Mark studied the live feed from the stealth drone with a grim feeling of dissatisfaction.

The scene before him was a nightmare, strewn with the remains of dozens of tanks and thousands of men. No one had an accurate figure - yet - for how many of his men had died in the opening hours of the battle, but he had a feeling that it was well over ten thousand. The fighting raged backwards and forwards as his men pushed their way into the outer layer of fortifications, only to be thrown back by counterattacks that evicted them before they had a chance to bring up reinforcements of their own, secure their position and continue the offensive. He hadn't expected immediate success - he'd seen too much to believe the defenders weren't serious about fighting to the end - but much of the attack had bogged down.

"Assault forces Beta through Gamma are requesting reinforcements," Ferguson said. "Beta is holding on to its gains, but Gamma is on the verge of being pushed back."

"Again," Mark said.

He gritted his teeth in frustration. His neatly-ordered formations had been torn to shreds. Soldiers were thrown together in scratch groups, regardless of where they'd been before the fighting, and pushed back into combat. Thankfully, their training was identical - a common headache in the Imperial Army - but it wasn't enough to make up for their problems. He needed time to regenerate his forces and consolidate his gains, yet the defenders had no intention of giving him any time. They were fighting like mad bastards to throw the attackers back out before it was too late.

"Mass reinforcements, then send them to support Beta," he ordered. He'd thrown thirty Landsharks into the teeth of enemy fire and they'd done a great deal of damage, but not enough to keep the defenders from wiping them out. No one had taken loss rates like that since…since ever. "Gamma is to hold as long as possible."

"Senior officers worry about morale," Ferguson warned. "A number of units have simply disintegrated."

Mark glared at him. Was Ferguson trying to establish a paper trail in the hopes of avoiding blame, if the offensive failed completely? Or was he just making a very clumsy point? No one had taken so many losses in such a short space of time for centuries. Normally, KEWs would clear the way and the soldiers would take possession of smouldering debris. Now… losing so many of their friends and comrades would undermine anyone's morale. It was a short step from that to outright mutiny. Or desertion. Anyone who wanted to desert could simply run towards the enemy positions, hands in the air.

They might get shot, he thought, morbidly. *But if they make it through the lines, they could tell the enemy a great deal about our current position.*

"Morale is not a concern right now," he insisted. It was true; his men had signed up to fight, not pick daises. "The concern is getting through the enemy lines."

Ferguson turned back to his console, allowing Mark to study the display. Cold ice ran down his spine at the mounting loss rates. The enemy's positions had taken a hammering, but they were solid enough to hold up under heavy shellfire and keep firing as his forces advanced. He really needed heavier penetrator weapons, he noted, yet their stockpile had been very limited and half the weapons he'd fired had been intercepted in mid-flight. In hindsight, it might have been better to rain shells down on the enemy rear, hoping to take out their point defence systems. But right now his gunners had to support the advance. The only hope of victory was to keep pushing forward, drawing the enemy into a kill-zone of his own...

The Admiral is not going to be pleased, he thought. Such losses were unprecedented in Wolfbane's history. Even a battleship being blown out of space only took a couple of thousand officers and men with it. *And nor is anyone else.*

"Beta has come under heavy attack," Ferguson warned. "The reinforcements may not get there in time."

"Then tell them to hurry," Mark snapped. "We have to break their lines!"

———

Emmanuel had seen hell, or so he'd thought. Lakshmibai had been a hellish place to live, even before it became a battleground. He still had nightmares about the extremes of wealth and poverty that dominated the world, starving children sold into slavery to well-fed aristocrats who happened to have been born to a higher caste. But the scene before him was far, far worse. The entire front line seemed consumed by fire, flames licking up as tanks advanced through the smog, only to be struck by missiles that destroyed them or forced them to fall back.

He peered through his binoculars, heedless of the danger. The Wolves hadn't randomly bombarded the city, as some had feared, but if they spotted him they'd assume he was a FFC and target his skyscraper for destruction. A handful of shells had already brought down a pair of skyscrapers, one of them toppling into another and sending both buildings crashing to the ground. Emmanuel hoped - prayed - that the buildings had been empty, although he knew the skyscrapers made ideal observation posts. There might well have been a spotter hidden in one of them...

The sound of bombardment grew louder as the enemy attack intensified. Men, looking as small as ants, ran forward, dozens falling as the defenders returned fire. The battleground was strewn with bodies, the attackers pushing the offensive over their fallen comrades. It was a staggering sight, utterly unprecedented in his experience. Surely, even religious fanatics couldn't keep up such an attack for long. And yet they just kept coming!

"This is madness," Angel said. She'd been reluctant to join him on the skyscraper and only a direct order from her superior had forced her into it. "They're going to burn the entire city."

"It looks like it," Emmanuel said. "But they haven't managed to get into the second line of defences yet."

He forced himself to keep watching, even though a voice at the back of his mind was yammering in terror, urging him to curl up in a ball and hide. A pair of missiles flared across the sky and came down somewhere amidst the defenders. There was a brilliant flash of white light, followed by a colossal fireball and a thunderclap that, just for a second, drowned out everything else. It looked like a plasma warhead, judging by the light, although he had no way to be sure. Everyone caught in the blast radius would be cooked before they had a chance to escape. The flickers of secondary explosions seemed almost an afterthought.

Sweat trickled down his face as the intense battle raged on. Another row of heavy tanks charged forward, crashing over the defence line and crushing fleeing defenders beneath their treads. His heart almost stopped beating before shellfire started to land amidst the tanks, destroying two of the giant vehicles and disabling three more. The remainder kept moving, only to run into missile fire that picked them off one by one. A line of enemy infantry, hoping to take advantage of the armoured assault, bogged down seconds later. He felt a flicker of sympathy for the men who'd been fed into the meat-grinder, mixed with a cool disdain for their leaders. Couldn't they think of any better tactics than just pressing the offensive at all costs?

"They're mustering another assault," he mused. It was hard to be sure - there was so much smoke drifting across the battlefield - but it looked as though hundreds of infantrymen were mustering near one of the captured fortifications. Behind them, he caught glimpses of armoured vehicles and self-propelled guns. "What are they doing…?"

He swore as he saw the gunners start to lob shells into the second line of defences. It wasn't a bad tactic either, he had to admit; the blockhouses were weaker to the front, where there were firing slits, than they were up top. A shell that made it through the slit would do very real damage. As if the defenders had realised the danger, counter-battery fire rained down on the self-propelled guns. Three exploded, a fourth was picked up and tossed backwards by the force of the blast. The remaining two hurried back, changing position while lobbing shells randomly towards the defence lines. Emmanuel rather doubted they'd hit anything, but there were so many shells in the air that the odds were in favour of a handful hitting something vital.

"We should get down," Angel breathed, as a shell landed within the city. Emmanuel felt the skyscraper rock slightly underneath him. "They're targeting the city."

"Maybe," Emmanuel said. There were no more shells landing nearby, as far as he could tell; it was quite possible that the shell the enemy had fired had been a mischance. "But this is still the best place to be."

Angel glowered at him, then strode over to the wall and sat down, wrapping her arms around her legs. Emmanuel shook his head in tired amusement and returned his gaze to the fighting as it grew even more intense. It looked as through the defenders were pushing even harder...

But they can't do this indefinitely, he thought. *How long can they keep it up?*

Deep inside, he wasn't sure he wanted to know the answer.

"They've kicked us out of sectors 4-13 to 4-15," Gwendolyn reported. She sounded frustrated at not being able to get into the battle, even though Ed needed her in the command bunker. "They're massing for a push at 3-14."

"Move reinforcements into position to relieve 3-14," Ed ordered.

He scowled as he studied the constantly-updating display. Thankfully, the enemy didn't seem to have achieved another breakthrough, although he knew it was just a matter of time. The sheer intensity of the assault was hitting the defenders hard, all along the line; it wouldn't be long before another fortification collapsed, allowing the attackers to surge forward. And when they did, he would have to split his reinforcements between two points of threatened weakness. Which one would the enemy turn into the main angle of attack?

"They beat back the counterattack at 4-19," an operator called. "They're in possession of the blockhouses, sir."

Ed swore. That hadn't been long at all.

"Reroute a reinforcement company to 3-18," he ordered, coldly. "Let them hold the line a few hours longer."

His scowl deepened. Maintaining an intensive assault for so long - the battle had gone on for four hours and felt like it had gone on for days - was an impressive achievement, particularly given the battlefield limitations. And yet, they had to be running short on everything from manpower to ammunition stockpiles and tanks. Ed could recall campaigns where Landsharks hadn't been so much as scratched, but by his count the Wolves had lost over a hundred. They had to be running short.

They couldn't have brought that many to the battle, he told himself. *Could they?*

He shook his head. Landsharks weren't designed for urban combat, unless one didn't give a shit about preserving the town and its population. Sending them into a network of fortified positions was about the worst possible use of the vehicles, although he had to admit there was a shortage of vehicles *designed* for such an assault. The Imperial Army had faced demands to put dozens of Landsharks in storage, simply because the planners had been unable to articulate why such heavy vehicles were necessary. Why *were* they necessary when KEWs could smash any enemy position from orbit, allowing the soldiers to take possession of blackened ruins?

Because KEWs aren't always available, he thought, darkly. Admiral Singh had hit the shield several times, no doubt hoping to batter it down, but the shield had persistently refused to break. *And now the Wolves are paying a price for their lack of imagination.*

"Reinforcements are moving up now," Gwendolyn reported. She gave him a sharp look, then lowered her voice. "I don't know how long our people can take this."

Ed nodded. Marines were trained to keep going, whatever happened, but the local militia hadn't had any such training. They'd done the best they could over the past two months, yet he was grimly aware that it wasn't enough. And realistically, the CEF hadn't had such intensive training either. They might break too.

"Keep an eye on the situation," he ordered. "It's all we can do."

———

Mindy hastily sipped flavoured water from the canteen - it was primed with nutrients to keep her going - and then passed it to Trooper Halls and picked up her rifle. It felt as if they had been fighting for weeks, if not months; they hadn't had a chance to rest when they'd reached the next blockhouse and hastily slotted themselves into the defence lines. Her uniform was askew, she knew, but she was really too tired to care. All that mattered was that she could still fight.

Her entire body felt weird, as if she had both passed the hump and yet could barely take one more step. She'd drunk too much, she thought; the energy drink could have unpleasant side effects if she drank too much of it. And yet, she somehow kept moving as the sound of enemy shellfire grew louder. Shells were smashing down on the bunker, warning her that it wouldn't be long before the Wolves attempted to break through the fortifications and cleanse the bunker of her and her comrades. The ground shook, time and time again, as the shellfire grew more intense. Some of the shells seemed to be targeted *behind* the complex...

They're trying to collapse the tunnels, she thought, tiredly. The tunnels were reinforced, but they weren't as strong as the fortifications. Collapsing them made sense, too; the enemy had to know that the hidden passageways were rigged to blow if the defenders lost control of the far end. *It'll keep us from counterattacking when they think they've secured the complex...*

The blockhouse shook, again, as something exploded within the next room. Mindy barely had a second to dive for cover as the door burst, allowing the enemy to hurl two grenades into her compartment. The explosions were deafeningly loud; she heard several of her comrades screaming in pain. She landed badly, letting go of her rifle and sending it skittering across the floor; she rolled over, just in time to see one of the lights flicker and fail. An enemy soldier advanced into the compartment, followed by a second. Their guns were traversing the compartment, searching for targets.

She knew she should lie still, pretending to be dead, but she had no idea how good their NVGs were. Her body temperature would remain constant, unlike those who had been caught in the blasts and killed. She picked herself up, yanked her ka-bar from her belt and hurled herself forward, stabbing the first soldier in the throat as he turned to face her. He staggered backwards as his comrade turned; Mindy shoved him into his comrade, trying to stab the second man. Too close to her to bring his rifle around, he shoved her hand aside and slammed into her, sending them both crashing to the floor. Mindy gasped in pain as her shoulder hit the concrete, her assailant landing on top of her with a grunt. She tried to muster the strength to fight back as he drew back his fist, intending to punch her lights out, but her body was aching too much. Her fingers touched the handle of a knife - *his* knife - as she twisted, barely avoiding a punch that would have crushed her throat. He shifted his weight, giving her a split-second opportunity to grab his blade and stab him with it.

He grunted again as she drove the knife into his chest. His body shuddered, violently, then flopped down on top of her. Mindy could barely force herself to breathe. Pushing him aside was beyond her. She heard shouts in the distance, followed by explosions…she had no idea who was coming her way. Friends…or foe?

"Clear," someone shouted.

He burst into the room, rifle in hand. Mindy moaned, trying to attract attention. She was past caring if she was about to be rescued or taken prisoner…if, of course, the Wolves were bothering to take prisoners. God alone knew what they'd make of her, if they saw her in such a position. She tried not to think about some of the other things that could happen to a female soldier, caught by the enemy and rendered helpless…

…It was hard to keep herself awake…she struggled against the weight of the corpse, but she couldn't shift it. Blood - his blood - was staining her uniform and pooling around her. She'd been in worse places, she reminded herself. She didn't think she had the strength to throw up without choking herself.

"Dear God," a male voice said. It had an accent that was distantly Avalon. She felt a surge of relief that drained the last of her energy. "What happened?"

Mindy tried to speak, but it required far too much effort. Her entire body sagged as she felt strong hands lifting the enemy soldier off her...

And then darkness rose up and claimed her for its own.

TWENTY-SEVEN

Indeed, one of the most dangerous officers faced during the battle was one who spent his entire career drugged out of his mind. His NCOs handled the unit and did quite a competent job of it. They actually held out for nearly twenty minutes before they were crushed by the CEF.

- Professor Leo Caesius. The Role of Randomness In War.

"Here they come," Buckley muttered.

Jasmine nodded as she stood by the side of the road, watching as the truck emerged from the darkness. Night was slowly falling over Corinthian, but the thunderous sounds of battle from the south had hardly diminished. She was morbidly impressed that the Wolves had kept up the battle for so long, even though it posed a major threat to her and her platoon. But they had to be feeling the effects of fighting for so long. Chances were the forces at the rear were nowhere near as alert as they should be.

She held up her hand, thumb extended, in the universal request for a pickup. They hadn't donned Wolfbane uniforms - they hadn't had any on hand - but marine battledress wasn't *that* different from standard-issue battledress. The gathering twilight would make it harder for watching eyes to pick out the differences, even if they were paying attention. This far from the front lines, it was unlikely the Wolves worried *that* much about infiltrators.

And this is technically illegal, Jasmine thought, as the truck slowed to a halt. She'd been worried about accidentally stopping a troop transport, but it looked as though they'd managed to catch a supply truck. *We could be shot for this.*

She snorted, inwardly. They'd be shot out of hand, the moment the Wolves discovered who and what they were. She forced herself to relax as the truck door slammed open, revealing a short balding man wearing a sergeant's uniform. No, a *supply* sergeant's uniform. She knew the type. He might call himself a sergeant, but he was no *true* sergeant. He was really nothing more than a beancounter in uniform.

He glared at them indiscriminately. "What happened to your unit?"

Jasmine glanced past him. There was a driver, but no one else. She walked forward and grabbed the sergeant, yanking him out of the vehicle and pushing him to the ground before he could draw his pistol or sound the alarm. Buckley hurried past her and covered the driver, who held his shaking hands in the air before being told to do anything of the sort. Jasmine couldn't help a flicker of contempt, as she drew her knife and held it to the sergeant's throat. The Wolves she'd ambushed earlier had fought back like men, but these supply officers hadn't even *tried* to fight! And the sergeant had wet himself like a child.

"If you lie to me, I will know about it," she growled, as she frisked the sergeant and secured his hands behind his back with a plastic tie. "Where are you going?"

"The gunnery position," the man stammered. "I…please don't kill me!"

Jasmine resisted - barely - the urge to simply cut his throat. She'd been through three different Conduct After Capture courses - and she'd been captured, once upon a time - and *she'd* done better than this overweight blob of lard. And she'd even hit a Drill Instructor - one of the few times when a recruit *could* hit a Drill Instructor - when he'd tried to convince her that the scenario was over and she'd passed! Instead, she gagged him with duct tape, bound his legs and dumped him by the side of the road. His superiors would deal with him afterwards.

"Get the others into the truck," she ordered, as she scrambled up into the driver's seat. "We need to move quickly."

She started the engine as soon as the remaining marines were in the truck, then drove off down the road. Thankfully, there were no changes from the trucks she recalled; the Wolves, it seemed, had simply continued to duplicate pre-collapse vehicles rather than improving on them in any way. She understood the logic behind it - the Marine Corps used very basic technology too - but it still surprised her. But then, it made life easier during wartime.

Buckley leaned forward. "Get in, bust some heads, get out again?"

"Yep," Jasmine said. Driving right into an enemy position took nerve, but they were already inside the security perimeter. Unless the guards were *very* alert, they'd be reassured by the simple fact that she was driving a Wolfbane truck. She'd walked through tougher security procedures before the exile to Avalon. "And we take out as many of their guns as possible."

"Got a lot of shells in the back," Stewart said. "I can rig these to explode, if you'll let me."

"Damn right," Jasmine said. "But don't detonate them until we're ready."

"Of course not," Stewart said. "*That* would be embarrassing."

"But funny," Buckley countered.

They must be desperate, Jasmine thought, giving Buckley a rude gesture. The Imperial Army had always shipped ammunition in heavily-guarded convoys...but then, it had been so inefficient that entire outposts had run out of ammunition before they could be resupplied. Unfortunately, the Wolves seemed to be a little bit smarter. *And their ammunition expenditure must be far higher than they expected.*

She felt cold ice gnawing at her heart, despite her words, as they approached the enemy position. It was larger than she'd expected, surrounded by barbed wire and a handful of armed guards. Dozens of guns sat within the wire, belching hundreds of shells towards Freedom City. Their fire wouldn't be very accurate - there were several gun models she'd never seen outside training simulations - but it hardly mattered. Forcing the defenders to keep their heads down was just as important as scoring hits.

"Very rapid rate of fire," Buckley noted. "Their gun barrels must be red hot."

"It won't matter," Stewart said. "They can just cast a new one on the MEUs. Any industrial node could churn out hundreds of guns and thousands of shells within a week."

"If they had the right programming," Jasmine agreed. "Keep your heads down, now. We don't want them to see more than two people."

She tensed as they rolled up in front of the gate. If the enemy was on the alert, they'd check anyone who wanted to enter the complex. There was no way either she or Buckley could pass for the supply sergeant and his driver. But the demand for shells was so high that the guards just glanced at the paper she'd found in the glove compartment, then opened the gate and waved them through the wire. Jasmine's lips twisted in bitter amusement, remembering the report she'd written after doing something similar on Han. *This* bunch were about to get something worse than a bad report.

The complex included a handful of MPs, who seemed to be directing operations, as well as the gunners themselves. She reminded herself not to get into a fist-fight with the gunners - they tended to be stronger than many infantrymen - and parked the truck where the MPs indicated. Her gaze swept the complex, searching for signs of prospective trouble, but it looked as though there were neither barracks nor heavy weapons emplacements in view. It puzzled her for a moment, then she realised that the gunners would probably be bussed away from the complex when they went off duty. No doubt they felt they needed their sleep.

"Go," she whispered.

She kicked open the door and jumped out, firing automatically as she moved her rifle from target to target. The MPs hadn't been particularly alert, she realised; they weren't even wearing body armour. She heard more gunshots cracking out as the other six piled out, picking off the enemy gunners and guards. A handful of enemy soldiers drew their weapons and returned fire, but it was already far too late. Her platoon swept them away before they could muster a coordinated resistance.

They searched the complex quickly as Stewart returned to the truck and moved it into position next to the heavy guns. There was little of value, although they scooped up hard drives and computer terminals in case intelligence officers could deduce something useful from whatever scraps of data they contained. The gunnery commander had apparently been fond of a woman back home, she noted; his makeshift office had dozens of photographs of the same girl hanging everywhere. And to think it would be just a temporary office...

She glanced up as she heard the sound of helicopters heading towards their position. She'd hoped the Wolves wouldn't have any chance to sound the alarm, but evidently *someone* had managed to get off an alert before it was too late. Or the guards had missed an hourly check-in or something. There was no point in worrying about it now; she barked orders to the remaining marines, then glanced at Stewart as he jumped out of the truck.

"The shells are primed," he called. "Everything's ready!"

Jasmine nodded, then bellowed orders for the marines to run. She glanced behind her as the sound of rotor blades grew louder, muttering curses under her breath. The helicopters were growing nearer, ducking low to avoid fire from Freedom City. Buckley unfolded a MANPAD as he ran, readying the weapon for immediate launch. If the helicopters pressed too closely they were in for a nasty surprise.

They slipped through the gate and went cross-country. Running down the road would have been suicidal. She looked at the helicopters again, then shouted a command to Buckley. He turned, locked his missile on the nearest target and fired. The helicopter twisted in mid-air, but it was far too slow to evade the missile. Its partner ducked backwards, keeping its distance, as flaming wreckage dropped to the ground. The crew hadn't stood a chance.

They must be running short of helicopters, Jasmine thought. *They're taking more care with the ones they have.*

She looked at Stewart as soon as they reached a safe distance. "Blow it."

"With pleasure," Stewart said. The marines dropped to the ground as he produced a detonator, unlocked the safety and held his finger over the button. "Three...two...one..."

He pushed the button, dramatically. There was a microsecond of pregnant silence, then a colossal explosion blasted out from the direction of the complex. The ground shook, violently; Jasmine could hear pieces of debris crashing down all around them. She turned, just in time to see an immense fireball rising into the sky. The remaining helicopter was picked up by the blast wave and thrown cart-wheeling through the air, spinning over and over again until it finally crashed into the ground. She found herself torn between hoping the crew had survived and hoping that they were dead, although they weren't so much of a problem without the helicopter. It was unlikely they were also trained infantrymen.

"Wow," Buckley said. "Good one."

"That's what happens when you fuck up with primitive shells," Stewart said. "I just rigged a couple to explode and they set off the others."

Jasmine smiled. "And now we'd better be going," she said. Darkness was falling, but she knew just how capable some sensors were in the dark. "I'd bet good money that there's a QRF on the way."

She took one final look at the burning complex, then led the way into the darkness.

———

"You shouldn't be up here," Hampton said.

Danielle scowled at him, but nodded ruefully. She was the President, yet she was also the leader of a coalition that might not stay together without her. Her death would start a political struggle that might completely reshape planetary politics, not something that could be tolerated in the middle of a war. And yet, she owed it to her conscience to take some risks. Hundreds - perhaps thousands - of young men who'd voted for her were now dead or seriously injured. It wasn't *right* that she should enjoy safety in the bunker while they fought and died on her behalf.

She sat next to him, peering out into the darkness. It brought no let-up, no pause in the storm; the enemy continued their advance, pushing the offensive forward as hard as possible. A giant fireball billowed up behind enemy lines; a thunderclap rent the air...and yet, the enemy just kept coming. She'd seen the reports and read between the lines. The outer edge of the defences was almost completely broken. There was heavy fighting within the inner defences now...

"They're trapped in a death match," Hampton said. He sounded pleased, despite knowing far too many of the soldiers personally. "They can neither push through our defences nor fall back."

"Unless they're willing to surrender their pride," Danielle pointed out. She saw a light moving through the darkness, then falling to the ground and disappearing. "They could always fall back and concentrate on keeping us trapped here."

"I doubt their higher-ups have any real comprehension of the problem," Hampton said. "It was a constant headache, back when I worked for the Empire. The people in charge didn't know what was going on, so they often pushed an offensive forward when it was pointless or stopped an offensive on the brink of victory. They'll be more concerned about saving face than saving lives."

Danielle nodded. She'd never been in the military, but she'd worked in a bureaucracy and recalled just how ignorant some of her superiors had been. The bureaucrats in high office hadn't understood the needs of their juniors, let alone how some of their policies had been very bad for their victims. And they'd always refused to believe that the endless problems were *their* fault.

But then, accepting the blame would be career suicide, she thought. The bureaucrats had been more interested in their careers than actually doing good. *And Admiral Singh faces far worse than merely being allowed to retire on full pay.*

She looked at him, grimly. "Can we hold them?"

"I think we're hurting them far more than they're hurting us," Hampton said. He waved a hand northwards. "Sooner or later, they're going to run out of men and machines to throw at us."

"Unless the shield fails," Danielle said.

"Yeah," Hampton agreed. "If the shield fails, Madam President, we fail with it."

———

"Emmanuel," a voice called. "Over here!"

Emmanuel blinked, looking around. There were dozens of injured men - and a handful of injured women - in the makeshift field hospital, but he didn't recognise any of them. And then he spotted Mindy Caesius reclining on a bed, stripped to the waist with a medical cast attached to her shoulder. She'd always been pale, he recalled - Jasmine had introduced them, back on Avalon - but now she was covered in bruises and cuts. He didn't want to think about what had happened to her shoulder…

But he had to ask. "What happened to you?"

"Landed badly," Mindy said, nodding to the cast. "They say I should be back on my feet within a day or two."

Emmanuel stepped backwards, studying her critically. A handful of medical packets were attached to her arms, save one that was positioned below her right breast. It looked as though she'd been through a nightmare, which he rather suspected she had. He didn't want to ask any more questions, but it was his job. And yet, he knew from experience that soldiers didn't always want to talk about what had happened to them. He'd be kicked out of the field hospital if he upset anyone, let alone made it harder for the medics to do their work.

"You should see the other guy," Mindy added. She sounded proud, yet hyper in a way that suggested she'd been drugged. "I knifed him with his own knife."

"Good for you," Emmanuel said. Behind him, he heard Angel gasp. "How…how bad is it out there?"

"Hellish," Mindy said, flatly. "They just keep coming and coming and coming. But it's much worse for them, I think. They have much less cover as they advance towards us."

"That's good," Emmanuel said.

He didn't ask any questions, just waited to see what she had to say. But she seemed more interested in staring at her pale hands than anything else. He watched her for a long moment, then stepped backwards as one of the medics inspected the medical packages. Mindy's eyes closed a second later; the medic gently attached a bracelet to her wrist, then turned to leave.

Emmanuel caught his arm. "How is she?"

"Badly bruised, but otherwise largely intact," the medic said. "We've given her something to help her relax, as well as feeding her. She should be discharged tomorrow, barring complications. We're going to need the bed for someone else."

"I understand," Emmanuel said.

He swallowed as he looked at the wounded. Military medicine operated on the triage principle, where soldiers who were too badly wounded to survive without intensive effort were given painkillers and left to die. It sounded heartless, but he understood the grim logic behind the system. The resources expended in healing a badly-wounded soldier might be better spent healing a handful of less-injured young men.

"We'd better go," Angel said, catching his arm. "There are too many wounded here. We'll just get in the way."

"I suppose," Emmanuel said. For once, she was right. "Let's go."

He took one last look at Mindy - she looked so fragile, lying on the bed - and then followed Angel out of the room. The corridors were lined with wounded men, some trying hard to keep their spirits up while others were clearly on the verge of death. Angel kept her distance from the groaning men, her entire stance suggesting she was horrified. Emmanuel didn't blame her. He was horrified too.

These men will be scarred for life, he thought, numbly. *Whoever wins the war, they lose.*

CHAPTER
TWENTY-EIGHT

As you can see, the question of just who is in command of a particular military force can cast a baleful shadow over the battlefield.
- Professor Leo Caesius. The Role of Randomness In War.

"Sir," Sergeant Rove said. "They're coming!"

Ryan staggered back to wakefulness, wishing he was dead. Or maybe he was dead and in hell. It certainly seemed plausible. He'd been fighting for hours, then practically collapsed in the enemy bunker. How long had he been asleep? It felt like bare seconds had passed between opening and closing his eyes. He glanced at his watch as he reached for his rifle and a stimulant tab, pushing the latter against his bare skin. Two hours. He'd slept for no longer than two hours.

"Fuck," he muttered.

He knew his duty. He was a lieutenant; he'd survived when countless others had died during the bitter fighting. For all he knew, he was the sole surviving officer. He was certainly the senior officer in the captured blockhouse. His body shuddered as the stimulant took effect, warning him that he was pushing his body too far. Too many tabs, taken too quickly, could cause addiction - or worse. The thought of spending the rest of his life dependent on the tabs was horrific. But he had no choice.

"Report," he said. His voice sounded shaky. He damned himself as he staggered to his feet, leaning on his rifle to remain upright. "What's happening?"

Rove didn't look back at him. "They're mustering for a counterattack," he said. "They know we're running short on reinforcements."

Ryan swallowed. He'd thought they were on the tip of the spear…hell, perhaps they *were* on the tip of the spear. And yet there were no reinforcements? He swallowed again, his mouth suddenly very dry. What if they were the last soldiers left alive? He retched, cursing his mouth, then forced himself to check the soldiers. They looked as battered and drained as he felt.

"Grab your weapons," he ordered, somehow. They weren't moving right either. A couple were wounded, but not badly enough to justify evacuating them. And even if he did, he had an uncomfortable feeling they'd never reach a field hospital. The enemy's shellfire wasn't as prevalent, but it was still pretty nasty. "Stand by to resist attack."

Grimly, he checked the terminal. Dawn was breaking; there were no reinforcements within easy reach. He hoped that meant that the other forces were doing well, punching through what remained of the enemy's defences, but he had a feeling that it meant that they weren't doing well at all. Or maybe he'd been locked out of the overall network, if the defenders weren't jamming it. Their damnable bunkers seemed practically *designed* to play merry hell with signalling.

He looked at Rove. "Any word from the others?"

"The attack through the second line of defences bogged down," Rove said. "They got caught in the open and slaughtered. And then half of the reinforcements were pulled back to comb the surrounding area for insurgents."

"Shit," Ryan said. The tab was taking effect, but it came at a price. His heartbeat was racing madly, erratically. He wondered, absently, just how close he was to a heart attack. "Can we send a runner back to beg for help?"

"I doubt there's any to send," Rove admitted.

Ryan closed his eyes in pain. He was too tired to care about showing weakness in front of the men. If there were no reinforcements, the remains of his company were dangerously exposed. The enemy would have no difficulty overwhelming them, either driving them back or crushing them like bugs. And yet, he had no authority to order a retreat. He might just be put in front of a wall and shot for cowardice in the face of the enemy.

He opened his eyes. "Start preparing for a fighting withdrawal," he ordered. If it was clear that *he* had issued the orders, his men shouldn't suffer. Besides, the regular chain of command had been shot to hell. He didn't know any of the men who'd attached themselves to the remains of his unit. "And then…"

A hail of gunfire echoed out in the distance. He swore, venomously.

"Too late, sir," Rove said.

———

Ed studied the reports, hoping desperately that they were reasonably accurate. *Marines* would have sent accurate reports, of course, and so would the CEF, but the planet's defenders had trained separately and didn't use the same nomenclature. He *thought* he understood what they were saying, yet if he was wrong…

"It looks as though the enemy has finally slacked off," he said. It had been nearly an entire *day* of fighting, at a tempo unseen since the Unification Wars. He dreaded to think just how much ammunition had been expended, even before Jasmine and her team had hit a gunnery station and blown it all to hell. "Do you concur?"

"Yes, sir," Hampton said. "They've finally lost their edge."

And plenty of material too, Ed thought. By his count, the Wolves had expended more material than an entire marine regiment would have had at its disposal. *Hundreds of tanks, armoured vehicles, guns…the list goes on and on.*

"Then it's time to launch the counterattack," he said. "Pass the word. I want a general counter-offensive, as planned, to jump off in twenty minutes."

"Yes, sir," Hampton said.

———

"Admiral," Mark said. He forced himself to speak calmly and clearly, even though his mouth was dry. "The offensive has failed."

Admiral Singh stared at him. He was relieved, more relieved than he cared to admit, that she was in orbit, rather than standing in the same room. He'd had too much experience with bad commanding officers to feel comfortable, particularly when he was admitting defeat on a terrifying scale. They'd expended more material than he cared to think about for nothing!

"Failed," she said, finally.

"Failed," Mark confirmed. He spoke on before she could say a word. "Admiral, we have over twenty thousand dead or wounded. Twenty *thousand*! We've lost over two hundred tanks and armoured vehicles and expended more ammunition than even our worst-case projections. I don't know if I can extract the forward elements before it's too late to stop the counterattack!"

"There is no counterattack," Admiral Singh said.

"There will be," Mark said. He forced himself forward. "Our shellfire has been slacking for the last two hours, Admiral. They will know they have the edge now. The battle is *lost*, Admiral. All we can do is save as much as possible and prepare for a second offensive."

"I will not countenance surrender," Admiral Singh snapped.

"I'm not asking you to surrender," Mark insisted. "I'm asking you to call off the offensive before it's too late!"

He cleared his throat, taking a moment to get his thoughts in order. "We pull back to our own lines, keeping the envelopment in place. Then we muster the forces for a second thrust into the city, using what we've learned to punch through the defences. We can still win the campaign, Admiral, but this battle is going to cost us everything! It has to end now."

"Hold as much as you can," Admiral Singh said, finally. "We do hold some of their defence points, don't we?"

"Not enough," Mark snapped. "Do you really want to explain why you threw an extra ten thousand men after *twenty thousand*?"

Admiral Singh's eyes narrowed, darkly. Mark braced himself, wondering just what she'd say. An order to Mark's subordinates, perhaps, ordering them to kill him? Or a command to her own people? He suspected that some of his aides were probably also her agents…

"Withdraw the troops as you see fit, but keep a stranglehold on the city," Admiral Singh ordered, finally. "They are *not* to have a chance to resupply themselves."

"Yes, Admiral," Mark said. He breathed a sigh of relief. "I understand."

Her face vanished from the display. "Send the word," Mark ordered, turning back to his subordinates. "Our forces are to pull back to their jump-off points, then start erecting fortifications of their own."

"Yes, sir," Ferguson said.

And lets pray that I did it in time, Mark thought.

———

Ryan gritted his teeth as the first wave of enemy attackers came into view, darting forward as quickly as they could while using the remains of countless Landsharks and other vehicles for cover. They had much more cover than the Wolves, he noted, as he fired on the first man to come into view; the remains of the battlefield provided all the cover they could possibly want. And they were well-trained too, one force providing covering fire while the other leapfrogged forward and then covered the other.

"Message from command," Rove shouted. "We're to fall back to the jump-off points!"

A hail of shells crashed down in front of the bunker, providing a limited amount of cover. It slowed the enemy offensive for a few seconds, then the enemy started their advance again, throwing grenades and missiles forward to push the Wolves back. Ryan thought fast, trying to decide how best to retreat. There was no way to avoid the fact that they'd be exposed the second they left the bunker, their backs to the enemy. He'd been a soldier too long to believe that shooting someone in the back was anything other than a honourable approach and he rather suspected the enemy would agree.

He glanced at the sergeant, then made up his mind. "Leave four men with me," he snapped, finally. "And then get the others back to safety!"

Rove gave him a sharp look. "I should stay with you."

"Don't argue, just go," Ryan snapped. He took aim at an advancing enemy soldier and fired, twice. The man dropped, but Ryan wasn't sure if he was dead or if he was merely taking cover. "You need to get them back to safety! We'll be along in five minutes."

He watched the advancing enemy for a long moment, firing rapidly towards prospective targets. They seemed more inclined to advance carefully now, perhaps wary of another hail of shellfire; Ryan wished, bitterly, that he had a FFC under his command. But he didn't and he'd just have to live with the missed opportunity. Carefully, he unhooked his belt of grenades and prepared to throw them towards the enemy. The explosions would provide cover for the retreat.

"That's five minutes," he said. He hurled the grenades, then ducked low. "Go!"

They turned and ran through the maze of corridors; behind them, the grenades went off in a single blast. Ryan prayed to a god he wasn't sure he believed in that the enemy would be delayed, just long enough for them to escape. They reached the other side of the giant blockhouse; he stared in surprise as he realised Sergeant Rove had sent the others on ahead and waited for him. There was surprisingly little enemy shellfire, although he could hear the sound of mortars being fired in the distance. And ahead of him...

He retched, violently, as he saw the bodies. He'd known, intellectually, that there had been thousands of casualties, but the sight of thousands of bodies strewn all over the field made him sick to his stomach. He didn't recognise any of them, yet he knew *some* of them had to be men he'd commanded, or men he'd served with during his career. They'd had good service records - on Thule, on Wolfbane, on countless other worlds - and yet they'd just been thrown away, attacking defences that might as well be impregnable. Cold anger burned within his gut, mixed with fear. What would happen when the offensive was resumed?

"Sir," Sergeant Rove said. "We have to move now!"

Ryan nodded. He could hear the sound of enemy soldiers behind him, making their careful way through the abandoned blockhouse. It was a pity there had been no time to rig a few booby traps, but if they were lucky the enemy would be delayed anyway, looking for traps that weren't there. And if they weren't lucky…

"Come on," he said.

He took a grenade from one of the soldiers and threw it into the blockhouse, then started to run as it exploded. The sound of gunfire was growing louder; he cursed as he saw a missile streak off the ground and strike a helicopter, blowing it out of the sky. It had to be a friendly helicopter, judging by its position. The defenders seemed to have an unlimited supply of HVMs…

Something slammed into his back, hard enough to throw him to the ground. The world spun around him as he landed hard, his stomach twisting brutally as violent pain seared through his body. He'd been shot, he realised; he'd actually been shot! He tried to cry out, as the world started to fade around him, but the words refused to form. Someone was talking very close to him…

…But he couldn't make out a single word.

"We've got most of our men out," Ferguson reported. "The enemy has reoccupied their blockhouses, what's left of them, but they're not launching a pursuit."

Mark nodded, curtly. The enemy had played it smart, so far; they wouldn't hurl themselves into the teeth of *his* firepower. Why throw away their greatest advantage? All they had to do was hold their position, knowing the battle wouldn't be settled until Mark had occupied their city or alternatively ground it into dust.

"Get the wounded up here as quickly as possible," he ordered. "And convert a number of local buildings into hospitals."

"Yes, sir," Ferguson said. "But it's not going to be enough."

Mark couldn't disagree. So far, the field medics reported that there were over seven *thousand* wounded, ranging from minor injuries to wounds that would be lethal, in time, if they weren't treated. But they couldn't be treated! Their medical supplies were grossly inadequate to handle so many casualties, forcing the medics to concentrate on the men who *could* be saved with what they had on hand. Mark silently promised himself that he would have the medical officers rebuked for their failure, even though he knew the root of the problem lay with him - and Admiral Singh. Pushing the offensive had been a mistake.

"Once the shooting dies down, send a messenger to the enemy," he said, pushing his concerns aside. "Tell them we want to collect the dead bodies and give them a proper burial."

"I don't know if the Admiral would approve," Ferguson said.

Mark rounded on him, feeling his temper snap. "Right now, you are under my command and you will do as I tell you," he snarled. Where was the *competent* Ferguson? Where was the man who had commanded the first troops to land on the surface? "You can complain to the Admiral later, if you wish, but you will do as I command or" - he put a hand on the holster at his belt - "you will be executed on the spot for disobeying orders in the face of the enemy!"

Ferguson paled. "I'll send the message now," he said. "Sir..."

"Go do it," Mark growled.

He glared at the display, forcing himself to calm down. He'd kept Ferguson in the FOB for too long, rather than allowing him to go back to the troops. And now Ferguson had become *political*, taking steps because he was afraid for his own prospects rather than because they were necessary. He was probably right to worry about his career, Mark admitted privately, but there were worse problems on hand. There were almost certainly wounded men on the ground, bleeding to death. They had to be recovered before it was too late.

Gritting his teeth, he sat back on his chair and watched as the reports came in. The death toll continued to rise as wounded soldiers passed away, despite the best efforts of the medical teams. He made a note to check the POWs for any doctors - he would be willing to pay, or offer parole, to anyone who was willing to help - but he suspected it would be futile. The enemy would probably have withdrawn any doctors before they could be pressed into service.

"The local CO reports that the enemy have accepted the message," Ferguson reported. "But they're insisting that the recovery parties be unarmed."

"Accept, then tell him to get organised," Mark ordered, curtly. "And make sure he knows the recovery parties are to behave themselves. They're not being sent on a spying mission."

"Yes, sir," Ferguson said.

"I mean it," Mark said. It wouldn't be the first time some mid-ranking officer had tried to be clever. "We do not want our teams kicked out for spying."

"Yes, sir," Ferguson repeated.

Mark nodded, then returned to his thoughts. It was maddening - and frustrating. There was no way to spin the battle as anything other than a defeat. They hadn't even captured enough room to bury their dead! The only real consolation was that the enemy had taken losses too, although far fewer than his forces. They still held the city, they still held their defence lines and they still held their damnable shield. His attempts to bombard the shield generator's prospective location had all failed.

He skimmed through the reports, one by one. If nothing else, they *had* learned a great deal about the enemy's defences. Their blockhouses were clever, but they were really very simple constructions. And they did have weaknesses...a thought occurred to him and he started to work, looking for possible alternatives. Maybe there were other ways to break through the defence line and get into the city itself.

It'll take time, he thought, grimly. It was workable, yet would the Admiral give him the time to make it work? He'd have to work hard to convince her to let him try. *And if it doesn't work, I can kiss my career goodbye.*

He shook his head, slowly. After so many lives had been lost, the Admiral would be desperate for a success. And yet, what if it failed a second time?

She'll be desperate for a scapegoat, he thought, with gallows humour. *And I would fit the bill perfectly.*

CHAPTER
TWENTY-NINE

The first type of officer would lose control of his unit very quickly, leaving his men a leaderless rabble scattered over the battlefield. This would naturally allow a competent enemy to wipe them out before they could reform (if indeed they did; a number of stragglers were wiped out by lower-caste bandits before they could return to safety.)

> - Professor Leo Caesius. The Role of Randomness In War.

"Hell," Ed said, quietly.

The scene before him was a nightmare. Hundreds of dead bodies were clearly visible, enemy recovery teams working hard to collect them, bag them up and carry them back to their lines for a decent burial. Dozens of destroyed or disabled vehicles lay within view, blown apart by missile hits or badly damaged by mines. Their blackened remains mocked him, even as he forced himself to remember that the battle was won. It was no consolation. He'd slaughtered thousands upon thousands of enemy soldiers, but their commanding officers were out of reach.

Poor bastard, he thought, looking at the remains of an enemy soldier. He seemed to be sitting upright, but his skull was broken and his brains were oozing down to the torn and broken ground. *What did you do to have such a commanding officer?*

He shook his head slowly. People would argue, in days and months to come, that the slaughter was his fault. He'd been the one who baited the trap, he'd been the one who'd lured the enemy into a killing zone. And yet, he hadn't started the war. He would have been happy to come to terms with Governor Brown, to recognise Wolfbane as a successor state equal to the Commonwealth. But Governor Brown, either out of an desire for power or a cool awareness of how technological advances would change the universe forever, had started the war. The men below him had paid the price for their master's misdeeds.

And now their mistress, he thought, looking up at the shield. It was nothing more than a faint shimmer in the air, barely visible to the naked eye, but it was there. The simple fact they were still alive proved it was there. *She couldn't begin to understand the horror she'd inflicted on her own people.*

The thought gave him no pleasure. Historically, the marines had enjoyed a considerable degree of freedom when it came to planning their operations. *Ed* would not have authorised a headlong charge into enemy fire, even if he'd had the entire Marine Corps behind him; *he* would have chosen to wear the enemy down piecemeal, while preparing a force to take advantage of any sudden weakness. But Admiral Singh, used to seeing planets fall quickly, had ordered an immediate attack. It would probably not have amused her, Ed reflected, to know that she had more in common with her former superiors than she cared to think.

At least we took some prisoners, he thought, sourly. *We'll learn something from them.*

He turned and strode back towards the inner layer of blockhouses. They were blackened by missile strikes and intensive shellfire, but remained largely intact. The wounded had already been shipped to hospitals within the city, placed well away from any defensive installations that might draw fire. There was still the risk of an accident, or Admiral Singh deciding to fire shells into the city at random, but there was no other choice. Admiral Singh was unlikely to accept any proposal to ship the wounded out of the city.

She's far too used to seeing men being healed overnight and springing back to work, Ed thought. So was he, but the medics were overwhelmed. Corinthian was an advanced world, yet it had already run short of medical technology and supplies. There were too many wounded who would bear the scars for the rest of their lives, unless they paid to have them removed in later life. *She doesn't comprehend what she's done to her men and ours.*

He nodded to the guard outside the blockhouse, who checked his ID before allowing him into the complex. Inside, the air stank of piss and sweat and human fear; soldiers manned the ramparts while others sat against the concrete walls, trying hard to catch a few moments of sleep before they were called back to duty. A lieutenant started, his face flickering though a dizzying series of emotions as he saw Ed. Ed waved him down before he could do anything stupid like waking his men to greet their ultimate superior. He'd always hated the officers who showed up for photographs, after the battle was won. He was damned if he was turning into one of those bastards himself.

A stab of guilt ran through him as he kept walking, reprimanding him for not sharing the dangers with his men. Marine officers were meant to lead from the front, to be first in the charge and the last in the retreat, but he'd been in the bunker during the battle. Cold logic told him that there had been no choice; emotion told him he should have been on the front lines, commanding the defence of a blockhouse and calling down fire on the advancing enemy soldiers. It had been far too long, he reflected as he clambered down a ladder into the lower levels, since he'd been in real danger. The ill-fated assassination attempt on Gaby, just before the war began, didn't really count.

You were on Lakshmibai, he reminded himself. *Does that not count?*

He sighed inwardly as he stepped into the command room. It wasn't much, merely a handful of terminals on tables and a pair of chairs. General Mathis was sitting on one of the chairs, issuing a calm series of orders to a pair of junior officers. Ed nodded to him as he looked up, then motioned for him to finish talking to his officers. He'd always hated it when a higher-up dropped in without advance notification, particularly when it was one of the officers who expected everyone to genuflect and prostrate themselves in front of him. Mathis could finish his essential work before talking to Ed.

"Colonel," Mathis said, when he had dismissed the officers. "Thank you for coming."

Ed nodded. If Mathis *meant* that, he'd eat his Rifleman's Tab. "I won't be staying long," he said, feeling another twinge of guilt. If he couldn't be on the front lines when the shit hit the fan, he owed it to himself to view the remains of men and women under his command. "I just wanted to see the repair work in person."

"We're holding back until the enemy have finished removing their dead," Mathis said, his tone flat. It was easy to tell that he expected Ed to overrule him. "I know they pledged not to send any spies, but I'd be surprised if the recovery crews aren't interrogated once the task is done."

"Almost certainly," Ed agreed. "Do we have a rough idea of just how many enemy died in the fighting?"

"We think around ten thousand, sir," Mathis said. Ed sucked in his breath sharply. He knew that thousands of people died each day on Earth - or *had* died on Earth - but he just wasn't used to such staggering losses. Enemy morale had to be in the crapper. Even the most fanatical of religious zealots had problems coping with immense casualty rates. "But there's no way to be sure."

Ed nodded, curtly. There were so many mangled bodies between the defence lines that it would be hard, if not impossible, for a WARCAT team to isolate just how many people had actually died. They'd have to use DNA testing, he thought, and even then it would be hard to give a *definite* answer. And that figure didn't include the wounded, the men and women who had been badly injured and died before receiving medical treatment; hell, it was quite possible that a number of enemy soldiers had deserted, once they realised just how little their superiors cared for their lives. He might never know for sure just how many Wolves had died in the fighting.

We'll have to compare notes after the war, he thought, grimly. *And the Wolves themselves might not know just how many people they've lost.*

He shook his head. "How quickly can you repair the defence lines?"

"The inner lines can be repaired fairly quickly, within a week at most," Mathis said. He snorted, rudely. "Repairing the outermost defence line is likely to be impossible, particularly if the enemy seeks to interfere with our operations. Sir...a single volley of shellfire per day would be enough to slow us down. We simply don't have enough equipment to soak up the losses."

"Or replenish the ammunition we used," Ed said. "How bad is it?"

"We shot ourselves dry in a number of places," Mathis said. "Sir, we were damn lucky it ended when it did. A few more hours and we might have been in some trouble. There was hand-to-hand fighting in some of the blockhouses too."

Ed rubbed his forehead. "And they'll know we're short on supplies too."

"They can interdict anything sent in by sea or land," Mathis agreed. "Our local industrial plant isn't capable of matching our demands."

"Yeah," Ed agreed. Freedom City was on a river, near the sea, but the enemy had sunk two freighters as they drew the noose tight around the city. Shipping in supplies would be impossible. "Let's just hope that they don't have the manpower to launch a second offensive on such a scale."

He sighed. "We still don't know how many enemy soldiers there are," he added. "Perhaps we'll learn something from the prisoners."

"Perhaps, sir," Mathis said. "But I would be surprised if they knew anything of importance."

Ed tended to agree. Soldiers were rarely told anything more than they needed to know - or, rather, what their *superiors* believed they needed to know. He remembered a pompous army general explaining that soldiers couldn't tell the enemy what they didn't know, but Ed had had enough experience of the Imperial Army to suspect that the truth was a little different - and far darker. Knowledge was power, after all, but only if it remained restricted to a handful of people. Sharing the knowledge weakened its value.

The Corps never embraced that attitude, he reminded himself. *And we were far stronger because of it.*

"I'll show myself out," he said. "Once the first set of repair works are completed, report to the bunker. We'll need to discuss changes in our tactics."

"Yes, sir," Mathis agreed. "One more battle like that and we are finished."

He was right, Ed knew. The casualties were bad enough, but running out of ammunition was far worse. There was no way they could replenish their supplies in time to withstand another offensive on such a scale. In hindsight, his calculations of just how rapidly they'd expend their supplies had been grossly optimistic. And to think he'd thought he was being *pessimistic*!

They'll have taken a bloody nose too, he thought. *But can they endure the losses long enough to force a victory?*

His expression darkened as he climbed back to the surface, one hand dropping to his pistol as he heard the rattle of gunfire in the distance. It sounded as though it was coming from enemy lines, well away from the defences. Enemy soldiers shooting animals to supplement their rations... or hunting insurgents? Jasmine had to have embarrassed them badly, when she'd sneaked into their gunnery position and blown the guns up in a single massive explosion. Ed recalled just how officers had exploded, when their precautions had been proved inadequate and his marines had sneaked into their bases. Now, with more at stake than embarrassment, he doubted the enemy officers would be lax in their hunt for scapegoats...

It all rests on Admiral Singh, he thought. *Which way will she jump?*

He wished, suddenly, that he'd actually *met* the woman. It might have given him a better feel for her personality. She'd taken hideous losses, losses she would need a victory to justify...but was she too proud to back away, if she believed she was losing? Or would she coolly calculate that the defenders had to be short on ammunition and launch a second assault, once she'd rallied her forces and resupplied them. It might take months to draw supplies from Wolfbane, but she had the time.

And she can keep sniping at us all the time, he reminded himself. *She may have lost the battle, but she hasn't lost the war.*

———

Mindy had long since lost the feeling of embarrassment - or vulnerability - that came with being naked in front of a bunch of men, even though it would have been the prelude to gang-rape on Earth. It helped that the doctor was thoroughly professional, inspecting her shoulder with a handheld sensor and then testing her blood before nodding to himself and motioning to her small pile of clothes. Mindy turned and donned them quickly, wishing there was some way to get a shower. She'd sponged herself down after recovering from the last bout of drugs, but she was ruefully aware of her own stench. It was a minor miracle that someone had managed to get her a clean uniform. The only thing missing was her service pistol.

"You should be fine, but watch that shoulder," the doctor said, curtly. He looked tired, too tired to care about her. "I'd recommend light duty for the next few days, but under the circumstances its probably unlikely."

"I know," Mindy said. She hadn't seen any of her fellow stormtroopers since she'd been dragged out of the blockhouse, but she'd chatted to a few of the other wounded and they'd all agreed the news wasn't good. They might have held the line, yet they'd paid a heavy price to do it. She couldn't afford to be lying around when her comrades needed her. "What happened to my pistol?"

"It'll be in the lockers," the doctor said. "We don't like leaving patients with their weapons, not here."

Mindy nodded, ruefully. The drugs she'd shot into her bloodstream to keep her going had produced any number of odd side-effects, particularly when combined with medical painkillers. She'd had all sorts of hallucinations before she'd finally crashed down into darkness, seeing visions of monsters and creepy shadows crawling over her bed. If she'd had her pistol with her, she might have started firing at random. In truth, she wasn't quite sure *what* had happened between her injury and her recovery.

She cleared her throat. "Do you know where I should report to?"

"There's a Command Post up top," the doctor said. He yawned, suddenly. It struck her that he must have had less sleep than herself. "They'll tell you where to go."

"Bloody MPs," she said. She tested her legs as she took a step forward, then sighed in relief as it became clear she could walk normally. "Thank you, doctor."

"Try not to get wounded again," the doctor said, sternly. "We ran out of medical packages shortly after you were treated."

Mindy swallowed as she walked to the door and left the room, the doctor already moving to the next patient. Outside, the corridor was heaving with wounded men, lining the walls as they waited for treatment. Mindy felt a flash of guilt as she saw men without arms or legs, knowing it would be months before replacements could be grown. They'd be crippled until then, she realised…and if their bodies rejected the replacements, they'd be crippled for life.

She shuddered as she stopped at the lockers and recovered her pistol, then hurried up the stairs to the command post. A handful of MPs stood there, working terminals and barking orders to a line of soldiers. Mindy joined the rear of the line and waited impatiently until the MPs finally got around to dealing with her. They checked her file, then looked up at her in some surprise.

"You've been nominated for the Purple Heart, the Knife Edge and the Medal of Honour," the MP said. "I'm not sure when the ceremony will be held, but they have already been added to your record."

Mindy winced. The Purple Heart was given to soldiers who were wounded on duty, the Knife Edge was awarded to soldiers who killed an enemy soldier in hand-to-hand combat…she would have cheerfully forsaken both of them, if she could. She wondered, absently, just who had nominated her for the Medal of Honour. She didn't *think* she'd done something particularly worthy of it.

"Thank you," she said. It wasn't important, not at the moment. She was sure that an award ceremony would catch up with her, sooner or later. "Where should I go?"

"Your unit is currently reconstituting itself at" - the MP skimmed the file for a long moment - "at Unit #4673," he said. "You don't have any specific orders, so I suggest you go there and report to your superiors. They'll know where to send you."

Mindy nodded in some relief. She'd feared being reassigned to CROW duty, to filling a hole in another unit. Instead, it looked as though her unit had survived largely intact. She took a printout of her medical record - she'd need to show it when she reached her destination - and then left the CP. Behind her, the MPs were already talking to the next soldier in line. She glanced at a map to orientate herself, then walked out of the building. The air drifting over the city tasted of fire and smoke and human flesh, burning to death. It took her a moment to realise that the skyline was different. A number of skyscrapers had simply vanished.

But at least we held, she reassured herself. *We held the line. The enemy didn't manage to break into the city.*

Steeling herself, she walked on.

CHAPTER
THIRTY

The second type would stop to loot and rape, thus ensuring that his men didn't get to the battlefield in time. A competent enemy would have time to crush the other regiments before the final regiment arrived, allowing him to defeat them all in detail. And, as a bonus, the second type would make themselves so unpopular that the locals could be relied upon for support.
- Professor Leo Caesius. The Role of Randomness In War.

"Admiral," Colonel Higgs said. "General Haverford is here."

Rani scowled to herself as she turned to face her advisor and bodyguard. Higgs had been with her since she'd taken control of the Trafalgar Naval Base, months before she'd moved her forces to Corinthian and turned the system into her base of operations. She trusted him as much as she trusted anyone, if only because he'd remained loyal when she'd been forced to flee into interstellar space when she'd lost control of the planet below. And yet, he didn't - he couldn't - give her valid advice. She didn't know anyone who could.

Save perhaps for Haverford, she thought. *And he has his own interests at stake.*

She met his eyes. "Show him in," she ordered. "And then leave us."

Higgs raised his eyebrows, but merely nodded and headed off to do as he was bid. Rani watched him go, grinding her teeth in frustration. She'd never found it easy to cope with people impeding her path to power, yet she'd always been able to manoeuvre around them and eventually take her revenge. Admiral Bainbridge had certainly learned the hard way not to leave her behind him, after he'd screwed her career for refusing to screw him! But Bainbridge had been a buffoon. The enemy below was far more dangerous.

She wanted power, she knew; power was *all* she had ever wanted. Power to protect herself, power to offer patronage on her own terms... she didn't want sex or wealth or anything but power. She would have been happy to work with Admiral Bainbridge, yet he'd never seen her as anything more than an attractive piece of meat. Her new enemies - her subordinates who would only remain loyal as long as she remained strong - wouldn't make that particular mistake. They wouldn't exile her to an isolated world; they'd kill her, just to make sure there was no possibility of a comeback.

The hatch hissed open, revealing General Haverford. He looked tired and mussed, for a man who had been safe in the FOB while his men went into battle. Rani couldn't help thinking nasty thoughts about REMFs - she'd been on the bridge of her flagship during several small battles - then dismissed the thought. Haverford wasn't *political*, as far as her spies could tell, but he did have a vast number of friends amongst the military. Turning him into a scapegoat might well work against her.

"General," she said, stiffly. "What happened?"

Haverford met her eyes, evenly. "The offensive failed," he said. His voice was very calm, but she was experienced enough to sense the consternation bubbling under his expressionless demeanour. "We threw everything we could muster at the enemy defence lines and failed to break through into the city."

"They were ready for us," Rani said. In hindsight...had the Commonwealth anticipated an attack on Corinthian? Had she been lured into a trap? The timing was suspicious. There was no way so many defences could be put together in less than a month, even with advanced technology. "Do you believe your forces gave it their all?"

"Yes, Admiral," Haverford said, flatly. "We could hand out hundreds of medals, easily. But most of them would be posthumous."

Rani scowled. She had no qualms about losing men and material in the service of a higher cause - unlike many of her officers, she understood that starships were meant to be risked in combat - but losses on such a scale were staggering. They would be covered up, of course, yet she knew all too well that the cover up would start to leak almost at once. Anyone who was anyone on Wolfbane had spies in the military, men and women who would hear fragments of the truth and pass them on to their masters. And they might well conclude that losses had been *far* higher than reality. The entire force might have been wiped out.

And telling them the truth won't make it easier, she thought, darkly. *They'll just say I got thousands of men killed for nothing.*

Her scowl deepened. No one had taken such losses for centuries, unless some of the more hysterical stories from the Core Worlds were actually *true*. If Earth's entire population was gone...her losses wouldn't even be a drop in the bucket. But no one could really grasp the sheer enormity of over eighty *billion* deaths. It was immense, utterly beyond comprehension; a meaningless statistic to men and women who had never visited Earth, nor seen it as anything other than a distant uncaring master. But twenty thousand deaths on Corinthian, men who had largely been recruited from Wolfbane, was anything but a statistic.

And I have nothing to show for it, she reminded herself. *They'll use that against me too.*

"Very well," she said, dismissively. "What is the current situation?"

"We have the city enveloped," Haverford said. His face twisted, too quickly for her to get a grasp on his thoughts. "They cannot get in or out of the city. Our gunners are hastily preparing to bombard their fortifications while half of our infantry are sweeping the area dominated by the shield for insurgents. Given time, we will starve them into surrender - or death."

Rani scowled. "We don't have time," she said. Besides, she rather doubted it was *possible* to starve the enemy out. Man might not enjoy living on algae-bars alone, but man *could*. "We need to have the matter concluded within two to three months."

Haverford leaned forward, meeting her eyes. "Then we need to rethink our approach," he said. "Our previous tactics proved disastrous."

"We didn't anticipate the shield," Rani said. She thought fast. Allowing Haverford his head might lead to victory, but it would be hard to steal even *part* of the credit. She didn't dare risk a challenger from among the military. And yet, she was short on options. "What do you have in mind?"

"We have gathered a great deal of data on the enemy fortifications," Haverford said, producing a datachip from his pocket. Rani took the chip and slotted it into her console, displaying a chart of the enemy positions. "They put together a massive network of bunkers and blockhouses, mainly woven from enhanced concrete and layers of hullmetal, then tied them together through a series of underground tunnels. It is a quite complex system, given the limited time they had to work, but it has a number of weaknesses. One of them - the tunnels - was revealed during the fighting."

"Our shellfire collapsed them," Rani said. She nodded, impatiently. "And the point?"

"We relied on basic weapons," Haverford said. "It made sense, given the time limits confounding us, but it ensured that most of the bombardment was wasted effort. I propose, instead, to use the MEUs to construct weapons specifically designed to smash through layers of protection and detonate inside the bunkers."

Rani's eyes narrowed. "And no one thought of this earlier?"

"No one ever had to fight on such a scale without KEWs," Haverford reminded her. "If we could drop KEWs on the defence line, Admiral, we'd smash it to rubble within a few hours."

He shook his head. "It will take at least a month or two to manufacture the weapons in sufficient numbers," he added. "I doubt we have any in stock on Wolfbane - I *know* we didn't have any on Thule. During that time, we build up our forces to take advantage of the second bombardment and harry the enemy positions with a bombardment of our own. We may even hit the shield generator, ending the campaign overnight. And then we take the city and put an end to the resistance, once and for all."

Rani nodded, thoughtfully. There was nowhere else on Corinthian capable of putting up a fight, as far as she could tell. Indeed, it looked very much as though the rebels who'd taken power had drawn all their forces into the city...a smart short-term move, given the existence of the shield, but a long-term disaster. Either the generator failed, allowing her to crush them from orbit, or her forces punched through the defences and wiped them out. The rebels might have been smarter to disperse their forces and settle in for a long insurgency.

She contemplated the plan for a long moment. It would take time, perhaps too much time, and require her to summon additional reinforcements. There was no way it would pass unnoticed on Wolfbane, although she *could* soften the blow by summoning recruits and conscripts from first-stage colonies that were otherwise useless. But they wouldn't be trained to the right standards...

It would require me to raise the stakes when I might be wiser to fold, she thought. *And I may be throwing good money after bad.*

She shook her head. Tactically, conceding defeat and withdrawing - after laying waste to as much of the system as possible - might be the smart choice. But it would be a disaster, a disaster that would be firmly laid at her door. Her enemies would draw their knives, while she couldn't purge them without causing all kinds of long-term problems. Wolfbane had lost too much when the shipyards were destroyed. The Consortium didn't need more problems as it struggled to rebuild. She had no choice, but to bet high and hope the dice fell in her favour.

"Very well," she said, slowly. "Your plan is approved."

"Thank you, Admiral," Haverford said. "I would also like to ship the wounded back to Wolfbane and..."

Rani shook her head. "Not now, General," she said. "They can be cared for on Corinthian."

"With all due respect, Admiral, they *cannot* be cared for on Corinthian," Haverford said, sharply. Rani tensed at his tone, but forced herself to show no other reaction. "Our medical supplies are already running out. I doubt looting the unprotected cities for supplies and medical staff will help, certainly not enough to make a difference. We have no choice, but to ship the wounded home."

"Not now, General," Rani said.

She saw his point, even though it was something outside her experience. Battles in space rarely saw many wounded; a badly-damaged starship was more likely to explode with all hands, rather than limp home to offload its crew. She was used to watching hundreds of men die with their ships, but not to seeing her crews wounded. But damnable politics gave her no choice. If her enemies saw a string of wounded soldiers making their way home, they'd be emboldened to speak out against her...

...And as long as she wasn't on Wolfbane, they'd have a chance to snatch control of the system defences and turn them against her fleet.

That would cost us the war, she thought. The Commonwealth would have all the time it needed to muster its counterattack while Wolfbane was consumed by civil war. *But do those bastards care?*

"Admiral," Haverford said. "This isn't a game...."

"I know," Rani said. She briefly considered explaining her reasoning, then dismissed the thought. Haverford wasn't a strategic thinker. He wouldn't understand. "But there's no choice."

Rani dismissed him, then looked at the planet, spinning in the holographic display. She'd made a mistake, she knew now. She had wanted to retake the planet, to crush the rebels who had chased her away; she'd allowed her plans for revenge to lead her into a trap. They were trapped now, forced to fight desperately to win...she didn't dare withdraw. Her career would come to an end along with the campaign. Retreat - and defeat - was unthinkable.

She made a vow to herself as she rose and walked towards the sleeping compartment. Corinthian would be hers again, whatever the cost. And then her enemies would pay for what they'd done.

———

Ryan jerked awake, every inch of his body screaming in pain. His vision was blurred, lights flashing around him so brightly that he thought, through a drugged haze, that he was *now* in hell. Each flicker of light *hurt*, the flashes digging into his skull and making him scream in pain. He closed his eyes, but that only made matters worse. And his body ached so badly that he could barely think. He started to struggle, feeling soft restraints tied around his wrists and ankles...was he a prisoner? Or was it just something to keep him under control?

"It's alright," a soft voice said. It was feminine, warm and welcome, but it hurt! "Lie still and relax."

Ryan tried to force himself to calm **down**, but his thoughts kept running in dozens of different directions simultaneously. It was hard, so hard, to think when a maelstrom was blazing through his mind, tearing his thoughts to shreds. He cringed as he felt a needle pressed against his upper arm…a *needle*? Needles had gone out of use on every single world, save for the most primitive. What had happened to injector tabs?

He must have blacked out, because the next thing he knew was that he felt a little better. His eyes opened, revealing that he was lying on a bed in a small room. It didn't *look* like a hospital ward, rather more like a hotel room. He puzzled over it for a long moment as he tested his restraints, realising that he was firmly tied to the bed. Movement was almost impossible, beyond breathing. His first thoughts flickered through his mind, again. Was he a prisoner? Or was something badly wrong with him?

The door opened. A young woman wearing a long white coat stepped into the room. A doctor, Ryan realised; the uniform she wore under the coat marked her as a starship doctor, probably called down from one of the orbiting ships. She was pretty too, he thought, despite the numbness flowing through his body. Her chest was covered, but her breasts were clearly large enough to be noticeable…

"Captain Osborne," the doctor said. Her voice was cool and professional, disrupting his fantasy before it had time to take root. "Do you know where you are?"

Ryan's lips worked incoherently for a long moment. "Captain?"

"You were promoted," the doctor said. "Do you know where you are?"

"Not a prisoner," Ryan managed. "Water?"

The doctor produced a bottle and allowed him to sip from it. "You were injured in the fight," she said. "Do you recall what happened?"

Ryan thought for a moment. His memory was flawed. All he recalled were flashes of impressions - and pain, lots of pain. They'd been in a bunker, he thought, and he'd been half-convinced he was in hell. But the angel beside his bed suggested otherwise. Unless, of course, it was just part of his torment…

"No," he said, finally. "I don't remember much."

The doctor grimaced. "You were wounded," she said. "Your sergeant brought you back here, to the makeshift field hospital. We did what we could for you, but a combination of the drugs in your body and the shortage of supplies made it difficult to do much…"

Ryan stared at her, then glanced down the length of his body. Everything seemed normal, as far as he could tell. And yet, he was covered and numb and…

"Tell me," he growled. He wanted to pull at the restraints until they burst, but he suspected they were too strong for him. "What happened?"

"I'm sorry," the doctor said.

An awful suspicion began to blossom in Ryan's mind. *"What happened?"*

"You took two bullets," the doctor told him. Her voice was flat, but he could tell she wasn't comfortable. "One of them went through your groin. By the time we got you here…"

Ryan jerked up, clashing against the restraints. "I…they blew off my balls?"

"We had to remove the remainder," the doctor said. She shifted backwards, as if she were preparing to run. "We don't have regeneration tubes on site."

"Untie me," Ryan growled. "Now!"

"You need to remain calm," the doctor said. "You're not in any immediate danger…"

"Untie me," Ryan snapped.

The doctor hesitated, then carefully undid the restraints on his wrists. Ryan pulled himself free and hastily sat upright, feeling between his legs. He hoped - prayed - that it was a nightmare, but his fingers touched nothing. His penis was gone. In its place, there was a pucker of flesh…

He stared at her in numb horror. His manhood was gone. He wanted to scream…he'd done everything right, he'd kept up the offensive when men were dropping like flies and yet he'd been unmanned? He'd been allowed to lie on the bed while his manhood was taken from him? He found himself torn between fury, horror and an insane urge to laugh. What was he now? A useless shell of a man? A woman?

"You can regrow dicks," he snarled, turning to her. "Regrow mine!"

The doctor paled. "It's not an essential requirement…"

"It fucking is," Ryan shouted. His temper surged out of control; he swung his legs over the side of the bed and stood. "I fucking lost my fucking manhood attacking that fucking defence line and you can fucking regrow it!"

He grabbed the doctor by the shirt and yanked her forward. "Regrow it!"

"I can't," the doctor stammered. "There are others who will die without urgent treatment…"

Ryan sagged, letting go of her as he stumbled back and sat on the bed. His rage vanished as quickly as it had come, mocking him. He was an eunuch. Nothing would ever be normal again. He was barely aware of the doctor hurrying out of the door, closing it sharply behind her. No doubt she was off to whine to her superiors…

Sitting on the bed, Ryan began to weep helplessly.

CHAPTER
THIRTY-ONE

And the third type (or the handful of competent officers) would actually stand and fight. They would pose a threat, forcing a competent officer to either bypass them or accept the losses inherent in defeating them.
                        - Professor Leo Caesius. The Role of Randomness In War.

"That's another freighter convoy, Captain," the sensor officer said. "She's heavily escorted."

Mandy pursed her lips in disapproval. Admiral Singh must have summoned reinforcements long before the Battle of Freedom City, if only because they were arriving before her messages to Wolfbane could have reached their destination. The soldiers on the freighters couldn't know what they were facing, but they would find out long before they walked into the meatgrinder and got themselves torn to ribbons. And there were too many warships escorting the convoy for her to risk an attack.

Admiral Singh learned from our first attack, she thought, grimly. *She's making sure that her positions are heavily fortified.*

"Pull us back," she ordered, reluctantly.

She shook her head in irritation. Popping off a missile or two towards the freighters was a tempting prospect, but she knew it would be pointless. The escorts would swat the missiles out of space long before they reached their targets. And Admiral Singh was too experienced an admiral to make basic mistakes, like insisting that all her convoys arrived on the same approach vector. Mandy had hoped she'd have a chance to scatter mines throughout space, but it would be nothing more than a waste of time. There was no way she could produce the sheer number of mines required to cover all possible approach vectors.

"Aye, Captain," the helmsman said.

Mandy nodded, then turned her attention back to the system display. Admiral Singh was running patrols around the planet, routinely detaching a pair of destroyers to sweep space for stealthed platforms and other surprises. It was largely a waste of time, but they *had* managed to stumble across one platform - which had self-destructed as soon as the enemy had locked on - and it kept the crews occupied. The only relief, as far as Mandy was concerned, was that Admiral Singh had detached two of her battleships shortly after occupying the system.

But that's not enough to reduce the KEW threat, she thought. *If the shield fails, the entire plan goes straight into the crapper.*

She gritted her teeth at the thought. There had been a brief - very brief - message from Mindy, transmitted out through the network of platforms, informing Mandy that she had been lightly wounded. Mandy had been in worse places - being on a pirate ship meant running the risk of being robbed, raped or murdered at any moment - but the thought of her sister being hurt was terrifying. Mindy might be a soldier now, yet part of Mandy would always see her as a helpless little girl, someone she needed to protect. But there was nothing she could do to protect her sister now.

"They're dispatching a courier boat," the sensor officer reported. "She's heading straight up towards the ecliptic."

"Plot an intercept course," Mandy ordered, although she suspected it would be hopeless. The pre-collapse courier boats had been the fastest things in space and even now they still moved at a respectable clip. Their acceleration rates were staggering. *Defiant* probably didn't have a hope of overhauling the craft, let alone bringing it to a halt. "Can we catch them?"

"They're moving too quickly, Captain," the helmsman said. "They'll be over the limit before we could get into firing range."

Mandy nodded, slowly. The war in space had effectively stalemated, unless she chose to bring the rest of the squadron into the system. And yet, she knew that would give the game away far too soon. Admiral Singh had enough firepower to make the odds even…and if there was one thing she'd learned from the pirates, it was that only a sucker sought even odds.

He might just *lose*. It was far better to have the odds stacked in your favour when you finally went to the mat.

"Keep us within sensor range of the convoy," she ordered, instead. "We may just learn something useful."

"Aye, Captain," the helmsman said.

It was frustrating, but it would keep her crew occupied. There had been a couple of fights below decks, between crewmen who were constantly on edge. She didn't blame the brawlers, even though she would have to stand in judgement of them soon. Skulking around the system while their friends and comrades fought for their lives didn't sit well with anyone on the ship. The rivalry between spacers and soldiers barely mattered when so much was at stake.

She shook her head in irritation. The only consolation, she thought, was that Admiral Singh was probably feeling the same way. Battles in space could be violent, staggeringly so, but they didn't take very long. One side either lost quickly or managed to break contact and escape. A long drawn-out conflict had to be frustrating to Admiral Singh, particularly when she had to worry about events right along the border. Who knew what was happening on Thule, or Night's Edge, or Rosebud while she was waiting at Corinthian?

But she has more time on her side than we do, Mandy thought.

It wasn't a pleasant thought. She'd looked for ways to sneak supplies through the blockade, but found nothing. Admiral Singh would intercept anything she launched into the planet's atmosphere, if she even managed to get that close. She would have been surprised if she had, given just how thoroughly Admiral Singh had seeded space with her own platforms. The Admiral probably knew the location of every grain of dust orbiting the planet.

She shook her head as the enemy convoy finally entered orbit, *Defiant* hanging back to avoid detection. No matter how she looked at it, the coming battle was going to be hellish. The Wolves didn't hold all the cards, but they held enough to put up a vicious fight. And all she could do was pray she was in time to save *something* of the forces on the ground...

And Mindy, she thought. *I don't want to go home and tell mother and father she's dead.*

Jasmine fought down, somehow, the urge to charge forward and run to the rescue of the unnamed town. Both sides had ignored it during the march to Freedom City, but that had changed as the Wolves started to sweep their rear much more effectively. Two whole companies of soldiers had surrounded the town, then summoned the inhabitants to come out or face the consequences. As soon as the town was empty, they'd fired the buildings and burned the entire settlement to the ground. It looked, very much, as though the Wolves were losing control.

"They're separating the young women from everyone else," Buckley breathed. Below them, the prisoners were being searched and then bound. "That doesn't look good."

Jasmine nodded, curtly. The Wolves had been remarkably disciplined, given the sheer size of their army; she knew their superiors had hung a number of men for mistreating the civilian population. And she'd killed four soldiers who might have gotten away with it, if they kept their mouths shut afterwards. But now, their army was crumbling at the seams. She'd stumbled across enough dead and mutilated bodies to know that their discipline was breaking down. She wouldn't have given a counterfeit credit for the fate of the young women below her.

They took too many losses in the battle, she thought. *Their command network has been shot to hell.*

She closed her eyes in pain, then forced herself to watch as the men were lined up and shot down, one by one. No doubt whoever was in command of the force below her would claim they were all insurgents or something along those lines…if, of course, anyone bothered to ask at all. Jasmine hated to admit it, but if discipline was that far gone their superiors would probably be hesitant to do anything to reassert their authority. The threat of a mutiny would be far too dangerous. She shuddered, wondering what would happen to the discipline of *her* unit if its commanding officers were killed and the remaining marines slotted into other units, with unfamiliar commanders. God alone knew how many of them had seen the field hospitals before they were pushed back onto the front lines.

"Jasmine," Buckley said, quietly. "They're going to gang-rape the women."

Jasmine glared at him. "And what would you suggest we did about it?"

She forced herself to keep her voice under control. "There's six of us and nearly two hundred of them," she added. "Even if we snipe at them, they'll have the strength to come after us in force."

"They'll also call for help," Buckley pointed out, in a tone that was so calm and reasonable she just *knew* he was trying to manipulate her. "And that will bring more witnesses to the scene."

Jasmine thought about it as she returned her gaze to the scene below her. The soldiers were laughing and drinking, taunting the women as they prepared themselves for the coming nightmare. If their senior officers *knew* what had happened, Jasmine asked herself, would they do *anything* about it? Or would they join in? She'd met Civil Guard officers who had been fond of indulging themselves. They'd been more savage than their men!

But the Wolves aren't that bad, she thought. *And if it triggers off a mutiny, it works in our favour.*

"Take aim," she ordered, switching her rifle to single-shot. "And make sure you don't waste a single bullet."

"Of course not," Buckley agreed. "Supplies are in such short supply these days."

"Very funny," Stewart snarled.

Jasmine scowled as she sighted her weapon, targeting an officer who was smoking something that she rather suspected wasn't tobacco. In her experience, isolated farmers out in the boondocks tended to grow all sorts of things planetary governments disapproved of; he'd probably taken it from a farm and kept it to himself. He'd probably also taken a great deal of alcohol and passed it to his men. She couldn't think of any other explanation for the sheer quantities the men were consuming.

"Fire," she ordered.

Her target dropped like a rock, the moment her bullet smashed into his head. Other officers fell, too careless or too drunk to remember the dangers of being obviously officers in plain view. Their men didn't show any reaction at first, then started to shoot madly towards the hillside as it dawned on them that they were being fired upon. Jasmine shook her head in disgust, wondering just what sort of punishment would be meted out to the survivors by their own superiors. Being drunk on duty - or stoned out of one's mind - was enough to ensure a dishonourable discharge from the corps, if the drunkard wasn't immediately dispatched to a penal world.

"Piss-poor shots," Stewart muttered.

"Bite your tongue," Jasmine said. One of the marines must have hit something explosive, because a truck exploded into a fireball. "And keep hitting the bastards!"

She swore as she heard the sound of three helicopters in the distance. *Someone* must have snapped off a distress call, even if they were too drunk to do anything else. Maybe there *was* a responsible officer amongst them…she shook her head, dismissing the thought. A responsible officer would have shot one of his men to regain control, if necessary, rather than letting them make preparations for a drunken gang-rape. She snapped out a command, ordering the marines to pack up and run. There was nothing they could do for the girls below, she knew; there was certainly no way they could escape in time. She just hoped that whoever arrived on the scene was ready to take control.

We did what we could, she thought, as they scattered into the undergrowth. HVMs were in short supply now, even though they'd stockpiled hundreds before the Wolves arrived. Hell, they were running short of bullets. *All we can do now is pray.*

––––––––

Mark was not given to brooding, as a general rule. He understood the realities of warfare and, although he would never have admitted it where spying ears might hear, he understood the realities of politics too. But it still shocked him to realise just how casually Admiral Singh was prepared to let thousands of men - thousands of *additional* men - die to cement her rule over Wolfbane. There was nothing that could be done for the men who had died in front of the blockhouses, yet the wounded and mutilated…they could be saved! But to do that, they'd have to be sent home.

And that would cause political problems, he thought, as he sat in his private office. *She's letting them die because it would threaten her position if she did otherwise.*

He studied the display, thoughtfully. The planning for the second offensive was well underway; the bunker-busters he'd designed were finally rolling out of the MEUs and being shipped down to the surface. Indeed, the defenders didn't seem to be fighting back with great enthusiasm. Were his bombardments so ineffective or were the defenders conserving ammunition? Mark had no idea just how long the Commonwealth had been plotting its stand on Corinthian, but he would have been surprised if they'd anticipated just how much ammunition would be consumed in a single day. *He* hadn't anticipated it either.

We could win this battle, he told himself. *But it could cost us the war.*

His intercom bleeped. "General, this is Ferguson," a voice said. "I have a vitally important report to make to you."

Mark scowled in irritation. He'd planned to reassign Ferguson, but he needed a skilled officer working underneath him. And yet, he had no doubt that Ferguson would betray him if all hell broke loose. He wouldn't want to hitch his star too closely to Mark's when there was a very real risk of losing everything. If Mark took the blame for the disaster, everyone close to him would suffer too.

"Come in," he said. "This had better be important."

He looked up as the younger man stepped into the compartment. At least Ferguson *should* be able to tell what was *important*. Mark had handled uniformed bureaucrats who thought a missing computer or a shortage of paper clips was a rather more serious problem than countless dead or wounded men. One of the few advantages of working for Admiral Singh, rather than Governor Brown, was the freedom to expel uniformed bureaucrats from the chain of command. He'd used it ruthlessly on Thule.

"It is, sir," Ferguson said. "There's been an...*incident*."

"An incident," Mark repeated. Ferguson should know to be blunter. Bad news didn't smell any better if it was wrapped up in flattery and butt-kissing. "Explain. Now."

Ferguson looked hesitant, as if he wasn't quite sure what had happened. "Captain Rask took a couple of companies on a search and destroy mission," he said. "They stumbled across a small town we had previously ignored..."

Mark nodded impatiently. He had a bad feeling about this. "And...?"

"They came under intensive sniper fire," Ferguson said. "Lieutenant Pella, the senior survivor, called for support. The reinforcements discovered that the companies had burned the town to the ground, massacred the male population and were on the verge of raping the female population when they were interrupted."

Mark stared at him. He'd known that discipline was a problem, he'd known that far too many units had been shattered by the fighting and their survivors parcelled out to other units, but a mass gang-rape? How badly had the companies been affected by the fighting? He struggled to recall the details...hadn't Captain Rask been promoted for surviving the assault on the blockhouses? He'd been so desperate for heroes that he'd jumped the man up a level and given him a company command. What had *happened* out there?

"Colonel Travis has assumed command of the scene," Ferguson said. "He reports that Lieutenant Pella has been placed under arrest, along with the surviving common soldiers, but he's not sure how to proceed from there."

"...Fuck," Mark said.

He tapped his terminal, bringing up the records. Captain Rask's two companies had been put together from the remains of a dozen other units. None of the officers had worked together before, very few of the soldiers had *fought* together before...and instead of a long period of training to smooth out the rough edges, they'd been thrown into a search and destroy mission in the midst of enemy territory. Captain Rask had either lost control or enthusiastically ordered the destruction of a town, followed by mass slaughter and rape. The bastard was far too lucky that a sniper had picked him off.

And I can't show any weakness, he thought, bitterly. Normally, isolated breaches of discipline would be handled by the MPs, but there were too many discontented - if not mutinous - men involved. Hatred of the locals was spreading, just as it had on Thule...but none of the units on Thule had been forced into a meatgrinder. *If I show weakness, discipline becomes a joke and we'll disintegrate.*

He took a breath. "Order Colonel Travis to have the prisoners shipped here, under guard," he said. "They are to speak to *no one* until I have had a chance to deal with Lieutenant Pella personally. I want them isolated from everyone else."

"Yes, sir," Ferguson said. "Do you want them assigned to a penal unit?"

"It's a bit bigger than that now," Mark said. On Thule, it would have been easy. The men would have been assigned to a penal unit so fast their heads would spin. But on Corinthian…he wasn't quite sure how to proceed. The locals might well already know what had happened. "Have them kept in isolation. I'll need to speak to the Admiral before taking any steps."

"Yes, sir," Ferguson said.

CHAPTER

THIRTY-TWO

Each type would ensure a different outcome, but there is no way to know which type would actually take command. Controlling one's enemy to the point where the right officers take commands is impossible.

- Professor Leo Caesius. The Role of Randomness In War.

Ryan lay on his bed, staring up at the ceiling.

He wasn't sure what he'd expected, really. He'd assaulted a doctor. That was a court martial offense, at the very least. He'd spent the next few hours lying on his bed, wondering when the MPs were going to come crashing through the door and haul him off to a cell. But nothing had happened and he'd eventually drifted off to sleep, only to be awakened by a female orderly - a press-ganged local - bringing him a tray of food. He'd glowered at her so badly she'd fled the moment she'd put the tray on the table.

It was hard, so hard, to keep himself under some form of control. He found himself weeping randomly, then shouting and screaming at the universe…and then sitting down numbly and just waiting to die. He no longer had *any* control, he admitted, when he could think rationally. Losing his junk was bad, but surviving when so many others had died… if he'd been promoted, did that mean that everyone above him was dead? He'd liked as well as respected the captain, the colonel had been strict but fair…were they dead? He wanted to ask someone, but the orderlies never stuck around long enough to answer questions.

He should be in pain, he knew; he **might** have felt better about himself if he *were* in pain. But the doctors had **done** a good job, given the limited time they'd had to work on him before moving to the next patient. He wasn't in pain; indeed, his body felt almost normal. And yet, the absence of his manhood tore at his mind. He could barely force himself to use the facilities, when he needed to pass water. It made him feel as if he were no longer a man.

Ryan sagged as he heard the sound of someone opening the door. He didn't *think* the door was locked, but he hadn't been able to muster the determination to open the door and step outside. Everyone would be laughing at him, he thought; they'd make fun of him for losing his manhood…his thoughts mocked him bitterly, even as he turned his head to see who had stepped into the room. It took him several moments, through the haze, to recognise Captain Gellman. He'd met him back on Thule…

"Captain Osborne," Gellman said. "Congratulations on your promotion."

"Fuck off," Ryan said. Gellman had been promoted - unless he'd pinched a major's uniform from someone - but he found it hard to care. "It came with too high a price."

"Yes, it did," Gellman agreed. "And that's *fuck off, sir*."

Ryan felt a surge of rage so powerful that he tottered forward before regaining control of himself. "Fuck off, sir."

"I can't go yet," Gellman told him, bluntly. "You have to return to duty."

Ryan couldn't help himself. He started to giggle.

"You have *got* to be out of your mind," he said, when he'd finished. "Do you know what's happened to me?"

Gellman scowled. "Do you know what happened to Captain Yates? Captain Benton? Or Major Shaw? Or Colonel Stewart?"

Ryan could guess. "Dead?"

"All save Shaw," Gellman said. "The poor bastard will probably never walk again. He's one of the few buggers who can't take regenerated bodily organs."

"I've lost *my* organ," Ryan protested. "They *can't* expect me to go back to duty."

"You can have your dick regrown once you get back home," Gellman said, bluntly. "And you will, which is more than can be said for Shaw. Right now, you can walk and you can fight and *that* means you can be slotted back into the army. We are critically short on experienced officers."

"Because most of them were killed, *sir*," Ryan said,

Gellman didn't bother to deny it. Instead, he walked over to the cabinet and threw it open, revealing a clean uniform and fresh underwear. "Get dressed," he ordered. "Or stay here and eventually be arrested for dereliction of duty. You'll be put in front of a wall and shot."

Ryan scowled, but did as he was told. He couldn't resist removing his gown right in front of Gellman, just to see how he'd react, but the older man showed no visible reaction to the gruesome sight. The uniform felt unnatural against his bare skin, after fighting for so long in a sweaty uniform that had probably been burned; he checked his belt, instinctively, and discovered that the pistol had been removed. No doubt someone had worried about him blowing his own head off after discovering he'd lost his manhood…

He stared down at the floor as he finished buttoning up his jacket. His entire body was threatening to shake. He'd been through uncounted skirmishes on Thule, from brief ambushes to house-clearance operations, yet now…yet now he felt as if he had lost his nerve once and for all. The thought of going back on the front lines, of going back into combat, scared him more than he cared to admit. His hands were shaking…angrily, he fought to bring them under control, knowing it would only be a matter of time before they started to shake again. Part of him was almost tempted to stay where he was and risk getting shot. At least that would put an end to the whole affair.

"I'm sorry," Gellman said, awkwardly. "If it was up to me…"

"If it was up to me, I would never have come here," Ryan snarled. "How many did we lose?"

Gellman said nothing. Ryan rounded on him. "*How many?*"

"Around twenty thousand," Gellman admitted. "Perhaps more, if some of the wounded die."

Ryan shuddered. He hadn't known everyone who'd landed on Corinthian, but he *had* known everyone in his company. Old sweats who'd been happy to help the stupid greenie lieutenant, young maggots scared out of their minds and trying not to show it…he'd known them all. And now they were gone, leaving him the last survivor. He wondered if that meant he had to write the formal letters, now he was the senior officer.

What the hell was he going to tell the mothers, fathers, wives and children? Their young men would never come home.

He said nothing as Gellman led him out the door and down a long corridor. The building had probably been a school, before the war; the corridors were lined with drawings that were very definitely childish. There were hundreds of wounded men, some lying on the floor and others sitting in chairs several sizes too small for them; he was glad, despite himself, that he couldn't see any of the locals. He'd saved at least one local girl from being molested, yet it hadn't stopped her comrades from taking his manhood...burning hatred flared through him as they walked down the stairs and stepped out into the remains of Cheshire. The town was crammed with armoured vehicles, emplaced weapons and soldiers strolling everywhere.

Should have just nuked the place, he thought, nastily. *Why play war when we could just crush the defenders and keep moving?*

A shuttle roared overhead as it dropped down towards the FOB. Ryan wondered, as Gellman led him to an AFV, why he hadn't been moved to the FOB itself. There was supposed to be better medical care there. No doubt the REMFs in their shiny uniforms were unwilling to gaze upon a wounded soldier. If they'd had problems with men in field uniforms striding around the FOB, and they had, he dreaded to think what they would make of him now. If he walked around naked...

The thought depressed him as they climbed into the AFV, which set off as soon as the hatch was slammed closed. Ryan had ridden in hundreds of the vehicles on Thule, but he couldn't help finding *this* one uniquely depressing. The driver said nothing to the officers, chatting only to the escorts as the small convoy headed back towards the FOB. They were constantly alert, Ryan noted, which didn't bode well for the war. If the enemy had managed to sneak into a gunnery position and blow the guns - and their crews - to hell, they'd have no problems sneaking through the forest and sniping at exposed soldiers. A single bullet pinged off the armour as they moved onwards, the machine gun answering the challenge with overwhelming firepower. Ryan couldn't help thinking it was a poor exchange.

He looked at Gellman as depression threatened to overcome him. "What's happening at the far end?"

"You'll get a new command," Gellman said. "But there may be something else to do first."

Ryan had to fight down the urge to start giggling, again. *He* would have a new command. If he'd been promoted - and he doubted the doctor would make such a mistake - he'd probably be given a company. Perhaps he'd be put in command of one of the penal units, a death sentence by any other name. Or perhaps they'd just pin a worthless medal on his chest before sending him back out to die. The thought of facing the enemy once again was terrifying. He couldn't help thinking that his nerve had died with the rest of his men.

The vehicle lurched, then came to a halt. Ryan stood as the hatch banged open and followed Gellman out into the FOB. Someone was *very* paranoid, he noted; the AFV had stopped within a wired compartment, isolated from the remainder of the FOB. A chemical stench floated through the air, strong enough to make him gag; outside the FOB, he could see tracts of wasteland that had once been trees and forests. The hillside he recalled from their first landing was just a blackened ruin, as if fire had swept over it so intensely that nothing had been left alive. There were clear fields of fire in all directions, he saw, as the guards poked and prodded at his body before allowing him to pass. He couldn't quite keep the resentment off his face at their attitude. Where the hell had they been while he'd been fighting for his life?

"This way," Gellman said, as they were finally waved through the gates. "I'll need to check in with HQ first."

"Of course, sir," Ryan said.

The FOB had expanded massively since his last visit, although - in all honesty - he hadn't been paying much attention to anything beyond the brothel and the bars. Countless warehouses had sprung into existence and countless vehicles were buzzing around, carting crates of supplies from the landing pads to the convoy assembly points. He shuddered in disgust as he saw some of the REMFs, walking along without a care in the world. Their nice clean uniforms had never seen combat, he was sure, any more than they'd seen it themselves. They probably hadn't even come under long-range mortar fire!

He glared at a pair of uniformed women who walked past them and had the pleasure of seeing them flinch. Women were rare in the combat branches, he knew; they were probably logistics officers or clerks, rather than anything *useful*. Their uniforms were so neatly tailored that he could just *guess* why they'd been assigned to Corinthian. No doubt they worked on their backs or on their knees, instead of crawling through trenches or even sitting in front of a desk. He glanced behind him to see the two woman hurrying away, as if they'd come face to face with a wild animal. Once, it would have bothered him; now, he no longer cared. The useless REMFs had no conception of what he'd faced.

"Here we are," Gellman said, with forced cheerfulness. They stopped outside a large building and waited, patiently, for the guards to check them once again. "We'll probably have to wait until the CO is ready to see us."

"Joy," Ryan muttered.

Gellman was right, he discovered as soon as they were shown into a waiting room. It was crammed with REMFs in fancy uniforms, all looking as if they'd just stepped off a recruiting poster. Ryan wondered if they'd run for their lives if he started growling, then forced himself to sit and wait as long as it took. And yet he found himself more and more aware of the bastards *looking* at him, as if they were wondering what he was doing here. He felt cold hatred flaring within his breast, demanding an outlet…

"Major Gellman, Captain Osborne," a woman's voice called.

Ryan allowed himself a moment of relief as Gellman led him through a door, following the woman. She had a nice ass, he noted; it was a relief, despite everything, to know he could still be interested. And yet, he could do nothing. His body twitched…he slowed to a halt, suddenly unwilling to walk any further. Court martial and summary execution seemed a great deal better than remaining where he was, a frail shadow of a man.

"Come on," Gellman said. "Not long to go now."

The woman turned to face them, her eyes wide. Ryan felt a surge of sudden hatred, a mad impulse to wrap his hands around her neck and squeeze. It was all he could do to remain still. Horror ran through his mind as he followed Gellman into the General's office. He hadn't been like this before, had he? He'd never even *considered* lashing out at someone, even a REMF, before the battle. What **had** happened to him?

"Captain Osborne," General Haverford said. Ryan had to force himself to remember to salute. "I'm sorry **about** your loss."

Ryan bit his tongue, hard, to keep from saying something he'd be made to regret. The General's uniform was **as clean** and tidy as every other uniform he'd seen inside the wire, where **there was** no danger of sudden death or prolonged mutilation. He'd seen actual combat, Ryan recalled, but he didn't *look* like a combat soldier. He **hadn't** even been under the shield, when the battle had begun. No, he'd been **safe** and warm in the FOB.

"If it were up to me, you'd be placed on inactive duty until you were fully healed," the General said. "You were the only survivor of your company. But I need you here and now."

"Yes, sir," Ryan grunted. He wondered, briefly, if he could snap the General's neck before Gellman could stop him. But that would just put an even more useless REMF in command of the operation. "I understand."

The General studied him for a long moment. Ryan stood still, finding it hard to care if he'd gone over the line or not. Death would be almost welcome. He couldn't bear the thought of going back into combat. And yet, cold hatred surged through him as he realised he was looking at the architect of the battle, the man who'd thought that throwing twenty thousand men into the teeth of enemy fire was somehow a good idea. There would be an opportunity to avenge the dead, if only he waited long enough. He was damned if he was blindly following orders any longer.

"We are developing new weapons to hammer the enemy positions and break through to the shield generator," the General said, finally. "Hopefully, we can clear our way through them with less casualties. Before then, I want you to take command of one of the reconstituted companies and prepare them for the attack."

At least it's not a penal battalion, Ryan thought.

"Thank you, sir," he said. He didn't mean it; he rather suspected General Haverford *knew* he didn't mean it. The man must be *really* short on qualified officers. "I'll take command of the company at once."

"A different issue, first," General Haverford said. "An officer lost control of his men two hours ago, Captain. They killed a great many enemy prisoners and were about to gang-rape many more. How should they be punished?"

Ryan scowled. The *old* Ryan would have been horrified. Atrocities - and word of the atrocity would probably have swept around the planet by now - only made it harder to win civilian hearts and minds. The guilty had to be punished. Worse, they had to be *seen* to be punished. But now, he found it hard to care. Let Corinthian be swept clean of life. The planet wasn't worth a single dead soldier.

"Throw them into the penal units, sir," he said, finally. It was the right answer, even though it wasn't what he wanted to say. "They'll have their chance to redeem themselves or die."

"I may have to hand the senior surviving officer over to the locals," the General mused, slowly. "They'll demand the right to try him."

"That would be a betrayal, sir," Ryan said, before he could stop himself. "You'd be giving us up to the enemy."

"Yes," the General agreed. "The Admiral said the same thing - and more besides. But atrocities like that aren't going to make us popular."

"We are never going to be popular," Ryan said, bluntly. The rage flared up in him again, so strong it was hard to think clearly. "They are going to hate us for thousands of years. But let them hate, as long as they fear."

The General blinked. "I'll take it under advisement," he said. "Dismissed, Captain."

Gellman elbowed him, outside. "You do realise you would probably have had a seat on the court martial board if you'd kept your mouth shut?"

"I don't care," Ryan said, bluntly. He'd spoken rudely to a General. *That* wasn't a mere prank like stealing weapons or selling information to the insurgents. "All I want to do is get this damned war over and done with."

"Fine," Gellman said. He didn't seem inclined to argue further. "Your orders should be waiting for you downstairs."

"Then let's go get them," Ryan said. "Shall we?"

CHAPTER

THIRTY-THREE

Furthermore, such concerns apply at all levels of warfare. A competent junior officer might be betrayed by his cowardly superiors, while a competent general officer might lose a battle because his juniors stopped to loot halfway to the battlefield.

- Professor Leo Caesius. The Role of Randomness In War.

Mark watched Captain Osborne leave the office with a profound feeling of dissatisfaction. It was obvious, blatantly obvious, that Osborne was on the verge of cracking up. Mark couldn't imagine what it was like to be castrated, particularly in such a manner, but he was sure it had to be traumatic. In an ideal world, Osborne would have had his manhood regrown long before he'd been allowed to wake up, or placed on medical leave until he was deemed fit to return to duty, if he didn't take a medical discharge. But Osborne was one of the few experienced officers to survive the battle, one of the few who could be put in command of the reconstituted units. There was no *time* to allow him to recover.

And he might not survive long enough to go on leave afterwards, he thought, as his intercom buzzed. *If he's that badly wounded inside...*

He sighed, then tapped the switch. "Haverford."

"Sir, this is Tallinn," a voice said. "I have Lieutenant Pella here, as you ordered."

"Bring him in," Mark said. "Now."

He'd taken the opportunity to glance at Lieutenant Pella's file while waiting for the meeting, but there had been little there of interest. Lieutenant Pella was too young, really; he should never have been kicked up a grade without some additional seasoning. But the battlefield was no respecter of high ranks, he knew, and Pella had been given responsibilities he was ill-prepared to handle. Captain Rask too, coming to think of it. The man had been a lieutenant before being promoted, after the battle. He'd needed more seasoning too.

But Rask is dead, he thought, as a young man - his hands cuffed behind him - was marched through the door, escorted by two burly MPs. Pella didn't look old enough to shave, Mark thought; his baby face probably hadn't made it any easier to impress his authority on the troops. And he probably hadn't had the nerve to contradict Rask either. *Pella is the senior survivor, the one we can hang.*

"Pella," he said, flatly. "What were you thinking?"

Pella stared at him, his eyes wide. "Rask...Rask said they deserved it!"

"Did he?" Mark said. "Are you aware that ordering the mass slaughter of two-thirds of a town's population and the gang-rape of the remaining third is an illegal order?"

He sighed, inwardly. Pella probably *didn't* know. He'd been recruited after the collapse, when Wolfbane had been concentrating on building up as large an army as possible. There hadn't been time to go over all the little niceties, particularly after the endless pile of red tape the Imperial Army forced upon its subordinates. The training officers, men who'd had to endure well-meaning interference from ignorant idiots, had probably thrown out some of the babies along with the bathwater. And Pella hadn't served on Thule. Corinthian was his first taste of combat.

"He said they were rebels, sir," Pella said. "And Sergeant Davidson agreed with him."

"Davidson is dead," Mark snapped. "*Rask* is dead. You're the one holding the bag, *Lieutenant.*"

He took a moment to clear his thoughts. "Tell me what happened," he ordered. "Start from the beginning and leave nothing out."

Pella paled. "We were thrown together after the battle," he said. "There were two companies glued together, with survivors from a dozen other units that were disbanded. I...Captain Rask gave me a platoon and told me - told us - that we would be going on a search and destroy mission. He said we'd be doing something to make sure the insurgents never threatened us again. He told us that we were going to destroy the town and punish the population for supporting insurgents."

"And you did nothing," Mark said, when Pella had finished. "Why not?"

"I was angry and scared," Pella admitted.

Mark groaned. It wasn't uncommon for soldiers on counter-insurgency duty to start loathing the local population, sometimes more than they loathed the insurgents themselves. Weeks of dealing with gormless morons who said nothing, yet went running to the insurgents as soon as the soldiers looked away, took its toll. It was impossible to accept that the locals had little choice when one was coming under attack, day after day. He'd worked hard to prevent atrocities on Thule, but there had been quite a few minor incidents. And yet, none of them quite matched what Captain Rask had set out to do.

And Pella was too scared to either stand up to him or scream to the MPs, he thought. *And now he stands condemned as the senior survivor.*

"Fuck it," he said, flatly.

He gritted his teeth. Relatively isolated atrocities on Thule could be handled without reference to outside authorities, let alone the enemy forces. But here, with the enemy already aware of what had happened... the last thing he wanted was a series of atrocities and counter-atrocities. The enemy might start targeting hospitals as well as barracks, medical supplies as well as ammunition carts. And yet, his own forces were already on the verge of breaking. If he cracked down too hard, he risked mutiny - or worse.

"The men under your command will be assigned to the standard one month of service in the penal battalions," he said, flatly. "If they survive, they will be returned to their previous ranks without any stain on their records. You, however, will face a significantly worse punishment. You will be hung this afternoon as a warning to others who might go the same way."

Pella stared at him. "Sir..."

Mark nodded, curtly. Admiral Singh had flatly refused to allow him to hand Pella over to the locals, pointing out that Pella might know all sorts of useful titbits. There was no choice, but to execute the young man. And yet it wasn't *fair*. Pella hadn't planned the mass slaughter; he'd merely been unable to stop it. If, of course, he'd *wanted* to stop it. Captain Rask might not have had to argue very hard to talk Pella into compromising himself.

"You will have the next few hours to do whatever you want to do, before you die," he said, flatly. "But you will die."

He nodded to the guards, who swung a dazed Pella around and frog-marched him out of the office. Mark sat back in his chair, feeling an odd mixture of guilt and shame. He was the army's commanding officer, the one who bore ultimate responsibility for its successes and failures. Pella should not have been promoted, any more than his dead superior. But now all he could do was cope with the situation the bastard had left him.

A good thing Captain Rask died, he thought, darkly. *I would have killed him personally, if I could.*

He forced the thought aside as he keyed his terminal, pulling up the death warrant. He'd never used the authority to kill one of his men before, even though he'd been familiar with the procedure from the Imperial Army. Indeed, he couldn't recall ever being involved in a case where *any* officer had used it. There were just too many legal quibbles over sentencing someone to death without a court martial or external investigation. The relatives of the dead man might sue…

Which isn't going to happen on Wolfbane, he thought. *And if his relatives are unlucky, they'll be hit with the bill for the bullets too.*

———

Danielle frowned as she read the message. "Do you believe this?"

Colonel Stalker scowled. "I don't know," he said, finally. "They had the hanging witnessed by a prisoner, who was then granted parole and permitted to return to the city, but it could easily have been a trick of some kind."

"They're playing with fire," Hampton observed.

"They killed over ninety people and were about to rape fifty more," Danielle said. She'd thought herself used to horror, but destroying an entire town…it was unthinkable. "How do we know they killed the right person?"

"They didn't," Colonel Stalker said, flatly. "The original report we received from our people stated that the officer commanding was killed by sniper fire, along with a number of other Wolves. The person they hung was probably the senior surviving officer."

Danielle looked down at the images. "And now…what?"

"There's nothing we can do," Colonel Stalker said. "Right now, there's no one to retaliate against even if we *wanted* to. The Wolves have killed one of their own as a sacrifice, both to appease us - I think - and to restore discipline among their ranks. I think we should accept it and move on."

"We could demand they handed someone over to us," Danielle said. It galled her to know that the person responsible would escape justice. But then, he was dead. "Would they concede the point?"

"Probably not," Colonel Stalker said. "I doubt they would give us anything, Madam President. What they've done, I think, is more about keeping their own people in line than making up for their crimes."

Hampton frowned. "And it will work too."

Danielle glanced at him. "How?"

"No one has taken such losses for centuries, certainly not in a single day of fighting," Hampton said. He nodded northwards. "I'd be surprised if their men weren't devastated by the fighting. Discipline has probably turned into a joke. Right now, I'd expect their commanders to be using every means at their disposal to restore order, even if it means shooting their own people. They cannot afford to show weakness in the face of disorder."

"And to think I thought the military was so disciplined," Danielle said. She felt a flicker of bitter amusement. "Admiral Singh wasn't so bad the first time around."

"It's a balancing act," Hampton said. "Too much discipline can lead to all sorts of problems, but so can too little discipline. In their shoes, I'd pull back a little and concentrate on regrouping my forces before I contemplated another offensive."

"And then we find ourselves asking a simple question," Colonel Stalker said. "How much time does Admiral Singh have?"

Danielle frowned. *She* knew, from bitter experience, that a person's political enemies could undermine someone very quickly, given sufficient cause. Admiral Singh desperately needed to prove that the expenditure - in lives, in equipment, in time - had been justified. Danielle had faced the same problem, admittedly on a smaller scale. But *she'd* never had the power to shoot her enemies.

"They're shipping *something* down to the surface," Hampton said. "We have to assume the worst."

"That they'll launch another attack as soon as they feel they can get away with it," Danielle said. "And if the attack threatens to break through the defensive lines...?"

"The starships will have to intervene," Colonel Stalker said. "And then we will know the outcome, one way or the other."

Danielle winced. The enemy might have pulled back, but they were still lobbing shells towards the defenders on a regular basis. Every day brought a report of a shell landing within the city itself, making it impossible to strengthen the defence lines any further. And the factories weren't even *remotely* keeping up with the demand for ammunition. She'd heard that the soldiers had been warned to limit expenditure as much as possible, conserving everything they could for the coming holocaust. The next battle would see her world free or crushed, once again, beneath Admiral Singh's jackboot.

"So we wait," she said.

"Yes," Colonel Stalker said. "The more men they shovel down to the surface, the better for us."

Danielle hoped, desperately, that he was right.

———

A dull crash echoed through the bunker as a shell landed somewhere nearby, jerking the soldiers awake. Mindy cursed under her breath as she grasped for her rifle, then glanced at the chronometer mounted on the wall. 0700. They were meant to be asleep for another hour, but she doubted she'd manage to get back to sleep. Cursing under her breath as her comrades settled down, she rolled out of the bunk and stood. Her entire body was aching from too little sleep.

Bastards, she thought, as another explosion echoed out in the distance. The enemy's new tactic was diabolical. Their random bursts of shellfire weren't hitting anything of value, but they sure as hell were keeping the defenders awake. A few more weeks of sleepless nights, she thought, would be quite enough to have her seeing things. *They could just charge the defence lines and get it over with.*

Pushing the thought aside, she paced out of the dormitory and into the kitchen. Some wag had scrawled A MESSY PLACE on the concrete wall, which Sergeant Rackham hadn't bothered to order removed. Below it, a smaller note warned the soldiers to be careful where they put their sugar, as the lower levels were infested with ants and cockroaches. Mindy wasn't too surprised, really. She recalled how both creatures - and rabbits - had proved a persistent bane during the early stages of interstellar colonisation. Her old tutors had called the introduction of rabbits a perfect piece of biological warfare.

Sergeant Rackham was sitting at a metal table, drinking coffee as he read the latest set of updates. The Wolves had gotten better, much better, at keeping unwanted personnel out of their fortifications, as well as preventing them from leaving the city. Mindy had seen the images - everyone had seen the images - of a ship ablaze and sinking in the river, making it clear that either interfering with the enemy or outright escape was no longer possible. And now the enemy were shelling at random, repairing the defence lines was no longer possible either.

"Trooper," he grunted. He cut her off before she could begin to salute. "Take some coffee, then sit down."

"Yes, Sergeant," Mindy said. Her body remembered, all too well, the mountains of push-ups that had been handed out to anyone who dared call a sergeant 'sir.' "Is it good news?"

Sergeant Rackham eyed her darkly. "Do you think there's any good news these days?"

Mindy shrugged as she poured herself a mug of coffee. They were still alive. The first enemy offensive had been beaten back with heavy losses. Mandy was out there somewhere, no doubt working to lift the siege of Corinthian as soon as she could. And they had nearly unlimited supplies of something that *passed* for food, as long as they didn't look at it too closely. She took a ration bar from the pile beside the coffee machine and sat down facing him. Someone had scarred his face during the brief period of hand-to-hand fighting and he hadn't bothered to get it fixed. She couldn't help thinking that it made him look less intimidating.

"We're alive," she said, finally.

Sergeant Rackham smiled, although it didn't touch his eyes. "We are," he agreed. "But there's no way we can tighten up the defence lines."

"I know, Sergeant," Mindy said. "We could sally out..."

"And get slaughtered," Sergeant Rackham said. He pointed a stubby finger at her. "Be grateful, soldier, that you didn't live through the days when your commanding officers had never fought in battles themselves. Those bastards would think that was a damn good idea too. *They* weren't the ones who bled and died."

Mindy studied him for a long moment. She'd never really been sure just how old the sergeant was, although he'd clearly been in service longer than she'd been alive. There was no way she'd be able to get a look at his file. She would have placed him at forty, perhaps a few years older, but rejuvenation technology could accomplish miracles. It was quite possible he was in his sixties or even older.

"I am glad," she said, finally.

She glanced up as she heard the rattle of machine guns in the distance, but ignored them as no alarms were sounding. The Wolves had started sending penal units to probe the defences, trying to determine what would and what wouldn't trigger a reaction. Part of her felt sorry for the bastards, part of her knew that trained soldiers were not sent to penal units without very good cause. Very few of them ever survived a month of clearing mines, probing enemy positions and digging ditches.

"So you should be," Sergeant Rackham said. "Let us just hope it stays that way."

He waved a hand at the concrete walls. She'd seen bunkers decorated with photographs and pornographic images on Avalon, but no one had had the heart to do anything of the sort on Corinthian. There was nothing homey about a bunker they might have to abandon when the enemy finally attacked. Pretending it was a home wouldn't do any good for any of them.

"This is war," Sergeant Rackham said. "This is the experience of countless men - and quite a few women - from the days when one caveman bashed another over the head with a rock until now. Long hours of boredom, followed by moments of screaming terror and months spent coping with the aftermath. And yet so many officers forget it."

"Yes, Sergeant," Mindy said. Why was he telling her this? "I understand."

He met her eyes. "Have you given any thought to your future career?"

Mindy hesitated. "I thought I would be a Stormtrooper," she said. "And just *stay* a Stormtrooper."

"But will you be an officer or an NCO?" Sergeant Rackham asked. "You'll have to choose soon, I think. We are short on experienced officers too."

Mindy hesitated. *Jasmine* had admitted, privately, that she wasn't suited to handle command of anything larger than a marine company. And Mindy was inclined to feel the same way too. But the Stormtroopers wouldn't allow her to stay where she was indefinitely...

"I don't know, Sergeant," she admitted, reluctantly. "But it all depends on what happens after this campaign, doesn't it?"

CHAPTER
THIRTY-FOUR

Indeed, the simple failure to train in unison would make it impossible for a large force to act as a single entity. Instead of a giant military, there would be lots of tiny units that can be defeated separately, in detail.
- Professor Leo Caesius. The Role of Randomness In War.

"They're moving into position, sir," Gwendolyn said.

Ed nodded, watching the live feed from a sensor mounted on a skyscraper. The Wolves had taken nearly two months to prepare their second offensive, but it looked as though they were finally ready. And this time, they were being careful. His forces had problems flying drones over enemy positions, even stealth drones, but it was clear that they were moving up tanks and other armoured vehicles as well as countless new weapons. No doubt they'd devised something to break through the blockhouses too.

He scowled, wondering if he'd made a mistake. Admiral Singh still held control of the high orbitals, allowing her to ship in reinforcements and replace her destroyed equipment. Maybe he'd miscalculated, maybe her position was stronger than he'd thought. Or maybe she was readying herself for one final attempt at the city, before retreating to save what she could from the maelstrom. There was no way to be sure.

"It looks that way," he said, reluctantly. "Did you get a message out to the Commodore?"

"She's as close as she can get to us," Gwendolyn said. "But she warns that the odds will be far more even than we had hoped."

Singh must be focusing on Corinthian to the exclusion of all else, Ed thought. *That should bite her hard, sooner rather than later.*

He frowned. On one hand, Singh probably had a point. Save perhaps for Thule, none of her other conquests were worth as much as Corinthian. But would her enemies on Wolfbane see it that way? Ed had far too much experience with senior officers who didn't understand that not all targets were created equally, that swatting a thousand insurgents could be less effective than picking off one or two who happened to be *very* well connected. It was quite possible Admiral Singh's position was already fatally undermined.

But there's no way to know for sure, he thought, shortly. *All that matters is holding the line.*

He looked at the display. "Are all our forces on alert?"

"The forward units are on alert," Gwendolyn confirmed. "Everything else is currently at stage-beta and will be snapped to alpha when the attack formally begins."

Ed nodded. Unless the Wolves had decided to unleash starship-level weapons on the defence line, in which case the entire city was doomed, it was hard to imagine anything that would break through the forward units in time to catch the rear units on the hop. There was no point in pushing his men too hard, not when the constant shellfire was a major hassle. The field hospitals were already warning that there were too many reported cases of shellshock for them to handle.

"All we can do now is wait," he said.

He peered at the sensor feed, wondering just what the enemy had invented. He'd worked out dozens of possible scenarios, but they were in uncharted waters. They might have hastily designed weapons intended to crack the bunkers open, one by one, or they might just have decided on another charge. It would be utter madness, but the ammunition shortage might just give them a chance of actually winning. They'd take hideous losses - again - yet they might just come out ahead.

And their victory may yet lead to total defeat, he reminded himself. *They would have to be insane to take the risk.*

"Yes, sir," Gwendolyn said, practically. "All we can do is wait."

———

"The advance units are in place," General Haverford said. His image flickered backwards and forwards on the display. The enemy, damn their souls, had been experimenting with new jamming systems. "The offensive will be ready to go tomorrow morning."

Rani leaned forward. "I want the offensive to jump off now," she snapped. "They'll be hurriedly making preparations of their own!"

"Yes, they will," Haverford said. He sounded tired, tired and bitter. Rani silently added him to the list of people who would be purged, after she had won the war and recaptured her former base of operations. She'd had too many reports of his growing discontent with her decisions. "There's nothing to be gained by pushing forward now, Admiral."

He was right, damn him. Rani forced herself to think clearly. The losses were staggering - and, according to her agents, word was already beginning to leak out on Wolfbane. She'd done what she could to hide it, by withdrawing troops from other worlds instead of summoning them from Wolfbane, but it was nowhere near enough. Word was spreading and, if she didn't find a way to justify the losses, she was staring a coup or a civil war in the face.

"Very well," she said, finally. "Once the attack begins, General, you are not to stop for anything."

"I understand," Haverford said. "I also request permission to move my command post closer to the front lines."

Rani considered it for a long moment. She'd been reluctant to let him move earlier because he'd be under the shield, ensuring she couldn't intervene if his command post came under heavy attack. And, she admitted in the privacy of her own thoughts, because it would make it impossible to bomb the FOB from orbit if he betrayed her. But if he happened to die, or betray her, she could use him as a scapegoat and *no one* could object. Haverford's death would secure her position once and for all.

"Very well," she said, finally. "But I don't want you in range of enemy guns."

Haverford looked irked. "I need to be as close as possible, Admiral," he said. "I need to have a feel for the battle."

"I don't want you to die," Rani lied. "And we can't risk command confusion at the worst possible time. Go close, General, but stay away from their guns."

"Yes, Admiral," Haverford said. "With your permission, I'll make the preparations now."

Rani inclined her head, regally. General Haverford's face vanished from the display, leaving her alone in her quarters. She took a long moment to compose herself, then turned her attention to the orbital display. Five battleships were more than enough to turn Corinthian into a slagheap, if its inhabitants rejected her once again. Let them hide under their shield, if they wished. She could render the entire planet uninhabitable within minutes. If she couldn't have Corinthian, no one else could have it either.

She sighed, then keyed a switch to summon her agents. It was time to start making a few contingency plans of her own.

———

"You need to keep your fucking head down," Ryan bellowed. "Don't worry about getting mud on your fancy uniform, you shithead! Keep your head down!"

He ground out a series of oaths as the platoon ducked down and crawled forward, ignoring the mud staining their uniforms. His company was a joke, a scratch unit consisting of a handful of combat veterans and a number of green reinforcements from various peaceful worlds. Hell, a number of them had actually been REMFs before they'd been thrust into a combat role. He would have found it amusing if he hadn't faced the prospect of taking them into combat. As it was, he was torn between fear of returning to combat and a desire just to put an end to it all.

And I would sell my soul for a sergeant, he thought. *Or two. Or three.*

A month of work hadn't done much for his men, he had to admit, although he hadn't really been trying *that* hard. He'd nearly strangled one man after he'd cracked jokes about officers who sat down to piss, which hadn't made winning their respect any easier. And yet, he found it hard to care. His condition hadn't really improved; he verged between fits of rage and a deep depression that made it impossible to move. He knew, on some level, that he was merely storing up trouble for himself, but he didn't care. Being relieved of duty would be something of a relief, even if it did lead to his execution.

"They reached their destination," Lieutenant Gordon said.

Ryan glowered at him. Lieutenant Gordon was so perfectly turned out that he could have stepped off a recruiting poster. His hair was neatly trimmed, his uniform was clean and his disposition was perfect. It hadn't taken long for Ryan to discover that the younger man had absolutely no combat experience at all, although he *had* earned a Purple Heart at some point in his career. The details were lacking, which made him wonder if Gordon had suffered a paper cut or some other ghastly malady. *No one* looked so good after weeks on the front lines.

"Yes, after being killed several times over," he snarled. "Do you think soldiers come back to life on the battlefield?"

He scowled as he blew the whistle, terminating the exercise. If there had been time to set up an *actual* blockhouse, he'd have used it to illustrate what they needed to know...but there hadn't been any time. The experienced men understood what sort of meatgrinder they'd be facing, yet the raw recruits - and former REMFs - were treating the whole thing as a game, one they could walk away from at will. They'd have been wiped out to a man within the first five minutes, he was sure, if the pretend blockhouse had been real. As it was, they didn't really comprehend the danger of a series of blockhouses covering one another.

"That was fucking awful," he bellowed. Even as a lieutenant, he'd left the shouting to Sergeant Rove. But Rove was dead and no one had sent him a replacement. The bastards didn't give a shit if his scratch company lived or died. "You'd all be fucking dead if that was fucking real, you idiots!"

He glared at them. "It doesn't matter if your uniforms are muddy," he snarled, lowering his voice slightly. "All that matters is staying alive! The bastards had you perfectly targeted the moment you ran forward, a single sweep of machine gun fire would be enough to tear you to shreds! You've seen the damned mass grave, haven't you? Do you want to end up in something just like it?"

The thought made him shudder. His former unit - even the captain - had been buried in the pit. *Every* recovered body had been dumped into the pit, rather than bagged up and saved for transport back home. It was just something else to resent, to mull over in the darkness of the night, when drink wasn't enough to numb the pain of his existence. The Admiral and the General seemed to believe it was more sporting to let the enemy kill his men, but they were happy to deny them a proper burial afterwards. He shuddered again, bitterly, and dragged himself back to reality. The men before him were going to die if they didn't learn the lessons he had to teach them.

"We're going on the offensive soon," he added, loudly. They'd been warned they would be moving to jump-off positions as soon as night fell, suggesting the offensive would begin in the morning. Ryan hoped desperately they weren't planning to launch a night offensive. It would be unbelievable chaotic. "If you don't learn these lessons by then, you'll wind up dead!"

But you don't really care, a thought whispered at the back of his mind. *Do you?*

He pushed it aside, angrily. "Dismissed," he bellowed. "Grab some food, then get your supplies for the offensive. Anyone not ready to jump off will be in deep shit!"

Lieutenant Gordon gave him a sharp look. "Do you *have* to keep swearing, sir?"

Ryan laughed, bitterly. "Do I *look* like a Drill Sergeant?"

He went on before Lieutenant Gordon could say a word. "These men have hardly any idea of what they're going to face," he snarled. "They think they can just rewrite the damned rules in their favour, time and time again. And the rules don't *work* like that! The enemy is going to eat them for breakfast!"

Lieutenant Gordon started to say something, but Ryan ignored him as a low rumble announced the arrival of a large troop of Landsharks, followed by boxy vehicles that looked like mobile missile launchers. He wondered, nastily, just how the tankers were coping with the brave new world. They'd been walking around in fancy uniforms on Thule, secure in the knowledge that nothing could hurt them, sneering at the infantrymen who'd cleared up the rubble after the tanks had passed through. But now over a hundred so-called invulnerable tanks had been destroyed in the fighting.

I might have been badly wounded but I survived, he thought. *They won't survive a missile exploding inside their armour or being gunned down when they try to flee.*

"Well," he said. He made a show of glancing at his watch. "Only fifteen hours to live, Lieutenant Gordon. Only fifteen hours to live."

———

"They're out there," Angel breathed. "I can *sense* them."

"Smell them, more likely," Emmanuel said. He wasn't sure *just* what the Wolves had used to clear the area of foliage, but the smell wafted over to them every time the wind changed. "I think they're getting ready to attack."

He smiled at the panicky look in her eyes as the sun dipped beneath the horizon, leaving a faint glow from the position of the enemy lines. A night attack was possible, but Colonel Stalker had said it was unlikely. The enemy would be charging right into the teeth of their fire - again - in darkness. Even the best night vision gear would have trouble coping with the scene. But tomorrow...Emmanuel had no doubt that tomorrow would see the next and final battle for Freedom City.

"There should be a good story in this for someone," he said. He'd recorded dozens of interviews and shot hours upon hours of footage... if he didn't return home, one of the editors would take the reports and turn them into a coherent story. "I was sure to record your good side, of course."

Angel gave him a sidelong look. "Did you?"

"I'm sure you will have a very big role in the flick," Emmanuel said, deadpan. He waved a hand towards the enemy lines. "Someone is going to make a movie of this, Angel; it'll be an uplifting story of heroism and human sacrifice, no matter who wins."

"Watching us all die wouldn't be very uplifting," Angel muttered. "The Wolves will still have won, won't they?"

Emmanuel shrugged. He'd interviewed a handful of the prisoners and they'd all been fairly demoralised, after watching hundreds of their comrades killed for nothing. If their attitudes were spreading through the rest of the enemy forces, it was quite possible that the entire edifice would collapse sooner rather than later. But no one knew better than a reporter just how easy it was to block news from spreading off-planet. Admiral Singh would do everything in her power to keep her enemies from learning the truth.

We'll be telling them, he thought, as the darkness deepened. There were flickers of light in the distance as the enemy hurled a handful of shells into the city, but otherwise the night was quiet. *A ship sneaking into one of their systems could broadcast a message, then run before anyone can catch up with them.*

"This could be our last night alive," Angel said, softly.

Emmanuel had to fight down a laugh. How many times had he heard that line on bad romantic flicks? One of the things he loved about Jasmine was that she was always ruthlessly practical. Romance wasn't something either of them enjoyed. She might die at any moment on duty, while he might be caught up in something he was trying to turn into a story and brutally killed. And as pretty as Angel was, he didn't find her appealing. There was something about her that bothered him.

"Yes, it could be," he said. "Why?"

Angel met his eyes. "Come to bed with me," she said. "No one will ever know."

Emmanuel hesitated. Maybe he'd done her an injustice. If she'd reached her current post through sleeping with her superiors, she'd hardly need to try to lure him into bed. Or maybe it was a gesture of defiance *against* her superiors by choosing her own bedmate. Or maybe he'd just been wrong all along. Jasmine was unusual even by the standards of most female soldiers he'd met.

"I'd know," he said, quietly. "And I do have a girlfriend."

He shook his head. "Go find someone," he urged her. "I'll be here for a while, then I'll go back to the bunker to get some sleep. Tomorrow may be our last day alive."

Angel smiled, rather wanly, and turned and walked off. Emmanuel smiled after her, then returned to staring out of the window towards enemy lines. The night was quiet, but the stench of defoliant still hung in the air. It seemed to be growing warmer too, or maybe that was just his imagination. The coming battle would be utterly savage.

He looked past the enemy camp, into the wilderness. Jasmine was out there somewhere, he was sure, although Colonel Stalker hadn't given him very many details. The enemy FOB was apparently impregnable, he'd said; Jasmine and her team would be of better service impeding the enemy when they launched their final attack. He hoped, desperately, that she would survive the coming struggle. It had been too long since he'd held her in his arms...

And yet I might not survive tomorrow either, he thought, grimly. Part of him was tempted to hurry after Angel, just to see if the offer was still open; he told that part of him to shut up. It was a natural reaction to the prospect of imminent death, but still annoying. *It might be the last day for all of us.*

CHAPTER
THIRTY-FIVE

And smaller factors can play a role. Did your enemy CO pay his men? Did your enemy CO allow them leave? Does he allow bullying to thrive within the ranks or does he crack down on it? Does he reward men who use their minds or does he see them as threats?

- Professor Leo Caesius. The Role of Randomness In War.

"It's time, sir," Colonel Travis said.

Mark nodded, slowly. The sun was already peeking over the horizon. He'd repeatedly considered a night attack, but his forces were already brittle. There just hadn't been *time* to reform the old units, train the newcomers and generally overcome the scars left by the last defeat. He'd taken every precaution he could, dragged up ideas from so far in the past that hardly anyone remembered them…and yet he knew he was gambling everything on one last throw of the dice.

But the enemy must feel the same way too, he thought. Their return fire had been sporadic, their counterattacks limited. Even given the opportunity to crush a handful of raiding parties, they'd been content merely to chase the raiders away from the defence lines. *Their ammunition must be on the verge of running out.*

He looked down at the chart, silently contemplating the enemy defences. There was far less detail than he preferred, even after a couple of unwary guards had been abducted and interrogated by his men. He'd learned more by debriefing the survivors of the first assault than by drawing answers from the prisoners. And yet, it was far from hopeless. The defence lines looked solid, but he knew that couldn't be the case. They'd already cracked one defence line during the first battle.

And he was woolgathering.

He scowled as he turned to face Colonel Travis. There was no way in hell he *wanted* to send his men back into that inferno. The defenders might only have enough ammunition to hold out for half an hour - he certainly intended to make them expend as much as possible - but it would be more than long enough for them to butcher thousands of men. Admiral Singh might win the battle, only to go back to Wolfbane and discover that even the normally cynical corporate overlords drew the line at victories that came at such a high cost. Who knew what would happen when the *next* world was invaded? That damned shield could hardly be unique. In their place, Mark would have tried to produce a shield that would protect an entire world.

And if that happens, he thought, *it will change everything.*

Colonel Travis met his eyes. "Sir?"

Mark sighed. "Contact the forward units," he said. "They are to begin the bombardment as planned."

———

Mindy rubbed her tired eyes as she peered out of the bunker, towards the blackened and broken soil some wag had started to call No Man's Land. The bodies might have been removed, thankfully, but it was still strewn with the remains of enemy tanks and various other assault vehicles. They provided a great deal of cover to anyone who wanted to sneak up on the defenders, Mindy thought, yet all attempts to clear them out of the firing lines had been unsuccessful. The enemy, as aware of their advantage as the defenders were of their weakness, had fired on anyone who tried to remove even one of the wrecks. It just created another problem for the defenders.

"There's no sign of them," one of the soldiers breathed. "Maybe they're not coming."

"Maybe they're just getting out of bed and into position," Sergeant Rackham snapped. "They don't *have* to launch a dawn attack."

Mindy nodded in quiet agreement. All the signs pointed to a major offensive being planned; the overnight shelling had been intensified, the sound of vehicles could be heard drifting out of the darkness and reports from observation posts warned that more and more enemy soldiers were being marched down from their base to their jump-off positions. And yet, it was quiet out across No Man's Land. A cool breeze wafted across the land, bringing with it the stench of defoliant and dead bodies. No one gagged now, not after a month of exposure to the stench. She wondered, absently, if it meant something was badly wrong with them.

But we're in trouble too, she thought. *Perhaps we should be glad they're planning to attack.*

She cursed herself for even thinking it, yet she knew she was right. Discipline was harshly enforced in the CEF, but she'd heard of discontent and even near-mutinies among the local troops. Their militiamen hadn't expected anything more than patrols and perhaps a parade or two, before Admiral Singh returned to Corinthian. A few more weeks of being under siege would be enough to allow the Wolves to win, without throwing themselves into the teeth of her fire. Freedom City might be able to feed itself, but it couldn't do anything about the shortage of ammunition or the growing mass of wounded who couldn't be given anything like enough medical help. The Wolves had flatly refused to allow the wounded to be transported out of the city.

Bastards, she thought. *They know the wounded put a strain on our resources.*

She glanced up, sharply, as she heard gunfire echoing across No Man's Land. The Wolves had started their bombardment, directing their shells into the city. She braced herself, just as the first shells came down on top of the bunker. It shook violently, dust falling from the roof and dancing in the light, but the concrete held. The enemy didn't seem to have changed their shells from HE to something more suitable.

"Hold your positions," Sergeant Rackham ordered, as more and more explosions shook the complex. "You don't want to let them get any closer than necessary."

Mindy nodded. She'd read the reports from the men and women who'd survived the first offensive. The enemy had often managed to get close to blockhouses, then roll grenades through firing slits to clear the way. It had been successful, very successful. Sergeant Rackham had even organised the platoon on the assumption that the enemy would try the same trick twice, keeping half the men in reserve to intercept anyone who broke into the bunker. She wondered, given how close she was to the firing slit, if she would survive long enough to see it, then pushed the thought aside. There was no point in fretting about it now.

"It's slacking off," one of the soldiers muttered. "They're running out of ammunition."

"They're hurling their shells further into the city," Sergeant Rackham corrected. "They'll be trying to target the shield generator."

Mindy paled as his words sank in. If the shield fell, they'd die within seconds. The Wolves would drop KEWs from orbit until the defence line had been smashed to rubble, then waltz in and take the rest of the city. She was tempted to run, but there was nowhere to go. Running north would take her straight into the enemy lines, running south would merely get her deeper into the city. And besides, she was damned if she was abandoning her squad. Mandy would never let her live it down.

Good thing you're not here, she thought, as the enemy shells continued to fall. Most of them would be hacked out of the air by the laser point defence stations, but statistically a number would get through and hit the ground. It would only take one lucky shot to put the shield generator out of commission. *At least mum and dad will have one surviving daughter*.

———

"They're firing into the city," Gwendolyn said.

Ed cursed. The enemy had to know that most of their shells didn't have a hope of finding a target, but they weren't being expended uselessly. He *had* to protect the shield generator, even if it meant exposing the defence lines to the enemy gunners. HE shells weren't that much of a problem - his men knew to stay under cover - yet he rather doubted the enemy would *keep* throwing HE shells. The Wolves had shown a disgusting willingness to innovate over the last few months. It wouldn't be *hard* to come up with something designed to punch through the bunkers, one by one…

He wanted to cover his men. But the cold equations demanded otherwise.

"Order the point defence units to protect the shield generator," he ordered, coolly. "They are to put its safety above all else, even their own protection."

"Yes, sir," Gwendolyn said.

Ed watched as she turned back to her console, then glanced at the constantly updating display. Enemy shells were coming down all over the city, striking targets at random; he watched in numb horror as a skyscraper shuddered, then toppled over. The falling building slammed into another building, knocking it over too. Ed couldn't tear his eyes away, half-expecting the collapsing skyscrapers to trigger a chain reaction of falling buildings, but it didn't spread any further.

"They hit a medical station," one of the operators called. "At least seventy men were inside."

"Shit," Hampton muttered.

"Yeah," Ed agreed.

He hoped, desperately, that it had been an accident. The Wolves had been far more ruthless ever since the first attempt at the city had failed - there was no shortage of reports about atrocities committed by their forces - but he didn't *think* they would be willing to slaughter wounded men. And yet, they didn't know where *any* of the hospitals were. They were firing at random, hoping to hit something vital. The hell of it was that, statistically, they had a very good chance of hitting *something*.

No time to mourn, he reminded himself. They'd bury the dead later, if there *was* a later. *We have to focus on the here and now.*

"The point defence is working, sir," Gwendolyn said. "But they'll start going after the point defence stations next."

"Probably," Ed agreed. It was what *he* would have done, particularly if he had a near-unlimited supply of shells. The Wolves had probably kept the guns so simple just to ensure their MEU knock-offs could keep up with the demands for ammunition. A single hit would be worth the expenditure of thousands of shells. "But we have to keep the generator safe."

He kept his eyes on the display. So far, the enemy hadn't started a general offensive, but it was just a matter of time. Unless they thought they could win through shellfire **alone**...it was a possibility, yet *he* wouldn't have gambled on a lucky hit if he'd been in command.

They're trying to soften us up, he thought, grimly. *And the hell of it is that it's working.*

––––––––

Ryan sat in a trench, his back to the enemy, fighting hard to keep his entire body from shaking helplessly. He hadn't been so scared the first day he'd seen combat or the day he'd led the charge into the teeth of enemy fire! Part of his soul had been lost along with his manhood, he realised slowly; he no longer had the nerve to stand up and force himself forward. And yet, he knew he had no choice. The presence of armed MPs, to the rear of the trench network, made it clear that any attempt to refuse to advance would be met with summary punishment.

He scowled as he heard two of the soldiers chatting, insisting that the bombardment would have swept the enemy out of existence. Had they learned nothing from him? No matter how many shells were thrown into the city, the enemy would survive! The enemy bunker network would have to be cleared piece by piece. His hands started to shake, no matter how desperately he fought to control them, as he remembered the hellish struggle to gain control of even *one* bunker. The idiots under his command were going to die, if they were lucky, in the next few hours. And if they were unlucky...

"The bombardment is picking up pace," Lieutenant Gordon said. He was standing by the side of the trench, using a pair of binoculars to sweep the enemy positions. Ryan wouldn't have given him good odds of survival - the enemy snipers were very good - but so far the damned fool seemed to have beaten the odds. "They're taking a beating."

"Not enough," Ryan muttered. He wanted to just lie back and cover his ears, but he knew it would just get him killed. "It won't ever be enough."

Lieutenant Gordon glanced at him. "Sir?"

"Never mind," Ryan said. The depression rose up, once again, threatening to sweep him away into numbness. Where was an enemy sniper when one was actually *needed*? A bullet though Gordon's head would teach him a short sharp lesson. "Just keep an eye on them."

He groaned as he heard the sound of tanks rumbling forward, the pressure of their passage threatening to collapse the trench. He'd thought the mere *idea* of building a trench was absurd, but he had to admit it had helped keep the men occupied and under control. And yet, it wouldn't be long before they had to leave the nice safe trench…

His hands were shaking, again. Frantically, he clasped them behind his back, fighting to still the tremors. But they refused to face…

He fought down the urge to start crying. Really, all he wanted was for it to end.

"Twenty minutes," Lieutenant Gordon said.

"Fuck it," Ryan muttered.

———

"They're switching their point defence to cover the shield generator," Colonel Travis reported. "As you planned, sir."

Mark glared at him. He was in no mood for brown-nosing. "Start launching the missiles," he ordered, bluntly. "They are to be covered by short-range fire."

"Aye, sir," Colonel Travis said.

———

Mindy gritted her teeth as the bombardment picked up, even though it was almost completely harmless. The shells seemed to be getting *smaller*, as if the enemy was running out of high explosive…or, more likely, was using its smaller guns to sweep the fortifications while keeping up the bombardment of the city itself. She didn't fault their tactics. By the time they finally launched their advance, the defenders would be too tired to fight effectively. One hand groped for the injector tab in her pocket, before she thought better of it. She wasn't that tired yet.

She heard a dull whistling sound, followed by a colossal explosion. The ground shook so violently that she thought, for a crazy moment, that there had been an earthquake. But no one in their right mind would build a city on a fault line…she heard someone shouting, dimly, as the ground shook again. Something was crashing to the ground in the distance…she glanced through the slit, just in time to see a massive explosion blowing one of the nearby blockhouses right out of the ground. Tongues of fire blossomed from its firing slits as the rubble crashed back down, burying any surviving occupants…

"Jesus," someone said. It took her a moment to realise that it was *her* voice. "What was…"

Training reasserted itself. The enemy had built something designed for use against the blockhouses. And they were now blowing the block-houses out of their way, one by one. It wouldn't be long before *they* were targeted and there was nothing they could do about it. She jumped up, grabbing her rifle, as Sergeant Rackham shouted at the men to run. There was a very real risk of being caught in enemy shellfire, if they left the bunker, but staying where they were was certain death. The bunkers and blockhouses were no longer impregnable.

Bastards thought of a way through our defences, Mindy thought. She remembered, suddenly, the couple of photographs of her family she'd left in the barracks, but there was no time to recover it. *They didn't want to make the same mistake twice.*

The hand of God picked her up and tossed her through the air, casu-ally. She barely heard the explosion as she braced herself for the landing, silently grateful that the enemy gunners had turned the land to mud. It would have killed her if she'd hit concrete or hullmetal. She rolled over as soon as she landed, slipping and sliding in the mud, just in time to see an immense fireball blasting out of the bunker. They would have been turned to charcoal if they'd stayed there a few seconds longer. Moments later, she saw a streak of light strike the next bunker, the explosion coming seconds later as the warhead punched through the reinforced concrete and detonated inside the complex. If there had been anyone in there, she thought numbly, they were gone now. There wouldn't even be anything *left* of them.

And the enemy shellfire was picking up…

"Fall back to the city," Sergeant Rackham bellowed. "Now, damn it!"

Mindy turned. His voice could barely be heard over the growing din. In the distance, she could see enemy tanks making their way towards the defence lines. This time, without solid defences backed up by missile fire, the Landsharks were likely to crunch their way through the defences and crush hundreds of soldiers under their treads. She took one last look, knowing that if she could see them they could probably see her, then turned to run for her life. It was all she could do to remember to keep her head down and run in a zigzag as she moved. She half-expected to feel a bullet between her shoulders at any moment, but instead - somehow - she made it to the outer suburbs without being killed. Hundreds of others hadn't been so lucky.

"Get into position," Sergeant Rackham ordered. Mindy nodded and took up a firing position. The defence line had crumbled, but someone had managed to strike the lead tank with an antitank missile, stopping the vehicle in its tracks. "They'll be sending in the infantry next!"

If nothing else, she told herself firmly, *we can at least sell our lives dearly*.

CHAPTER
THIRTY-SIX

And what about the condition of his equipment? Are his logistics in good order? Is the quartermaster honest or corrupt? Does he have enough technicians to maintain his weapons, vehicles, aircraft and everything else he needs? Is his force fighting fit? Or does it need a long refit before it can take the battlefield?

- Professor Leo Caesius. The Role of Randomness In War.

"Sir," Colonel Travis said. "The enemy defence line is collapsing!"

Mark allowed himself a moment of relief. It had been hard to convince Admiral Singh to let him expend so much of his limited productive facilities on the bunker-busters, not least because no one had used anything of the sort for centuries, but it had paid off. By God, it had paid off! The enemy lines were crumbling under the weight of his fire, even as some of their point defence stations tried to switch themselves back to covering the remaining bunkers. It was too late. Even if none of the remaining bunker-busters found their targets, and he had to admit it was possible, there was already a gaping hole in the enemy lines.

He smiled as he studied the first set of reports, then sobered. The Landsharks had done a great deal of damage, but they weren't designed for urban combat. Nine more tanks had been disabled or destroyed, once the enemy reacted to their presence. He'd hoped to use them to tear the enemy's inner lines wide open, but it was clear that it wasn't likely to happen. It was time to send in the troops.

"Order the infantry to advance," he said, curtly. "They are to secure the suburbs, then march onwards."

He shook his head as Colonel Travis hurried to carry out his orders. The entire battle was absurd; normally, he would have his men securing the roads in and out of the city, then capturing vital locations until the enemy surrendered or starved to death. But here, he needed to capture or destroy the shield generator. Once it was gone, he was sure the enemy would surrender...if, of course, they trusted his men would *accept* their surrender. He cursed Captain Rask under his breath, hoping the bastard was enjoying the fires of hell. He'd ensured that a great many more people, on both sides, were going to wind up dead.

"The infantry is moving forward, sir," Colonel Travis said. "Victory is at hand."

"Shut up," Mark snapped.

————

"Sir," Lieutenant Gordon said. "That's the order to advance."

Ryan shrugged. It was *comfortable* at the bottom of the trench, comfortable and *safe*, despite the slowly pooling water. The shelter had been relatively dry until the tanks had roared past, churning up the soil and tipping puddles of water into the trench. There was probably some obscure regulation against sitting in water, but he found it hard to care. He just wanted to sit and wait until the end of the world.

"Sir," Lieutenant Gordon insisted. "We have to move."

Ryan wondered, absently, just what the LT would do, if Ryan refused to do anything, but sit in the trench. Drag him to the ladder? Hurl him over the side of the trench? Draw a gun and force him to walk into battle? Or just take command of the company himself and leave their nominal commanding officer behind. Once, he would have hated the thought, but now...now it was almost tempting. It wasn't as if he'd bothered to get to know the men under his command. Why would he waste the effort when they would all be dead by the end of the day?

"Sir," Lieutenant Gordon said. "You have to move."

Ryan felt a sudden hot flush of anger that launched him to his feet. Lieutenant Gordon stepped back, hastily. He'd been on the receiving end of Ryan's temper more than once, over the last month; Ryan had even punched him for asking too many stupid questions. Indeed, Ryan was rather surprised he hadn't been reported to the MPs. A sergeant clouting a particularly idiotic soldier was one thing, but one officer punching another was a very different thing. And besides, both of them were technically illegal.

"Fine," he snarled, checking his rifle. "Let's go, shall we?"

He cast a jaundiced eye over his soldiers as the bombardment started to slack off. They looked terribly young, so young he'd been tempted to ask if the military had started to recruit from schools. It wasn't impossible, either. Wolfbane had plenty of opportunities for young men and women, but many of the other worlds that had been snatched up after the Collapse were nothing more than farming communities. Fighting for Wolfbane probably seemed more attractive than spending one's life staring at the back end of a mule and marrying a distant relative. It probably would have been too, if their officers weren't trying to get as many of them killed as possible.

"Keep your fool heads down and make damn sure they're all dead," he ordered, curtly. The higher-ups wanted prisoners, but as far as he was concerned they could come take the prisoners themselves. He wasn't risking whatever remained of his life so the bastards could feel good about themselves. "Put a bullet in their heads, even if they look dead to you."

He heard a whistle blow and turned to the ladders, then glanced behind him to see the approaching MPs. They looked out of place amidst the trenches, wearing white uniforms and red berets that should have made them easy targets. He was surprised the enemy hadn't already picked them off. Hatred of MPs was damn near universal among soldiers, after all; he saw no reason why the Commonwealth should be any different. And besides, shooting the MPs would almost certainly slow the advance...

The whistle blew, again. "Go," he ordered.

Lieutenant Gordon led the way, followed by Sergeant Kais. Ryan had hoped the Sergeant would be able to do most of the work, but Kais had been promoted after everyone above him had been killed in the first battle. His experience of being a sergeant was on a par with Ryan's experience of being a captain, which made him a disaster waiting to happen. A sergeant who played the bully was one thing, but a sergeant who actually *was* a bully was quite another. Ryan had to admit, privately, if he'd had to deal with the man before his injury he would probably have summarily demoted him back to the ranks. Or worse.

He reached the top of the trench and ran forward, using the remains of the earlier attack forces as cover. The enemy blockhouses were little more than smouldering piles of rubble; bodies, *enemy* bodies, lay behind them, mostly torn and mangled by shellfire. He shuddered as he saw a blackened corpse kneeling on the ground, its arm extended and pointing south, towards the enemy lines. Ahead of him, there were dozens of small houses that had been turned into strongpoints…

The sound of gunfire rattled out. He threw himself down and kept crawling forward, allowing his instincts to guide him. The houses wouldn't make *good* strongpoints, not for very long. But they'd hold long enough to trap his men and slaughter them. Bullets snapped through the air above him, suggesting that the defenders had already taken aim. He winced, despite his constantly shifting mode, as he saw a young man - barely out of basic training - fall to the ground. There was no point in attempting to help him. The bullet had struck his forehead.

Shit, Ryan thought.

The sound of shooting was growing louder as he crawled towards the first house, a small cottage with a neat little garden and - of all things - a garden gnome in the middle of the flowerbed. He found himself giggling at the sheer absurdity of the sight, wondering why he hadn't seen anything like it on Thule. But then, most of the people who resisted the Wolves came from the inner cities or the countryside. The cottage before him probably belonged to some wealthy couple who worked in the city, but didn't have to live in it.

Lucky bastards, he thought, as he spied the shooter firing through a window that had long since cracked and broken. The enemy gunner had a solid position, but he couldn't see anyone crawling up from the side. *And now I'm about to wreck their house.*

He nodded to two of his men, then unhooked a grenade from his belt and hurled it forward, into the window. It exploded seconds later, throwing *something* up against the side of the wall as Ryan hurried forward and kicked down the door. Inside, pieces of debris lay everywhere. The grenade had done a lot more damage than merely fuck up the enemy soldier. He crunched over pieces of china as he probed forward, then sighed in relief as he saw the enemy soldier lying on the ground. She - the breasts were unmistakable, even though her stomach was a bleeding mess - gurgled once and died. He kicked her head anyway, then motioned for his men to search the house.

"Clear, sir," one called.

Ryan nodded, looking towards what had once been a comfortable armchair. The room suggested *age*, age and experience. There were no hints that any children had lived in the house for a very long time. Maybe the owner was a grandfather instead of a father, he thought, as he peered carefully out the rear window. There was an entire row of cookie-cutter houses ahead of him, all practically identical. A couple had been hit by stray shells and badly damaged, but the remainder were intact. He found himself shivering, although he wasn't sure why. The homes were normal, perfectly normal. And then it hit him. The houses were practically identical. They even had the same decorations in the garden!

And they'll all have to be cleared, he thought, numbly.

Ryan keyed his radio as he led the way back out of the cottage. There were hundreds of bodies - new bodies - lying on the ground, men gunned down as they ran across the ruined defence line and into the city. He shuddered, sinking to his knees as he realised that it was happening again, that hundreds of thousands of men were going to die, leaving him the only survivor.

He took a deep breath, unable to force himself to rise. His entire body felt drained, deprived of energy. He didn't want to move, he *couldn't* move. He just couldn't face going any further, not when it would only get hundreds of men killed. And yet, somehow, he knew he had to keep going. The MPs would kill him when they pushed forward, funnelling the men into the killing zone. He could hear the sound of gunfire as the forward units pushed onwards, followed by AFVs. Their machine guns provided cover as the infantry inched forward.

Gritting his teeth, he forced himself to take the injector tap and press it against his skin. A surge of energy shot through his body, driving him back to his feet. He glanced around as the energy burned through him, even though he knew it was a lie. The combat drug wouldn't last long, not when his system was already weak. But it would have to be enough.

"Forward," he shouted. "Now!"

———

"They're through the main defence lines," Gwendolyn reported. "Sir...?"

"I heard," Ed said. Bunker-busters. He'd expected the enemy to come up with *something*, but this time they'd surpassed themselves. Explosive enough to blast entire blockhouses out of the ground, simple enough to be put together in a matter of days. And they'd punched a hole right through his defences. "Shift reinforcements to meet the main thrust of the enemy advance."

"Aye, sir," Gwendolyn said.

Ed glanced at the timer. It was a race now, a race to chase Admiral Singh away from the planet before the shield generator could be destroyed. The enemy had already knocked out two point defence units, making it harder to intercept all of the remaining shells before they struck the ground. If they were monitoring the firing patterns, he suspected, they'd probably be able to tighten their estimate of precisely *where* the generator was located. He'd thought about trying to create a false impression, to try to convince them that the generator was located somewhere else, but far too much could have gone spectacularly wrong. A lucky hit could have disabled the generator once and for all.

"Mandy?"

"No word," Gwendolyn confirmed.

He looked at the display for a long moment. His forces could keep the Wolves tied up for weeks, fighting their way through the city, as long as the ammunition held out. But he doubted they'd *have* weeks. The prospect of a lucky shot grew more and more likely with every passing hour. And even if it didn't, he'd soon lose the ability to resist.

"General Hampton, take tactical command," he ordered. "I'm going up there."

Danielle gasped, but he ignored her. He was damned if he was leaving men to fight when he wasn't by their side, not any longer.

317

Besides, he didn't dare risk being taken prisoner. The Wolves would forget all good intentions regarding the treatment of prisoners when they realised who they'd caught. He knew far too much to risk being interrogated.

"That's not wise, sir," Gwendolyn said.

"It's not debatable," Ed said, firmly.

Mindy gritted her teeth as she took up position in the makeshift strongpoint, peering down the street towards the advancing Wolves. They were taking their time clearing the last set of suburban houses, but she had to admit they were doing a professional job of it. No doubt the handful of IEDs the retreating defenders had left in their wake had concentrated a few minds, not to mention the handful of troopers who'd hidden amidst the debris and then opened fire on the Wolves from the rear. They were being very careful indeed.

But it isn't going to be enough, she thought, as she slotted the magazine into place. There were ammunition stockpiles scattered throughout the city, thankfully, but it was depressingly clear that they were running short. The facilities just hadn't been able to replenish the hundreds of thousands of rounds expended during the first round of fighting. *We're waiting for them here.*

A dull boom echoed over the city as someone tripped over an IED. She smiled grimly to herself, even though she knew it wasn't funny. Anything that slowed the enemy down, if only for a few minutes, was fine with her. She wondered, absently, if Jasmine was wreaking more havoc in their rear, then decided it was unlikely. The Wolves had been stung so badly, in their first attack on the city, that they'd taken extreme precautions against another commando raid. Jasmine was good - she'd kicked Mindy's ass around the sparring ring when Mindy had challenged her to a *friendly* match - but even she and the marines couldn't break into an impregnable stronghold.

They'll be shipping men and supplies up to consolidate their advantage, Mindy thought, numbly. The Wolves seemed to have unlimited ammunition, judging by the rate they were expending it. *She'll have plenty of opportunities to wreak havoc.*

"Here they come," Sergeant Rackham said, as a handful of grey figures appeared at the far end of the road. They were followed by two Landsharks, the massive tanks rumbling forward and crushing garden walls under their treads. "Get down and take cover."

Mindy realised what was about to happen and hastily did as she was told, covering her ears as Sergeant Rackham produced a detonator. His hand pushed down on the button and the ground shook, the roar of the nearby explosion so loud it drowned out everything else. Her ears were ringing afterwards, despite the implants; she turned, just in time to see the flaming remains of a tank crashing to the ground. The tank behind it had been flipped over, crushing a number of enemy soldiers beneath its massive bulk. Other soldiers were walking around, dazed. Blood was spilling from their ears...

"Shoot them," Sergeant Rackham bellowed. "Now!"

Mindy hastily lifted her rifle, retook the firing position and opened fire.

———

Ryan stared in disbelief as the remains of one Landshark tank crashed down, nothing more than a pile of scrap metal, while the other flipped over and came down hard. There was a giant crater below where the first tank had been, suggesting that the entire street had been rigged to blow! And if he'd taken one less minute clearing the last house, finding nothing apart from a handful of rude taunts scrawled on the wall, he would probably have been caught in the blast and killed...

Bullets started cracking through the air, picking off men who'd been far too close to the blast and were too dazed to take cover. Ryan stared in horror as Lieutenant Gordon, trying desperately to get one man out of the enemy gunsights, was shot right through the throat, his blood splashing down to the ground as his body collapsed. He'd been an ass, but he'd been *trying* to do something useful.

He turned and saw a pair of MPs, advancing forward. He'd seen them at work over the last two hours, urging some men forward and arresting two more for self-inflicted wounds. Cold hatred flared in his heart as he saw them eying him, clearly wondering if he'd decided he didn't want to go on any longer. And they'd be right, he thought, as he raised his rifle. The flicker of sudden alarm in their eyes, as he pulled the trigger twice, was gratifying. They weren't *real* soldiers. *Real* soldiers would have realised the danger and jumped for cover at once.

"No more," he shouted. His company was already coming apart at the seams. Like before, he'd found himself in command of men from a dozen different units, men who'd been fed into the sausage grinder by unfeeling superiors. "No more!"

His men took up the cry as he led them away from the enemy position. "No more!"

CHAPTER
THIRTY-SEVEN

Indeed, the Imperial Navy squadron that lost the Battle of New Preston did, at least in part, because its quartermaster was selling off supplies on the black market. They were not expecting to go to war, so the quartermaster saw no harm in allowing the stockpile of spare parts to drop to a critically-low level.
- Professor Leo Caesius. The Role of Randomness In War.

Rani allowed herself a cold smile as the enemy defence line started to crumble. It gave her very little pleasure to admit that General Haverford had known what he was doing when he insisted on deploying the weapons, but there was no way to avoid it. Her forward units were already advancing into the city, cutting a bloody swath towards the shield generator. It didn't matter, in the end, just how much of the city was destroyed before the generator was finally smashed. All that mattered was stamping her iron will on the city and forcing its population to acknowledge her.

Not long now, she told herself. *And then it will all be worthwhile.*

She leaned back in her chair, watching the reports as they were put together by her analysis crews. The enemy fire was already slacking, some said; it was clear they were on the verge of running out of ammunition. Others warned that the enemy were attempting to shorten their defence line, fighting to the last to keep her from reaching the generator. It didn't matter, she told herself, as she watched shells striking down within the city. Either her forces captured the generator or they destroyed it. She would come out ahead whatever happened.

And then I can crush my enemies, she thought. The latest set of reports from Wolfbane - three weeks out of date, despite the best efforts of her courier crews - had made it clear that her supporters were in trouble. Her enemies weren't making any overt moves, but they *were* repositioning themselves to snatch power or protect themselves in the case of a general revolution. *I have to prove that taking Corinthian was worth the effort.*

Her console chimed. "Admiral, this is Henderson in Communications," a voice said. "I just picked up an urgent message from the surface. There's been a mutiny!"

Rani leaned forward, shocked. "A mutiny?"

"Yes, Admiral," Henderson said. "A number of units have refused to advance against the enemy positions."

General Haverford didn't call me, Rani thought. Cold suspicion flowed through her mind. If *she* was planning to dispose of Haverford, and turn him into a scapegoat for hundreds of thousands of deaths and billions of credits worth of destroyed equipment and property damage, he might be planning to do the same to her. *Is he up to something?*

She glared at the display. "Do we have any detailed reports?"

"Not as yet, Admiral," Henderson said. "The report came from a source within FOB II."

Haverford's new base, Rani thought. *And that means...?*

She forced herself to think, despite the growing urge to just contact Haverford and order him to put the mutiny down with extreme force. Mutineers *knew* they faced execution, if they were taken alive. It was one of the few Imperial Navy regulations that Governor Brown had kept in force, without rewriting it to avoid all the pesky little quibbles the lawyers had inserted to earn their pay. And Haverford would have to be mad if he was planning to turn against her. He had no way to get an assault team onto her flagship and, without that, she could simply destroy his forces from orbit.

And he may be dealing with the mutiny already, she thought. *He may think he doesn't need to inform me.*

"Put me through to General Haverford," she ordered. "And be quick about it!"

"Aye, Admiral," Henderson said.

General Haverford's face appeared in front of her moments later, slightly fuzzed because of the jamming and the enemy shield. "Admiral," he said. "We have a situation."

"So I hear," Rani said. There was no point in hiding the fact she had agents on his staff. She rather suspected it would make it harder for him to put together a conspiracy. If, of course, he didn't have one already. Soldiers wound up loyal to their commanders, after all; it was how she'd bested Admiral Bainbridge and taken Trafalgar for her own. "What - *precisely* - is happening?"

"We have small mutinies in a dozen sectors," General Haverford said. "I sent in the MPs to restore order, but they were greeted with gunfire. Right now, the enemy doesn't seem to have realised our weakness…"

Rani jerked as the alarms sounded. "Red alert," Captain Gowon bellowed. His voice echoed through the giant battleship. "I say again, red alert! All hands to battlestations! Admiral Singh to the CIC!"

"It seems I have a situation too," Rani said, rising. "General, do whatever you have to do to squash this mutiny and resume the offensive. Do you understand me?"

"Yes, Admiral," Haverford said. "I understand perfectly."

———

"They have us, Captain," the sensor officer reported. "They've locked on."

Mandy nodded, curtly. She hadn't expected to get *that* close to the planet, even though her squadron was masked by the most advanced cloaking devices known to exist. Admiral Singh *had* seeded local space with countless sensor platforms, after all, and it only needed a single flicker of turbulence to betray their presence. And yet, it suggested Admiral Singh was rather more concerned about allowing her squadron anywhere near the planet than Mandy might have expected. A cunning officer might just have quietly tracked her ships with passive sensors, then opened fire without warning.

"Drop the cloaks," she ordered. They were of only limited value, now the enemy knew where they were. "Deploy sensor decoys, launch probes."

"Aye, Captain," the tactical officer said.

Mandy felt a flicker of relief. Admiral Singh had concentrated her ships above Freedom City, as if she'd hoped to cow the inhabitants from orbit. Or, perhaps, intervene at once if the shield generator failed. Now, the four giant battleships and supporting units were altering position, shifting away from the planet to gain manoeuvring room. No, Mandy realised as the enemy ships picked up speed. They were heading right towards her!

"Enemy ships on attack vector," the tactical officer said, confirming her thoughts. "Enhanced missile range in seven minutes, standard missile range in twelve."

"Lock enhanced missiles on the battleships," Mandy ordered. She had twenty-four ships to Admiral Singh's forty, but her advanced weapons would make up for her shortage of warships. Or so she hoped. Admiral Singh would have problems replacing any losses in a hurry, if Jasmine was right, yet the Commonwealth wasn't much better off. "Prepare to fire."

She thought fast as the two fleets converged. What was going through Admiral Singh's mind? Did she see a chance to crush a sizable enemy force while she had the advantage or was she planning a long-range engagement before breaking off and escaping across the phase limit? But Mandy was reasonably sure she could break off the engagement herself, on her own terms, if things went badly wrong. If nothing else, a long drawn-out engagement worked in her favour. She could hammer Admiral Singh from beyond her effective range.

"Weapons locked," the tactical officer reported. "Missiles armed, ready to fire; point defence network up, ready to engage."

Mandy sucked in a breath as the timer ticked down to zero. "Fire."

"Aye, Captain," the tactical officer said. "Firing...*now*."

———

Rani swore inwardly as the two fleets converged. The Commonwealth Navy had picked a particularly bad time to arrive, if only because of the threatened mutiny. She didn't dare allow them a chance to take control of the high orbitals, but - at the same time - she didn't dare risk allowing them an engagement on their terms. And she couldn't simply withdraw because there would be no way to spin it in her favour.

"Admiral," the sensor officer said. "The enemy fleet has opened fire."

Impossible, Rani thought.

She quashed the impulse a moment later. The enemy wouldn't have wasted upwards of three hundred missiles without reason, which suggested that they *knew* they could hit her at this range. And they were well outside *her* range. Even if the two fleets continued converging, there was no way she could engage them now. Her missiles would burn out long before they reached their targets.

"Bring the point defence network online," she ordered. The enemy missiles weren't just longer-ranged than hers, they were faster too. Thankfully, she'd had her crews training on the assumption that better missiles were not only possible, but plausible. "And then..."

She thought with desperate speed. If the missiles carried standard warheads, it was quite likely her fleet would survive long enough to get into engagement range and return fire. But if they didn't, if their warheads were as advanced as their drives, they might inflict serious damage outside her own range. She'd done it herself to pirate ships, back in the day; the Commonwealth would have no qualms about doing it to her. Only a sucker sought a fair fight when she could tip the odds in her favour instead.

Morton's Fork, she acknowledged, silently saluting her unknown enemy. If she fought, she might lose everything; if she ran, she'd never be able to convince her enemies that it had been nothing more than a prudent move. *Whatever I do, it may not rebound in my favour.*

"Continue on our current course," she ordered, finally. "Engage the enemy missiles as soon as they come into range."

They were targeted on her battleships, she realised, as the missile vectors shook themselves down. Her smaller ships had been completely ignored, which made it easier for their crews to concentrate on keeping the missiles from striking the battleships. But there were just too many warheads, some of which were spewing out jamming pulses as they closed in on their targets. She gritted her teeth as she realised just how cunningly the system had been designed. There was no hope of hiding the missile's existence, so the jammer was making it hard to pin the missile down to a precise location. It required several shots to be sure of taking down each missile, which ensured that others would make it through the defence grid and strike their targets...

"*Furious* has taken fifteen hits," the tactical officer reported. "She's..."

He broke off as *Furious* vanished from the display. Rani stared, shocked. No battleship had been lost in combat for decades! The heavily-armoured ships had been designed to be virtually invulnerable. Poor maintenance was a far worse threat than enemy fire. She knew better - no battleship had ever faced another battleship in combat for centuries - but it was still shocking. The enemy had something new.

"Report," she growled, as red icons lanced towards *Orion*. "What happened?"

"I'm not sure," the analyst admitted. "There were some...oddities... around the missiles as they plunged into their target, but..."

Orion shuddered, violently. Rani grabbed her chair and held on for dear life as red lights flashed up on the display, reporting that the battleship had taken two hits. It looked as through the Commonwealth had come up with something that went through armour - even hullmetal - like a knife through butter. Her mind raced, wondering what it could be, as damage control parties scrambled to the gash in the hull. Even superhot plasma cannons couldn't do more than scorch hullmetal. Cutting through the immense slabs of armour protecting her battleship required heavy lasers. It was why she'd always dreaded having to repair a battleship, when she'd been assigned to System Command. Even the simplest task was a nightmare.

"Keep us on course," she growled. *Furious* was the only battleship that had been destroyed, but *Hammerhead* and *Powerful* had both taken damage. The only consolation was that the second enemy barrage was much weaker than the first. "And prepare to engage the moment we enter missile range."

"Aye, Admiral," the tactical officer said.

Rani forced herself to sit back and relax. The enemy had shown off a new surprise, but they hadn't had enough missiles to make it decisive. A barrage twice the size of the one she'd faced would have wiped out her entire fleet. Hell, if they'd fired on the smaller ships, they would have destroyed at least a dozen warships. And now she knew what she was facing.

This isn't the end, she told herself, firmly. *This is not the end.*

"They're still advancing towards us, Captain," the tactical officer said.

Mandy raised her eyebrows. She'd expected - hoped - that Admiral Singh would break off after the first missile strike. Losing a battleship and two thousand trained spacers had to hurt, even if the other three battleships had survived blows that would have killed anything smaller. Indeed, as reluctant as she was to admit it, there was no way to avoid the simple fact that the battleships were *very* well built. Their acceleration curves were pathetic, they moved through space like a whale through mud, but they were tough. And planets, their targets, could neither run nor hide.

The second strike is going to be a great deal less effective, she thought. Admiral Singh's crews might be stuck with primitive gear, compared to some of the wonders she'd seen emerge from the Commonwealth or the Trade Federation, but they weren't stupid. Their point defence had already adapted to the advanced warheads. Given time, they might even figure out how the trick was done and counter it. *And we're running short of advanced missiles.*

She watched, grimly, as the range closed. The second strike had been a *great* deal less effective than the first. Her crews were already updating their targeting systems, but it was too late. She just didn't have enough missiles to batter Admiral Singh to rubble before the Wolves entered their own range. And at that point, she'd have to keep the range open to keep from being overwhelmed herself.

"Captain," the tactical officer said. "The enemy are entering missile range."

"Reverse course," Mandy ordered, as the battleships opened fire. The design wasn't just tough, she recalled; it was armed to the teeth. Each battleship was spitting out more missiles than all of her squadron put together. "Hold the range as open as we can."

"Aye, Captain," the helmsman said.

"And continue firing," Mandy added. "Don't give them a moment to relax."

She forced herself to watch as the enemy missiles roared towards her ships. They'd be operating on the extreme edge of their range, but it probably wouldn't be enough to save her from taking damage. The only saving grace was that it would keep Admiral Singh away from the planet, preventing her from doing something drastic. Mindy was down there, along with Jasmine and hundreds of others she knew. She didn't dare let Admiral Singh lash out at the planet. She'd kill billions in a split-second.

"The enemy have updated their own seeker heads," the tactical officer noted. "Their targeting system is roughly thirty percent better than it was during the Battle of Tazenda."

Mandy nodded, unsurprised. Admiral Singh wasn't *stupid*, after all, and she *did* have possession of a fairly large industrial base. The Grand Senate might have been able to slow innovation to a trickle, but Admiral Singh couldn't possibly do anything of the sort. She'd be crushed by the Commonwealth when something new and deadly - or even an improved weapon - was put into service against her. Even the Trade Federation might be able to come up with something that would obliterate her navy in an afternoon.

"Take out as many as you can," she ordered. No matter what she did, she was going to lose ships and spacers. "And continue firing."

———

They must be desperate, Rani thought. It was odd to be *pleased* at losing a battleship, along with spacers she couldn't easily replace, but enough things *hadn't* happened to convince her that the enemy was on the ropes. They should have kept their new missiles in reserve long enough to lure her into a trap and crush her with overwhelming firepower. Instead, the cat was out of the bag far too early to give the enemy a decisive victory. *They know I'm going to take Corinthian off them.*

It was stupid, she noted: stupid and sentimental. An advantage like that shouldn't be thrown away, even if it meant surrendering an industrialised world to her. The Commonwealth could have won the war within months, if they'd kept their weapons a secret until it was too late for her to come up with countermeasures. Instead, they'd lost their best chance at kicking her ass.

She smiled, coldly, as the battle slowly evolved in front of her. The enemy's hasty decision to reverse course was far from stupid, but they just hadn't had time to get back out of missile range before it was too late.

Their point defence was an order of magnitude more capable than her own - it was clear their sensors were excellent - yet that was why she'd fired so many missiles. And their hulls weren't any tougher…

Their force shields are eating up some of our missiles, she thought. She'd expected as much, of course. *But we have ways to get around it now.*

"Admiral," the tactical officer said. He sounded pleased, but there was an edge in his voice she didn't like. "Three enemy ships have been destroyed, two more have been crippled. A number of others have also taken minor damage."

Rani nodded. There would be a chance to capture the ships soon enough, if the crews didn't abandon ship and trigger the self-destruct. Even if they did, she'd take the lifepods and have the crews interrogated. They might just know something useful about how the shields worked. Or, for that matter, how so many other pieces of technology worked. And then…

"Admiral," the communications officer said. "I'm picking up a signal from the planet."

He swallowed, hard. "I'm afraid it's bad news."

CHAPTER
THIRTY-EIGHT

But when the squadron was suddenly called to war, they were utterly unable
to meet the challenge. They lost, decisively.
                              - Professor Leo Caesius. The Role of Randomness In War.

"The 23rd Assault Regiment is also reporting problems," Colonel Travis
reported. "An officer has been killed and two more have been forced to
run."

Mark swore, venomously. He should have anticipated the possibility of a general collapse, even at the very hour of victory. He'd known
there were problems, he'd known his men were brittle...and he'd thrown
them into battle anyway. Defeatism and mutiny were contagious, too; as
panic spread, more and more units would collapse into chaos. Normally,
he could have brought up intact units and sealed off the contagion before
it spread further, but now...now he no longer had the reserves in place.
He'd thrown everything into the battle for the city.

Damn it, he thought. They were *winning*! The inner enemy defence
lines were crumbling before them. And yet, his force was coming apart at
the seams. It wouldn't be long before the enemy noticed and counterattacked, if they didn't just use the time to take a breath and get their forces
ready for the next offensive. *We were winning!*

"I can order the gunners to shell the mutinous soldiers," Colonel
Travis suggested. "Sir..."

"Shut up," Mark snarled. Sending Ferguson away had *definitely* been
a mistake. The man was probably dead, after taking command of a unit

that had charged into the teeth of enemy fire. And if he wasn't, chances were Ferguson had been badly wounded himself. "I'm not going to shell my own positions."

An operator looked up from her console. "Colonel Bateman has been killed, sir," she said, grimly. "Captain Rostock reports that he has been forced to abandon his post after some of his men turned on him."

Mark rubbed his eyes, then glanced at the system display. Admiral Singh was battling the Commonwealth Navy, which seemed to have inflicted significant damage on her forces even though she was pressing the offensive. Did she want to get herself killed? No matter what happened, Admiral Singh was going to have real problems staying alive, let alone holding on to power. Tens of thousands were dead, a number of irreplaceable starships had been destroyed…and for what? Taking Corinthian now would hardly make up for everything they'd lost.

And going down in a blaze of glory will get my remaining troops slaughtered, he thought. *I won't let them die for nothing!*

———

Jasmine crawled through the sewer, silently thanking the gods that protected marines that her nasal implants were working perfectly. The sewer hadn't been cleansed in weeks, perhaps longer, and the stench was practically unbearable. If she hadn't had the implants, she suspected she wouldn't have been able to force herself into the pipe and crawl along it towards their destination. As it was, she was grateful she wasn't claustrophobic. Coming apart midway through the mission would have gotten the entire team killed.

She allowed herself a flicker of relief as she saw the grate at the far end, nothing more than a grid of metal allowing inspectors to peer into the system. There didn't seem to be anyone on guard duty, but she was careful not to make a sound as she reached the grate and used a sonic screwdriver to unlock the screws and carefully lower it to the floor. The inspection chamber was empty, thankfully; she inspected the door as Buckley followed her out, looking as if he'd crawled out of a bog. Stewart, behind him, didn't look pleased at all.

"Remind me," Jasmine muttered. The door should be easy to open from the inside, even though it was locked and bolted. "Whose bright idea was this?"

"*Yours*," Buckley said. He produced a debonder from his belt and held it out to her. "I thought my idea was better."

Jasmine smiled as she tested the debonder against the door, making sure they could get out without using explosives. The enemy command post was heavily guarded; there were guard posts, three layers of barbed wire, a dozen AFVs and four companies of armed soldiers on constant patrol outside the fence. She'd watched them long enough to know they weren't incompetents either, unlike some HQ guard companies she could mention. Everyone who went in and out of the command post was thoroughly inspected, no exceptions. She'd watched with some amusement as a protesting senior officer was patted down by the guards before he'd finally been permitted to enter. No doubt he'd already been planning a futile complaint to his superiors.

She'd tried hard to come up with a way to breach the defences, but found nothing. Her platoon was better trained than the enemy soldiers, yet they'd be unable to inflict enough damage to win if they attacked from the outside. If someone in Freedom City hadn't checked the plans and discovered the sewer, she wasn't sure *what* she would have done. Taking out the enemy command post was desperately important, but even a suicide mission had no guarantee of success.

And if we're wrong about where the enemy CO has based himself, she thought, *we're screwed.*

She checked her rifle, then glanced at the remainder of the platoon. They were ready, weapons in hand. Jasmine held her k-bar in one hand as she pressed the debonder against the lock, disintegrating it into dust. She kicked the door open and lunged out into the corridor, eyes scanning for enemy soldiers. A young woman in uniform gaped at her, her eyes going wide as Jasmine pitched the knife at her, striking the poor woman in the throat. She tumbled to the ground, gurgling in pain as she died. Jasmine recovered the knife, wiped it on her stained uniform and led the way down the corridor. The longer they could keep the enemy from realising that they were under attack, the better.

Poor bitch, she thought, as they found the stairwell. If they were lucky, most of the defences would be on the outside. *But she was in our way.*

They ran into a pair of armed soldiers as they hurried up the stairs, two men who snapped up their rifles with commendable speed. Jasmine opened fire, killing them both instantly; they staggered backwards and fell to the ground. She swore as she stepped over their bodies and hurried further up the stairs. The entire building would have heard the gunfire. They'd be starting their emergency procedures at once, putting the officers in the panic rooms while elite troops swept the building for the marines. It wasn't as if they'd have difficulty finding them, either. Jasmine suspected all they'd have to do was follow their noses.

Four more guards appeared at the far end of the corridor as she reached the top of the stairwell, opening fire at once. Jasmine ducked as Buckley unhooked a grenade from his belt, then threw it down the corridor. The building shook as the grenade detonated; Jasmine picked herself up and hurled herself forward, sweeping the corridor for surviving enemy soldiers. One of the young men was badly wounded, so badly wounded he didn't have a hope of survival; the others had been caught in the blast and killed. She felt a stab of pity as she put him out of his misery, then pointed to the final door. It had been blown off its hinges by the grenade.

Inside, a handful of senior officers were stumbling around in panic. Jasmine allowed herself a tight smile as she led the way into the chamber, watching in grim amusement as the officers hastily raised their hands. REMFs! No doubt they'd felt safe, surrounded by so much firepower and armed guards. But then, they *had* been safe in their original FOB. It was coming so close to the city, where there were plans and charts for every building, that had defeated them. *She* wouldn't have made such a careless mistake.

She searched for the senior officer and blinked in surprise as she recognised him. General Haverford had accepted her surrender on Thule, a lifetime ago. She hadn't been impressed at the time, even though she suspected she had him to thank for being dispatched to Meridian, instead of being summarily shoved out an airlock. Admiral Singh would not have hesitated to kill her if she'd known who Jasmine was. The combat uniform he wore was unmarred by extensive collections of medals and campaign ribbons, but it was also clean and tidy. He hadn't been in the field for months.

"The battle is over," she said, confidently. Dirty and smelly as she was, she'd walked right into the heart of the enemy CP. "Order your troops to surrender."

———

Mark stared at the figure before him, momentarily lost for words. She - he wasn't entirely sure of the gender, let alone anything else - was covered in filth, but she was holding him at gunpoint. Her team was covering his senior officers, most of whom were holding their hands in the air as if they were afraid that one false move would result in a massacre. How the hell had she gotten into the base?

He took a breath, despite the stench. "Admiral Singh..."

"Admiral Singh is not here," the figure said. She jabbed her rifle towards him. "*You* are."

Mark nodded, curtly. They'd lost. The mutinies had been bad enough, even though he thought he could have put them down in time, but the enemy commando team could wipe out his entire command staff. His army would come apart, allowing the enemy to wipe them out piece by piece. And Admiral Singh seemed to be doing her best to get herself killed, rather than either escaping or coming back to succour the groundpounders.

He forced himself to meet her eyes. "What guarantees will you offer for the safety of my men?"

"The same you offered us on Thule," the figure said. "We will take your men into custody; they will be held in a POW camp until the end of the war or our superiors agree on a prisoner exchange. They will be treated in line with the standard conventions, provided they don't make trouble. Officers such as yourself will be held separately from the men, but otherwise unharmed."

Mark wondered, grimly, just how much of that was true. The Commonwealth might *want* to keep its word, but there were a great many people on Corinthian who would want revenge against his men. God knew there had been far too many incidents in the last month, despite the draconian measures he'd used to keep order. None of his men went out alone, not after finding the remains of a particularly stupid soldier who'd been lured away from his post by a local woman. His killers had been particularly imaginative.

But he knew the battle was lost. All that remained was to save as much of his manpower as possible.

"Very well," he said. "But I must inform Admiral Singh of my decision."

The figure nodded, slowly. "Order your men to surrender first," she said. "And then you can inform your superiors."

He walked over to the terminal, keying in the override code. "This is General Haverford," he said. He'd be heard by everyone with access to a radio. "You are ordered to cease fire and surrender to the nearest enemy unit. I say again, you are ordered to cease fire and surrender to the nearest enemy unit. Obey all enemy orders consummate with the laws of war and common decency."

"Thank you," the figure said. "Tell your guards to surrender too, General. We don't want to have to fight our way out of here."

"Of course," Mark said.

He sighed, inwardly, as he was prodded back to the centre of the room. There had been no time to input a destruct command, not when he was held at gunpoint. The standard procedures for surrender allowed for the destruction of classified material, but somehow he doubted his captors would permit him to do anything of the sort. There was little classified data for them to recover, yet some of it might prove disastrous in the wrong hands. He'd just have to hope his subordinates had the wit to destroy it themselves.

It's over, he thought, numbly. *And yet we are still alive.*

Somehow, it didn't make him feel any better.

Rani forced herself to think, coldly and logically, as her fleet closed in on its opponents. General Haverford had surrendered, damn the man. The timing was perfect, too; there was no way she could reverse course to punish him without being defeated by the Commonwealth Navy. Had he been a traitor all along? Or was it just sheer bad luck?

She studied the display as a dull quiver ran through the battleship, another barrage of missiles spewing from its inner tubes. She'd taken damage, but so had the enemy; she could win, if she pressed them hard. And then she could turn back to Corinthian and scorch the world clean of life. But it would come with a cost. Victory might just go to the side that had only one or two ships left. There was a very good chance she wouldn't survive either.

I can blame the defeat on Haverford, she thought, coldly. It wasn't much, but it would keep her alive long enough to tighten her grip on Wolfbane. *He can be portrayed as an enemy spy or merely a coward, a traitor who sent hundreds of thousands of men to their doom.*

She cleared her throat. "Fire a final barrage, then alter course and take us out of the system," she ordered. A flurry of relief ran through the CIC. "Send a general signal to occupation forces in the industrial nodes. They are to trigger the self-destructs, then abandon the facilities and make their way to the pre-planned pick-up points. We'll pick them up as we leave."

"Aye, Admiral," the communications officer said.

Rani nodded, curtly. It was a defeat; there was no way to hide the fact it was a defeat. No one but a complete idiot would think otherwise. And trying to blame everything on a damnable traitor wouldn't save her from some very hard months. Haverford had been *her* choice for ground-side commander, after all. Her enemies wouldn't let her forget that in a hurry.

But at least they got chewed up, she thought, as the enemy broke contact and drove towards the planet. *They took heavy losses in the fighting too.*

She scowled. The only consolation was that Corinthian was finished as a manufacturing centre, at least for a decade. She'd known precisely where to target to do maximum damage to their economy, an economy she'd been partly responsible for building the first time around. Their trained manpower might have survived, but it would be more efficient to distribute them around the Commonwealth than return them to Corinthian. The planet was looking at an economic disaster that would make them *wish* she'd won the war…

It wasn't much of a consolation, she told herself. But it was something.

––––––––

"It's confirmed, Colonel," Hampton said, through the communicator. "Admiral Singh's fleet has broken contact and is heading towards the phase limit at speed."

Ed nodded, rather ruefully. He hadn't done much, once he'd reached the front lines. He'd merely taken command of a reserve company and directed them into battle. But at least it was *something*. Gaby wouldn't be pleased, when she heard about it, yet he thought she'd understand. He couldn't allow others to go into danger without sharing it himself. If nothing else, it would keep him from becoming as useless as some of the commanders he recalled from Han. Admiral Valentine had been so fat he'd had to waddle from his princely quarters to the CIC and back again.

"It's over," he said, quietly.

"It looks that way," Hampton agreed. "The organised enemy forces are surrendering, Colonel, and the mutinous ones are offering no resistance. We should have the bastards in POW camps by the end of the day."

"For their own safety, if nothing else," Ed said. He had no doubt the CEF would remain true to its training, but the Corinthian Militia was quite another story. By now, *everyone* knew someone who had been killed in the fighting or heard horror stories about how women had been raped and little children had been gunned down for sport. "We need to avoid atrocities."

"I know," Hampton said.

Ed nodded ruefully, staring out over the remains of Freedom City. A third of the towering skyscrapers he'd seen on arrival had been knocked down, while many of the remaining structures had taken damage and

337

CHRISTOPHER G. NUTTALL

were dangerously unsafe. The suburbs on the outskirts of the city had practically been destroyed, while the spaceport had been devastated by two hours of savage fighting. He'd arranged for the shuttles to be moved elsewhere, saving them from destruction, but replacing the facilities was going to take months. Corinthian didn't have an easy time ahead of it.

The only thing sadder than a battle lost is a battle won, he thought. He'd been taught *that* at the Slaughterhouse, although he'd never understood it until his first taste of combat. The battle had been won, but the war itself was far from over. *And now we have to clean up the mess.*

He stood there for a long moment, watching as sergeants hastily organised men into smaller units to take and guard prisoners, then turned and headed back to the bunker. There was no time to stand around wool-gathering. He needed to get the final report from Mandy, then consult with Jasmine...

And then plan the next step, he told himself. *It will be months before Admiral Singh recovers, if she can. And that time is ours.*

CHAPTER
THIRTY-NINE

Randomness plays a greater role in wartime than we care to admit - or want to believe.

- Professor Leo Caesius. The Role of Randomness In War.

Ryan knelt on the broken ground, hands laced behind his head.

It was hard, so hard, to feel anything as more and more of his former comrades were corralled together by the enemy soldiers. He knew he should feel shame, he knew he should be planning his escape, but in truth he felt nothing. He'd committed mutiny in the face of the enemy, a court martial offense if ever there was one, yet he felt no urge to run or face up to his crimes. There was a part of him that had broken, he knew now. His nerve had shattered, once and for all, in the final battle.

He looked up at the enemy soldiers, looking as tired and battered as he felt. There were few real differences between the two sides, he saw; the only *real* difference was that there were a handful of female soldiers among the Commonwealth troops. General Haverford had been strongly against recruiting women, Ryan recalled, although he had no idea why. The General hadn't bothered to discuss his decision with a lowly lieutenant. Maybe, if some of the stories he'd heard about the Imperial Army were true, he'd just thought that female soldiers were more trouble than they were worth.

A loud whistle echoed through the air. "Attention," a tough-looking sergeant snapped, in unaccented Imperial Standard. His rank insignia, Ryan noted, was identical to Sergeant Rove's before his death. It was far too soon for the various successor states to start taking on their own iden-tities. "You are being separated into two groups: mutineers and loyalists. If you declare yourself when you are processed, you will be sent to the right camp; if you refuse to state a side, you will be sent to the loyalist camp by default."

Ryan would have rolled his eyes, if he hadn't been so tired. The Commonwealth was wise to separate the mutineers from the loyalists, although no one - not even himself - could genuinely separate one from the other. But then, a loyalist might not survive an hour in the mutineer POW camp or vice versa. He had no doubt that many of the REMFs would blame the mutineers for costing them the war. It struck him, suddenly, that there might be a chance to murder General Haverford if he went into the loyalist camp, but further reflection told him it was unlikely. The Commonwealth would probably isolate the officers from the men, both to deprive the men of leadership and prevent them from taking bloody revenge.

He smirked as a female soldier motioned for him to rise. *Getting rid of the officers will probably improve unit morale fivefold.*

The smirk refused to leave his face as she prodded him past the other guards and up to a desk, manned by a grim-looking NCO. Ryan could practically read the REMFs mind; he was pissed, very pissed, at having to register prisoners. It probably wasn't what he'd signed up for, although he wasn't sure *what* REMFs had signed up for, beyond committing treason by making it harder for the fighting men to actually *fight*. Two guards, equally grim, frisked Ryan thoroughly, then bound his hands behind his back with a plastic tie. Ryan hadn't planned to use any of the tools they'd taken, but it was still annoying. He'd scrounged them personally, back when he'd been promoted for the second time.

The REMF eyed him nastily. "Name?"

"Captain Ryan Osborne," Ryan said. He'd considered declaring him-self to be still an LT, but knowing his luck the enemy had seized the FOB's records. The REMFs were supposed to have destroyed them, once they received the command to surrender, yet he wouldn't have bet a fake credit on the bastards actually doing something useful. "14th Assault Regiment."

He waited, patiently, as the REMF worked his way through the files. They wouldn't find anything, Ryan was sure. The Empire had had a passion for recording everything and distributing copies of the files to every last planet in known space, but he hadn't been a serving soldier until after the Collapse. If what the old sweats said was true, he had good reason to be grateful. Unless he'd joined the marines…

"We have no record of you," the REMF said, finally. "As an officer, you will be directed into the officer detention centre."

"Oh, thank you," Ryan said. He pushed as much sarcasm into his voice as he could. "Do we get lobster dinners and wine with our breakfast?"

The REMF ignored the sally. "You will be held in the detention centre until the end of the war or until a prisoner exchange swap is agreed," he said. "If you wish to declare yourself a mutineer, or are willing to turn into a usable asset, now is the time to do so."

Ryan considered it for a long moment. Interrogating POWs, or attempting to induce them to defect, was technically illegal. But then, it wasn't as if anyone had much *experience* in coping with POWs prior to the Collapse. He thought about it, wondering just what he should do. There was nothing waiting for him on Wolfbane, save a death sentence if Admiral Singh knew he'd started the mutiny. And if he declared himself a mutineer, it would make damn sure of his death if he ever returned home.

"You want me to defect," he said, finally.

He wondered, absently, why the thought didn't bother him. No, he *knew* why the thought didn't bother him. He couldn't face the thought of returning home, let alone going back into combat. Intellectually, he knew he should be reluctant to switch sides so casually; emotionally, he no longer had any attachment to anyone. And if the Commonwealth was prepared to help him…

"I need medical assistance," he said. "In exchange for a new pair of balls, I'll defect."

The REMFs expression darkened. "This is no time for joking around…"

"I'm not joking," Ryan said. He nodded to the guards. "Get your pet goons to pull down my pants and you'll see."

He found it hard not to start giggling as the guards did as they were told, recoiling in shock when they realised he hadn't been joking. What competence! One could hardly pass through a checkpoint without being groped in a staggeringly unprofessional manner, yet the guards behind him had completely failed to notice his missing cock! Or had they thought he was simply a small-breasted woman? It was possible…he had to bite his tongue to keep from laughing out loud at the thought. If the guards were like any of the HQ troops he'd seen back home, they'd probably been contemplating a little *more* than a grope while they marched him to his new home.

"Very well," the REMF said, finally. His face was very pale. Losing one's manhood was every man's worst nightmare. "I'll put you on the list for medical treatment."

Ryan lost it. He started to giggle inanely.

"And I hope you'll be useful," the REMF added. "Welcome to the Commonwealth."

And pray the Commonwealth doesn't lose the war, Ryan thought, as he was marched to the camp. *I'll lose more than my balls if I get recaptured now.*

———

Ed nodded curtly as he stepped through the door and into the small chamber. General Mark Haverford sat in a chair, his hands cuffed to the armrests and his feet shackled together. It was paranoid, Ed had to admit, but he'd seen docile prisoners turn violent when they thought there was a chance to inflict some real damage. Killing the Commonwealth's highest-ranking military officer might be worth the deaths of every last POW.

"General," he said, curtly. "You wanted to speak with me?"

Haverford looked up. He was a short man with brown hair and an unshaved face, wearing a simple uniform. Ed silently applauded the touch, knowing it would appeal more to professional soldiers than REMFs. Haverford had been making a statement all along, although it was largely meaningless. He hadn't surrendered his men until Jasmine had shoved a weapon into his face.

"Colonel," Haverford said. He sounded tired, tired and relieved. "Thank you for coming."

"I'm very busy," Ed said. There was no point in moderating his tone. "I assume you had some *reason* to want to see me?"

"Admiral Singh has gone mad," Haverford said.

"And yet you did nothing to stop her from sending hundreds of thousands of men to their graves," Ed snapped. He wasn't in the mood for self-pity. The collective death toll - both military and civilian - was well over two hundred thousand. It would be higher still, he suspected, before the planet recovered from the war. "Why did you even join her?"

"I believed in Governor Brown," Haverford said. "He offered me a chance to shape the army for *genuine* combat missions."

Ed shrugged. "Get to the point."

"I'm offering you my services," Haverford said. "Admiral Singh has to be stopped."

"You're offering to defect," Ed said. It wasn't as if Haverford had much choice. Swapping him in a prisoner exchange would only put him in Admiral Singh's hands, assuming he survived captivity. He'd been isolated from everyone else for his own protection. "That's...quite an interesting choice."

Haverford leaned forward, despite the cuffs wrapped around his wrists. "Colonel, Wolfbane was a joke," he said. "The *army* was a joke. You know that to be true. Governor Brown gave us back our dignity, our confidence that we could be more than colonial enforcers..."

"And then led you in battle against the Commonwealth," Ed sneered. "Forgive me for not being *enthusiastic* about him."

"Governor Brown was a rational man," Haverford said. "You could talk to him, negotiate with him. I believe he would have accepted a limited victory in the war or pulled back and come to terms if it became clear he was losing. Admiral Singh wants it all for herself. She will happily let Wolfbane burn if it boosts her personal power. When she gets home..."

He took a breath. "When she gets home, Colonel, she is likely to purge her enemies and start a civil war."

"That isn't exactly a problem for *me*," Ed pointed out. "Why should we care?"

"A civil war on Wolfbane will give the Commonwealth a very definite advantage," Haverford agreed. "But it will also destroy much of the system's industrial base, making it harder to rebuild the Empire. You'd be throwing thousands upon thousands of trained workers into the fire."

Ed scowled. He hated to **admit it**, but Haverford had a point. Wolfbane represented a sizable percentage of the known surviving industrial base. Given time, the Commonwealth could replace it with more advanced systems...yet he didn't know if he *had* the time. Wolfbane was large, but there had been systems towards the Core that had had more firepower at their disposal. Who knew what had happened to *them*? His worst nightmare was discovering that one of the Core Worlds had survived and had now gone on a conquest spree.

"I can help you break down Wolfbane," Haverford said. "You need information I have locked up in my head."

"We do," Ed conceded. "What do you want in exchange?"

"I want to feel as though I'm on the right side," Haverford said. "Does that make sense?"

Ed scowled. No one reached high rank without being ambitious. Haverford wanted something for himself, even if it was just a command of his own. He'd be in a good position to replace Admiral Singh after she died, if the Commonwealth backed him. And yet, he understood Haverford's point. The Imperial Army had rarely been on the *right* side during the final years of the Empire.

"You will be shipped back to Avalon," he said, choosing not to answer the question. "Once you are there, you will be debriefed extensively. We will discuss future options after your debriefing is completed. I need not add, I hope, that we will take it amiss if you lie to us."

Haverford nodded. He knew as well as Ed that a defector who was caught lying would be killed out of hand. Ed wouldn't make him any promises, not yet, but he'd keep Haverford in mind when he considered the next step in the war. They'd knocked Admiral Singh back on her heels, but now they needed to follow up before she recovered herself and did something drastic. An all-out attack on Avalon could still win her the war.

"Thank you," Haverford said. "That's all I can ask."

"Indeed," Ed agreed.

Her bodyguards had objected, citing the danger of isolated enemy hold-outs or angry civilians, but Danielle had insisted on leaving the bunker and walking through the city. It was a chilling sight, even though she'd done her best to steel herself; large parts of the city were empty, completely deserted, while other parts were in ruins. The military was doing what it could to clear the way, to allow the repair crews to start work, but she knew it would be years before the city returned to normal. It would probably be *decades* before the entire planet recovered from the brief savage war.

She ran her hand through her hair as she strode down towards the defence lines, where white-coated men were pulling out bodies, bagging them up and preparing them for transport to the nearest mass grave. They'd be taking fingerprints and DNA patterns, she knew from one of the innumerable briefings, but some of the dead would never be identified. There would be hundreds of families who would never have closure, who would wonder if their loved ones were still alive, even though the odds were against it. The repair crews would be finding bodies for years to come. She caught sight of a dead woman, wearing the grey urban combat uniform of the planetary militia and shuddered. The poor girl had died to defend a planet that couldn't even be bothered to give her a proper burial.

I'm sorry, she thought, grimly. *There just isn't time.*

She found Colonel Stalker standing outside one of the command posts, issuing orders to his frightening Command Sergeant. Danielle had honestly wondered if Gwendolyn Patterson was even *female*, despite the name; her voice and mannerisms were distinctly masculine. If she hadn't seen the woman in the showers, one day in the bunker, she would still have been a little confused. There was something about Gwendolyn that marked her out as *different*.

"Colonel," she said, as Stalker turned to face her. "Can we have a word?"

Stalker nodded, then dismissed Gwendolyn and led Danielle into the command post. Inside, it was cool and dry; a large map hung on the walls, showing the remainder of the defence lines. No doubt they'd be dismantled soon enough, once the booby traps were carefully removed or detonated under controlled circumstances. Danielle knew she should be worried, but right now she found it hard to care. The city she loved, the city she'd built, had been devastated. And the remainder of the planet wasn't much better off.

"Madam President," Stalker said. "What can I do for you?"

Danielle looked him in the eye. "Was it worth it?"

She'd expected a snappy reply, but Stalker did her the honour of giving the question careful consideration. "I don't think we had a choice," he said, finally. "Admiral Singh could not be allowed to take this planet."

"Tens of thousands of their soldiers are dead, tens of thousands of ours…God alone knows how many people are going to starve in the coming weeks and months," Danielle snapped. "I know, we can feed them…if we can get the food *to* them. Taking care of the POWs alone is going to be a major headache, even if you *do* ship most of them back to Avalon. Was it worth it?"

"We defeated her," Stalker said. "We knew it would come at a cost."

Danielle nodded, slowly. "Why?"

She waved a hand towards the devastated city. "Why all of…*this?*"

Stalker frowned. "There's a theory - I heard it at the Slaughterhouse - that states that humanity can be divided up into three categories: sheep, wolves and sheepdogs. The sheep cannot fight; the wolves prey on the sheep; the sheepdogs *defend* the sheep."

"Hum," Danielle said. It sounded absurd to her. Humans were humans. And yet it was an insight into Stalker's character. "You see yourself as a sheepdog?"

"Most marines do," Stalker admitted. He shrugged. "The thing is, my tutors didn't consider the theory to be very valid. Humans are thinking and emoting beings. Someone can switch from being a sheep to being a wolf at any moment, given the right incentive. The mindset that makes someone a wolf can turn them into a sheep, if they meet someone bigger and nastier than themselves. A sheepdog…can turn into a wolf, if the sheep remain constantly unappreciative of what the sheepdog does for them."

Danielle scowled. "And your point?"

"The Empire collapsed," Stalker said. "It unleashed all sorts of forces when it fell. Admiral Singh, who would never have been anything other than a footnote a century ago, saw a chance to become a wolf and take power for herself. Other would-be wolves took their own chances. And sheep who thought themselves secure, protected by the Empire, were suddenly forced to take up arms and become sheepdogs. Or get killed by the wolves."

He sighed. "The wolf cannot be stopped without force," he warned. "And that always comes with a price."

"A price paid by the people of my world," Danielle said. "Did they deserve it?"

"The universe isn't fair," Stalker said. "What someone *deserves* rarely has anything to do with what happens to them. All we can do now is make sure they didn't die in vain."

CHAPTER
FORTY

Or, as the old rhyme has it, 'for want of a nail, a kingdom was lost.'
- Professor Leo Caesius. The Role of Randomness In War.

"He wanted to be buried here, sir" Jasmine said. They stood together, near the unmarked grave that held Rifleman Gavin Jalil. "His will specifically stated that he wanted to be buried on the world that finally killed him."

"And so he will be," Colonel Stalker said. His voice was very calm, something that worried her more than she cared to admit. "The President was quite happy to leave him in his grave, if we wanted to leave him here, or move him to somewhere else."

"I think he'd prefer to remain undisturbed," Jasmine said, after a moment. "He died to make this planet free."

The Colonel nodded. "It will be years - decades, perhaps - before this part of the planet is turned into towns and cities," he said. "His body will have plenty of time to decompose in peace."

He glanced at her. "Did you handle the rest of the ceremony?"

"Yes, sir," Jasmine said. "His Rifleman's Tab will be returned to Castle Rock and his handful of possessions have been shared amongst the platoon. A handful of letters he wrote to his girlfriend have been saved; we'll see to it that she gets them when we return home."

And we'll hold a wake for him too, she thought. *See how many of the remaining marines can make it.*

"Very good," Colonel Stalker said. He looked past her, down towards where Emmanuel was interviewing a pair of local soldiers. "Are you going to offer me your resignation again?"

Jasmine blinked in surprise, then understood. She'd tried to resign twice now, only to have her resignation rejected. And, deep inside, she was relieved. The Marine Corps was the only home she had, now the Empire was gone. Getting home would be tricky as hell. She'd heard of plans to send starships back towards the Core Worlds, just to see what was going on, but nothing had come of it. The demands of the war consumed everything else.

"No, sir," she said. "I didn't fuck up so badly this time, even if I still stink."

The Colonel smiled. "Your young man doesn't seem to care."

"He has no sense of smell," Jasmine said. She'd showered as soon as she decently could, scrubbing her body so hard that her skin was raw, but she could still smell herself. None of the other marines were any better off, either. They'd be getting into fights all over Castle Rock if they stunk when they returned home. "We'll get better, even if we have to drown ourselves in perfume."

She shrugged, dismissing the thought. "When are we heading home?"

"General Mathis and two-thirds of the CEF will be remaining here to provide assistance and look after the prisoners," Colonel Stalker said. "The remainder of us will depart in a week from now, barring accidents. That should give us plenty of time to find a way to take the war to Admiral Singh."

"Unless some kindly soul assassinates her for us, sir," Jasmine said. "If half of what we got from the defectors is true, Admiral Singh was balanced on top of a very unstable structure."

"If," Colonel Stalker said.

Jasmine nodded. She'd brought General James Stubbins back to Avalon from Meridian, where he'd been a prisoner after Governor Brown had taken control, but everything he'd been able to tell the debriefing officers had been at least two years out of date. Jasmine didn't fault him for that - it wasn't as if he was trying to lie - yet she knew she couldn't take anything he said for granted. The new crop of defectors were far more up to date.

"I hope there'll be a role for us, sir," she said. "1st Platoon performed very well."

"So it did," Colonel Stalker agreed. "Do you want to be reassigned to the CEF...?"

"No, sir," Jasmine said. "I think I'm much better off as a small-unit officer."

"Understood," Colonel Stalker said.

He shrugged. "There's no immediate call for your services, so feel free to take the next couple of days off," he added. "We're trying to rotate everyone through some leave, now the fighting is over, but it isn't easy."

"Good for morale, though," Jasmine said. In the last two weeks, hundreds of soldiers had been flown to other cities, just to be reminded that there was more to Corinthian than a badly-damaged capital city. "They'll need more leave on Avalon."

"We'll see to it when we get them home," Colonel Stalker said. He smiled at her, rather tiredly. "And there will be much more for us to do."

Jasmine nodded. Shore leave suddenly seemed a very good idea. She had no interest in visiting a brothel or watching flicks that were already several years out of date, but stealing a tent and going hiking with Emmanuel sounded like fun. It would be *relaxing*, insofar as she *could* relax. She had no idea how Mandy could endure going to the spa to be pampered for a couple of hours. It was absurd.

"Thank you, sir," she said, as Emmanuel turned and walked towards them. "I'll see you in two days."

"Take care of yourself," Stalker agreed. "Have fun."

He turned and strode off, heading down the hill towards the road. "Jasmine," Emmanuel said. He glanced around to make sure they weren't in earshot, then kissed her hard. "What was that?"

"Shore leave," Jasmine said. She smiled at him, warmly. "You want to grab a tent and go wandering?"

Emmanuel smiled back. "Why not?"

———

"Welcome back," Sergeant Rackham said. "Did you enjoy your leave?"

"Yes, Sergeant," Mindy said. "I had a very good leave."

It was hard not to smile at the question. She'd spent the first day with Mandy - her sister had shuttled down to the enemy FOB to meet her - and then spent the second and third day in Chimayo City, where she'd met a militiaman who'd been *very* impressed with her. They'd spent so much time in bed together that she'd almost missed her flight back to Freedom City, which would have ended very badly for her.

"Good, good, glad to hear it," Sergeant Rackham said, exhausting his grasp of the social niceties. "Do you remember our last conversation?"

Mindy took a moment to remember what he'd said to her, on the eve of the final battle. "You asked if I wanted to be an officer or an NCO," she said.

"Close enough," Sergeant Rackham agreed. "And have you made up your mind?"

"Not yet," Mindy said. "Is now the time?"

Sergeant Rackham shrugged. "You're *career*," he said. "I don't think you'd be happy, getting out of the military when your first enlistment expires, marrying some farm boy and having a dozen kids. The military is your *life*. You need to think about your career, soldier; you need to think about where you want to be in ten years."

Mindy nodded, slowly. "And if I stay an enlisted soldier," she said, "I might not be able to leave when the enlistment officially ends."

"This war may go on for years," Sergeant Rackham said. "And you are enlisted for five years - *or* for the duration. If you plan on the assumption you will be able to leave in five years, you may find yourself trapped - unable to leave and unable to advance. But you don't want to leave, do you?"

"No, Sergeant," Mindy said.

"There's also the simple fact that you are now an experienced soldier," Sergeant Rackham added. "What you learned here" - he waved a hand towards the battleground in the distance - "is knowledge the military must not lose. The battle here may only be the first of many, once the Wolves duplicate the force shields. We may find ourselves fighting to liberate a dozen worlds, rather than simply driving away the fleets and taking the high orbitals."

Mindy shuddered. They'd seen just how many enemy soldiers had died - or had been savagely maimed. She wouldn't forget the castrated soldier in a hurry.

Sergeant Rackham cleared his throat. "You'll be shipping back to Avalon with the Colonel," he said. "When you arrive, you will have an opportunity to go to NCO School. You may not pass, but you can give it your best shot. Or you can go to OCS and try to get high rank. The choice you have to make, now, is which one you want."

Mindy hesitated. She admired Sergeant Rackham - and Command Sergeant Gwendolyn Patterson. The idea of becoming like them was both tempting and terrifying. And yet, she was tempted by the thought of becoming an officer too. It would mean more responsibility, but also more independence. And the Stormtroopers were new enough that she could make her mark on them.

She looked down at her hands. Officers led men in combat, but they sometimes sent men to their deaths to accomplish the tactical objective. She wasn't sure she could do that, even if the alternative was losing everything. Sergeants, on the other hand, took care of their men; she'd see men she knew, men she liked, die in front of her time and time again. It was a heavy burden - Sergeant Rackham wouldn't have suggested NCO School if he thought she couldn't cope - but she wasn't sure she *wanted* it.

But if you don't become an officer, she thought numbly, *you'll have to watch someone else take command of your men.*

She looked up. "NCO School."

"Very good," Sergeant Rackham said. His voice didn't show any hint of approval or disapproval. "I'll put your papers in at once."

"Thank you," Mindy said. She was committed now. "Do you have any words of advice?"

"Never forget what you are," Sergeant Rackham said, dryly. "That's something I was taught when *I* started."

Mindy frowned, then nodded in understanding. A sergeant was *always* a sergeant. Sergeant Rackham couldn't be anything else; he wasn't a common soldier, he wasn't an officer…he was a sergeant. Looking after his men was his job - hers too, if she passed one of the hardest training courses in the military. He was *always* on duty, even on leave.

"Thank you," she said.

"And if you fail, at least you will have tried," Sergeant Rackham said. "And then you will know more about yourself."

"Yes, Sergeant," Mindy said. "And thank you."

———

"That's the completed records, Colonel," Gwendolyn said. "Ninety-seven men dead; forty-three too badly wounded for immediate treatment."

"But only from the CEF," Ed said. "The number is a great deal higher for planetary militia."

"Yes, sir," Gwendolyn said.

Ed sighed, inwardly. The Committee for the Conduct of the War would be pleased, no doubt, that the CEF had avoided high casualties. They'd been furious over the disaster on Thule, even if it *had* been mitigated soon afterwards with the escape from Meridian. This time, at least, there wouldn't be a major dispute over the decision to send the CEF into danger. But it would also make them overconfident, more inclined to demand immediate results. He knew, all too well, that they had only won a tactical victory. It remained to be seen if it could be converted into a strategic victory.

And they won't see the dead here, he thought. *They'll just be relieved they won't have to pay a political price for the dead there.*

"No matter," he said, rising. "We'll be on our way home tomorrow."

Gwendolyn smiled, although her eyes told a different story. "You're looking forward to seeing the baby?"

Ed blinked. "He won't be born yet, will he?"

"Not yet," Gwendolyn said. "But you'll see him soon."

"Unless I get called away again," Ed said. He shook his head. "We need to find a way to end the war before it's too late."

"Maybe we *should* encourage a civil war," Gwendolyn said. "It would give us time to put more of the new weapons into production, then mop up whoever's left."

Ed shrugged. "We will see," he said. "It all depends on Admiral Singh now."

———

Rani sat in her cabin, brooding.

Defeat happened. It was a fact of life and only an idiot - or a politician - would believe otherwise. Battles could be won and lost by nothing more than random chance or simple misfortune. She'd rolled the dice and lost, but bad rolls of the dice were inevitable. All that mattered was how one coped with the results. She had lost a battle - she conceded that in the privacy of her own thoughts - but she had not lost the war.

She wondered, absently, just how much was already known on Wolfbane. A courier boat could outrace her fleet and get there weeks before she could, no matter how hard she pushed the drives. Her enemies might well have bribed someone to tell them the news, if they'd seen signs of looming disaster before it was too late. For once, the never-to-be-sufficiently-damned time it took to send messages from star to star worked in her favour. By the time they knew the truth - if she was lucky - she'd be there with the remainder of her fleet.

And then I will take full control, she told herself.

It had been a mistake, she knew now, to keep Governor Brown's political structure. She understood the logic, she understood the concerns, but it had been a mistake. Wolfbane was not set up for total war, unlike the Commonwealth. The Commonwealth put victory first, ahead of political considerations or corporate concerns. And it had paid off for them, in everything from military tactics to technological innovations. The missiles that had mauled her fleet could not have been designed, let alone built, on Wolfbane.

And if we don't start innovating soon, she told herself, *we will lose.*

She scowled at the thought, but it had to be faced. If the enemy had brought more missiles to the battle, her entire fleet would have been destroyed without being able to fire a single shot in its own defence. And that would have been the end. The Commonwealth would have crushed Wolfbane and then expanded all the way to Earth, without meeting any significant challenges. Who knew what would have happened then?

But there was still a chance to win the war - and win everything.

Impatiently, she glanced at the terminal, where her plans awaited implementation. She would not hesitate any longer, no matter the risks. There was no time to waste. She would take full control of Wolfbane, rebuild her forces and then go on the offensive one final time.

She'd lost the battle. She conceded as much. But the war was still very much in the balance.

The End

Coming Soon!

CULTURE SHOCK

AFTERWORD

There's a line you may have heard quoted, originally attributed to Lloyd George, that war is far too important to be left to the generals. He was, on one hand, entirely correct. War is a tool, one of many, used by the nation-state in its quest for survival and dominance; wars are (or should be) fought with a clear goal in mind. But on the other hand, he was entirely wrong. Politicians - both uniformed and not - have very little understanding of the nature of war. Taking the decisions out of the hands of the professional military and attempting to micromanage a war from long distance is a recipe for eventual - certain - disaster.

And yet, the tendency to micromanage has only grown stronger in this, the second decade of a dark new century. Worrying signs of this were evident as far back as 1914, of course, when the British Admiralty harassed the naval officers commanding the pursuit of two German ships in the Mediterranean. (Those ships eventually made it to Turkey, bringing the Ottoman Empire into the war.) The Royal Navy's commanders were used to holding sweeping authority to take whatever measures they deemed fit, as they were often out of contact with London, but the development of radio made it suddenly possible for London to peer over their shoulders and demand updates. This was also true of British officials in India and other British possessions. Once, the man on the spot could make decisions without reference to London, because it could take weeks (at least) to get a response. Now, he was really nothing more than a mouthpiece for his superiors in Whitehall.

This problem has only grown worse as technology advances. Even during the later years of the Cold War - and the Falklands War - the officers on the spot had some freedom, but it was often very limited. I cannot imagine a competent naval officer being particularly pleased with orders not to touch enemy ships that posed a very real threat to the task force, yet British submarines in the Falklands were forbidden to go after enemy vessels for political reasons (and, when the heavy cruiser was finally sunk, it turned into a political headache in Whitehall.) Now, in the second decade of the War on Terror, micromanaging politicians in Washington DC and London have made achieving ultimate victory considerably harder.

Consider this: enemy targets move, particularly when the 'target' is nothing more than a person on foot or a small convoy. In the time it takes for a sniper, a drone or even a jet aircraft to receive permission to engage, the target may move or do something like move close to innocent civilians. (Terrorists are fond of human shields because they can rely on the media to give anyone who accidentally kills a civilian a very hard time.) Even with the best will in the world (which is often lacking) the time it takes to get authorisation to engage can prove fatal.

But it gets worse. Politicians are often under the delusion that they, operating with the benefit of hindsight, are more capable of making decisions than the person on the spot, at the time. That person, of course, is operating from incomplete knowledge. The politicians, therefore, second-guess the man on the spot (particularly when his actions cause political problems) and often hold him to a standard that is not only unfair, but impossible to meet.

Imagine yourself a soldier on guard duty, somewhere in the middle east. You know the enemy doesn't play by the rules. The veiled woman walking nearby might be a man concealing a submachine gun, the child running past might be raised to kill infidel soldiers, the local soldier next to you might be an insurgent, ready to stick a knife in your back the moment you turn away. You know that the terrorist shitheads have no qualms about killing their own people to get at you.

You're on edge, of course. Soldiers who aren't on edge die. And then a car comes screaming around the corner and drives straight at your checkpoint. The driver ignores warning signs and shouted orders.

What do you do? If the car is carrying a bomb, the closer it gets, the greater the chance of being killed or maimed. You need to stop it as quickly as possible. But if the car is driven by a lunatic and carrying his family, you're about to kill a number of innocent civilians. The driver may be a madman, but his family doesn't deserve to die. So what do you do?

And you have bare seconds to decide.

The safe choice is to open fire, to try to disable the vehicle or kill the driver. This isn't as easy as the movies make it look. But maybe you succeed. The bomb detonates at a safe distance or is simply never detonated. Or maybe you inspect the wreckage and discover, to your horror, that a civilian has been killed. The reporters descend so rapidly you become convinced the whole affair was a put-up job. Before your superiors can begin to investigate what happened, the media back home is already screaming about atrocities.

And then the politicians throw you to the wolves.

This is not an idle scenario. It has happened, time and time again. War is messy; accidents happen, yet politicians simply do not begin to understand it. And when something goes wrong, as it always will, politicians will start looking for scapegoats.

————

Earlier, I called war a *tool* and that's exactly what it is. Wars are not fought for fun and games, certainly not these days. War has the sole purpose of imposing one nation-state's will on another, regardless of the stated goal. One may go to war to obtain natural resources or remove a dictator, but the overall purpose is still the same. A country fights to get something it wants, be it conquests or independence from another country.

War, for the purpose of this essay, has four aspects; *geopolitical, strategic, tactical* and *operational.* Operational can be defined as small-unit manoeuvres; *this* is how we're going to take *this* house. Tactical scales it up a little; *this* is how we're going to capture *this* city or defeat *this* army. Strategic operates on a much bigger scale; *this* is how we're going to conquer and pacify *this* country. Geopolitical operates on a global scale; *this* is how we're going to accomplish our overall objectives.

It should be noted that the four aspects tend to be a little more expansive than you may think, from my very brief description. Tactical may be concerned with winning battles and taking territory, but it also touches upon logistics and other related issues. They also tend to have complications when they interact. A nation may successfully occupy another nation, but in doing so bring itself into conflict with a *third* nation - a strategic success but a geopolitical failure. For example, Adolf Hitler's pact with Stalin in 1939 was a strategic masterstroke - it ensured that Poland didn't have a hope of resisting the invasion - and yet it also opened his back for Stalin's knife. He could (and did) go east, but Stalin could have gone west. Indeed, there are people who believe that Stalin *did* have a plan to strike westwards first.

In order to plan military operations, one must have a realistic understanding of the physical and political terrain, a realistic understanding of the forces involved, a set of loose contingency plans for any eventualities and a willingness to pay the cost of war. This is a complex topic, but one that has to be comprehended by anyone considering a war. Hitler's failure to do any comprehensive strategic evaluation of his targets eventually doomed Nazi Germany to defeat. What had worked - sometimes more by luck than judgement - against small targets like Poland and France failed spectacularly against Soviet Russia. As a warlord, Hitler was more interested in the daring masterstroke than solid planning.

First, however, one must consider the goal. Evicting Iraqi forces from Kuwait or Argentinean forces from the Falklands were both relatively simple goals, with clearly-defended end conditions. Liberating Afghanistan, Iraq and Libya from their governments and then building a set of secure and peaceful democratic states were far more complex. There was no reason to believe that the mere act of removing the odious governments would automatically result in a better nation. Instead, destroying the governments (and not taking control from the start) led to social collapse and civil war.

It is politicians who must define the goals of a war. This is their job. It does not matter if they're democratically-elected leaders or dictators who seized power by force. *They* are the ones who must define the goals of the war. Once the war is underway, the politicians must grit their teeth and ignore setbacks, keeping their eye on the ultimate goal. Losing a battle is hardly disastrous; abandoning the war midway through *is*.

It is the senior military leadership who must figure out *how* to fight the war, then carry it out. They must consider the objective and calculate how best to accomplish it. Once they have a realistic appreciation of just what will be required, they must explain to the politicians just what will be required in terms of commitment. Destroying a Third World army, on one hand, can be accomplished in weeks; occupying and fundamentally transforming its country is a task that will require decades. And once the war is underway, the senior leadership must run interference between the politicians and the officers on the spot, the ones actually commanding the war.

It is the junior military leadership that actually has to lead troops into battle. They are focused on small objectives, instead of being aware of the *greater* objective. Their task is to take and hold territory - a bridge, for example - without needing to know how it fits into the overall plan. In order to do this, to take advantage of fleeting opportunities, they have to have considerable freedom of action.

This is an idealised view, but it is not what happens.

The speed with which messages can be flashed around the globe, these days, have resulted in a mangling of the abovementioned separation of responsibilities. Politicians lose sight of the greater picture as they grow more and more involved with *tactical* or *operational* decisions; because they lose sight of the overall picture, they see relatively small setbacks as utterly disastrous. (The Tet Offensive is a good example; the US won everywhere, save in the sphere of public relations. Unfortunately, that was the decisive sphere.) Where politicians such as Churchill or Franklin Roosevelt (or Stalin, for that matter) gritted their teeth at failures and set-backs, while keeping their eyes on the prize, modern-day politicians have become risk-averse. They want to accomplish complex and difficult tasks without a single major setback or even a comparatively minor one.

They also waste their time meddling in the military sphere. Politicians back home have often interfered in military operations, both before and after the war. Donald Rumsfeld, for example, had a nasty habit of dictating which army units were permitted to embark for Iraq and Afghanistan, playing merry hell with the TOE. Indeed, I believe that one of the reasons for the prisoner abuse scandal in Iraq was that *dedicated* units were not permitted to enter the conflict zone. Putting a cap on the number of deployable soldiers in both countries limited the kind of operations that could be undertaken, forcing the US to rely on air power to make its opinion felt. And consulting lawyers during combat operations (themselves a risk-averse breed) only caused more and more delays. I recall a report in which a prominent Taliban commander, targeted by a drone, was allowed to escape because the lawyers thought engaging him would not be legal.

But a more dangerous aspect of the changing face of war is the rise of hindsight-driven prosecutions. A soldier who makes the wrong decision (as in the example above) can now be charged in a civilian court, even though he took precisely the *right* course of action based on what he knew at the time. There is a difference - a strong difference - between an accident, however tragic, and a deliberate atrocity. Soldiers understand the difference. I doubt you'll find many American soldiers willing to defend the conduct of Steven Green and his comrades. But watching a soldier get hounded through the courts because of a genuine mistake - one blown out of all proportion by the media - is destructive for one's morale.

These are not the days when warfare had to be left in the hands of the generals. But putting it in the hands of the politicians (civilian and uniformed) has been disastrous.

Right now, we face a fast-moving enemy who understands our weaknesses very well. Our forces are the best in the world, but their hands are tied by their political superiors; our weapons are vastly more destructive, yet they cannot be deployed without bureaucratic nonsense and other delays. Our enemies have no qualms about provoking incidents they can turn into atrocities (with the willing assistance of a media that has lost its sense of right and wrong.) On one hand, outright defeat seems unlikely; on the other, we may lose either through death of a thousand cuts or simply surrendering our morality and embracing a final solution of our own. Steering a path that allows us to win without losing ourselves is not going to be easy...

...And, right now, our current crop of politicians are not up to the task.